THE TOMAHAWK AND SABER SERIES

Language of the Bear
Through the Narrows
Untitled Book 3 (Fall 2015)
Untitled Book 4 (Spring 2016)

Also by Evan Ronan

OtherWorld

The Unearthed Series

The Unearthed
The Lost
The Accused and the Damned
The Hysteria
The Traveler

THROUGH THE NARROWS

EVAN RONAN &
NATHANAEL GREEN

CALHOUN PUBLISHING

THROUGH THE NARROWS

Calhoun Publishing

ISBN-10: 0-9964958-1-9

ISBN-13: 978-0-9964958-1-3

Edition: October, 2015

For my girls.
Evan

To Callum and Owen.
Nate

“PER ANGUSTA AD AUGUSTA.”

ONE – THE THINNING

The smoke curled like a shriveling, scorched husk from the end of Wolf Tongue's pipe. He took a long draw on it, pulling the tobacco smoke into his mouth. The bowl of the pipe surged red, then darkened. He held the smoke in his mouth, eyes closed. It tasted too bitter, like a bite on his tongue with little of the usual sweetness of his tribe's sacred plant.

He blew out the smoke and waved it to the spirits with one hand and a silent prayer. The tobacco was off, but not so unpleasant for him to stop.

Wolf Tongue took another draw and settled the pipe with his folded hands in his lap. He stared at the bowl, yellow-brown and shaped like a tulip, its innards faintly red. Smoking tobacco was supposed to bring good thoughts. Let his soul relax. Let his problems mingle with the world of the spirits and help him clear away the caked mud on his eyes.

But today, Wolf Tongue only tasted bitter tobacco and felt his muscles itching to tuck his pipe back in his bag and go do something. Anything.

The Susquehannock had been fading as long as he could remember. Since the English and French first arrived, his people's hold on the lands, the rival tribes, and their tributes of goods had slipped out of their grip. His people had once been known as the fiercest warriors, and with an immense spread of land to prove it.

But their power and their numbers had begun to shrink a long time ago. And it had only gotten worse in the past year.

He twisted to look over his shoulder at his village. He saw no one else. The longhouses all still stood, though half of them had holes with no curtain on their doorframes. The former home of the Bear Clan stood only as a skeleton, its inner timbers exposed like the ribs on a carcass of a massive beast. The people who still remained had removed the exterior bark and timbers to fix their own longhouses or burn in their fires. Grass, still stunted from the winter, grew out through the gray timbers.

When movement caught Wolf Tongue's eye, he watched as his mother-in-law, Sits-by-the-Tree, hurried along the mud and ice between the longhouses and the central fire. She clutched something to her chest with her chin and shoulders drawn to it, not to shield whatever she carried, but seemingly to seek comfort in its closeness. She stayed close to the blank faces of each house before she finally pushed through the curtain of her own doorway.

Wolf Tongue took another puff from his pipe and blew the smoke out before rising to his feet. He'd come away from the village to look over what was left of their lands, hoping the air and the scene would bring him some idea or plan. Here, on the wooden palisade that guarded his village, he could see across the fields of soggy snow where they would plant squash and corn in the spring, if enough of them remained in the village to do the work. Beyond the fields, the forest bristled with the bare branches of trees under a low, gray sky.

As he stepped down off the planks, they thumped beneath his feet. At least something about the Susquehannock had some stability, he thought.

Wolf Tongue wound his way past the empty houses, peeking in at the cold, black fire pits. Once, the air moved, winter's fingertips trailing across his scalp and neck. As he arrived at his doorway, he brought his pipe to his lips only to find the fire had died, untended in his hands.

Tucking his pipe away, he ducked beneath the curtain to the longhouse. Inside, it was dark and heavy with the smell of wood smoke, salves, and the fainter mustiness given off by the puckered remains of their winter's food stores. Sits-by-the-Tree stood to the left, hunched over the shoulders of her husband. Lifting Smoke sat on a pile of blankets, his head tilted toward the ceiling as his wife rubbed something onto his chest.

Lifting Smoke had been a chief of the Susquehannock for more than ten years, and to Wolf Tongue, it seemed like his health followed the fortune of his people. Lifting Smoke had never been an exceptional warrior or particularly large or strong. But Wolf Tongue had always remembered him as intimidating in the way his eyes flashed and how his voice, rough like the scrape of a flint knife, could hush a quarrel in council.

Now, his voice was ragged and dull, worn by a cough that seemed to have no cure. His neck seemed all strings beneath a drape of skin, leading down to two fragile lumps of clay that had once been shoulders.

Wolf Tongue looked away.

As he turned, a sudden movement caught his eye and he reflexively braced himself. He grunted and twisted his body as a boy slammed onto his back. Wolf Tongue rolled, swinging the boy over his shoulder and locking him in a hug against his chest.

Root Cutter, Wolf Tongue's nephew, struggled against the grip for a moment before Wolf Tongue released him.

The boy turned to face his uncle and lifted his chin high. He was growing quickly and strong, one of the few who seemed to be. He almost stood to Wolf Tongue's shoulders and had a sharp jaw and quick hands. Like his uncle, he wore his hair shaved on all sides and with a lock of hair at the back crest, but today he wore a tight cap dyed red and black. His nose, like that of his mother who was taken by the pox, was arched like a hawk's beak.

Root Cutter straightened his leather tunic. "You never saw me hiding there. If I'd had a knife ..."

Wolf Tongue winked. "If you had a knife, I'd have a new one for my collection."

Root Cutter's haughty mask didn't fade as he picked up a loose stick from beside the fire. He stood straight-backed for a moment, then lunged at Wolf Tongue with a short cry. Wolf Tongue shuffled around the attack, spun the boy around and pulled the stick from him.

In a quick wrangling of limbs, Wolf Tongue spun behind his nephew and pinned the boy's hands under his knees along with the stick. Root Cutter struggled for a moment, grunting in frustration.

"Now," said Wolf Tongue. "You Seneca dog. You get what you deserve." With one hand, he held Root Cutter's arms clamped tight against the backs of his legs. He raised the other high in the air and brought it down, fingers clamping into the boy's side below his ribs.

Root Cutter struggled quietly for a moment before he finally burst out in laughter. He wriggled and broke free with strength that told Wolf Tongue this might be the last time he could hold his nephew so easily.

As Root Cutter rolled away, Wolf Tongue cuffed his head.

Wolf Tongue smiled as he turned toward the back of the longhouse where his wife sat watching him, her eyes squinted with a smile.

Root Cutter rushed back to Wolf Tongue's side. "Uncle, tell me again about the battle and how you saved the village. But start with when you challenged Kicks-the-Oneida." His fierce mask was gone and he was again the curious boy who followed his uncle around the village.

Wolf Tongue clasped the boy's neck and pulled him against his side. "You've heard it so many times that you know it better than I do. Go now. I need to talk with your aunt."

Root Cutter looked at him a moment with crafty eyes, then ducked as Wolf Tongue swatted at his ear. Wolf Tongue watched him jog around the longhouse fire and slip through the curtain.

Fox's Smile was watching him as he turned back to her.

"How are you feeling?" he asked as he settled onto the blankets beside her.

His wife didn't set down the cradleboard she was decorating, but still held it in one hand and put the other to her rounded stomach. “I’d be better if you’d stop worrying about me and stop moping.”

Wolf Tongue held back a chagrined frown.

Fox’s Smile slapped his arm. “You were never this serious. If I wanted an old man to father my child, I’m sure I could have found one. Maybe Bone Snake’s father? I think he had an eye for me.”

Despite his mood, Wolf Tongue laughed. Bone Snake’s father was older than Lifting Smoke. Though currently in better health, the old man was toothless, bent, and so lecherous that he often made even Wolf Tongue uncomfortable. He was also one of the sweetest, kindest people Wolf Tongue knew, and much like his son, Bone Snake.

The laughter came and went on the wind. Then Fox’s Smile set her hand on Wolf Tongue’s leg. “I know you put on your mask when you fight with Root Cutter or talk to anyone else. You’re still upset.”

Slowly, Wolf Tongue nodded with a wry twist on his lips. He blew out a breath and ran a hand across his face. “Who’s left of the Susquehannock? Just us few straggling idiots too stubborn to beg another tribe for a place.” He took a breath. “And those who are smart enough to, but too weak to try.” He waved his hand. “We’ve talked about this before, and I’m not getting any smarter. I don’t know what to do.”

Wolf Tongue felt his stomach churn. As a Susquehannock with an English father, he’d fought so hard to be seen as one of the tribe, to become a leader in their fate, to become part of these people and care for them. It pained him to see so many people shed the Susquehannock name he loved, to desert and join other tribes, or to take on the Christian god and settle into a British town.

But what pained him even more was the suffering of those like Root Cutter’s mother who stayed through the vomiting fits and the pox that seemed to be hacking through the tribe. To see dozens die, fevered, covered in sores and shrinking away from their families. To watch his own mother’s flesh shrivel until her eyes, always so sharp and quick, clouded and closed.

To see his friends and family abandon the village was like a fire against his heart, but if the sickness that took his mother along with so many others was still here with his wife and their child …

“The pox won’t get me, Wolf Tongue.” Fox’s Smile turned back to her work as if she’d finished their conversation.

Wolf Tongue rubbed his hands across his scalp and let out a breath. “If it did, I’d have to find a new wife. Though, maybe an old lady this time so I can let her do the worrying for me.”

Fox’s Smile snorted. “Old ladies are too smart to lie with the likes of you.”

“I can be persuasive.” Wolf Tongue attempted a joke out of habit, but his tone was more dour than he intended.

Fox's Smile looked at him from the corner of her eye. Her voice was softer, more serious when she spoke. "It's not old ladies on your mind. So who are you trying to persuade?"

Wolf Tongue blew out a breath and thought about the tribe again as he looked to the front of the longhouse. Lifting Smoke now held a cup in his hands, a blanket draped over his shoulders. His face, storm-gray and creased with sagging lines, stared quietly at the drink he held. His wife sat beside him, fussing at a blanket of her own.

Wolf Tongue thought of all the decisions the old man had made for the village. The help from the English, the cessation of raids and the old wars, his quiet acceptance of his friends' decisions to leave the village. When Wolf Tongue looked back to his wife, he saw Fox's Smile watching him with narrowed eyes. She glanced at her father, then with a deliberate motion ran her tongue along her teeth behind closed lips before looking down at the cradleboard in her lap.

Wolf Tongue took a breath and cleared his throat before he spoke. "I'll start with Bone Snake. He's smarter than I am and gets along with more people. Maybe he can help me keep those we have. Maybe even persuade some of those who left to return after the pox has passed."

Fox's Smile set her hand on his knee again. Her smile was small, and though her words were encouraging, her shoulders slumped slightly and she turned her head in the way she might when offering condolences for the death of a loved one.

"Do what you have to do, lover."

Wolf Tongue found Bone Snake outside his family's longhouse. His uncle wore a similar fitted cap as Root Cutter, though his had four hawk feathers tied to it. He was walking toward his house, a bundle of smoked fish slung over one shoulder on top of a gray, wool English blanket he wore over his shoulders. He turned and smiled when Wolf Tongue called out to him.

Bone Snake was not so tall as Wolf Tongue, but broader in the shoulders and fifteen years older. Bone Snake was of the Porcupine clan and had married one of Wolf Tongue's aunts. His uncle had been one of his closest companions as he grew, and the older man had taught him more about battle, romance, politics, and life in general than anyone else. He had an odd habit of talking with his bottom lip, which seemed to only add to the delivery of the raunchy jokes he passed along from his father.

"You look like a dog just shat you out," came Bone Snake's greeting.

Wolf Tongue shrugged. "At least I'm making it out the other end."

The two embraced. Though the village housed only about two hundred people when it was full, and now it was less than half that, it felt to Wolf Tongue that he hadn't seen his uncle in weeks.

"Come in for a bite? Have a smoke?" asked Bone Snake.

Wolf Tongue shook his head. "No. Thanks. I want to get back to Fox's Smile."

"She feeling all right?"

Wolf Tongue nodded. "She's better now. She was sick in the mornings for a while, but that's better and she's back to herself again."

"Is that good or bad for you?"

Wolf Tongue laughed and looked away for a moment. Then, he said, "I need to talk with you."

Bone Snake sobered. "Everything all right? You sure you don't want to come in?"

"No. Thanks." Wolf Tongue sought the right words for what he was thinking. He knew the sense of loss and helplessness that came with each family that left their village, but he wasn't sure how to say it or what he wanted.

"So many people have died," he began. "And it seems like the remaining sick are getting better. But people are still leaving."

"Wolf Tongue," Bone Snake interrupted. "We've talked about this at council. I know how you feel, but ..." he looked around at the village. "Do you see what's happening? The Bear Clan's house is coming apart. The Turkey Clan is empty. The people who are left are sick and want to belong to a tribe again. It's only a matter of time before someone attacks us for what little we have left. The Susquehannock had our fire, and now we're almost ash."

"But we don't have to be. We can still raise a hundred warriors if we need to. The sickness is passing and so many of the others who left can come back when it's safe. If people want to belong, they have a place here. They belong among the Susquehannock, not beside the Cayuga or the Mingos. But I need your help to rally people together. Keep people here, as Susquehannock, and we'll work together to make the village strong again."

Bone Snake shook his head. "You're going to be a father. You know how it feels to want to protect your family. You go and take your family with you. Make the Mingos a little less dirty when you join them."

Wolf Tongue stared at his uncle for a moment. They'd had this discussion before. Bone Snake had always seemed the most sympathetic to him, but he still held his own idea that those leaving weren't deserters, but just people looking to survive the slowly-growing storm.

This time, though, there was something different in his uncle's posture, in the tone of his argument. He stood a little too defensively, one shoulder turned farther away.

Wolf Tongue truly noticed for the first time the heft of the smoked fish Bone Snake held on his shoulder. When he looked back into his uncle's eyes, he knew it.

"You're leaving, too."

Bone Snake licked his lips, then let out a breath with eyes closed. When he opened them, he said, "Yes. In a few days."

"Where?"

"The Mingos. North and west a few day's walk."

Wolf Tongue nodded. His old rival, Kicks-the-Oneida, had gone to them as well. A group of *iomwhen* from different nations grouped together to form their own bands and villages in the Ohio Valley, farther away from the British. They were an assortment of nations bound into a new one.

Bone Snake opened his mouth to say something, to offer some apology or explanation, but stopped and simply looked back at his nephew.

Wolf Tongue nodded again, managing a smile this time. He clapped his uncle on the arm. "I hope they're good people. Come by before you leave. We'll eat and smoke and have a night of it."

"I will." Then, with another clap on Wolf Tongue's arm, Bone Snake turned and slipped into his home.

Wolf Tongue stood alone for a moment, listening to the sounds of twilight before he turned around to trudge back to his own home.

TWO – JENKINS TOWN

Lieutenant Hugh Pyke waited impatiently in the hall as the builders hurried in and out of Colonel Bennett's house. They were running out of daylight and they were months behind schedule—like all builders. Because they were in and out so much someone had propped the doors open, letting the drafty cold of March transform the hall into an icehouse.

He'd been waiting an hour for his appointment with the colonel, which was thirty minutes longer than the usual. Pyke could hear the colonel meeting with someone in the study, though he could not understand what was being said. Occasionally he heard what sounded like laughter and he smelled tobacco smoke escaping under the door. The colonel's dog, Cerberus, padded silently into the hall to lie on the cool marble tiles. The dog flopped to its side and let its huge tongue hang out of its mouth.

Pyke had served with honor and distinction for two years now in the Colony and the colonel had vaguely hinted at a promotion. Pyke felt he was due, overdue in fact. His father had told him his just rewards would come his way if he served well and acted the gentleman. But that was proving not to be the case and Pyke was now ready to press the issue. Because of his strained history with the colonel, he feared his career as an officer was not progressing, despite his commendable service. He yearned to take up the burgeoning fight with the French. After Washington's resounding defeat at Fort Necessity and the continued French encroachment on English territories, all the talk in the Province centered around war. Even the Quakers, ever the peace-lovers, were now at least considering raising a colonial militia to counter the attacks on the frontier, though of course there was disagreement about how the effort should be funded. The older Pyke grew, the more he thought that everything came down to money.

As a gentleman he thought about money only as much as he needed to. He sent what he could home to his family and thought nothing more of it. What he longed for was to serve the Crown and he'd come to the Province to do just that. He knew he was a capable officer. If only he got the opportunity, he knew another senior officer would appreciate his service, perhaps even General Braddock himself. He'd heard talk of an expedition Braddock planned on leading deep into the frontier to challenge the French and push them out of English territory once and for all.

The door to the study opened, snapping Pyke out of his reverie. He expected to see the colonel's liveried footman, a long-time sergeant who'd served under the colonel for years.

But instead, Lieutenant Smith appeared in the hallway, pipe in his mouth. He was out of uniform, having returned to Jenkins Town very recently from leave – his fourth extended absence in as many months.

"Ah, Pyke. Good to see you. You can be the first to congratulate me."

Pyke forced a smile. "Likewise, Smith. What good news for you, then?"

No doubt the man had been busy apple-polishing as was his wont and in the process had earned some small kindness from the colonel, which he was now going to embellish. Smith advanced his career not by being an exceptional officer but rather by knowing how to curry favor.

"My promotion." Smith's mouth twisted into a smile. "*Captain* Smith. It has quite a ring to it."

"Captain …"

Smith kept talking but Pyke didn't hear a word of what was said. Pyke had been given his commission prior to Smith and had spent the better part of his service on dangerous missions, while Smith usually landed routine patrols and found ways to dally in Philadelphia. Pyke had seen real action on the frontier, risking life and limb to protect the fragile peace of the Colony, not to mention his commanding officer's reputation.

Across the sea, Pyke would have been made captain a year ago and would have been on track for the rank of major by now. Whereas a man like Smith would have …

Smith had finished speaking and was waiting for a response.

Pyke realized he was frowning. He stopped but couldn't bring himself to smile. "Yes, well-deserved. Congratulations."

Before he said anything rash, Pyke moved past Smith and headed for the colonel's study.

"Sir."

Pyke stopped dead before he reached the study and looked over his shoulder at Smith.

Smith's mouth smiled but his eyes did not. "I am your ranking officer now, Mr. Pyke. Not to rub your nose in it, I'd never do a thing like that, but you should call me *sir* so the men don't get any ideas. I'm sure you understand."

Pyke held the man's stare for a long time. Ever since they had met, Smith had dogged him and sought to undermine him at every pass. Smith would use his new rank to press every advantage he had to keep Pyke under heel.

"Congratulations. Sir."

"Thank you, Mr. Pyke. Now you better get in there. The colonel is a very busy man."

Pyke felt his nails dig into his palms and realized he was making fists.

The colonel had always been portly but now he was rotund. Rarely did he leave his home and only then to dine or to meet Penn's officials, which was an excuse to gluttony. His command was peculiar and suited him well. Most of the work involved patrols, defending Jenkins Town, mediating disputes, and offering support to neighboring British settlements. He had his lieutenants—and now one captain—to do this for him so his desk was his home and his hobby, cartography, was slowly consuming his life.

"Mr. Pyke, good to see you." The colonel said it in such a way that it was clear he was not. "At ease."

Pyke fell into parade rest and spread his feet. At ease meant he could look the colonel in the eye, which he did now.

"Good to see you, Colonel. By way of quick report, last night's patrol proved fruitless. Our men discovered signs of a temporary camp but no Indians. The farmers are telling the truth about the raids. My recommendation, sir, is to station a squad near the farmland where they will be in a better position to capture any marauders."

The colonel took a long pull on his pipe. "Just as likely these Prussian farmers created the illusion of an enemy camp so they can tie up more of the Crown's resources."

Pyke didn't see what the local farmers had to gain by the supposed deceit. No money was changing hands and the soldiers wouldn't assist with the farming. He was about to say as much when the colonel spoke again.

"We have a much more pressing matter to discuss, Mr. Pyke." He moved some sketch maps on his unruly desk aside and found the report he was looking for. Pipe ash fell all over his desk as he did this. "There is a mission that I think you are best-suited for given your qualifications and history with the local tribes."

"I stand ready to serve, Colonel."

"Spare me the platitudes, Pyke. You and I haven't always seen eye-to-eye and our history is bleeding through your tone. If you're not going to be sincere, then keep your bloody bone box shut. Understood?"

Pyke was taken aback. He hadn't intended to put any tone in his voice. But apparently one had come across anyway. He had to measure his words better. The enlisted men respected him, but when it came to people with any authority he had few allies in the Colony. His commanding officer wasn't one of them.

"Sir, my apologies but I did not intend to—"

Bennett held up his pudgy hand. "Save it. Now then. Reports are coming out of Millers Town of Indian raids. This latest report states the Susquehannock are the cause."

Millers Town. The Susquehannock. Pyke had history with both. He'd befriended a Susquehannock warrior by the name of Wolf Tongue and together they had tracked down a renegade Englishman on the frontier. Their violent, dangerous journey had taken them through Millers Town, giving them an opportunity to meet the townspeople.

Based on what Pyke knew, the report did not make sense. "The Susquehannock are our allies. They have a good relationship with us, trade frequently with our settlements including Millers Town, and have no love for the French. They would not raid, not unless they were provoked. I know many of them personally."

The colonel harrumphed. "You weigh your history with the savages more than the word of an Englishman?"

"Sir. You might recall from my report on the late business with the Susquehannock that we encountered scalpers from Millers Town. Ample provocation if the Susquehannock were so inclined."

"I recall your prolix, verbose report very well, Mr. Pyke. I also recall from that same report that you put the scalpers to the death. All of them loyal citizens, by the way."

One of the scalpers, a man by the name of Nederwue, had been Dutch, actually, but that wasn't worth pointing out. Pyke and the colonel had waged this battle before and Pyke knew he would never win. He could only hope not to lose the argument.

"They were murderers and they were jeopardizing the mission, sir."

"You cannot murder a savage, Pyke. You can only kill them. And besides, as rational beings, the villagers would have heeded you had you better explained the critical nature of your mission."

The colonel would hold this history over him always. Scalpers had followed Pyke and Wolf Tongue from Millers Town and surrounded them at the worst moment: when they were within striking distance of their quarry. The scalpers promised to leave Pyke unmolested but in exchange they wanted Wolf Tongue's head. Wolf Tongue might have been a savage but that didn't excuse Pyke's obligation, or the fact that scalping was an evil practice. So Pyke and Wolf Tongue had turned the tables on the scalpers, sending them all to early graves.

Later, Pyke had grown to respect and even admire the Indian. Wolf Tongue was a great warrior, an honest man, and a good friend. His brand of honor differed from Pyke's, but at least he had a code.

The same couldn't be said about many an Englishman.

Pyke said, "I was under orders of confidentiality from you so I explained what I could to the scalpers. They did not heed me. I needed Wolf Tongue and without him and the Susquehannock, Azariah Bennett would still be stirring up trouble."

At the mention of his dead, rebellious grand-nephew, the colonel stiffened. "Don't think yourself so powerful, Mr. Pyke. If you had failed—and you nearly did—I would have found someone else to handle Azariah."

Pyke bristled. The mission had been a wild success in light of how the colonel had mismanaged the overall strategy by sending only two men after a charismatic rogue rumored to command dozens. And now Bennett was making it out to be a near-failure!

The colonel said, "Have you gone native? Maybe I should send Captain Smith instead, as he'll be more predisposed to trust our own people."

Pyke knew he was overstepping, but he opened his mouth anyway. "Captain Smith does not know which end of his musket is the working one."

The colonel's eyes bulged and his fist rattled the desk. "Captain Smith is now your superior officer. Any more insubordination like that and I'll turn you into a Junior Grade!"

A *demotion*? When he should have been awarded the rank of Captain? Pyke was beside himself but forced a calming breath down his throat.

"Sir, I am best suited for this mission. I know the parties and I have a rudimentary understanding of the Susquehannock tongue."

The colonel slowly leaned back in his seat, sated by Pyke's response. He brought his pipe to his puckered lips and puffed.

"That's more like it, Mr. Pyke. Likely we would find a chest of French sols buried in the Susquehannock village, no doubt the damn French have put them up to this latest series of raids. Now I'd like you to get out there posthaste and find out what's going on. Report back to me immediately."

"Where will I find the man that filed this report?"

"He will meet you at first light at the armory. His name is Fletcher."

Pyke knew the man from his short time at Millers Town. "Sir, if I may make a request?"

The colonel sighed. "Go on."

"These townfolk likely suspect Wolf Tongue and I killed their kin."

"A sin you will now have to atone for, Mr. Pyke."

"I will go to my grave with a clear conscience," Pyke said, hard-pressed to keep the edge out of his voice. "My point is, they will not receive us with open arms. At best they'll be neutral. At worst they'll undermine me at every turn. With the men by my side, the townfolk will be forced to accept my authority."

"With the bloody French threatening war? With all these other raids by the bloody savages?" Bennett shook his head somberly. "I'm not going to send what few soldiers we have to Millers Town to settle this petty dispute."

Pyke could see where this was going, so he changed tacks. "But, sir, if there is any truth to the rumors, the town may need interim defenses until we can settle the matter properly with the raiders. I would request five men for this mission. In fact, I have some thoughts on who they should be."

Damn the colonel! Pyke did not want to be in the same position as last time, when he and Wolf Tongue were two men challenging a small army.

"*Captain* Smith has an important mission that requires what men we have in the regiment. These damn Quakers refuse to raise a militia, so you will be satisfied with Sergeant Davies alone. Conclude any local business you have this evening and leave at first light. I expect your report in three days. That is all."

"Sir?"

"What is it, Pyke?" The colonel had purposely left out the *mister*.

Pyke squared his shoulders and forced the colonel to meet his eye. "I've been in your service for quite some time now and have, I believe, served honorably."

"As all officers should."

"Yes …" Pyke already could tell he wouldn't get anywhere with the colonel. Still he had to raise the issue to satisfy his own self-worth. "For that reason I wanted to discuss my career with you. I was given my commission more than—"

"You saw Smith and now you want a promotion too? Really, Pyke, I thought you a bigger man than all that. You're acting like a jealous second-born whose older brother was just given his first horse."

Deep breath. "Sir, I already had these thoughts in mind before Captain Smith shared his good news with me."

"Oh, so your sin isn't jealousy. It's pride and greed?"

"Sir, back in England commanding officers regularly discuss these matters with their junior officers to—"

The colonel was out of his seat. "You presume to tell me how to soldier?"

"No, sir, I was only saying—"

"Get out of here!"

Great Britain warred with France in all but name in the New World and it seemed to Pyke that everyone but the men under Colonel Bennett had seen action. He'd heard stories of Robert Rogers's heroics and of Washington's failures. Long had Pyke looked forward to proving himself on the field of battle and if he could do it against the ever-poisonous French, all the better.

Of course, he had proven himself one year ago in Penn's Woods against a madman leading a ragtag army. But Colonel Bennett had quickly pushed that mission back into the closet, barely commending Pyke for a job well done under extreme circumstances. Robbed of any recognition, he'd looked forward to marching against the French but so far that opportunity had proven elusive. Instead of getting his chance at a proper mission, once again the colonel was shuffling him off to a thankless job on the frontier away from the real action.

Pyke stood in his small room in the boarding house after packing his supplies for the next morning. He surveyed the room once, then tucked his pistol into his belt, but left his saber where it lay against the dresser. On his way out the door, he eyed the tomahawk, a souvenir from his time with the Susquehannock. He tucked that under his belt. Though his conversation with the colonel had been unpleasant, it had stirred fond memories of his mission with Wolf Tongue. By now the man was surely married and his wife probably with child.

The evening was cold. Lanterns lit York Road, which had turned sloppy with ruts as snow melted and refroze beneath horses' hooves and wagon wheels. Pyke took the street, waving to people he knew as he went.

Officers normally irrigated at Molly's Tavern but last week some low-level Philadelphian official had gotten drunk as an emperor and negligently started a fire that had consumed Molly's and threatened to take the Magistrate's office next door. The taverners had formed a line from the closest well to the tavern and passed buckets back and forth throughout the night to stop the inferno.

The upshot of this was that Pyke and the other two officers, Smith included, were forced to imbibe at The Brown Cow where the enlisted men drank. Pyke didn't mind being around the men but he liked to give them their space when they weren't on duty so they could bark at the moon without an officer's eyes on them. By dining there Pyke was forced to watch over them and they were forced to be on their best behavior, an arrangement neither party wanted.

Pyke entered The Brown Cow. Tobacco smoke hung stubbornly in the air and with the fire going, the tavern was easily twenty degrees warmer than the outside. At the corner table a lively game of John Bull ensued where gamblers tossed coins with noisy clinks onto their grid and won, or lost, small fortunes. The enlisted men waved or nodded at him and Pyke returned the gestures. He took a table by himself and away from them so they had their space. Sergeant Davies took up one whole side of their table himself. He was a big fellow with a booming laugh that rattled mugs. He was probably three drinks ahead of everybody, though he could handle it better than anyone Pyke had ever met.

Pyke hadn't eaten since breakfast so he was gut-foundered. The server brought him a mug of small ale. Everyone said the Jenkins Town water was unpolluted but few were brave enough to drink it. Five minutes later the server was back with spoon bread and a bowl of whatever they had caught and found this late in the winter—it seemed to be squirrel and some brown-stained root vegetable.

Pyke declined that strange gray loaf concoction their Prussian butcher seemed to have no shortage of, *scrapple*.

Men came and went and the conversation remained lively. Pyke enjoyed two small ales, knowing they would aid him in digestion and also maintain his strength. He kept his own company, a company he enjoyed. He ordered one last drink. The ale had taken the edge off the day and that was enough. Pyke was careful not to bung his eye, as he'd seen many men ruined by drink.

He called the server one last time and requested he fill his wine skin with cider. He returned a few minutes later and he thanked him and put it away. He enjoyed cider but the drink was not for him.

As he took his last sip of ale, the conversation around the tavern suddenly died down. Men turned in their seats to look at the entrance.

Damaris Bennett had entered the tavern and was looking at him.

He had loved her. He had approached the colonel to ask permission for her hand in marriage, and the colonel had approved. But all that had transpired before he truly knew her. At that time she'd just been a red-haired beauty with dazzling eyes and a sensual air.

She had been spoiled and romantic and overstepping, but he'd written that off to her youth and the influence of the Colony on her. But then ... then she had sided with Azariah, her cousin-removed against her own father. She had even fired a pistol at Pyke, though whether she was actually trying to shoot him, he could not say. She had missed him from inside ten feet.

Her actions had forced Pyke's eyes open. He'd been wrong in his appraisal. He'd brought her home to the colonel and cut ties with her, though he'd continued to serve her father honorably.

The sight of her still stirred something inside him. Pyke didn't know what to label his feelings. He had been in battle and knew the strange experience of later reliving each gory detail in his mind, the memories forcing him to relive his emotions. He wondered if the same thing were at play when he saw her.

She wore a blue satin gown with lace around her forearms and neckline. She adjusted a thick shawl over her shoulders as she came toward him and settled into the chair next to him. The Brown Cow was no place for a woman of her class. And all men were watching them. As much as the colonel tried to keep the rumors from swelling, eventually the truth outed and Pyke figured that everyone in Jenkins Town knew their tortured history.

"Lieutenant Pyke," she said. "It is so good to see you. How have you been?"

"Miss Bennett." He was aware of the air around him, of his arm against the table. "I was just about to leave. Could I escort you home?"

"This is the first evening my father has permitted me to roam the town since …" She looked down as if embarrassed. " … since you saved me, Hugh. I figured you were in here and was wondering if we could enjoy each other's company?"

She put her gloved hands on the table.

"Your father would not approve. I wouldn't either." He couldn't stay here. But all the same, he didn't want to leave. He had so many questions for her. If she could just explain why …

He forced the useless thoughts from his mind. He knew it was foolish to open himself to her again. She was more unpredictable than an Indian and more dangerous than the whole French army to him.

"Have you read my letters?" She kept her eyes on him. He felt rooted to the spot.

"Damaris …" He hadn't opened a single one, afraid of reentering her world. He searched for the right words, but to find the right words he needed to understand his feelings. He didn't.

"Hugh, I spoke to my father about you. I reminded him of what you did. Sometimes he forgets that because my actions spoil the memory of everything during that time. He forgets that you stopped Azariah."

"The Susquehannock stopped Azariah."

"With you leading them. You and your friend."

She smiled warmly and he felt a tightness in his chest.

She said, "My father is a stubborn man, but he could see the force of my argument, Hugh. He knows what you did. I think he can be convinced you are due for a promotion."

Pyke said nothing.

"Hugh." Damaris lowered her eyes and her voice grew heavy. "I know you won't believe me but I was … not myself. I was going through a very difficult time in my life and I fell under Azariah's spell. I know now he was not a good man. I know now you did what was necessary. And I know now part of why you did it was for me. You're a good man, Hugh, an honorable man. You've been too good to me, better than I deserve. Some nights I have terrible dreams that you were killed in your duel defending my honor."

Pyke still said nothing.

"You loved me once, Hugh. I was wondering if you could find it in your heart to love me again. I'm sorry about what transpired, all the things that went so horribly wrong. I've thought about it these many months, endlessly, night after night. Could you ever forgive me?"

Pyke stood. She was a viper disguised as a beautiful woman. Of course she wanted to marry him now, as her reputation had driven any other prospects to the four corners of the Earth. And he was certain the colonel and she had plotted this whole conversation. It was no coincidence this was the first night she'd been permitted to roam free, hours after Pyke had tried to discuss his career with her father and hours before he began another dangerous mission. If he agreed to the engagement and then was killed, the colonel could dispel the rumors swirling around his daughter—see, the man she was accused of wronging asked for her hand! Then her prospects, at least some of them, would return.

Pyke said, "I forgive you. But I won't marry you to obtain a promotion."

He left her in The Brown Cow and ignored the stares of everyone as he left.

The next morning, Sergeant Davies was waiting for him outside. Davies was a pot-bellied man who hadn't seen a razor in months. Across the sea, his slovenliness wouldn't be tolerated. But they were not across the sea.

"Sir, good to see you."

Pyke smiled. "Did you go to bed last night, Davies?"

"I attempted to go to bed twice, sir. But neither woman was obliging." Davies laughed.

They started down York Road. The sun was just now melting the frost and a fine dew covered everything.

"The colonel has shared the nature of our mission with you?"

Davies belched. "Savages are raping and killing people in Millers Town."

"Aren't one for details, are you, Davies?"

He tapped the side of his head. "Got it all up here, sir. Officers usually only want to hear the summary, not the details."

Pyke laughed at the truth of that statement. As they approached the armory, Pyke spotted the quartermaster, a wizened old colonial, and Fletcher, one of the men he'd met at Millers Town. Fletcher, a thin man of about twenty-five with his brown hair pulled into a tail at his shoulders, waved at him like they were old friends. The quartermaster chewed his tobacco and hawked a big gob into the street.

Pyke lowered his voice. "Sergeant, there is more to this story that I will share with you. But not in front of Fletcher."

Davies said, "Quite right, sir. Quite right."

They reached the armory and Fletcher greeted him with a smile and handshake.

"Lieutenant Pyke, good to see you." Fletcher spoke in that slight, strange colonial accent Davies had.

"Likewise, Mr. Fletcher. How is your wife? I have not forgotten her, or her delicious cider."

At the mention of alcohol, Davies groaned.

Fletcher smiled. "You remember she was up the duff? She gave birth to a healthy baby girl. Ain't nothing wrong with that girl's lungs I can swear."

Pyke shook the man's hand again. "Congratulations to you and your family."

Fletcher thanked him but his face darkened. "That is really the only good news to share, Lieutenant. Millers Town is at a crossroads what with the raids. We were just getting on our feet but then the savages came. Stolen crops and cattle and anything left outside. This week one of ours was left for dead. It's a miracle from God that Carter survived."

Pyke had a vague recollection of Carter. He clearly remembered Millers Town. They had not been eating high on the hog, but they also weren't impoverished. He'd seen many worse frontier towns.

"I'm sorry to hear of your troubles," Pyke said. "Sergeant Davies and I will work to resolve this quickly."

"We're in your debt, sir."

Fletcher excused himself to saddle his horse. Davies and Pyke went inside the armory, which also served as a grainery, with the quartermaster, a man named Strange. The old man was seventy years old if he was a day.

Strange walked with a noticeable limp. One leg looked longer than the other. "Two days' supplies. Approved by the colonel. I've got the boy to get the materials for you." He pointed along the wall at the sacks of food and artillery.

Pyke smiled. "Thank you. But we'll need five sacks of grain, five muskets, and two more horses."

"The colonel only approved two days of supplies." Strange went to his desk. It took him ten seconds to walk as many feet. He produced a slip of paper with the colonel's unmistakable handwriting on it.

"That is correct." Pyke smiled at the old man. "But we'll be joining several others on the road for this mission. We need two days of supplies for all of them."

The quartermaster reread the orders from the colonel, even though he'd just read them off to Pyke. "Doesn't say anything about these other men on here."

Pyke nodded. "The colonel is very busy so his orders are short and to the point."

Strange mumbled something about the unintelligibility of the colonel's orders. Pyke bit his tongue. Davies was openly staring at him. Pyke didn't meet his eyes.

Strange scratched at his balding head. He was weighing his options. Pyke had been careful not to ask for anything absurd.

Finally the quartermaster shrugged. "Take what you need, then."

Pyke and Davies loaded the supplies onto the extra horses and thanked Strange. They met Fletcher on York Road minutes later. All were quiet as Pyke and Davies led the horses. When York Road degenerated into the narrow Indian trail, Fletcher spoke.

"Has the colonel seen fit to send us extra supplies?" He nodded at the horses and the additional things Pyke had requested from Strange.

Pyke smiled. "These are for the Susquehannock."

Both men stared openly at him.

"Sir?" Davies said.

"You're taking them gifts?" Fletcher said.

Pyke didn't care for the insolent tone in Fletcher's voice but he kept his voice light. "I know the Susquehannock well. I don't doubt you were attacked but I believe you are mistaken they are responsible. I will get the truth out of them. If I'm wrong and they're responsible, then these goods will serve as payment for whatever their injury, be it real or perceived."

Davies wanted to say something but Pyke shot him a quick look to be quiet.

Fletcher was at a loss for words.

"Do you foresee a problem with that, Mr. Fletcher?" Pyke said as innocently as possible.

Fletcher paused like he was thinking about it. Pyke got the sense he was holding back something, or didn't know what to say.

"No, it's worth the try. I'm no soldier, just a poor miller. So if it's all the same to you, I'd rather straight home to my wife and daughter. The Susquehannock are bloodthirsty savages. They see me traipsing into their village and they'll look like God's revenge on murder and come for my scalp."

"Fair points. Sergeant Davies and I will meet you in Millers Town."

Fletcher seemed relieved. They rode the Indian trail another five miles before Fletcher took his leave and turned north. Davies and Pyke stopped to rest their horses and take a drink. The sun was high overhead and its warmth felt good coming through the barren branches.

Davies pulled out his wine skin.

Pyke said, "Didn't think you were fit to drink today, Sergeant."

"A drink to repair. Besides, don't trust the water." Davies tipped the skin at him. "Sir?"

"I have my own, thank you." Pyke sipped the cider he'd gotten from The Brown Cow last night. It was watery and had a sharp, bitter bite to it. Molly Fletcher's was much better.

Pyke took the opportunity to recount his experiences with Millers Town, especially his killing of the scalpers. Though Davies couldn't read, he made up for this shortcoming with an excellent memory, and Pyke knew he would retain all the details and nuances of the story.

Davies's pot-belly, scraggly appearance and unseemly gait proved perfect camouflage. He would always be underestimated and he was cunning enough to use it to his advantage. Pyke enjoyed his company very much, despite Davies's poor habit of ignoring the finer points of soldiering.

"So you're taking us to the savage's village?" Davies said.

Pyke nodded. "They are our allies."

Davies shuddered, and Pyke knew why. As a young boy, Davies's camp had been raided by one of the tribes. Davies had seen his mother cut down with a tomahawk. He was a good soldier but utterly terrified of Indians. He believed they possessed superhuman strength and practiced witchcraft. Davies's fear was probably why the colonel had assigned him to this mission. No doubt Davies had angered the colonel at some point because Davies was lax and the colonel had a short temper.

"We camp there tonight?" Davies gave Pyke a sidelong look.

"Sergeant, you have nothing to fear."

"I'd rather see the stars from Millers Town tonight."

Pyke smiled. "Sometimes, Sergeant, you must speak the language of the bear. Especially if you don't want it to eat you."

THREE – AN OLD FRIEND

There was little alarm as Pyke and his soldier arrived at Wolf Tongue's village. A few dogs barked and a few children hailed to the elders that *quhanstrono* were riding in. And then Pyke came near the gates of the palisade and waited.

Wolf Tongue cringed at the reception. When the English soldiers had come to the village years ago, there had been sentries by the palisade, women working the fields surrounding it, hunting parties and fisherman in the surrounding woods who would raise an alarm. Usually, the arrival of strangers signaled an event worth interest, if not outright danger, and most of the village would rush to investigate.

Now, Wolf Tongue, Fox's Smile, and fewer than a dozen others came to the palisade where the two soldiers waited, holding the reins of their horses.

Wolf Tongue's embarrassment only soured when he saw that it was his old friend waiting patiently to be invited into the village. At least Pyke had the courtesy to wait to enter. Would that the Susquehannock had the presence and consideration to make an event of his visit.

Still, the arrival of his friend made Wolf Tongue smile. He jogged forward and grabbed Pyke in an embrace that seemed to discomfit the Englishman, though when Wolf Tongue let go, Pyke's demeanor remained unruffled.

Pyke was shorter by a head than Wolf Tongue, like most of the whites were when standing next to a Susquehannock. The Englishman smiled slightly and genuinely, a look that Wolf Tongue had rarely seen in their time together. Even though they had only spent a few days hunting Storm-of-Villages, Wolf Tongue knew he'd seen much of this Englishman's soul.

And though Pyke smiled, he seemed much older than the year apart should have made him. He had always been sturdy, and he was still, perhaps more so. His seeming aging hadn't diminished his stature or strength, it seemed, but rather sharpened his jaw, thickened his shoulders, and given to his eyes some wry knowledge or look that Wolf Tongue might have seen only in older men.

"Wolf Tongue, my friend. It's good to see you again."

"And you. Have you finally come for my wedding? You missed the ceremony, but maybe we can find a Susquehannock woman for you."

Pyke shook his head. "I'm sorry I couldn't be here for your wedding. I had other matters to attend to."

"Eh? That woman you led home on a leash?"

Pyke's eyebrows raised and he cleared his throat. "She's not for me, no."

Wolf Tongue leaned closer. "She's probably better for you because you already know she wants to kill you. With my wife, I never know when the knife will come."

"I can speak English," came Fox's Smile's voice over Wolf Tongue's shoulder.

Wolf Tongue winked and his wife shook her head.

"I come bearing gifts." Pyke changed the subject. "But first, this is Sergeant Davies."

Wolf Tongue went to the other man and extended his hand in the way of the British. Davies was shorter than Pyke and more solid around the trunk. He wore a short beard and a grimace of one who seemed about to vomit. He shook Wolf Tongue's hand heartily, eyes wide.

"Davies," repeated Wolf Tongue in greeting. Davies nodded in return and removed his hand. He glanced over Wolf Tongue's shoulder and then again at him as if unsure of where to settle his eyes.

"The good sergeant has not met any *iomwhen* before," said Pyke with a slight lilt in his voice.

Wolf Tongue grinned and looked back to Davies. "Oh, and we'll pray the Susquehannock are all you meet so you're not disappointed in the rest, Davies."

Pyke chuckled as he rifled through his horse's pack. He pulled free a wine skin and tossed it to Wolf Tongue. The container was smaller than a water skin Wolf Tongue would carry, and he caught it easily and uncorked it. He eyed Pyke over it as he sniffed. Then his eyes widened.

"A gift just for you, though I have more to share. Not as good as what we had before, perhaps. But I hope it suffices."

Wolf Tongue closed the skin. "It will, if you'll drink with me." He waved them toward the village. "Come, take a rest, eat, clean the dust from your animals. We'll talk and smoke after."

Wolf Tongue and Fox's Smile walked alongside Pyke as they passed through the palisade gates. Davies trailed slightly behind. As they passed into the open area, Wolf Tongue noticed a slight hesitation in Pyke as the Englishman looked around. His gaze lingered on the abandoned Bear Clan longhouse, but he said nothing and quickly increased his speed to match that of his hosts.

Wolf Tongue cleared his throat. "This cider." He held up the wine skin. "You say it's not good?"

Pyke half-smiled. "It's not bad, but it's the best I could do without going to Millers Town to see Mrs. Fletcher. Still, I thought you might like some."

Wolf Tongue rolled his eyes. "I wouldn't go back there, even for ten barrels of her cider." A crawling sensation went up Wolf Tongue's neck as he remembered being followed by some of the townspeople, hunted to be killed for his scalp to be sold to the French.

Pyke sucked in a breath as if to speak, but then stopped as a sudden noise drew their attention. Ahead, a group of Susquehannock came striding toward them, shouting.

"Get them out! We don't want them here!" called one woman who held her toddler in her arms. The woman's husband pushed to the fore and shouted, "Keep your dirty friends out of our village."

A few others shouted insults and curses. Beyond them, two younger men not yet blooded in battle came running forward with tomahawks and knives in their hands, calling out threats in Susquehannock. "I'll kill the *quhanstrono*!"

Pyke stopped and laid his hand on a pistol. Wolf Tongue put one protective hand on his friend's chest and held the other palm-out toward his people. Pyke gave him a questioning look before turning his gaze back to the other Susquehannock.

Wolf Tongue growled in their own language. "These men are friends. They fought Storm-of-Villages beside me and now come with gifts."

The older man scowled and stared at Pyke. "The *quhanstrono* are not our friends anymore. They poison their gifts to us while the Dutch and the English fight over our lands. And where do you think the Shawnee and Seneca get their muskets?" He looked back to Wolf Tongue and shook his head. "Wolf Tongue, he may be your friend, but none of his people are mine. We'd be better without them here."

One of the younger men stepped forward and pointed at Davies with his tomahawk. "That one grows fat by stealing from us. His blood will regrow our village."

Wolf Tongue looked briefly at Davies. The sergeant, to Wolf Tongue's surprise, had lost his nervousness and now watched them all with narrowed eyes, his musket held lightly in both hands before him.

Wolf Tongue looked back at the young men. He hadn't seen him before, but his nephew, Root Cutter, stood a few paces behind them with a long, pointed British dagger naked in his hand. He could see hunger in all their eyes, in the boniness in their elbows, the strands of sinew in their necks. They hungered for glory and vengeance as much as they did for food.

Wolf Tongue lowered his hand from Pyke's chest. "These men are my friends.

If you attack them, you attack me. There was a time when the Susquehannock feared no one and now you jump at visitors like dogs on a wounded bird." Both young men bristled.

Wolf Tongue softened his tone. "You want blood, I know. I felt the same taste when I fought Kicks-the-Oneida to lead the battle against Storm-of-Villages. This man helped save our people and ate with us at our celebration. He's not your enemy. Soon enough, I'm afraid, you'll need your weapons when the Seneca attack. Save your hunger for them."

The two young men scowled, but seemed pacified with Wolf Tongue's admonishment. Root Cutter looked at his feet with a chagrined frown. The others shook their heads and returned to their work or else crossed their arms and frowned as they watched Wolf Tongue and his visitors pass.

Fox's Smile touched Wolf Tongue's arm. "Maybe we had better eat inside."

The day was surprisingly warm for the season, and Wolf Tongue had hoped to sit out of doors. But Fox's Smile was right.

When he turned to Pyke, he could see the questions in his eyes, but the Englishman didn't say anything.

"Come. We'll rest in our longhouse."

"It's not the Susquehannock."

Wolf Tongue leaned forward, elbows on his knees. A small flame burned lonely in the center of the fire pit between him and his friends. Fox's Smile took a small sip of the cider Pyke had brought, made a face, and passed it back to the lieutenant.

Wolf Tongue reached for the stick he'd taken from his nephew and poked at the ashes. "It's not the Susquehannock," he repeated.

He'd heard Pyke's tale and his mission. Pyke's chief, his *colonel*, had sent him to protect the dirty *quhanstrono* of Millers Town from the raiding Susquehannock. Except Wolf Tongue knew, almost with certainty, that this was no band of his nation.

"I told the colonel that it wasn't Susquehannock."

Wolf Tongue snorted. "It may well have been in my grandfather's day. But not now." He looked from the twisting flames to Pyke's eyes. "You saw what's left of us, of our village."

Pyke blinked and looked to the wine skin in his hand for a drink.

"But there are others? Other villages?" asked Davies. The man had taken to the food heartily and still sat with his cup filled with beans and broth long after everyone else had eaten. There had been only talk of small things and jesting during the meal, but eventually Pyke had suggested they talk of serious matters, despite his sergeant's continued appetite.

"Yes," said Fox's Smile. "We still hold to three villages. Though, the last I heard, people were deserting those, as well. South past the swamps there were two villages that I heard were joining into one, though even then they'll be as few as we are here."

Davies moved to speak, but seemed to think better of it and spooned more beans into his mouth. Pyke voiced his thoughts. "So even though it's not from this village, it could still be Susquehannock?"

Wolf Tongue shrugged his shoulders. "It could be. But I doubt it. All our people's villages look like this one. The children who haven't died or lost their strength to the pox watch as their neighbors attack their parents. And every day, more and more people slip away to find a new home among the Cayuga, the Lenape, or even or the Mingos. There's little spirit left in the Susquehannock. They've taken their fire and given it over to the Iroquois nations, or else picked their side to live by the British or the French."

"Dirty French," muttered Davies.

Pyke huffed a laugh and took another drink. He passed it to Wolf Tongue. "I don't doubt you, my friend. But that sounds like all the more reason to attack a settlement. You're losing your home. Your children are sick. Your old enemies are armed with French muskets. They might be taking what fire they have and using it to get supplies and reunite themselves, rather than letting it flutter out."

Wolf Tongue looked sharply at Pyke, but the lieutenant did not seem to notice his words' effect. Instead, he stared at the fire and rubbed one hand on his chin. "Still. Millers Town is mostly English, and we've not had any trouble between us. And I trust your judgement."

Wolf Tongue narrowed his gaze and puckered his lips as he watched Pyke. Pyke stared into the fire for another few moments and Wolf Tongue was sure he'd finally read what Pyke was after. He had not said it explicitly, possibly to measure out Wolf Tongue's thoughts, or perhaps only to leave the decision to Wolf Tongue. Or perhaps to plant the seed for Wolf Tongue to think it his own idea.

"You want me to come with you."

Pyke looked up without any hint of guile. "If you would. Your help would be invaluable. Whoever they are, you probably speak their language. And if we need to track and scout, I know no one better. And if they are Susquehannock," Pyke licked his lips and inclined his head, "I'd rather have you there for any … negotiations."

Wolf Tongue rubbed his neck and looked up. The wood interior and roof that arched over him were stained dark from smoke. The faces carved into the main poles that held the bark together, though, seemed as though they'd just been cut the week before and leered back at him with wild eyes and gaping mouths.

The four sat in silence, the fire snapping between them. Then, Wolf Tongue turned his eyes to Fox's Smile. His wife sat watching him with her hand on her stomach. He knew her face better than anything and he searched it for some reaction or hint of her feeling. Somehow she kept all her emotions hidden. Just polished-walnut eyes waiting for his reaction.

"Negotiations?" he asked.

"I hope negotiations only. There's no mission beyond that. I'm to investigate, try for a simple cessation, and report back to Jenkins Town. Any military action would be done by the regiment."

Wolf Tongue tossed the cider to Pyke. "If it'll help, I'll go. Especially if Davies will be there to protect us." He winked at the sergeant. Davies, now with a mouthful of boiled bread paused in his chewing and looked to Pyke.

Pyke didn't look to Davies, but smiled his gratitude. Again, Wolf Tongue noticed the past year seeping through Pyke, not in his appearance, but in the curve of his smile, as if his thanks were more genuine for the lack of other things to be thankful for. Wolf Tongue wondered how his own smile might look.

Pyke took another drink of the cider, then held the skin aloft. "I'm afraid it's empty."

"You told me you brought other gifts. I would've made the cider last longer if I'd known it would take you this long to give them out."

"We might need the remainder of the supplies for someone else," Pyke said.

Pyke and Davies were outside tending to their horses when Wolf Tongue caught his wife's hidden smile. They both laid out blankets to arrange bedding for their visitors and as she turned away, her eyes crinkled.

"What are you smiling at?"

"You."

Wolf Tongue stared at her in silence. Fox's Smile finished arranging a deer hide before she faced him again. "As soon as I saw it was Pyke, I knew you'd be off soon."

Wolf Tongue furrowed his eyebrows.

Fox's Smile laughed. "If men aren't away hunting, they're away hunting something else. I can manage on my own. The baby won't come when you're gone. And even if she does—"

"*He* does."

"Even if *she* does," repeated Fox's Smile. "You won't be able to help me anyway."

"I know. But. The British think we're attacking them, and if they decide this village is a threat ..."

Fox's Smile held up a hand. "Lover. I know. We'd be pressed to fight off a flock of turkeys." Though he knew she joked, Wolf Tongue grimaced. She leaned closer. "But it's not your fault and you're doing what you think is right. And it is. If the British think we're a threat, they'll attack, and we can't stand up to that now."

Wolf Tongue sighed. Again, the emptiness of his village, of the hole that seemed to come from the abandonment of so many people, blew through his body like the breath from the great bear of the north.

"And," she continued. "You'll go because you love adventure."

Wolf Tongue swallowed. He knew her words were true, but the thought brought up a surge of guilt. That he could run away for adventure when his people were dying. But the adventure would, he thought, help protect his people from an attack by the British.

After a long breath, Wolf Tongue felt a small smile creep onto his face. "That's why I live with you."

FOUR – LIMES BRITANNICUS

As they walked, Pyke, ever the quiet man, listened to Wolf Tongue's tales of adventures he'd undertaken since their last mission together. Each one grew more outlandish than the last. It made Pyke recall the celebration in the Susquehannock village after their defeat of Azariah Bennett, where Wolf Tongue recounted their dangerous tale and no detail was left unembellished.

Davies, for his part, grinned nervously whenever Wolf Tongue made a joke but also kept his distance, always making sure to put Pyke between himself and the Susquehannock.

Wolf Tongue, sensing Davies's unease, brandished his tomahawk.

"Davies, this is a sacred weapon and has split fifty skulls. You have spilled blood?"

Davies shuddered. "I've fought enough."

Wolf Tongue's eyes turned mischievous. It was a welcome sight for Pyke. The man he'd met a year earlier had been carefree and easy. Now the Susquehannock warrior was different. Guarded, less playful. Pyke sensed the weight of the man's village bearing down on Wolf Tongue's shoulders. Lifting Smoke had grown enfeebled, Pyke hadn't seen too many elders or warriors left, and death seemed to linger in the village. Wolf Tongue carried a heavy burden and it had aged him. It was good to see his old friend, if only for a moment, ignite that teasing smile.

Wolf Tongue said, "How many *savages* have you killed, Davies?"

Davies grunted. "All men are savages, not just Indians."

Wolf Tongue nodded. "I like you, Davies. I hope someday my tomahawk doesn't have to split your skull too."

Davies looked to Pyke for direction.

Pyke grinned. "Don't mind the savage, Sergeant. He enjoys banter and puffs himself up."

The day couldn't decide what it wanted to be. In the morning, it was foggy and overcast. Then the clouds gave way to a blazing sun that hinted at spring and had only just begun to warm them. Now the clouds had gathered again and a cold wind swept in. They had taken this trail last time, so Pyke knew they drew close to Millers Town.

Wolf Tongue nodded at him. "What happened to that girl who tried to kill you?"

Pyke bristled, and his own reaction surprised him. "As soon as Miss Bennett was herself, I set her free."

Davies's eyes bulged.

"Did you marry her?"

Pyke couldn't tell if his friend was joking. Davies had developed a fascination with the ground at his feet.

Pyke said, "I did not have the honor of taking Miss Bennett's hand."

"Did you have the honor of taking her to your bed?"

Davies blanched and hacked a fake cough.

Pyke shook his head. "I would not tell you if I did." Really, the Indian went too far.

Wolf Tongue shrugged. "Shame. That woman had fire in her."

Davies jaw fell open.

Pyke slowed his horse and looked at Wolf Tongue.

"Now that we are away from your village, I would ask again. Are the—"

"It's not the Susquehannock," Wolf Tongue said grimly.

"If it *were*, would these goods be sufficient recompense?" Pyke gestured at the materials they'd gotten from the quartermaster. He'd given some to Wolf Tongue and his village but had kept the rest for negotiations with the raiders, just in case.

Wolf Tongue glanced over at him. "The Pyke I knew would tell the savages to go to hell."

His friend was right. Pyke smiled at the thought. His time in the Colony had changed him. For better or worse, Pyke didn't exactly know.

"The savage I knew would tell me to pay the blood money, rather than risk his life defending those he didn't know."

Wolf Tongue pointed at him. "You finally learn from me."

Pyke smiled. "The last time you and I faced an army, we very nearly died."

Wolf Tongue smiled. "You nearly died."

Davies gave Pyke a disbelieving look. He didn't need to say what he was thinking. Pyke had been just as taken aback by Wolf Tongue's sharp words the first time he'd met the warrior. He understood now it was mostly harmless bravado.

"Sergeant." Pyke gave Davies a sharp look. "What's said on the road shall not be repeated. That is an order."

"Quite right, sir. Quite right."

Pyke looked back to Wolf Tongue. "As much as I'd like to take the fight to the savages raiding this settlement on the arse-end of the British Empire, I recognize our limitations. We are three, the townsfolk are no soldiers, and the colonel ..." Pyke's eyes fell on Davies. "The colonel will not be willing to send any of the little reinforcements we have. He has other plans, unknown to me. He wants this mission done quickly, quietly, and without fuss."

Davies nodded to Pyke. They had never shared their feelings of the colonel with each other, but Pyke could see Davies harbored the same sentiments. An understanding had passed between the two men.

Wolf Tongue said, "Your colonel is more concerned with the French."

Pyke said nothing because Wolf Tongue was right, though it was no secret. The British military was always concerned with the French. That provincial major from Virginia, Washington was his name, had launched a surprise attack on the bastards last year, and only a few months later he suffered a devastating defeat at his aptly-named Fort Necessity. Though the Crown had not officially declared it, for all intents and purposes, they were at war with the French. Hamlets like Millers Town now occupied a sort of no-man's land, a frontier where the boundaries were in constant flux. Pyke did not envy the hard-nosed frontiersmen that lived out here.

They took another bend as they came at Millers Town from the east. Ahead a tree-covered hill dove sharply toward the town, its slope severe enough to make it impassable. Pyke figured no Indian would stage a raid from this front. He remembered there was a plain separating the hill from the town which removed any advantage the high ground would have afforded.

"This way." Pyke motioned north.

It took them another fifteen minutes to round the hill and reach the northern plain. They waded through the creek and turned to Millers Town.

It had grown in the last year. Before it had been barebones, most of the homes just huts. Now the houses were timber affairs and Pyke figured the town had tripled in size. He estimated thirty, maybe forty homes. A church house rose above the mill, which churned on the bubbling waters of the creek. The townsfolk had begun construction of a wall that would ring the town. From what Pyke could see here, though, it barely stretched across the width of the northern edge.

Smoke lifted from a dozen chimneys in the town. Pyke smelled meat cooking. As they drew closer, the church house grew more impressive. It had two stories and in likelihood also served as the town hall. A knot of children rolled a hoop down the street, while others played ninepins in the dirt.

"This town grows," Wolf Tongue said.

Pyke knew what Wolf Tongue had left unsaid. Millers Town grew, while Wolf Tongue's village withered.

Then Pyke saw the woman.

She carried a basket and the three boys playing ninepins, instead of letting her pass, made her walk around them. One bumped her intentionally and she almost lost her basket. Pyke scowled at their lack of manners and wondered if this were a product of living on the frontier, away from the better influences of polite society. Then, one of the boys rolling the wheel broke away from the group to grab a scarf that had fallen out of the lady's basket. He ran it up to her and she pinched his cheek as he dropped it in.

Even from this great distance, Pyke could tell the woman was a beauty. She brought her forearm up to her head to shield her eyes from the glare of the afternoon sun and watched them as they approached.

Davies followed the woman with his eyes. "Lord, thank you, and I pray she don't have the flapdragon."

Wolf Tongue didn't understand so Pyke explained. "The sergeant hopes she does not have any disease."

"A pox?" Wolf Tongue recoiled.

Pyke chuckled. "No, not exactly."

Wolf Tongue still didn't understand but they were too close to the lady now to speak of such matters. She stared up at him. She was young, probably Wolf Tongue's age, and the sun had tanned her skin. Up close, Pyke could see something continental in her features. She didn't look English.

"'*Allo*," she said.

She was French.

Davies shot Pyke a look, which he ignored. If she was French, then there was a good likelihood she *did* have the flapdragon. Pyke's father had been warning him off French women ever since Pyke had been old enough to understand what he meant.

Even outside carnal concerns, Pyke didn't trust the French in general. He wondered just what in the hell a madame was doing here, at the ends of the British Empire, especially when a war simmered, if not raged.

"*Bonjour, madame.*" Pyke stopped his horse. "I am Lieutenant Hugh Pyke, here on the Crown's business. What is your name?"

She put her basket of laundry down beside the bubbling creek and did a mocking curtsy. "Madame Fleur nee Bonheur Nederwue."

With her thick accent, it took Pyke a moment to make sense of her words. *Nederwue*.

Wolf Tongue stole a glance at him, having realized it as well: they had killed this woman's husband one year ago in self-defense.

Pyke remembered to smile. "*C'est une plaisir de faire votre connaissance.* May I present Sergeant Davies and Wolf Tongue of the Susquehannock."

She looked up at the three of them with a playful smirk, brazen like all French.

She had been in the middle of doing laundry. Her dress was wet and clung to her side.

Davies smoothed his beard and straightened his coat. "Madame." The word sounded funny coming from him.

Wolf Tongue stepped forward. "I am Wolf Tongue of the Wolf Clan of the Susquehannock."

"Oh my." She batted her eyelashes. "I have seen no man taller."

Pyke rolled his eyes. The last thing the savage needed was flattery. His pride already burst at the seams.

The boy that had picked up the madame's scarf peeled away from the rolling wheel to watch them. He looked to be eleven or twelve, but small for his age.

Pyke smiled at him. "Nice to meet a gentleman out here on the frontier."

The boy smiled at back. "You're a soldier!"

Fleur turned as he ran up to them and pinched the boy's cheek again. "Boone will break many hearts in a few short years."

The boy blushed and looked up at Wolf Tongue. "What tribe are you?"

"I am Wolf Tongue, of the Wolf Clan, of the Susquehannock, the greatest, fiercest tribe the world has ever known."

Davies laughed. "And I'm just Sergeant Davies."

Boone couldn't take his eyes off Pyke and Wolf Tongue.

"Nice to meet you too," Davies said, smiling.

Boone said, "Are you here to kill all the Indians?"

Wolf Tongue laughed. "I hope not all of them."

"We're here on Crown business." Pyke jumped off his horse and shook the boy's hand. Boone could barely contain his elation. He looked ready to float away. "We need to speak with Mr. Fletcher, Boone. Would you be so kind to take us to him?"

Fleur pointed. "They'll want to talk to you first."

Four men formed a V by the newly-built log wall, Fletcher not among them. Two carried muskets. They looked to be brothers, both tall and gangly. One man carried a pitchfork like it was no heavier than a pencil. He had a beard thicker than sheep's wool and his forearms were knotted with muscle.

But the man who made the biggest impression on Pyke was unarmed. He stood ahead of the others, clearly in charge. His wool breeches and matching wool vest looked new, as did his silk cravat.

Pyke wondered two things. Why had Fletcher come to Jenkins Town and not this man, the apparent leader of the community? And why was Fletcher not here now?

The man in front of the others had intelligent, appraising eyes and Pyke realized the man was taking measure of him.

Pyke turned back to the boy. "Boone, you go on back to your game now. It was nice to meet you. And you as well, Madame Nederwue," Pyke said.

Fleur did another mocking curtsy and he found it impossible to keep his eyes from her bosom. She hitched her skirt and hiked past them with her laundry basket, the sun turning her clothes almost transparent. Pyke caught Davies gawking. Fleur proceeded further downstream and waded in to do her wash.

"I don't like these men already," Wolf Tongue said.

Pyke turned and together they met the four men just outside the wall. Boone walked past, turning a dozen times to look at Pyke and Wolf Tongue on his way. The children playing ninepins stopped their game to stare as well. The tallest put on a brave face and held up an imaginary musket and fired it at Wolf Tongue.

Wolf Tongue, for his part, smiled and tapped the tomahawk at his belt. The child's eyes went wide and they scurried away, leaving their ninepins in the dirt.

"Welcome," the man in front said. He extended his hand. "Robert Sutler, but every country-put around here calls me Dob."

Pyke shook Dob's hand. "Lieutenant Hugh Pyke."

"We've been expecting you, Lieutenant!" Dob pumped Pyke's hand. "Welcome! I have great admiration and respect for the military. As my surname implies, my grandfather sold many supplies to the army in his day."

Pyke had met a few sutlers in his time and didn't much care for them. They profited from war but never seemed to take part in it. While other men died, they made money.

Dob said, "And who might your friends be?"

Pyke motioned. "This is my friend Wolf Tongue, of the Susquehannock tribe." He carefully measured Dob's reaction to the name of the tribe. The man's expression didn't change, but his friends carrying the muskets couldn't hide their shock. "And this is Sergeant Davies."

Dob turned to the tall, gangly brothers first. "These two Dukes of Limbs are called Kit and Quill. They're brothers, in the event you forgot your spectacles."

Dob laughed at his own joke. Kit and Quill wore polite smiles.

Dob said, "And this bearded one is called Josiah. Everyone calls him Si, but he doesn't much care for it I think."

Josiah rested his pitchfork against his shoulder and nodded at them.

Pyke regarded Dob. "Mr. Sutler, we have ridden a long way and would like to get off our feet. Where could we get our horses fed and watered and sit down to eat?"

"Of course, I'll show you. But first, I must ask. Any news of getting a proper road out this way?"

Pyke smiled. They had asked him the same thing last time he was here. It was the same everywhere.

"I am happy to renew the town's request with the colonel. But as you know Mr. Sutler, the Crown's resources are tied up in defending towns such as yours and in establishing more trade routes with the natives."

"I appreciate that, sir. And please do call me Dob."

"With clothes like that," Wolf Tongue said, "a man like you could build his own road."

Pyke hid his smile. He'd been thinking the same thing.

Dob frowned, for just a moment. He quickly regained his composure. "A trader is only as impressive as his clothes, believe me."

"Not the trader's goods?" Wolf Tongue said.

Dob's mouth was going to catch flies. It was very clear no one spoke to him like this, let alone an Indian.

Pyke secretly enjoyed Wolf Tongue asking difficult questions as it gave him a chance to gauge Dob's reaction. But he decided to step in to keep up appearances. "You'll forgive Wolf Tongue. He knows English, but not English manners."

Dob closed the oak door to the church and they were alone. The dank beams smelled of incense. Pyke took in the two-story building, impressed by the rafters that arched overhead. It felt like England here.

"Where is Mr. Fletcher?" Pyke asked as Dob led him to the front. They sat on a bench next to each other. The afternoon light filtered in through high windows and hit the interior in random places.

"With his wife and daughter I presume," Dob said, but offered nothing else.

Pyke pressed the issue. "I was expecting to see the man who filed the report, that is why I ask."

Dob chuckled and leaned in. "Lieutenant, there is nothing sinister at play here. Fletcher I'm sure is busy attending to that darling little girl of his. We did not know when you would be here so he couldn't wait outside the walls."

"Mr. Sutler, who is that French woman?"

Dob wagged a finger at him. "I caught you looking at her apple-dumpling shop! Hard not to, isn't it?"

Pyke did not care for the man's familiarity, not one bit. It was the Colonial way, and though he'd been in the Colony for two years now, he was still not used to it.

"I ask because she is French, not because she is a woman."

Dob held out a palm. "My apologies. As an officer I should have known you would place duty above anything as vulgar as that. She was married to one of the men who lived here."

For a moment Pyke wondered if she might have been a spy. Though Millers Town offered no strategic military advantage as it was small and boasted little in the way of goods, Pyke wouldn't have put it past the French. But what information could she have even gathered out there that would be of use? And in a village this small, surely the townfolk would have shared their suspicions with him, if they had any, of her.

It was unlikely she spied for the French, but Pyke figured it was safer to treat her with suspicion than not.

He asked, "Where does she come from?"

"Her background is vague, the rumors aplenty."

"Such as?"

"Excuse me for saying, sir, but one rumor went she was a piper's wife."

"Do you think this Nederwue fellow would have married a whore?"

"He was Dutch." Dob laughed. "But no, probably not."

"He is gone?" Pyke asked innocently.

"He is dead." Dob looked away. "Good man, at that. Left one night to trade with some Iroquois. Never came back."

Pyke acted surprised and went along with the story. Nederwue was in fact one of the scalpers who'd nearly killed Pyke and Wolf Tongue on their last mission.

"How long ago was this?"

"A year. We have not seen him since."

"How do you know he is dead?" Pyke said.

"Have you seen the man's wife?" Dob broke into laughter. "Any man who doesn't come home to her must be dead."

Pyke smiled, just enough to be polite. "Do you have proof he is dead?"

Dob shook his head. "No, sir. No proof. Just common sense. A man that goes missing in this place, at the edge of the British Empire, where savages lurk behind every pass, the lowest form of men, closer to animals than we ... a man who leaves a wife behind like that, that man is surely dead. Surely murdered for some reason or other."

Pyke couldn't tell whether Dob knew more than he was letting on. "I'm sorry to hear about Mrs. Nederwue's—and the town's—loss."

"Thank you, sir."

Pyke bobbed his head. "When I last was here, there was no church house and the town was half its size. I'm very impressed."

A new voice sounded from behind him. "The Lord provides."

Pyke turned. The town's pastor, dressed in a plain black smock and collar, came slowly down the aisle. Pyke figured he was Anglican, whose doctrines were more palatable to those of the strict, humorless New England Puritans he'd met before. The man had white hair and walked with a limp.

"Lieutenant Hugh Pyke." He offered his hand.

The pastor extended a bony hand that trembled almost violently. "Keith Baldwin. This is my flock."

Pyke carefully shook the man's delicate hand.

Baldwin couldn't seem to keep his head still. Pyke wondered what affliction plagued him.

The reverend said, "I hope you will kill these savages quickly. Teach them a lesson."

Pyke couldn't believe the words coming out of the man's mouth. Surely the man was familiar with the Commandments?

"I will get to the bottom of this trouble and hopefully I can resolve it peacefully, without the need for bloodshed."

Baldwin shook his head. "I admire that, Lieutenant Pyke, but the savage is a lower form of animal. He has no soul and like the beasts of the plains must be put in his place."

The man was old and feeble and losing his mind. Pyke did not feel the need to educate him though he smiled at the thought of Wolf Tongue's reaction to these sentiments.

"Thank you, Reverend." Dob moved behind the old man and aimed him at the doors. "Now you go rest up. We will need your help in the coming days so you must have your strength."

Without much argument, Baldwin let himself be shuffled to the door. He went outside.

Dob came back to Pyke. "He has served the Lord God for a long time, God bless him."

Pyke said nothing.

Dob sensed his dislike of the pastor but said nothing about it. "And surely God has blessed us. So far we have been lucky, luckier than many. But don't let outward appearances fool you, much like my dress fools those I do business with." Dob smoothed his wool overcoat. "We are struggling of late and these raids bring a lot of uncertainty. Any interruption to trade and our buyers are inclined to go elsewhere."

"The town does look prosperous. Perhaps that is driving the raids?"

Dob shrugged. "Who knows what goes on in the mind of the savage?"

Pyke had to acknowledge that. "Yes, who knows. From Mr. Fletcher's report, the attacks appear more personal in nature, as if the raiding tribe feels it has been aggrieved."

"I can assure you, sir, such is not the case."

"I understand that, but still there is always a reason behind what they do, believe me. Has a chief approached you? Have they attempted to communicate?"

Dob was too quick to shake his head no. "They have not, lieutenant. These are unprovoked attacks."

Pyke pretended to think. Then, "Does anyone in the town trade Indian scalps for coin?"

Dob's eyes never left Pyke's face. "No, sir. No, sir, we do not. We are peaceful men: farmers, and traders, Christians all. We only want be left alone."

Pyke nodded and carefully considered his next words.

"The colonel sent me here because I am familiar with the area and because I know the Susquehannock. They are warriors, but they haven't been known to attack English settlements without provocation."

Pyke let the words hang in the air.

Dob sat up on the bench. "What are you saying, sir?"

"I'm saying what I know, Mr. Sutler. The man I brought with me is of them and he is honorable. He would tell me if his tribe was raiding this village—and why. But he tells me they do not."

Dob thought about that. Then he smiled again. "Lieutenant, I am no expert on the savage. Neither are my people. Perhaps we are wrong about the tribe, I'll concede that much. But the raids are fact.

"Just two nights ago a war party attacked Hezekiah Morris. Broke his arm and took his one good horse. Go meet with him, and he'll tell you. The raids are getting worse. I fear Hezekiah's broken arm is only the start of the violence. I fear men—good men—will be killed. They are animals, lieutenant. They are brutes, ignorant of culture and morals. And they have no regard for us, no regard for women or children. I've heard stories you wouldn't believe, lieutenant. Stories that will haunt you in your sleep the rest of your life, of the pillaging, infanticide, raping and slaughtering. There is no reason to their actions, either. One day they do not even bother to look at you and the next day they descend upon your town with arrows and fire ... Lieutenant Pyke, I know this from personal experience. When I was a boy, they came and took my mother. There was nothing I could do."

"Well, sir?" Davies asked.

Pyke had met them outside Fletcher's home. Wolf Tongue had made it a point to track down Molly Fletcher and inquire about her cider.

Pyke checked the immediate area for eavesdroppers. "Sutler lied to me."

"About what?" Wolf Tongue said.

"He said there were no scalpers in this town."

Wolf Tongue smiled. "Maybe there aren't. Anymore."

Pyke shook his head. "I doubt it. He made up a story about Nederwue's disappearance. We can't trust him, and he's the man in charge."

"What next then, sir?" Davies asked.

Pyke surveyed the town. Fletcher's hut sat on a hill so he could see most of the town. He saw thirty or forty men, all of them laborers, just as many women, and maybe twenty children. Most the men probably knew the musket, but unlikely they had one for each or the discipline to use them. Against a war party they stood little chance. And the town itself was only half-fortified. The wall was not finished, not by a long shot. Forest all round. Really only two ways out quickly: north and south.

Seeing the town and its surroundings from this vantage point, taking stock of the townspeople, all of it confirmed what he'd been thinking when they'd set off on the journey.

"We need to talk to the chief and settle this without bloodshed. Blood money if necessary."

FIVE – MINQUA

Wolf Tongue shrugged his shoulders. "This is a long way to make me walk if you're just going to hand out your gifts and hope everyone wanders away."

Pyke, unruffled, looked at Wolf Tongue. "I'll need your help to talk with them. I'll be able to talk with them if they speak English."

"Or French, apparently," murmured Davies. The sergeant quickly cleared his throat and issued an apology at a sharp look from Pyke. Wolf Tongue watched the exchange, wondering at the give-and-take between these two.

"But," continued Pyke, "even if I can talk with them, I would like your help understanding them."

Wolf Tongue grunted. "I don't know what I can tell you that you can't see yourself. Someone wants something that these people don't want to give up. And you say this Sutler lied to you?" He shook his head. "This place is sour to begin with. We came to help a year ago, stayed, shared food with these people. And then their friends tried to kill us both for our scalps."

Davies sat up with a jolt. He quickly relaxed, but still looked at Pyke with clear questions in his eyes. Clearly, Pyke hadn't shared his full history with his sergeant.

Wolf Tongue felt the ire like metal in his mouth. "And now their leader is lying to you about the scalpers? What else will he lie to us about? And how long until someone here tries to sell our heads to the French again? This place is filled with dirty *quhanstrono* who don't care for us, even after we come to help them a second time. I say leave them."

Pyke looked at Wolf Tongue for a moment, then turned his eyes to some distant thing and worked his jaw.

Wolf Tongue took a breath, then, "I came with you because you're my friend and you asked for my help. But these people are not our friends. Many aren't even

English and I wouldn't doubt that they're fully deserving of any death that comes their way. I know it's not the Susquehannock. And whoever it is is probably already allied with the French, and we both know the French are much more generous with their muskets than the English. If they want to attack in force …" he let his thought drift off.

Davies made a show of resettling himself in his seat. Pyke looked at him for a long moment, considering. Then said, "And you, Sergeant? What do you think?"

"Never thought I'd say it, sir, but I agree with him. The town's nearly indefensible. Forest is too close. Wall's not up. Not much high ground here by the creek, you know. If it comes to puffs of smoke and flashing steel, a smart man would bet on the savages."

Pyke's shoulders sagged very slightly and he nodded. "Noted, Sergeant."

"Sir. If I may." Davies leaned forward, his voice lowering even more. "I didn't know nothing about them scalpers coming after you, and I don't pretend to know what you were at on that mission you keep so tight in your pockets. But if I'm hearin' right, it sounds to me like this is a den of vipers here. If we're in danger from the people as much as from the savages, I say we take a long, slow road home and let Millers Town and the savages figure out their own bickering."

Davies seemed to be finished for his bit, but a breath later, he raised his hands. "But, sir. I don't know what the colonel's orders specifically are. And I know orders is orders."

Pyke looked down and fiddled with the hilt of his saber for a moment, then looked back up at Davies. "Sergeant, my understanding of my orders is … ambiguous. I understand your concern. But I cannot leave without knowing for certain that I'm not abandoning good Christian folk."

Wolf Tongue leaned in. "Is that because they're so few you've never seen any before?"

Pyke pushed at his cheek with his tongue and ignored the comment. "We'll stay and help how we can. Perhaps we can talk to the raiders and end it all with some gifts from Colonel Bennett. Then we take the long, slow road home."

Wolf Tongue crossed his arms. "You feel obligation to people who lie to you when you come to help? People who've tried to kill you."

Pyke took a long breath, his shoulders rising and falling with a grimace on his face. "Jesus said, 'But I say unto you, that ye resist not evil: but whosoever shall smite thee on thy right cheek, turn to him the other also.'"

"A cheek is one thing, but I doubt this Jesus offered up his scalp."

"Actually—"

A scream from outside interrupted Pyke.

All three men rose immediately, hands on their weapons, when the screams became distinct: "Indians! Indians!"

Wolf Tongue tore through the door first. Outside, it was dark, but the screams and rattle of battle turned his head to the left. Not thirty paces away, he saw the spit of fire from a musket and heard its crack.

He ran, his musket in one hand and his tomahawk in the other. Just beyond the man who fired the musket, a fire had started inside one of the houses and was throwing off a low light that showed shadows running before it. Flashes of dark bodies tangled against one another, twisting, engaging briefly and then turning away. Farther into the town, to Wolf Tongue's left, he saw two more fights. He heard the *thrack* of muskets being used as clubs and the war whoops of the attackers.

Both Pyke and Davies brought their muskets to their shoulders.

Wolf Tongue veered to his left, sprinting for the nearest melee and hoping Davies would aim toward the edge of the town.

The muskets behind Wolf Tongue fired almost simultaneously. He didn't look to see what happened, but closed on a man from Millers Town who used his musket like a spear. He fended off the knife-swipes of a young man who wore his forehead shaved with long hair in the back in the Shawnee fashion.

The young man swatted away the probing musket and seemed about to lunge when he looked to Wolf Tongue. Confusion flashed across his face, slowing his attack for a heartbeat. Then, he stumbled back as the muzzle of the musket jabbed him in the jaw. He staggered a few steps, then gathered his wits enough to turn and run toward the larger group gathered by the fire.

Another muzzle-blast cracked in the night as Wolf Tongue slowed his run to stop. The man with the musket seemed shocked to see him and pointed his musket at him. Wolf Tongue hammered the end of the musket to the ground with a swipe of his tomahawk and glared at the man. "Fight your attackers, fool!"

The man only blinked, confused.

Wolf Tongue shook his head and turned back toward where the fight sounded the biggest. He saw Pyke draw his saber and run toward the burning building where a dozen men struggled hand to hand. Davies was reloading his musket.

Wolf Tongue searched for an opening, a shot on one of the attackers, but in the flickering dark among the knot of men, he couldn't pick out a solid target. He saw Pyke engage with another invader with a clang of steel on steel. With a grunt of frustration, Wolf Tongue ran again toward them.

If only Pyke would stay out of it, I could just leave them to fight it out.

A moment later, he stood alongside Pyke. He'd wounded his man, who scrambled backward with a bleeding gash cut into his shoulder, even through the thick fur wrap he wore against the cold. Wolf Tongue's left arm twitched as he instinctively readied his musket, but then he lowered it and narrowed his eyes at the wounded man as he ran for safety.

Seneca, he thought.

The wounded man ran past another pair of fighters as the invader hacked at the *quhanstrono's* neck with his tomahawk. The Millers Town man fell to his knees, blood black across his white shirt. Another musket blast cracked and the man standing over him jerked and dropped his weapon.

Pyke ran toward the main knot of fighting and Wolf Tongue followed. More than a dozen men were fighting now, axes against war clubs, butcher knives against tomahawks. Metal clanged and grated. Dogs yelped and growled. And a woman was screaming.

"Raise the town!" bellowed Pyke as he slammed his saber against a Seneca's musket. "Bring your guns!"

Wolf Tongue surged forward to block the way of another Seneca running toward Pyke's side. The Seneca feinted, then ducked down low as he swung his war club. Wolf Tongue danced away, still taking a knock against his knee. In a heartbeat, Wolf Tongue and the Seneca were locked in combat. Wolf Tongue dropped his musket and loosened his tomahawk as the Seneca came in close, pressing hard with his short war club. The weapons cracked as they hammered against one another. Wolf Tongue felt the whoosh of air as he leaned back from a slash at his face. Another swipe and Wolf Tongue parried with his tomahawk, hooking the blade around the head of the war club. He yanked, pulling the weapon free and stepping close for a punch with his other hand.

The Seneca's head snapped to the side and he dropped to one knee. Wolf Tongue recovered his momentum and raised his tomahawk, but the man had continued his fall and rolled away. Wolf Tongue took a step toward the man, who was now scrambling to his feet, when he recognized the yells.

"Back to the camp! Back to the camp!" came the Seneca calls in their strange accent.

Then more shouts came in another tongue that sounded something like Unami, the language of the Lenape.

One man still fought with a pair of Millers Town men farther away, beyond the flaming house by where Wolf Tongue stood. The rest were fleeing, running into the surrounding field and woods with their taunts and whoops echoing. A musket fired, then a second, though they seemed to hit nothing but the night.

Pyke ran toward the only two men still engaged in a fight. The Millers Town men, with now almost all of the village present, all seemed too absorbed with other tasks to join him. Some crumpled to the ground to examine their own wounds, while others bent over their fallen neighbors. Others still simply stared out at the retreating *iomwhen*.

The lone invader dove against his attackers, knocking into them both, and pulled a musket from one of their hands. As he spun away, he whirled, swinging the musket in a huge arc. Wolf Tongue heard the crack as it smacked into one man's head. The villager crumpled to the ground as his friend stumbled and ran to escape the huge attacker.

The invader stood upright and turned slowly around. His eyes fixed on Pyke, still running, then he turned and with long strides sprinted out into the night.

As the man passed the glare of the fire, Wolf Tongue felt his breath catch in his throat. He thought the men had been Seneca. Most wore the wrapped, knee-length skins and furs like their people and cried out in their awkward tongue.

But this man was no Seneca. At least he hadn't been the last time Wolf Tongue had seen him.

For a moment, Wolf Tongue doubted his eyes. But then, he was sure. There was no way he could mistake the huge man he'd lived in the same village with and then fought for leadership of the Susquehannock.

That was Kicks-the-Oneida.

SIX – THE SPOILS OF WAR

In the darkness, Pyke saw Fletcher cut through the crowd and approach with a torch. The man's shirt and breeches were torn, blood smeared on one side of his face, but he walked as if unharmed.

"Your Indian was right," Fletcher said. "They stole our corn stock."

Pyke nodded. For once he'd hoped his friend, Wolf Tongue, had been wrong. The Susquehannock had explained that Seneca very often used raids as feints to hide their true aim.

Only this raid had been both an attack and a feint.

"Any others hurt?" Pyke said.

"Thompson and Hines, dead. The rest of us, cuts and bruises."

Pyke put his hand on the man's shoulder. "I'm sorry. Attend to your family."

Pyke saw Wolf Tongue and Davies waiting for him. He excused himself and gestured at Wolf Tongue and Davies to follow. Men and women still ran helter and skelter down the main street as the house fire continued to rage. A dozen men had pitched water from the creek but Pyke hadn't seen a one try to put out the flames. Instead they had ringed the tiny home with dirt and were apparently letting it burn to the ground. Pyke guessed the water they had collected was being saved to protect the nearest cabins in the event the fire jumped.

Pyke led Wolf Tongue and Davies away from the crowd. Behind him, Pyke heard Dob Sutler shouting his name, but he ignored the calls. The three men huddled near where they had entered the town, Davies propping one boot on the half-built wall.

"Wish this were a little farther along in the construction," Davies said.

Pyke looked at Wolf Tongue. "Who were they?"

The Susquehannock blew out a breath. "They are many."

Pyke frowned.

"Many are Seneca, I think. But they aren't alone. There are others with them. Wyandot, even Shawnee."

He ran his hands over the shaved sides of his head and looked at the ground before continuing. "Many of the *iomwhen* want to move west. Remove themselves from all this." He waved a hand at the town. "Some of the strongest warriors and families leave their tribes and band together to move into the Ohio Valley. Closer to the French and open land with new villages. I hear they'll accept warriors from other tribes if those men can prove themselves. The Lenape call them all *minqua*, the treacherous."

Wolf Tongue drew a long breath, and when he spoke, his voice had lowered as if too heavy to bear. "Some of the Susquehannock were supposed to have gone to them. Tonight I saw one."

Davies, not appreciating Wolf Tongue's heavy heart, cut in. "The Mingo? Never heard of 'em, but it explains why the townfolk thought the Susquees were attacking them."

Wolf Tongue nodded gravely. "Kicks-the-Oneida."

Pyke remembered the man. Tall, broad, proud, with a bevy of warrior's scars and twice as many souvenirs of death. A warrior surpassing all others amongst the Susquehannock, with the exception of Wolf Tongue. The two men had vied for leadership in the community and loathed each other. He had, in fact, nearly cost the Susquehannock their battle with Azariah Bennett by failing to heed Wolf Tongue's strategy. By the grace of God and a desperate, near-miracle rally, Wolf Tongue and Pyke seized that day. But it could have just as easily gone the other way. Pyke was very nearly in heaven, courtesy of the man's foolishness.

"Kicks-the-Oneida," Pyke echoed.

Davies examined his musket in the fire light. "Who's he?"

"Our best warrior." Wolf Tongue smirked. "Until I came of age."

"But still a man that commands respect," Pyke said.

Wolf Tongue nodded. "He had many—what did you call them?"

Pyke said, "Apple polishers."

"Ah yes," Davies said. "I'm familiar with the type."

Pyke could hear what the sergeant had not said: *Captain Smith.*

Wolf Tongue said, "If Kicks-the-Oneida has joined them, other Susquehannock have as well."

Pyke said, "The man led many when he was still of your people. Have they all gone?"

"Yes. A dozen left with him, many of them our best warriors." Wolf Tongue had a faraway look in his eyes. "I was supposed to stand shoulder-to-shoulder with these men, not against them."

Pyke felt the conflict in his friend's heart. And like all good soldiers, he knew a man's heart was his most important weapon.

"Wolf Tongue, this is not your fight. I would not ask you to stand against your own people."

The Susquehannock warrior slowly turned his eyes back to Pyke. For a moment, he said nothing.

"They're not my people anymore. Because they raid with the Seneca and Shawnee, British soldiers consider war against the Susquehannock. If they had stayed, things would have been different for our people. Now we're sick and dying and accused of treachery."

Much as he needed his friend's help, Pyke did not want the man to stay out of loyalty alone. "Then perhaps you should attend to your people, rather than be here."

Wolf Tongue shook his head. "I help my people by being here. The British are strong and I hope they remember this favor. Before this is done, I'll send Kicks-the-Oneida's soul flying."

Pyke nodded, even more grateful for his friend's assistance. "Davies, how did the townspeople handle themselves?"

"Like monkeys on horseback without their tails tied, and half the lot were Peter-gunners." Then Davies shrugged. "Then again even soldiers can be like that when the air's on fire, sir. All in all, they were fair, but not used to the fight. A few weeks' training would harden 'em, though."

Which meant it was worse than Pyke had originally hoped. He could forgive them their lack of discipline in the skirmish, but he had hoped they would have had more training or cohesion. According to Davies, half were poor shooters, and Pyke had hoped the hunting would have sharpened their eyes. Though, shooting a deer and gunning down a six-foot-tall murderous Indian were a far cry apart.

"Wolf Tongue, what do the Mingo want?"

"It must be blood." Wolf Tongue turned and gestured at the town. "This village grows but there are more profitable towns to raid. They seek blood. Or else to just harass the British."

"Will they return tonight?" Pyke said.

Wolf Tongue thought about it.

"Lieutenant!"

Pyke looked past Davies and saw a silhouette approaching. He could tell it was a woman and a second later knew exactly what woman it was.

"Mrs. Nederwue ..." Pyke was at a loss for words. "Are you hurt?"

"Lieutenant, can we speak? Privately?"

It still took him a moment to register the words through her accent. "Madame, we are in the middle of—"

"It is urgent. *S'il vous plait.*"

Davies gave him a long look from across his face, and Wolf Tongue did the same thing. Pyke had no idea what this could be about, but he doubted she was interested in carnal pleasures at this moment. He ignored the charged looks of the sergeant and the savage.

Pyke said, "Sergeant, establish a perimeter and assign watches to span the evening. We don't want to be hit again with our breeches around our ankles."

"Permission to speak—"

"Don't stand on ceremony with me, Davies."

"Thank you, sir. We soldiers would divide the night into halves. But the townfolk ain't no soldiers. I think three watches."

"Sound idea. Make it happen."

Davies hurried off. Wolf Tongue stepped beyond the wall to give Pyke and Fleur some privacy. The Susquehannock peered into the night and Pyke wondered what the man could see. And if he could anticipate the Mingos' next move.

Fleur wore her dress but had also wrapped herself in a shawl and seemed to be bracing against the cold. Pyke was still sweating from the battle.

"Mrs. Nederwue, we have urgent problems to attend, so if you'll forgive the informality, please come to the matter quickly."

She harrumphed. "We French come to the matter better than you Rosbif, who would rather three left turns instead of one right."

In the fire light, her face looked soft, her eyes not as daring as earlier. The French were so very different than the English, and yet, Pyke knew his history. At times their kingdoms and peoples had been one.

Pyke would have welcomed the distraction from his duties of Fleur on a routine mission, but this was no routine mission. Pyke didn't have time for such things.

"You cannot trust Dob Sutler."

Pyke kept his face expressionless. "Why do you say that?"

"It is for the scalping. This." Fleur gestured toward the town. Villagers were still acting crazed and the flames lifted high into the sky. Pyke spotted Davies rounding up some men, or trying to.

Pyke didn't want to show his hand. "There are scalpers in this town?"

"*Oui.*"

"How do you know?"

"Because my husband was one."

Pyke said nothing.

"Some men in this town trade for Red-men scalps. My husband was one of them. They brought them north. It is how he and I met."

The English and French had learned scalping, an evil and barbaric practice, from the savage. And they had used the gruesome ritual for their own ends, promising coin in exchange for scalps. Pyke objected to the idea on Christian grounds, and because Wolf Tongue had shown him that some savages had a strong moral code.

The French, it was rumored, offered a lot of money for the scalps of Indians belonging to tribes sympathetic to or allied with the English. Their way of stirring up trouble within the territories controlled by the Crown. But the thought of British subjects profiting from such a venture knotted Pyke's stomach.

Pyke said, "They traded these scalps with the French?"

Fleur frowned. "I do not know, he would never tell me with who. All I know is, the Red-men scalps were worth something."

"How did you not know? You lived in a French settlement, did you not?"

Fleur's mouth formed a thin line and Pyke saw that famous Gallic pride in the locking of her jaw.

"What happened before is none of your business."

Her response prompted Pyke to only inquire further, but he hesitated. Who the scalpers traded with did not matter at this moment. More urgently, Pyke needed to understand whom he could trust within Millers Town.

He said, "Dob knows about this?"

"He knows everything."

Pyke shook his head. Part of him wanted to file his report with the colonel and leave these wretches to their fate. No doubt the Mingos were retaliating. These men had brought about this violence. Pyke saw no good reason to risk the lives of Wolf Tongue and Sergeant Davies in this senseless squabble.

Over the shouts and confusion, Pyke heard another wail rise. A child. He looked past Fleur and saw a woman hurrying with a young girl cradled in her arms. At first he could not tell if the child was injured or scared, then realized the woman would not be rushing somewhere if the girl were simply frightened.

The sight reminded him of the other children he'd seen, and the many women living here. This was not a soldier's fort. Men and women lived here as families. And the children …

"Do all men here engage in this trade?" Pyke asked.

"Many do not know." Fleur shook her head. "When I discuss it, I am told 'be quiet.'"

Pyke faced the full reality. Many in this town were innocent. And the Mingos would show them no mercy. The savage was different than the English. The savage viewed guilt and responsibility from a tribal, not an individual, perspective.

They would massacre the entire town, innocents be damned.

"Thank you, Mrs. Nederwue." Pyke nodded. "Now you should return to your home."

"Impossible." She drew the shawl more tightly around her and pointed at the hut no one was trying to save. "It burns."

Pyke didn't know what to say, so he stammered, "I am sorry."

She suddenly stepped forward and spoke as if she had read his mind. "Do not leave us. Please. Do not leave me."

Wolf Tongue wore a sly grin as he watched Fleur walk away. "I like that one, for a white."

That was the Susquehannock warrior. The town burned and another attack could be imminent, but the man was joking.

Davies returned to the half-finished wall, out of breath. "Sir, many of the fathers won't leave their families to stand watch."

Pyke took that in. "Damned fools. Their families would be safer if they stood proper watch."

"I know, sir, but like I said, they ain't no soldiers."

Wolf Tongue shook his head. "Like children, they think if they cannot see the danger, there is no danger."

Pyke turned to Wolf Tongue. "Why hasn't their chief come to us, if they are so aggrieved?"

The Indian thought about it. "Some chiefs send warriors to scratch their own arses. Though I wouldn't follow anyone who wasn't first into battle, so he may have been in the attack. If he wants to talk, he'll make himself known."

Pyke cursed. Davies was doing his best to keep his composure, but Pyke could tell the man's mind was racing with thoughts of murderous savages descending upon the town.

"So then we must go to them," Pyke said. "Make it known we wish to talk."

Davies shuddered.

Behind them, the fire still raged. Fleur's house, destroyed. Pyke found himself wondering where she would sleep tonight, and live tomorrow. The way the boys had shown her no respect earlier, the way the men had not even tried to save her home, they treated her like an outcast. This town's Mary Magdalene.

Wolf Tongue said, "You'll need more than what you have left if you're looking to send them away with gifts."

Davies scratched at his beard. "No time to ride to Jenkins Town and requisition more materials. We'd likely come back to a dead town."

"Then these people will have to choose. Either fight or pay."

Wolf Tongue said, "An English does not part with his possessions easily."

"Nor an Indian his pride." Pyke smiled. "We must convince the town."

Davies looked from Pyke to Wolf Tongue and back again. "Aside from the obvious, how do we do that?"

Wolf Tongue nodded. "I'll tell them of the savage. They will pay."

Davies's eyes became very white.

Pyke said, "Before I forget, you should dress yourself so these people can tell you from the Mingos."

Wolf Tongue smirked. "And if we ever face the French together you will have to do the same."

SEVEN – THE BRITISH GOD

Wolf Tongue crossed his arms and leaned against the doorjamb of the church. This place was where the English god was supposed to live, though he saw nothing to inspire awe here. Rough wooden benches in rows faced a slightly elevated platform. On the platform was a table beneath two beams attached cross-wise. The walls were whitewashed with blocks of black where the windows of the church blocked out the night.

This was the place of the god of the French and the British. The god of Wolf Tongue's father, though he had spoken of him seldom. Briefly, Wolf Tongue wondered whether his father had reluctantly stepped away from his god to be with the Susquehannock, or whether he'd fled his religion and found refuge.

He drew his eyes and his focus back to the men arguing at the front of the place. He smirked as he watched Pyke. One of the townsmen was saying something about his godliness and Christian blood. The soldier stood at the base of the dais, his hands clasped behind his back, chin down as if in severe conference with the other man's words. The muscles in Pyke's jaw clenched and unclenched.

When the other man, gaunt with gaps where a few teeth should have been, finished speaking, he looked around for a moment as if unsure how to end his tirade, then stomped to a bench and flopped down. Pyke raised his chin and, with what seemed like an effort to Wolf Tongue, politely thanked the man for his thoughts.

"But, good sirs," Pyke continued, "the Indians do not yet care for our pleas of Christian love. I, for one, pray that they do learn of Our Lord and take His teaching to heart. But those who attack now must be placated." Pyke reiterated his argument with the tenacity of a badger. "We drove them away because they only intended to harry us. And even at that, we are wounded, and two men are dead."

"Harry us? Their raids would be bad enough, but tonight's attack was no raid. It's murder and chaos!" cried another man.

Fletcher stood and raised his hand. The man had been thin a year ago, but now his skin seemed to sag away from his eyes and mouth. "Lieutenant. Joseph is right. When I came to Jenkins Town it was because a dozen Indians would swoop in at night and steal livestock and supplies. We had some clashes with them and Carter met the worst of it with a broken arm. But this was different. They've never come in to attack us directly like this before."

"All the more reason to give the savages nothing!" cried another man on the other side.

Pyke nodded to Fletcher as if in thanks and then looked to the others. Pyke did not raise his voice, but his words came out sharp and cold with annoyance. "I only recommend that we treat with these Indians to learn their grievance. If something has changed to provoke them, I will meet with their chief with your representatives. But we must be prepared to offer a gift to show our good will—our Christliness—and settle their ire."

"They have no reason for ire! We till our fields in peace and only want land to feed our families. Why must we pay savages to keep our food and our lives?"

Pyke again raised his hand and patted the air. "I hope that it does not come to that, but I only recommend that we prepare ourselves for a negotiation. Well prepared is well armed."

Wolf Tongue smiled as he suddenly saw the arc of Pyke's argument.

"And, incidentally, gentlemen, we are not. Well-armed, that is. You defended yourselves bravely and well last night, and I have no doubt you men would fight like Hell unleashed if it came to it. But the truth, gentlemen, is that we have too few men, too few muskets, and a half-built palisade around our town that's settled in the low ground by the creek."

The same gaunt man spoke again, "We're not soldiers, Lieutenant, but we'll fight as well as any militia."

Pyke nodded, tensely. It seemed that the questions and hesitancy were draining his patience. "I believe you, sir. But even the best militia cannot stand an attack from higher ground, with overwhelming numbers, better armament, and better—" he broke off, briefly, but Wolf Tongue saw his chagrin as his carefully-cultivated politeness and subtle flattery cracked. In a breath, Pyke had regained himself. "Better trained warriors."

"Those savages?" Sutler, the man they called Dob, leaned back and crossed his arm. Many of the other men watched him with interest.

"Yes." Pyke's flattery was gone, seemingly replaced by direct honesty. "The nations in this area are trained for war from youth. This is a group of some of the strongest warriors from different nations. The Mingos. They are the Spartans of the savages."

"Filthy, ignorant buggerers is what they are."

Wolf Tongue pulled away from the door and stomped toward the benches. "Filthy, ignorant buggerers we may be," he called. The men turned suddenly, shock on some of their faces as they twisted over their shoulders to see him. "But we are warriors. The men of my tribe, all the men of my tribe, are raised from the moment we can walk to carry a weapon, bear a beating, fight, wrestle, run down a deer, stalk an enemy."

Wolf Tongue bared his teeth as he sneered. "You men tend to your fields and chase your animals around in fences. Our women do such things because the men are hunting, raiding, and making war. As boys, our elders train and beat us with sticks. Cut us with knives and attack us with brands so that we know pain. Chase us naked into the wilds so that we learn the value of our own strength. Before I had hair between my legs, I had the blood of my enemies on my knife."

Wolf Tongue pursed his lips as he looked into the eyes of a few men. Each blinked and looked down. Then, he gestured toward the crosswise beams. "Your god preaches peace. But our gods demand blood. So we give it to them by spilling it into the earth like rain." He paused again as he jolted one finger out toward the night. "That is what is waiting for you if you choose to fight."

He stared for another moment, then let his arm drop. With one more baleful glance around, he turned and stalked through the doors. Wolf Tongue walked until he heard the rumbling of the men begin again. Then, he slipped away into the darkness and circled back toward the church.

As he returned, he picked up the conversation again. He leaned against the exterior and crossed his arms.

"... nothing here but what we grow and harvest," the lanky man was saying. "What do they want? Jewelry? Gold? We certainly don't have any of that. And supplies? As the lieutenant so aptly clarified, we have only a few muskets, and most of them poor. Our farm tools?"

"Remember," said Pyke. "When we meet, I need only a small gift to offer in good will. I will talk with them to try to dissuade their anger. But. If it comes to negotiation to prompt them to leave, I will need to know what you will be willing to part with."

"We can offer our harvest." It was Fletcher this time. "Split the stores. Wool. Butter. Corn. Whatever we have salted, pickled. Whatever keeps and you can divvy. They can carry it away with them. It's all we can offer."

"But then what will we eat? We haven't even begun to plant our crops yet."

A moment of silence before Fletcher spoke. "The Lord will provide."

Wolf Tongue listened for another few minutes as the men detailed their stores and how much they might part with. Many seemed grudgingly to do so and Wolf Tongue sneered silently at them.

Then, his sneer drained away as he thought of his own village. His people were under attack, too. By the pox, by deserters. And increasingly, by the Iroquois. Wolf Tongue knew he would fight for his people, for his village and his nation. If a thousand men came down at him and demanded his musket, his tomahawk, and most of his food, he would have died in battle and brought glory to the Susquehannock.

But now there were too few Susquehannock. And glory needs a fire-bearer to keep it alive. If Wolf Tongue died today protecting his village, there would be no ember of glory to carry on his name because his village was almost already nothing but ash.

As he thought of what he would do to save Fox's Smile and their child, Wolf Tongue looked again at the crosswise beams at the head of the church.

A moment later, the men rose with shuffling noises of scuffing shoes and hissing fabric. In groups, they filed past. Many muttered in growls to one another with hunched shoulders. One man shuffled by as he rubbed absently at his elbow, eyes downcast. Davies came toward the back of the crowd with his head shaking as he watched them.

The sergeant tensed when he saw Wolf Tongue, then relaxed slightly. "Didn't know you were there," he muttered as Pyke joined them.

The three of them turned toward their own quarters and separated from the dispersing men.

"Do you think they'll actually give anything if it comes to it?" asked Wolf Tongue.

Pyke shook his head. "I don't know. They really don't have much to offer, but I hope it's enough. I still hope to avoid more bloodshed here."

A rough throat-clearing from Davies turned Wolf Tongue's attention his way. "Wolf Tongue," he began. The sergeant still pronounced his name hesitantly, as if he weren't sure how to address him, or whether he should. "Is it true? All that you said 'bout becoming a warrior? The burning and cutting and all?"

Wolf Tongue stopped to look fully at Davies. After a breath, he said, "It's worse. I would not give up our secret training to the *quhanstrono*, and if I did, it would make them weep to hear it. There was no reason to scare them that much. But, Davies, believe me when I say that it's much worse."

Davies licked his lips and drew a very long breath. Finally, he attempted a resigned nod and continued walking.

Wolf Tongue turned to follow when he felt Pyke's hand on his arm. Pyke looked at him with furrowed brows. "It is true?" he whispered.

Wolf Tongue finally let a quiet laugh break out as he shook his head. "Well. Maybe some of it."

EIGHT – THE AGGRIEVED

Fleur visited Pyke in his dreams.

She spoke to him in French, which he understood better than he could speak, and wore a tattered smock. They were sharing a table at the tavern in Jenkins Town. Pyke felt the eyes of the colonials watching them. Damaris Bennett entered the pub and did her best not to glance in their direction, but Pyke knew she was watching. She was always watching him.

Fleur pleaded with him not to leave. *I am in mortal peril and no one protects me,* she said in French.

Pyke reached across the wooden table and put his hand in hers. Her skin was rough, callused, and it betrayed the hard frontier life that she led. He knew nothing of her past, nothing of her lineage, but sensed she had come from much better circumstances and her family had perhaps fallen on difficult times. Not unlike his own.

Pyke squeezed her hand and spoke in French. *I will protect you.*

Her dark hair shined and her eyes were knowing and mischievous. *Have you ever known a French woman?*

The tavern disappeared, and they were in his room at the boarding house. She stood in front of his bed and unknotted her smock at the neck, revealing the delicate flesh between her breasts. She smiled playfully at him and raised her arms, waiting for him to remove her clothes.

Pyke stepped forward and put his hands on her sides. Her hips were fleshy and yielding. Before he could pull her smock over her head, though, the expression on her face turned grim.

She spoke in English this time. "They must not know."

"Know what?"

"They will kill you. Then they will kill me."

Pyke didn't understand.

Fleur said, "They must not know you killed my husband and his friends."

The dream dissolved.

Pyke's head jerked up from a nod.

He'd been falling asleep on his watch. A young officer's mistake. He cursed his carelessness.

Slowly he started to gather himself. In the night he had sunk to the ground and put his back against the half-built palisade.

"Sir," Davies said.

Pyke immediately jumped to attention. He didn't want Davies thinking he'd fallen asleep.

"Mr. Davies, excuse me."

Davies scratched absently at his beard. His eyes were focused beyond the palisade, searching the plain for Mingo warriors.

"Sir, your watch was over and you wanted to rest here," Davies said.

Pyke frowned. Had that actually happened, or was Davies allowing him to save face? His memory was foggy, almost as foggy as the plain fronting Millers Town, which they now faced. Their visibility was severely limited. Pyke couldn't see more than twenty feet ahead.

"Thank you for reminding me, Mr. Davies," Pyke said. "Thicker than soup out here."

"It is," Davies grumbled. "I moved some of the men forward."

"Good man, Davies."

"Good training, sir."

Pyke yawned. He retrieved his musket and saber. It was a cold, brisk morning and the air was heavy. The wind was a reminder of the hard, long winter. Pyke's joints cracked as he stretched.

Davies half-turned to relieve himself. Pyke did the same thing. In Britain, he would never have considered doing such in front of a sergeant, but familiarity was the norm as opposed to the exception in the Colony.

"They're here!" someone yelled.

Pyke quickly finished and peered into the mist.

"Over here!" another yelled.

"Here!" someone else shouted.

"Here!"

"Here!"

"Here!"

Pyke couldn't see a damned thing. The fog hung like a curtain. He heard men scampering in the mist, coming toward him.

"Sergeant," he said.

Pyke and Davies shouldered their muskets.

A Millers Town man suddenly appeared, no more than ten feet from them. Pyke took his finger off the trigger and aimed away. Davies did the same.

"They're coming!"

The man went to run right past them, but Pyke cuffed his arm.

"How many?"

"Too many!"

"You must stay," Pyke said.

Pyke realized the man was really a boy, no more than sixteen and quite possibly as young as thirteen. He was rail-thin and looked like he'd never needed a razor before.

"Rouse the men," Pyke said. "And get Wolf Tongue, right away!"

The boy nodded and ran off.

Pyke faced the fog again. It was beginning to dissolve. He could just make out dark shapes in the mist, the Millers Town men backing toward him.

Davies groaned. "Damned fog. Is it this bad in London?"

Pyke grinned, briefly. He'd been to London several times. It was a grand, awe-inspiring city, the seat of the Empire's power. He wondered if he'd ever see it again, or if fate had brought him to this town that was about to be destroyed and would never appear on any map.

"Yes, Sergeant. I've heard it's worse in London."

Davies nodded.

Five townfolk had backed out of the fog and now took cover behind the palisade. Little good it would do them. It was half-built, the men were outnumbered, and the fog rendered the approaching Mingos invisible. By the time they fired one volley, the savages would be inside.

"Davies, anybody else?" Pyke asked.

"Missing one bloke, sir."

Then Pyke heard a horse coming.

"Stand ready!" he ordered.

They might only get one shot in, but he was going to make sure it was a good one. Pyke stepped forward five paces and listened intently. It was only one horse approaching at a canter. He slung his musket over his shoulder and drew his saber. In this fog he wouldn't be coolly shooting anyone from afar. They were about to engage in a close-quarter battle.

Then the horse stopped.

Pyke listened, saber ready. The horse snorted and stomped. Then Pyke heard something heavy hit the ground. He crouched, ready for the blind attack through the fog.

But no one came.

Then he heard the horse galloping away.

Pyke looked over his shoulder at Davies. The sergeant shrugged.

Pyke turned back around. Slowly, the fog continued to lift, leaving a thin sheen of dew everywhere. Pyke took five more steps into the blindness and saw the body.

The eyes were squeezed shut in horror, in pain. The Mingo had opened the man's neck. His clothes were blood-soaked, his hands red-stained. He must have put his hands to his throat in a last-ditch, futile attempt to stem the flow.

Pyke said, "Davies, the missing man is dead."

Davies cursed. "Sir, you should come back here."

"Hiding behind this half-wall will not help."

Pyke turned as Wolf Tongue came running toward him. The Susquehannock looked down at the dead man briefly, then his eyes met Pyke's.

"Now what?" Pyke said.

"Now we wait."

Pyke lowered his voice so the others would not hear. "For how long?"

Wolf Tongue tensed and drew his tomahawk. "Not for long."

Pyke followed the savage's eyes. He could now see halfway across the plain.

It was filled with Mingos. More warriors than people in Millers Town. As the last of the fog peeled away, he saw more, and more.

And more.

So many.

Muskets and tomahawks. Like Wolf Tongue's tribe, the Mingos painted their faces. One man wore a beaded cap with deer antlers on his head and had colored his face ghostly white. Other warriors were bald except for a line of hair that ran down the middle of their heads.

Davies had come up alongside Pyke. "How many?"

Wolf Tongue answered. "Too many."

A troop of Mingos warriors began a slow, methodical dance. They stooped and shouted and cried while other men shook rattles, beat drums, and blew whistles.

"This is how they prepare for war," Wolf Tongue said.

Davies shuddered.

Pyke stepped forward and held his saber over his head.

"Sir?" Davies said.

Pyke said, "We will lose a battle, so I must speak to their man."

"He is here," Wolf Tongue said. "Nyakwai."

"Fletcher," Pyke said. "Hold here with the men. We will discuss terms with their chief. If the negotiation fails, be prepared to defend the town. They might strike right away."

Fletcher gripped his musket and nodded. He shifted his weight back and forth between his feet. Behind him, the men readied themselves. The palisade wasn't long enough to provide cover for everyone. They had decided to let the boys who were old enough to fight position themselves behind it.

Pyke nodded at Fletcher and then turned. He led Wolf Tongue and Davies across the plain. The fog was gone and the sun had pierced the clouds. It had been cold overnight but the March day was growing warmer by the minute.

"Tell me about him," Pyke said.

"Nyakwai." Wolf Tongue spoke the name with reverence, an emotion Pyke had never heard the savage express before. "An old warrior, as old as Lifting Smoke but still capable of splitting any man's skull. They say his tomahawk has tasted the blood of a thousand men. He is father to more than twenty warriors, both men and women."

"You said they were here for blood. What about Nyakwai?"

Wolf Tongue grimaced. "If he is here, he has come for blood."

"This is an impressive show for what must be a very few scalpers."

"But who owned the scalps they took? And would you do any less?" Wolf Tongue answered.

They crossed the field and the Mingos continued their dance. As they passed the enemy line, the warrior-savages folded behind them. They shrieked those ear-piercing cries and screamed in their alien tongue at Pyke, Wolf Tongue, and Davies.

But especially Wolf Tongue. Pyke wondered if they saw his siding with the English and these colonials as some kind of treachery. He worried Wolf Tongue's actions would bring even more trouble to his dying people.

"Keep walking," Wolf Tongue said.

Davies's face was flushed. Sweat ran down his jowls and dripped from his beard. His knuckles were white around the barrel of the musket, and his eyes never stopped moving.

The drums continued and the rattles shook. The Mingo warriors rushed at them, stopping inches short of attack, before dancing away. More than once, Pyke nearly drew his saber.

"Nyakwai," Wolf Tongue said.

The knot of warriors ahead parted and Pyke laid eyes on the chief.

Deep lines creased his face and he lounged rather carelessly on a felled tree, his eyes almost skyward like he didn't have a care in the world. He wore his hair like the warriors, bald everywhere except down the middle of his head. But Nyakwai's hair was startlingly white, a testament to his many years.

Though his face gave away his age at nearly sixty, the chief looked as strong as a man half that. He held the biggest tomahawk Pyke had ever seen loose in one arm draped across the tree. Its blade was chipped and worn, but shone silver.

Pyke was ten feet away when the chief raised his palm.

"No closer."

His English was difficult to understand. Once again, Pyke was glad to have Wolf Tongue with him.

"Nyakwai, I am Lieutenant Hugh Pyke of his Majesty's Army, serving under Colonel Bennett in the Commonwealth."

Nyakwai barely looked at him. His eyes shifted to Wolf Tongue. "You."

"I am Wolf Tongue of the Wolf Clan of the Susquehannock."

Nyakwai stared long and hard at Wolf Tongue. "Your tribe is no more. All the warriors beg to fight for me, like dogs with tails between their legs. I take pity on a few and accept them."

Laughter erupted among the Mingos. Pyke wondered where Kicks-the-Oneida was. That proud man wouldn't take kindly to that comment.

Nyakwai motioned for silence. "The Susquehannock have no warriors. Without warriors, there are only women and old men. No tribe. Your people are dead."

Wolf Tongue grinned. "We kept all of our great warriors and sent the weakest to you."

Pyke figured now wasn't the best time to insult the chief, when they were standing in the midst of the man's army. But he had learned to trust the Susquehannock warrior.

Nyakwai didn't register the insult. He looked right past Davies, back at Pyke.

"Your English take our scalps. Men, women, and children. This angers me."

Wolf Tongue had told Pyke what to expect and so far had been right. He had predicted the Mingo chief would taunt him and slander the Susquehannock, explain the purpose behind his raids, and then expect Pyke to offer blood money.

Nyakwai motioned impatiently at Pyke to begin. "Speak what you have."

Pyke kept his hands open at his sides. He was angry and scared and not a little intimidated by the Mingo chief.

"You have attacked a British settlement on British land," Pyke said. "I march under Colonel Bennett's orders to—"

"Colonel Bennett is a worm-ridden dog."

Pyke had no love for the colonel, but had to act the part. "Colonel Bennett protects His Majesty's interests in the Commonwealth. I understand you are aggrieved, sir, and I can appreciate that. There were scalpers in this town before, but they have since gone. These good people drove them away. They do not wish to make war on the Mingos."

Nyakwai grunted.

Pyke continued. "If you were not aggrieved, sir, Colonel Bennett would order the entire militia to hunt you down and slaughter your warriors."

Nyakwai grinned. "Have the fat English send his dogs. Our children could split their skulls and our men will enjoy English women."

Pyke kept his voice steady. "Millers Town is prepared to make offerings so that we may avoid a costly battle. There is no reason for anyone else to die here."

Nyakwai motioned with his hand for Pyke to hurry up.

Pyke said, "We can offer crops. Half the corn stock and a quarter of our wheat. Two cows, ripe with milk for cheese or slaughter for meat. We have fifty pounds of grain available as well."

"Guns. Horses," the chief said.

Pyke nodded. "Five new muskets, straight from the manufacturer in Philadelphia. One horse trained to gallop into battle, unafraid of guns, arrows, and men."

Nyakwai grunted like that wasn't enough. "Coin."

Pyke held out a purse. "Spanish dollars."

The chief ripped it out of his hand and spilled the few doubloons into his palm. With a look of contempt on his face, Nyakwai said, "More."

Pyke shook his head. "Millers Town has no more to offer."

"I do not care."

Pyke locked eyes with the chief. "There will be no more. We have offered you just payment. You have already killed three men and injured more. If this is unacceptable, we are prepared to fight and we will kill every last one of your warriors."

Nyakwai laughed mirthlessly. "How will you do that?"

Pyke put some steel in his voice. "I would be happy to show you."

Nyakwai looked away before he spoke. "I accept your offerings."

Pyke forced himself not to smile. He didn't wish the chief to know how relieved he was there would be no fighting.

"And the coin."

Pyke nodded. "Then I will have the townfolk prepare the offerings for you."

Pyke turned and started walking. Wolf Tongue and Davies followed.

"But what about my daughter?"

Pyke stopped. He wasn't sure he'd understood Nyakwai. He looked over his shoulder.

"This will be her thirteenth summer and she is more beautiful than all stars in the sky."

Pyke turned back around. "Your daughter?"

Wolf Tongue's hand went to the tomahawk on his belt.

The chief got to his feet. He moved with the ease of a man half his age. He was taller than Pyke and almost as tall as Wolf Tongue. Nyakwai moved forward, gently swinging his tomahawk.

"You must give her back to me," Nyakwai said. "Or I will kill all English here."

The war cries erupted again, but the chief's face was stony.

Then he looked at Wolf Tongue. "And I will kill the last of the Susquehannock warriors with my own tomahawk."

NINE – HE WHO IS WITHOUT SIN

Wolf Tongue lowered his chin to stare at Nyakwai through his eyebrows. In his own tongue, he said, "You're too used to our weak cast-offs if you think you can kill a Susquehannock."

He felt Pyke's hand on his forearm and heard the Englishman speak. "The Crown's soldiers have only just arrived, and we haven't heard anything about a missing girl."

Nyakwai shifted his glare to Pyke. Before, the old chief had seemed bored with their visit, but now, he glared with hate. "The English from your village take her. If you do not know, she is dead. If you see her, you would know she is my daughter."

Nyakwai took a step forward and Pyke reached for his saber. He did not unsheathe it, but gripped the hilt and lifted his left hand in a calming motion toward the chief. "If she is in the town, we will find her. If she's not in the town, the people may know where she is and we can still help you find her."

"She should be returned already. If she is there, we come in and find her ourselves."

"Give us time," said Pyke. "If you attack now, you know many of your own people will die. Let us go and learn what we can and I, personally, will return by the end of the day."

Suddenly, a different voice called at them from Wolf Tongue's left. He spoke in Susquehannock. "You've talked enough, *quhanstrono*! It's time your people were here no more!"

Amid the shouts and war cries, Kicks-the-Oneida stood unmoving. His words addressed Pyke, but he stared directly at Wolf Tongue.

Wolf Tongue's mouth tasted bitter at the sight of his old rival and the defector from his tribe. "Why haven't you looked for the girl? Did you go tracking her?

Or maybe your master doesn't let his slave do anything more challenging than attacking women and little boys."

Kicks-the-Oneida bared his teeth and began to step forward when Nyakwai raised a hand. Kicks-the-Oneida stopped and growled in frustration as he stared at Wolf Tongue.

"We looked as soon as she disappeared," said Nyakwai in his own tongue. "They went to the village. If she is not there, then she is dead. And everyone else will be soon, too." He paused, his eyes shifting between Pyke and Wolf Tongue. In English, he said, "Return in one hand of the sun."

Wolf Tongue frowned. That wasn't enough time to harass the obstinate people of the town into giving up information they might not even have. But Pyke seemed appeased. "Done," he said and turned.

Wolf Tongue didn't miss Pyke's urge to return to the village. With an agreement with some time and free passage, the lieutenant seemed appeased enough and ready to remove himself from the hostile Mingos.

Wolf Tongue looked once to Kicks-the-Oneida, who glowered at him, his chin jut out. Wolf Tongue puckered his lips and kissed the air in his direction before walking alongside Pyke back toward Millers Town.

None spoke until they were almost to the low wall around the houses. Beyond it, a handful of men and boys stood wide-eyed. Not all had muskets, and instead held wood-axes or butchering knives. Most stood in groups of two or three, a man with a musket and a son or two by his side. Then, another five paces down the wall stood another man with his boys.

Before they reached the wall, the three men stopped.

Pyke narrowed his eyes slightly and looked at Wolf Tongue with a tilt to his head. "What just transpired?"

"Kicks-the-Oneida wants to make more trouble for all of us. But Nyakwai has enough of his own."

"I judge by their reactions that you insulted them."

Wolf Tongue smiled. "We all have our talents."

Pyke looked to the village with a frown. "I don't think it helped us."

"There isn't much that is going to help us. And I'm afraid these people aren't going to know anything about the missing girl. And if they do, they'll not give it up easily. But if you want to find her, we've got to move quickly."

Pyke nodded slowly, his eyes scanning the town in thought.

"Sir, what is a hand of the sun?" asked Davies.

He'd addressed Pyke, but Wolf Tongue answered. "The time it takes for the sun to travel the width of your hand. And you don't need to call me *sir*, Davies."

Pyke's lip curled in the slightest movement of a smile. "Just under an hour, Sergeant."

Davies let out a long, low whistle that voiced Wolf Tongue's own resignation.

Finally, he shrugged. "These people won't give much up, and I don't trust the dirty *quhanstrono* anyway. Scalpers and slavers, the lot of them. But that probably means there's one of them in some groundhog hole with the girl. Or ready to sell her to the French, if she's still got her scalp." He grimaced. "We might be lucky that she's a young girl. It's likely she's still alive."

Pyke frowned in distaste. "Not so lucky for her."

Wolf Tongue nodded. He hoped that for all their sakes, the poor girl was still alive an unmolested. Perhaps a healthy slave might fetch a higher price.

Pyke nodded and cleared his throat. He looked back at Wolf Tongue and Davies. "Let the Lord be good, then, and protect her. Even if her father doesn't deserve it. Let's go find out what our good people know about this. But we need to be quick and firm with them. We have less than an hour to return to Nyakwai."

He didn't say it, but Wolf Tongue knew Pyke was still chafing from the council in the church. Too much talk, too much bantering, and too many lies. Wolf Tongue smirked. "You be quick in the talking. And if need be, I'll be firm."

Pyke led them back over the wall with a quick step. He called out to the men guarding the town, "Stand fast and keep your guard! The Indians hold for now. Where is Fletcher? Dob?"

In a matter of moments, the two men, along with a fair number of others, trotted over to where Pyke stood just inside the protective wall. Pyke frowned at the four other men who came along. Without raising his voice he glared at them. "I said to stand your guard by the wall, men."

One of the men, a young one dressed in a fine tunic and holding a new musket sniffed. "We are free men, Mr. Pyke, and not your soldiers. If we're to talk of the fate of our town, I'll be here to hear it."

Wolf Tongue clenched his teeth and held back a biting remark followed by a punch.

Pyke cocked his head and replied, his voice quiet and slow. "Then, sir, your fate is as good as death. I have come by the goodwill of the Crown who hopes to protect its people and offer my help. But if you will not heed my advice, then I am tempted to leave you to the savages. If you would like protection from a soldier, do as I say."

The young man snarled and took a breath to retort, but Fletcher stepped between them. "He's right, Joseph. Go, guard the town. And the rest of you, too."

Joseph glared at Pyke then turned and stomped off. The other three men grumbled as they, too, returned to their positions. Wolf Tongue shook his head. These men had a chance to save their people, and they might be too stupid to do it.

As Fletcher watched the men walk away, Pyke spoke without preamble. "What do you know about a missing Indian girl?"

Fletcher glanced quickly at Pyke, his eyebrows constricted and his head tilted back. "An Indian girl?" he asked.

Dob wiped a hand across his mouth as he looked at Fletcher out of the corner of his eyes.

"What do you mean? What's this have to do with ..." Fletcher stammered for a moment, shaking his head.

Wolf Tongue broke in, pointing to Dob. "You. What do you know?"

Dob seemed to notice his hand was at his mouth and with a cough, lowered it. "How should I know what the savages do with their own kin?"

Pyke eyed both Dob and Fletcher. "The attackers claim that their chief's daughter, a thirteen-year-old girl was taken by someone in this town. We have one hour to return her to him or they'll attack. What can you tell me to save your town? Save your lives?"

Fletcher scratched his beard and looked off at nothing in particular. "I don't know," he said. "I can't imagine anyone here would do anything like that. And I haven't heard any rumors from anywhere lately. Why do they think it was someone here? It's got to be a mistake. Maybe we can explain to them—"

Pyke cut him off short with a gentle wave of his hand. "Mr. Fletcher. These men are convinced that the girl is here. Or that someone here took her. They've accepted our offer of goods as payment as long as they also come with the chief's returned daughter."

"What if we offer more?" asked Dob. "Would they leave us be?"

Fletcher seemed to wilt, shoulders drooping with a sigh. "We don't have much more, Dob. It'll be tough to make it through to any kind of harvest with even what we've got. It's only the beginning of March. If we get another storm or frost, we'll all starve before anything's ready."

"It wouldn't help," said Wolf Tongue. "Most of the Iroquois, the Lenape, even the Susquehannock often take blood-wite as payment for a murder. But Nyakwai cares for blood, not vegetables."

Pyke crossed his arms. "Can you tell me anything? Anything you've seen, heard? Maybe someone's acting strangely or there were strangers through here recently?"

Fletcher frowned. "No. But wait." He looked to Dob as if suddenly remembering. "Robert Burgess hasn't been around for a few days. But he comes and goes so often, I never know when he's around."

Dob nodded. "Aye. Rab's gone, but that's nothing unusual."

"Could he have taken this girl?" asked Pyke.

"No," they both said at the same time. But as soon as he said it, Fletcher paused, sucking air through his teeth. "Well ..." he said, then paused.

"Mr. Fletcher. I need to know. We don't have time."

Fletcher wiped his hands on his shirt as he spoke. "Lieutenant, I'm not one to bear false witness or indulge in idle rumors. 'Let he who is without sin—'"

"Die beneath a tomahawk," finished Wolf Tongue. Already these talks were taking too long, and clearly these two men knew something they weren't sharing.

Wolf Tongue drew his knife from his belt with a quick *thhhup*. "Pyke, this fat one knows more than he's saying. Maybe he'll indulge us in some idle rumors."

Dob's face drained of color as he stumbled backward a single step before he regained his composure. Still white, the man straightened his shoulders. "There is no need for hostility, sir. And of course I will do what I can help." He coughed a little cough, then, "Rab is … an odd sort. Didn't get along well with the folks. Has a little house he keeps on the north side of the town, but he's not often there."

"Do you think he'd kidnap an Indian girl?"

While Dob stammered, Fletcher seemed to slump and gnaw on his lip until he finally spoke. "I hate to say it, Lieutenant, because I don't know whether it's true. May God forgive me if I'm spreading lies, but if it'll help us … people whisper that Burgess goes in for children and he's doing the Devil's work when he disappears for days. Now I don't know if all that talk is true. But what is true is that the folks around here never wasted their kindness on Mr. Burgess. Tacitly unwelcome, you might say. And no surprise he goes wherever he does so often."

Pyke sighed and set his shoulders as he looked around the village. Finally, after a long silence, he said, "Thank you, gentleman. Please return to your guard posts and let me devise some plan of action. I'll come to speak with you in just a few moments. And please, if you think of anything else you can tell me, or know of anyone else to answer my questions, please do so immediately."

With a curt nod, Pyke turned away and strode away from the wall. Wolf Tongue slipped his knife back in its sheath and followed.

When they were alone, Davies spoke first. "I don't like that Dob."

"We don't need to like these people, Sergeant. Just protect them."

"Makes a soldier's job hard, sir."

"That it does." Pyke turned to Wolf Tongue. "What's your feeling?"

"I'm with Davies. Dob's not telling us everything, though I'm not sure about Fletcher. Sounds to me like this Burgess is the most likely one. And if you consider what kind of people live in this town … or rather, *lived* in this town?"

Pyke nodded. He looked to his sergeant and asked, "And you, Mr. Davies. What would you do now?"

"Me, sir? I'd leave the lot of lying, whining shit-sacks to their own." Davies composed himself with a scratch at his neck. "Sorry, sir. I guess we already had our talk about that. So now?" He blew out another whistle. "We don't got the girl to return and we don't even got the man who maybe took her. So if we can't run or convince these people to run, we fight."

Wolf Tongue watched Pyke's eyes rake the town and the fields beyond. An attempted escape would kill them more surely than an outright battle. The people couldn't flee quickly, and it would be uphill and disorganized. Pyke grimaced, and Wolf Tongue knew he was imagining the arrangement of defenses.

"I'll track Burgess down."

Pyke and Davies both looked at Wolf Tongue. He continued, "If you can convince Nyakwai to give us more time, I'll hunt down Burgess. And, I hope, the girl."

Pyke shook his head slowly. "No. My friend, you've already done too much here. You're in danger now and you needn't be. You have been a good friend, and you have saved my life more than once. Now you have a family and need to take care of your own people. If you can get away now, I say you go. Davies, you, too. Two men might be able to get away. Take the horses."

Wolf Tongue shook his head. "No. You saved my life, too. There's a thing to be done, and I'll do it. I don't care if most of these *quhanstrono* die in the dirt, but there are some good ones. And it's not right that you need to protect them."

He took a long breath and looked out to where the warriors hid among the fog and the barren trees. "And it might give me a chance to embarrass Kicks-the-Oneida again." He thought of how many of his people had followed the warrior when he left the village, how he had begun in earnest the dwindling of his people.

"Davies," Pyke began, but his sergeant waved him off.

"Pardon, sir, but we already had this talk, too. The time to run's gone, ain't it? And if you're a godly enough man to stay, I'll follow your example. I just hope the Lord will judge me by my company."

Pyke considered them while his left hand, missing most of his little finger, drummed on the hilt of his sword. "What will you do?"

"Maybe I can convince someone to talk to me about Burgess. His trail is too far gone now if he's been out more than a day. But if I can learn something, I might be able to find him."

Wolf Tongue had a sudden thought. As much as he wouldn't abandon Pyke in this fight, it might seem like running off for a washed-away trail was, precisely, abandoning his friend.

He looked at Pyke. "Unless you want me here. If you have a fight, you'll need me."

Pyke smiled. "More boasting, Wolf Tongue?"

"Just sad honesty."

Pyke lowered his head to look at the ground, but kept his smile. "Go. I'll do my best to hold off Nyakwai until you return. And Davies, work with the townfolk to get the agreed-upon goods to that savage."

"I will. And sir?" Davies suddenly sounded excited. He looked around and lowered his voice. "If I catch your meaning from earlier, this town is filled with scalpers selling to the French. Well, if they're selling, they need to know where to go to find a market, so to speak. Someone might know exactly where that is."

Pyke smiled more broadly. "Sergeant, if we don't die today, I'm putting you in for a promotion."

Wolf Tongue nodded. "Right. I'll find someone to talk to. I might sweat something from them by myself."

As he turned to go, Pyke called to him. "Wait. We need haste, but how do I talk to Nyawkai? What will make him listen and offer us more time?"

Wolf Tongue thought for a moment. "Beware his pride—he wants his daughter, but he also will want to keep his power and face. He'll still want the offered tribute, so perhaps take a portion as good will, but hold back on all of it until I have the girl. Tell him we'll bring him the girl, the kidnapper, and whatever else you can offer. He'll expect respect, but don't flatter. Be like a dog—growl, but don't bite, and stay on your feet. The moment you roll to your back, he'll gut your belly."

TEN – NEGOTIATING WITH THE BEAR

"*Monsieur.*"

Pyke put his extra pistol in his belt as Davies and one of the villagers hoisted the last sack of corn over the horse's back. He turned to see Fleur coming down the lonely dirt road toward them.

Pyke felt the eyes of all men standing at the wall on him. Fleur had let her raven hair down, and it tumbled almost to her waist. She held her skirts up as she rushed to meet him to avoid the mud.

"Mrs. Nederwue," Pyke said, unable to keep the edge out of his voice. "You are always catching me at a most inopportune time."

And there was no time to waste. Wolf Tongue had gone hut to hut, house to house, building to building, around the small town as quickly as his legs could carry him to discover if someone had secreted the chief's girl away and not taken her anywhere. Neither he, nor Wolf Tongue had missed the disapproving and offended frowns.

Pyke had waited by the wall as long as he could, hoping against hope Wolf Tongue would appear with the girl and Pyke could take her and the offerings and the money to Nyakwai.

But the sun had almost moved the width of Pyke's hand. There was no time left. Pyke hoped Nyakwai's palm was broader than his.

"I come to help you." Fleur shot him a scathing look, offended by his dismissive manner.

"What is it, then?" Pyke said. "Quickly."

Her bottom lip jutted out and for a moment, Pyke thought she would turn around and leave. He hadn't met many French, but so far what his father had told him was true. They all suffered from the sin of pride.

But she motioned for him to come closer so they could speak in private. Pyke ignored the stares of practically every man on the wall, and especially the look Davies was giving him, and stepped closer. Fleur faced away from the wall and spoke in a low tone.

"Rab Burgess is a pig." Fleur almost spit the words out. "I keep a pistol in my skirts when he is around."

Immediately Pyke found himself picturing the weapon where she had described. He forced the image from his mind.

"He is ... presuming?"

"He forces women and prefers Indian *poupee*, *tres jeune*."

Pyke didn't know what *poupee* meant, but *tres jeune* he understood well: *very young*.

"This man has been forward with you?" Pyke said.

"He is forward, backward, and sideways to anything with tits."

Pyke's eyes betrayed him and strayed down Fleur's neck at the mention of a woman's bosom. He forced himself to look her in the eye.

"He likes young Indian girls?" Pyke said, wanting to be sure he understood her.

"That is what I say." Fleur nodded. "And they all know, Dob knows. If they did not tell you, they lie. Rab has the girl."

"What does he do with them?"

Fleur made a disgusted face. "I found him bread and butter with an Indian girl once ... when he has had his fun, he takes them north for selling."

Pyke was disturbed at the thought of Rab Burgess forcing himself upon a young girl, but also perversely happy that it could be Rab that had taken the chief's daughter. At least there was an outside chance they could return her to the chief. Pyke would gladly hand over the libertine, Rab, along with the girl and let Nyakwai torture the bastard to death.

Pyke looked over his shoulder. They were all watching him, as if they knew Fleur would share their secret.

He quickly turned back to her. "Madame, would you do me a favor?"

She nodded.

"Find my friend, Wolf Tongue, and tell him this. But don't tell anyone else you shared this with me."

Fleur smirked. "You think I am stupid?"

She was petite but her spirit overwhelmed him. Pyke found himself wondering again at her origins and how in God's name she had come to marry Nederwue, the Dutch scalper, and end up in this little town, where no one liked, or even trusted, her.

"No, I do not. Thank you, madame."

"So formal." Her eyes twinkled. "You Rosbif."

She turned and Pyke wished very much to watch her rush back into town.

But there was no time to enjoy the simple pleasure of watching a woman move.

Davies tucked his knife and a pistol into his belt and checked his musket for probably the hundredth time. The sergeant stuck his chin out stubbornly and nodded.

"Sergeant, do not be careless with your life," Pyke said.

"Don't got to tell me twice, sir."

At the wall, the townfolk parted. Dob and Fletcher hovered just beyond. Davies took the reins of the horse carrying the offerings and they reached the wall.

Pyke nodded at Dob and Fletcher as they left. "Gentlemen, this wall here is now your life. Defend it with everything you have and do not let them move you off it."

Ahead were the Mingos.

Fletcher called out. "Lieutenant, what if we cannot hold this wall?"

Pyke turned and leveled his gaze on Fletcher. "Run for your lives."

Pyke watched as Fletcher gulped and Dob looked behind him, as if he were already preparing to run.

"Be strong," Pyke said, before turning back around.

"Just aim them muskets here." Davies put his hand on his gut. "And you won't miss. You lot will be fine."

Davies gave Pyke a little nod and they set off again. The day had grown still warmer. Pyke felt a sweat on his back, though he knew not all of it was borne out of the weather. He glanced at Davies, who stuck his chin out defiantly as they approached the Mingos again.

Pyke knew how much the savages terrified Davies, but the man refused to let his fear rule him. He'd also given him the opportunity to leave but the sergeant had declined, knowing full well his own life was in serious jeopardy now. If there were a battle, they would likely die.

Pyke shook his head. When he'd first come under Colonel Bennett's command, he had judged Sergeant Davies much too harshly. The man was unkempt, pot-bellied, and lacked the military air Pyke had witnessed back in England and come to expect from all soldiers. Davies also had a tendency to drink and ignore orders he found silly, and to offer an opinion where none had been called for.

But having served with the man now for some time, Pyke had come to regard him with respect. And when Davies spoke out of turn, Pyke made sure to chide him publicly while also considering his opinion privately. He knew how to soldier, even if he didn't appear a soldier, and he was, against all outward appearances, the most reliable enlisted man under Colonel Bennett. And yet again, Davies had surprised Pyke by refusing to leave when it was in the man's own interest.

Davies must have felt Pyke's eyes on him. "Sir?"

Pyke smiled. "It is amusing how wrong we can be of other people."

"Right. When you first appeared, I thought you a skulker like Lieutenant Smith."

Pyke couldn't help but laugh. Davies would have been flogged for such a remark under normal circumstances, but the two men marched to the gallows. So gallows humor it was.

"That's *Captain* Smith," Pyke said.

Davies grunted and made it sound like a curse. "Being we're not long for this world, I figure a soldier like me has a right to say what he thinks."

Pyke nodded. "What is your excuse normally then?"

Davies looked over at him, as if surprised by Pyke's assessment of him. "*Captain* Smith ain't no captain. I couldn't in good conscience call the man a Saturday-soldier even."

Pyke agreed but said nothing. They were within the Mingos' ranks again. The warriors picked themselves up off the ground. No war dance commenced this time, no drums were beaten.

Now they were grim-faced, serious, and scowling. Anxiously excited to battle. None challenged Pyke or Davies as they walked through the makeshift camp, on their way back to Nyakwai once more.

They found the chief where they had left him, on the felled tree. This time he smoked a pipe and watched them with fiery eyes. More than a dozen warriors ringed him. Pyke noted Kicks-the-Oneida among them.

"Where is your pet Indian, English?" Kicks-the-Oneida said.

Pyke ignored him, which he knew would insult the man just as much as words.

"Nyakwai." Pyke bowed his head, but only an inch.

"I see a horse but my daughter is not on it," Nyakwai said.

Pyke remembered Wolf Tongue's advice. *Offer respect, but not flattery. Be like a dog. Growl, but don't bite.*

"We are committed to this deal," Pyke said. "So I offer you half what was promised to show we are serious."

Nyakwai suddenly hurled his pipe behind him. It hit the man standing next to Kicks-the-Oneida square on the chest and left a mark of ash before falling to the ground.

The chief stomped forward, till he was a foot from Pyke.

"I do not see half my daughter anywhere!"

Pyke knew he had to offer Nyakwai the truth. At least, some of it. He had to show the town hadn't kidnapped her. Rather, this had been the act of one man.

"We believe a man named Robert Burgess took her. He once lived in this town, but the good people forced him to leave. They knew his ways were evil."

Pyke figured a little lying wouldn't hurt. Besides, it was close enough to the truth. From Fletcher's and Fleur's accounts, the *good* people of the town didn't like him and were glad to see him gone. But Pyke wondered about the *bad* people.

"I will kill all your dogs," Nyakwai said. "Then fuck their wives and daughters. When I am done, my warriors will have their turns. And when they are done, we burn this town."

Pyke didn't once look away. "In four days, we will bring your daughter to you, along with this man to do with as you please. At that time we will also give the rest of the offerings."

Nyakwai studied Pyke for a moment. "I don't need your help to track a man. Tell me where he goes and I might spare your whore-women and bastard children."

Pyke cursed himself for not anticipating this answer from the chief. "He trades in the north, possibly with the French. Our search party will be able to find her and negotiate her safe return if necessary. If you send warriors, Rab will hide. And if you show your arms against the French, it will threaten your alliance with them."

Pyke had spoken as confidently as possible, but the words sounded hollow. It was a weak answer to the chief's challenge.

Nyakwai turned and walked back to the tree. He motioned at Kicks-the-Oneida to retrieve his still-smoking pipe for him.

Kicks-the-Oneida bit back his response and bent a knee to pick up the pipe. Then he walked it over to Nyakwai.

The chief stuck it back in his mouth. The smoke curled into the sky. Pyke stole a glance at Davies. Rivers of sweat poured down the sergeant's face, but he maintained his military bearing, for once, keeping his shoulders squared and back and his eyes forward.

Nyakwai took the pipe out of his mouth. "Tomorrow at this time, you will either bring my daughter or five from the town."

"Any more death and Colonel Bennett will send ten regiments to hunt you down."

"I do not fear the fat dog, or the bitches he sends to do his work."

The chief scratched himself absently, while his warriors cried with excitement.

Pyke did not take his eyes off Nyakwai. He recalled Wolf Tongue's advice, and thinking of his friend, gave him an idea of how to respond.

"Those bitches would make cats out of your men."

Nyakwai pretended to yawn. "Your talk bores me."

"Even if you don't fear the English, you must respect us. We will make life miserable for you if you continue to engage this town."

"Life is misery. *Your* life will end in misery." The chief paused to let those words hang in the air.

Pyke buried the fear that gripped him and scowled at Nyakwai. But the chief's point had struck home. Before Colonel Bennett raised a company, let alone ten regiments, Pyke, Davies, Fletcher, and the rest of Millers Town would be long dead. Little good Bennett's retaliation, if he deigned to deliver any, would do them.

Pyke's job was to keep them alive, for as long as it took to find Nyakwai's daughter. Bennett would deal with the aftermath. Or not. Pyke didn't think the colonel much cared for Millers Town. He had his own town and career to worry about and the encroaching French. Millers Town was nothing to him.

Pyke was nothing to him.

He settled on one last threat of English might. "They have guns, and more horses than you can imagine, and cannons. You do not want to incur His Majesty's wrath."

The chief said, "I do not fear the English before me, so I will not fear the English I cannot even see."

"If you do not fear us, why ally with the French?"

The Iroquois seemed to favor the English, but Pyke guessed Nyakwai and his band would support the French if they were moving west toward the Ohio Valley. When the chief hesitated, Pyke knew he had scored one hit. A moral victory, though, nothing more.

Nyakwai said, "I am friend to the French because it pleases me."

Pyke looked past the chief at his dozens of warriors. They were sixteen to thirty years old and looked like they had been whelped to go to war. Perhaps there was truth to Wolf Tongue's stories of the savage customs. If the chief had half the number of men, he would still have enough to take the town.

Pyke said, "We need more time than a day."

Nyakwai waved his comment away. "Then pick five skulls for me to split. And you will have another day."

Pyke didn't answer. Both men knew that Nyakwai held the advantage in numbers, so he could dictate the terms.

The chief said, "You may send dogs for my daughter. But I will watch them. If they go to get more dogs, they will die."

Pyke had considered sending several men and instructing two to secretly ride hard for Jenkins Town for reinforcements once out of range of the Mingos. But Nyakwai had wisely anticipated this, so Pyke hid his disappointment.

The chief pulled on his pipe and exhaled a cloud of smoke. "Five skulls will bring you another day. After that, I will burn the town to the ground."

They had one day to find the girl, and so Pyke and Davies jogged to the church.

Wolf Tongue, Dob, Fletcher, and two other men who appeared to be brothers waited. Pyke recognized one as the man he'd dressed down in front of his neighbors not an hour ago: Joseph Adams. His expression was dark as his eyes watched Pyke come down the aisle.

"Well?" Dob said. "You talked him out of it?"

Before Pyke answered, he saw Wolf Tongue shake his head impatiently. And Pyke felt much the same way. The chief's daughter had been kidnapped, probably violated, and was on her way to be sold. And yet, Dob expected Pyke to have talked the chief out of his anger.

"We have one day to find her."

"One day!" Dob exclaimed.

Fletcher and Adams expressed their disbelief also.

Wolf Tongue interrupted. "Be thankful Nyakwai offered one day. He is not usually this generous."

Dob pointed at Wolf Tongue. "That means we should engage him again. Perhaps he can be made to listen to reason." He turned back to Pyke. "Lieutenant, you must go back out there and do a better job at convincing the savage to accept the original terms of our deal."

"That is wasted air," Wolf Tongue said. "Once the bear offers terms, you do not return to ask for better."

Dob ignored him. "I mean, we're happy to assist him in finding his daughter ... but if we're unsuccessful we shouldn't be ... we shouldn't be punished for one man's actions."

"One man?" Pyke said. "I have it on good authority that scalpers resided here."

"Did that *French* woman tell you that, Lieutenant?"

Pyke frowned and took a long, steadying breath.

"Colonel Bennett maintains good intelligence on this area and knows all that goes on. I *know* there are scalpers operating here. You kept that from me, which calls into question everything you have said!"

Dob was at a loss for words. Pyke watched Fletcher and Adams to see how they reacted. Fletcher looked embarrassed more than anything. Adams kept his steely eyes on Pyke.

Did they all know? Bloody likely, in Pyke's estimation. In a town this size, everyone knew their neighbor's business. It would have been difficult not to.

Dob said, "Lieutenant, you are wrong. But I can understand your frustration."

Pyke said nothing.

Dob went on. "The Colonel's reports *were* correct. There were scalpers here in the past, but they have since left. Much like Rab Burgess left. We did not want them here. We are peaceful, God-fearing people living on the frontier. We can ill-afford to invoke the wrath of the savages."

"That much is obvious," Pyke said. "Why did you keep this from me?"

"Because small towns like this are judged by their worst people, not their best."

Pyke had had enough of this man's double-talk. "If we cannot produce the girl in one day, he has asked for five people to kill."

The room fell silent.

Pyke went on. "If not in two days, he will burn the town. And anyone in it."

"So we must find the girl," Wolf Tongue said.

Dob took a lingering look at Wolf Tongue before he turned to Adams and the other man. "Is two days enough time?"

Wolf Tongue stepped between them. "That is all we have, so it must be."

Pyke watched the exchange, wondering what Wolf Tongue had done or said to goad these men into action. "Who are these men?" Pyke asked.

"You know me," Joseph Adams said. "I wasn't good enough for you to talk to."

Pyke ignored the man's hostility and turned to his companion. "And you?"

The other man had trouble meeting Pyke's eyes. "I'm his brother. Everybody calls me Dirch. We … offered to help find Rab."

"You must know where he travels then?" Pyke said.

Dirch looked down at his feet.

The older Adams answered. "Yeah, and what of it? It don't mean we helped him kidnap that girl."

Davies stepped forward. "It don't mean that, but it pretty much does."

Adams turned to Dob. "I offered to help! And this is how me and my brother are treated?"

Dob held up a palm. "Gentlemen, our tempers are a little short. Very understandable under the circumstances. Let's let cooler heads prevail here."

Wolf Tongue stepped away from them. "We don't have time for heads to cool. I'll be outside."

Pyke and Davies followed him out.

Clouds had rolled in and blotted the sun and now it was cold again. A winter wind swept through the town as the three men put some distance between themselves and the town hall. They passed a few houses and stopped at the crossroads.

Wolf Tongue said, "How will you sneak the people out?"

Pyke nodded. He and Wolf Tongue had been thinking the same thing.

Davies answered. "The creek becomes more a river at the other end of the town. The sound of water obscures other noise."

Pyke smiled. "Good thinking, Sergeant."

"Even a blind squirrel finds an acorn."

Pyke turned to Wolf Tongue. "My friend, two days is not enough time. If by then you have not found the girl, do not return. There will be nothing here but death."

Wolf Tongue grew thoughtful. "I go to the gods, one way or another. And I won't run from Kicks-the-Oneida, even if he has an army behind him."

Pyke was about to object, but Wolf Tongue spoke over him.

"My path has always been to face him in battle. He'll fall under my tomahawk for the Susquehannock that he corrupted and for the Susquehannock he abandoned to die."

Pyke nodded. "Thank you, my friend."

Wolf Tongue's grave face broke into that wicked smile again. "Besides, you cannot win this battle without me."

ELEVEN – THE HUNTERS

Wolf Tongue smiled as he said it, but he knew it was true—Pyke would need every weapon he could get if he intended to survive a real attack from Nyakwai. Though, with that many warriors attacking, even Wolf Tongue wasn't sure he'd be able to change the town's fate.

He hoped Pyke's plan would work. He'd bought time from Nyakwai, and if he could sneak most of the people out through the dark, they might at least live to return to Jenkins Town or wherever they came from. But if it didn't work, Wolf Tongue would try to return as quickly as possible because even with Pyke and Davies organizing the men, a battle would be little better than a slaughter. And in that case, at least, Wolf Tongue might get a chance at Kicks-the-Oneida.

Though even that thought was troublesome now. The air around him reeked of a dying people, a village about to become blood and ash. As much as Wolf Tongue longed to humiliate and defeat his old rival, Kicks-the-Oneida had once been Susquehannock.

"Lieutenant!"

Wolf Tongue, Pyke, and Davies all turned to see Dob, Fletcher, and the Adams brothers come scurrying out of the church. Dob clutched a white handkerchief in his hand and it fluttered through the air as he stomped toward them.

He huffed as he stopped just sort of Pyke. "Lieutenant, Joseph and Dirch here have agreed to guide this Indian of yours in hopes of finding Mr. Burgess."

"I'm no slave, dandy," growled Wolf Tongue. "Forget it again and you'll need your own guide back from the dead."

Dob stuttered and paled again. "I'm … I'm …" He looked to Pyke for reassurance, but the soldier ignored the exchange.

Wolf Tongue scowled at the man, but secretly was surprised at his angry retort.

"I thank you, gentlemen," said Pyke. "I would hope that one of you might suffice. If it comes to a fight here, Mr. Adams, we'll need every piece of steel we have."

"No," spat the older Adams, Joseph. He scowled like he'd drunk piss and stared at Pyke. The younger, Dirch, gnawed on a lip and looked at the ground. The brothers were of a size, a few inches shorter than Pyke, and with brown, lank hair tied neatly at the base of their necks. Both wore stained jackets over their tunics and carried seemingly new muskets.

"Me and my brother go together. That was the deal we made with Dob. We got Indians killin' our kin here, and I don't trust another Indian to be alone with my kid brother where no one can see him. We go together."

Wolf Tongue looked sidelong at Pyke. These brothers would be two man-sized holes in the town's defense. Though Wolf Tongue guessed they wouldn't be steadfast and fierce in the fight even if they stayed.

Pyke frowned for a heartbeat. "Fine," he growled. "We don't have time to argue. And if you're fast enough, we won't come to a fight anyway."

"How far are we going?" asked Wolf Tongue.

"It's just—" Dirch began to speak before Joseph took a step and spoke over him.

"Not sure," he called a little too loudly. "I think Burgess travels up north a ways. There's a trader's outpost, Harris's Ferry, about a half-day northwest. Could be he stopped there or passed through."

Wolf Tongue narrowed his eyes on Dirch. The younger brother held his musket in one hand, and his other crossed across his body to rub at the other elbow.

"Then why do I need you?" Wolf Tongue's eyes snapped back to Joseph. Harris's Ferry was what the *quhanstrono* called the *peshtank*—the still waters where Susquehannock, Shawnee, Munsee, and others would congregate to trade. "If you don't know where Burgess is, I know the outpost and can find it myself."

Joseph snorted. "Suit yourself. But if I were Burgess and I saw a seven-foot-tall Indian come asking about me, I'd slink away to the nearest hole and sit in it with only the muzzle of my longrifle sticking out."

Dirch shifted and spoke, his voice quieter than his brother's. "We know what he looks like. And he knows us. If we can ask around and go the right places, he might let us find him."

Wolf Tongue looked to Pyke. The soldier's stone face barely changed, but Wolf Tongue saw it, and nodded in agreement.

"Fine, then," Wolf Tongue said. "Go gather your things now. We'll travel quick and light."

The Adamses exchanged a look, then loped off toward one of the squat houses. Wolf Tongue watched them as they leaned in toward one another to exchange curt words while Pyke issued orders for the town's defense to Dob and Fletcher.

Wolf Tongue wondered at the interaction between the brothers. Again, he had the sense that there was much more they weren't telling him. They would take him somewhere, but he wasn't convinced it was the trading outpost Joseph had mentioned. It seemed too vague. If they were to find Burgess and bring him and the girl back within two days, they would need to either have a much more solid plan, or be incredibly lucky that Burgess might just still be lazing about a dingy outpost.

"Don't trust them," said Pyke.

Wolf Tongue still watched the brothers until they disappeared inside a doorway of a rough, clapboard house. When he looked back, Dob and Fletcher were well away, sent on some errand by Pyke in preparation.

"What other choice do we have?"

Pyke shook his head slowly, but said nothing.

Wolf Tongue sighed. "They know more than they're saying. The way I reckon it, there are two paths. They won't admit being friends with this Burgess, but they know right where he is so they'll take me to him and let me do the work. Or they're just taking me somewhere to try to scalp me and then run away so they don't die here."

Pyke's sad expression didn't change. "For all our sakes, I hope they do something helpful and right. Everyone here knows more than they're saying, and those two especially. Maybe once you've gotten away from here, they'll be more candid."

"Sir," said Davies. "Do we have any bait to be sure they'll come back? Wives, another brother, anything?"

Pyke shrugged. "I don't know, Sergeant. I'd hoped that I could get one of them to stay. It might have given the other brother at least a moment's pause before he fled. And given us a new musket behind the wall, too. But after this morning, I knew that stubborn cad wouldn't settle without some small victory over me."

Wolf Tongue lifted his arms and stretched. "So the brothers might lead me right to Burgess and the girl so we can bring them back. Or they might decide to save their own lives, run from their burning town, and maybe sell a Susquehannock scalp to buy a few days' provisions."

Pyke and Davies exchanged a dark look before the lieutenant spoke. "Be careful, my friend. In any event, I do not trust these men, even if they do help bring us the girl. But I hope all goes well."

Wolf Tongue knew the weight of Pyke's unspoken words. The safe return of Nyakwai's daughter was the best hope anyone in the town had of surviving into the next season. If Wolf Tongue failed, the town, and his friends, would likely be dead before he returned.

Wolf Tongue clapped his friend's shoulders with both hands. "Hold them off, and I'll return as fast as I can. I'd be forever jealous if you kill Kicks-the-Oneida."

As he released Pyke's shoulders, he saw the Adams brothers coming from their house, each carrying a wadded bundle. Wolf Tongue turned to Davies and held out his hand.

Davies took his forearm and rested his other hand on it, in the Susquehannock fashion. Wolf Tongue smiled. Pyke must have taught him this.

"Davies. Go with the spirits. And don't die."

Davies chuckled. "That's good advice. I'll do my damnedest."

Wolf Tongue grasped Pyke's arm the same way and the two looked at each other for a moment. "I'll pray for you, my friend," he said.

Pyke smiled. "And I for you."

"With so many gods, then, we can't fail." Wolf Tongue slapped Pyke's shoulder once more, then turned from his friend in the direction of the Adams brothers.

TWELVE – THE BATTLEFRONT

Once Wolf Tongue and the Adams brothers had gone, Pyke and Davies went back to the church where they could speak in private. It was fast approaching evening now, so there was no time to lose.

Pyke said, "We need men we can trust in this god-forsaken town."

Davies nodded. "We got each other, sir. And maybe Fletcher. And maybe that Frenchie with the flapdragon."

Pyke was about to object to Davies's characterization of Fleur, then wondered why he'd been so quick to take offense. She was French, after all, and they warred with France in all but name. He owed her nothing. He owed the town and the British subjects everything.

That was how he should have felt.

But the world was upside-down. Pyke didn't trust the townfolk, especially Dob, and felt they had brought the wrath of the Mingos upon themselves, by taking scalps they had then gone on to sell to the French, the Crown's gravest threat in the Province. These people had shown no loyalty to His Majesty and had incited the savages to murder. He was duty-bound to protect them, though he didn't much relish the thought. And he would protect the women and children. They had no part in this but Pyke knew the Mingos would be merciless.

He *shouldn't* have trusted Fleur. But he did, despite the fact she was French and had been married to one of the scalpers. He would gladly protect her from Nyakwai and his warriors, because he *knew* she was innocent and no other man would stand up for her.

"Maybe Fletcher, I agree," Pyke said. "And we can trust Fleur. She is no friend to Dob and the people do not care for her. She has no loyalty to them and so we can trust what she says."

Davies looked like he wanted to say something.

Pyke ignored the look. "What about those men we met when we arrived, Kit, Quill, and Si?"

Davies shook his head. "They're Dob's men."

Pyke stretched. He was stiff from having slept on the wall last night. He'd grown too used to sleeping in a soft bed in Jenkins Town.

"Well, Davies, we have our work cut out for us."

"Sir, how are we going to protect these people?"

Pyke pictured the town in his mind. It sat in a hollow between three small hills. The Mingos filled the plain to the west. Forest to the north where the creek came into the town, then flowed into more forest to the south. To the east, beyond the mill and the water, was another field of a few hundred yards ending in a nearly vertical slope of trees and scrub.

Nyakwai would watch everywhere. Unless Pyke gave him something specific to look at.

He smiled. "We start with the women and children first."

Davies nodded. "But how?"

"We fortify."

They gathered the men quickly and fifteen minutes later were back in the church. Pyke recognized most of them: Fletcher, Kit, Quill, Si, Dob, and a few other men from the minor skirmish last night. The rest were a ragtag bunch, either too old or too young, too scared or not scared enough. Many had that look in their eye, like they would flee at the first chance they got. Pyke did not sense much loyalty among them.

He was used to leading soldiers. Men who expected to receive orders and knew they would be flogged if they did not follow them. Men who were expected to work toward a common goal and who understood the basics of defense. Pyke knew it would be different with these men. He was glad to have Davies with him for this, as the sergeant would back him up in the face of any opposition.

"We must fortify the town," Pyke said.

A middle-aged man in the back with incredulous eyes spoke first. "Didn't we send Joseph and Dirch to find the squaw? They'll get her. If Rab done took her, they won't have a problem."

"We also sent Wolf Tongue, the fiercest warrior I know," Pyke said. "But one day is not much time. And if we do not have the girl by then, Nyakwai will come for us."

The same man said, "Should we draw straws?"

Pyke thought he was joking, but no one laughed.

"You're not serious, are you?"

The man nodded. "Life is a negotiation. Maybe the brute will take one person tomorrow and be happy. I say we hand over the French bitch. One whiff of that cunt and he might forget all about his daughter."

A few others voiced their agreement.

Fletcher cut in to counter. "We can't hand him anybody."

Another man joined to back Fletcher up. "No honorable fellow hands over a woman to die."

Pyke was still stunned they were even discussing this. He raised his voice. "We are not handing anyone over to that savage. We will fight first."

"Your orders were to protect the Crown's subjects. She is French. You protect us by handing her over."

"Do not presume to tell me, or interpret, my orders."

"You'd prefer we all die?" the man said. "Where's the sense in that? I say we start with the old and sick and work our way backward."

Davies raised his voice and moved his hand to his pistol. "Like the lieutenant said, we are not handing anyone over."

Pyke waited for the murmuring to die down. "So if they are not back—"

"They will be. We must remain hopeful," said another man. "And if they aren't, we should just ask for more time. He'll have to listen to reason."

Pyke shook his head. Obviously the man was just repeating what Dob had told him to say. He had coached everyone prior to the meeting, no doubt.

Pyke said, "Hope is not a strategy. If you want peace, prepare for war."

"Quite right, sir. Quite right," Davies announced.

"So we will fight. And in order to fight, we must fortify the town."

Si raised his pitchfork so he could have the floor. "If we spend all night fortifying we'll be too tired to fight tomorrow and the Mingos will overrun our town. We should just conserve our strength for the fighting."

Pyke said, "A man is never too tired to fight. And the fortifications serve two purposes. The first and obvious: to aid us in the defense. But the second, and perhaps more important: to serve as a distraction this evening."

Dob finally spoke. "What do you mean, Lieutenant?"

"Right now, Nyakwai watches. His hundred of warriors watch. They are waiting for us to attempt escape. And when we do, they will hunt us down. On the road we will be without the protection of the town or the wall. We will be utterly defenseless. So we will fortify and be obvious about it."

Pyke looked around the room to gauge the crowd. Some had figured out what he planned to do. The rest waited for him to go on.

"The Mingos will believe we are preparing for a battle, while we secret our people out of the town."

Pyke waited for the inevitable challenge.

Dob folded his arms. "Who gets to go and who stays?"

Pyke smiled. "I like the suggestion from the man in the back. We draw straws."

Pyke and Davies walked the perimeter.

Millers Town sat in a hollow through which the creek wended north to southeast. To the east, three hundred paces separated the creek from a severely-sloped, tree-covered hill that rose high enough to delay morning for the townfolk by a good ten minutes. To the west, a plain gently rose to meet the forest on the other side.

Houses lined the north and south boundaries of the town. They were no more than small huts, but Pyke knew they could be used as weapons as a last ditch effort. They could be burned to pose a blockade on one side.

He hoped it didn't come to that.

The church house sat in the middle of town. It was solidly built, spacious, and two stories, which would make it their stronghold.

"When all else fails," Davies said, reading Pyke's mind.

Pyke nodded.

The two soldiers completed their sweep. They talked for a few minutes of the town's geography but their walk had unearthed nothing new. The east hill would have afforded the enemy a great advantage, but it was covered in trees and too much open field separated it from the town's eastern edge and the creek. To the north and west, the forest was much closer, the trees providing perfect cover for the savages. Likely they would come from those fronts first.

Pyke had hoped for inspiration during the walk, but only a precious few ideas had come to him. They returned to the palisade along the north side of town.

"Davies, I want all food stock, guns, and gun powder moved to the church," Pyke said. "Our horses will corral outside. If it comes to it, they can ride two women or two children. I want all supplies as close to the church as possible."

"Sir."

"The young men will be runners. Find out how many of those we have."

"Sir."

Pyke paced for a few moments. "Now how the hell do we fortify this town?"

Davies said, "Ain't no mysterious science at play: ditches and fire."

Pyke nodded. "A ring of fire on the western plain."

Davies smirked. "I always knew you were devious, sir."

Pyke said, "We draw their attention to the wall. It is half-built, so it would be the obvious thing for us to attempt to finish."

Davies turned east. From their vantage point, they could just make out the edge of the creek as it slipped between the pass. "While we work west and north, our people escape south."

"Precisely."

"Nyakwai is a heathen but he ain't no beef-head."

"Then we shall have to be convincing."

"Sir."

"Hand out the assignments," Pyke said. "Keep Dob's men apart. Kit on the wall, to the west, Si to the south. Or however you want to do it. Just keep them separate."

"Sir."

"We need men working on the north wall the entire evening. Long enough to spirit the rest of the town to the east. They will have to escape in small parties, sticking to the river, perhaps even in it."

"Sir."

"Once you have everyone situated, make sure to get yourself some dinner," Pyke said. "We have a long night ahead of us."

"You're not joining me, sir?"

"I will eat later."

Davies's eyes were full of questions.

Pyke said, "I need to speak to the one person we can trust."

"Brushing up on your French, then?"

Pyke found Fleur rooting around the piles of burnt wood where her small house had stood, not more than a day ago. She carefully stepped from plank to plank and was hunched over, searching for something.

"Mrs. Nederwue?" Pyke said.

Fleur stopped what she was doing and stood. She wiped her hands on her waist and looked over her shoulder at him. In the light of dusk, she looked otherworldly. Her dark hair was tangled and fell to her waist. She'd hiked her skirts to walk through the rubble, displaying her calves and the back of her legs when she bent over.

"Lieutenant Pyke." She smiled. "Hugh."

When she said his first name, it sounded like *ewe*.

"Madame, I was wondering if I could have a few minutes of your time."

"*Oui*."

She carefully picked her way over the scorched wood. Pyke stepped forward and offered his hand. She batted her eyelashes at him playfully and took his hand as she stepped off the last plank.

"Madame, if you'll forgive my saying so, you seem awfully carefree at the moment."

Fleur let go of his hand and brushed her dress off. It was mud-stained and covered with ash. Her palms were black as pitch.

"We are not dour like the English."

Pyke pointed west. "There are a hundred warriors making camp on that plain. Tomorrow they will come. And the day after that. And the day after that. Until this town is no more."

Fleur shrugged. "Maybe they will rape me or kill me. What can I do?"

Pyke said, "I won't allow that to happen."

"Ah, *tres bien*. Then I have nothing to be fearing of. You see?"

Pyke couldn't help but smile. "Earlier you said Rab had taken the girl."

"Yes."

"Did you see him with her?"

Fleur shook her head. "No, but everyone knows."

"What do you mean, everyone knows?"

"Most of the men do. The rest look the other way. But to ignore something, you must know not to look."

"Yes." Pyke started walking and she fell in step with him. How long had it been since he'd enjoyed the company of a woman? Months.

After his very brief engagement to the colonel's daughter had ended, Pyke had tried making the acquaintance of a few women, most of them friends to distant relatives or associates. At most, he'd shared a meal with them at some gathering but they quickly lost interest. Pyke had always suspected the colonel of spreading rumors about him, the dissolute man's petty form of revenge for Pyke having rejected his daughter. But sometimes, Pyke looked in the mirror and wondered if it was just him. Perhaps he didn't interest women. He'd never considered himself good- or bad-looking. A gentleman wasn't supposed to concern himself with such things, as they were a mark of vanity.

"Who is she?" Fleur said.

"Who is who?"

"I know that face you make. For the woman you loved."

Pyke frowned. "I have loved no woman."

"*Monsieur,* you prefer men?"

She pouted playfully and Pyke found himself smiling.

Fleur pursed her lips. "You English are like children when it comes to love. Always hiding your feelings and playing pretend."

"And you French …"

"Are what?" She nudged him on the shoulder.

Pyke shook his head, but he was smiling. "How in God's name did you end up here?"

"You want to know if the rumors are true?"

"I don't know what the rumors are," Pyke said. "And I don't care to hear them, honestly."

"Ah, but they are so much more romantic than the truth."

Pyke nodded. "Somehow I doubt it."

"It is okay you do not trust me," she said. "Our countries have warred for very long."

Pyke said nothing. As a rule, he didn't like the French and preferred open war with the bastards, rather than this skulking around in the New World, courting the Indian tribes between them in the Ohio Valley. But this woman intrigued him. He should have been thinking of the fortifications more but instead he'd come here, ostensibly to speak to her about the town. Somewhere along the way, she had altered the direction of his thoughts.

"Madame, I need to know whom I can trust in this town. How many are Dob's men?"

"Where Dob goes, most follow. Fletcher is one exception. He is a good man and his wife was nice to me after my husband did not come back. Fletcher has a brother here and I think he is a good man also."

Pyke said, "This town seems prosperous, but they all cried poor. Dob himself dresses like a Philadelphian."

"Scalps," Fleur said. "They trade for scalps. They trade for Indian women … they trade for everything."

Pyke frowned. "They had hardly any money to offer Nyakwai."

"That is what they told you."

He nodded. "Where are they hiding it?"

"*Je ne sais pas*." She looked at the ground. "When you were here last time, did you meet my husband?"

Pyke was instantly on his guard. "I did."

"I miss him so much."

Pyke stopped walking. They had reached the south edge of the town and stared out over the field to the woods beyond. It was getting dark, but Pyke thought he could see them, the Mingos, slipping quietly through the trees. Already getting into position for what was looking like an inevitable fight.

An inevitable slaughter.

"I'm sorry for your loss," Pyke said, without thinking.

Her head turned and she stared at him. "You know he is dead?"

Pyke calmly faced her. "I doubt any man would leave you of his choice."

"Ah, Hugh … you see, you Rosbif can be romantic."

Again she batted her eyelashes and stepped into the field. The bottom of her skirts were mud-lined and her dress was threadbare at the elbows.

"He was not a good man, but he was good to me." She looked at him. "And I loved him, even though he was not good."

Pyke didn't know what to say to that. His parents enjoyed a good marriage, but his father had shared sobering stories with him of men and women married but miserable in their union. The thought of a life like that terrified him and had given him the courage he needed to refuse taking Miss Bennett's hand.

"Where do you think the money is?" Pyke asked.

"The church." She looked over her shoulder at him. "Probably."

Pyke shook his head. "They would have expected us to meet in the church. They may be brigands but they are not fools. They would have hidden it elsewhere."

She shrugged and looked away. To the woods. He wondered if she saw the same shadows moving into place behind the trees. He wondered at how well she hid her true emotions. The woman must have been terrified. The Mingos would not spare her.

Pyke went on. "Besides, we have impressed upon them the dire nature of this situation. Only mad men would not part with their money to save their lives."

Fleur shook her head. "Money drives some men mad."

Pyke's family had once had a lot of it. But they had fallen out of favor and … perhaps Fleur had a point. It had driven his grandfather mad. The man had spent the end of his days worrying about it, worrying about the family's future. Pyke remembered his father saying money had driven the man to an early grave.

Pyke said, "What else are they not telling me?"

Fleur sighed and turned to face him again. In the twilight, her beauty was stunning. Being this close to her reminded Pyke he had been alone for these many years. He had slipped away to Philadelphia on two occasions, out of uniform, to enjoy a drink and a whore in a place where no one would recognize him. But the pleasure had been fleeting and had left him feeling hollower after.

Fleur walked up to him and stuck her forefinger in his chest. "The moment you are no longer a help, they will turn on you."

Judging by the tone of her voice, Pyke knew she was speaking from bitter personal experience.

"Is that what happened to you?"

"I am French." She turned and gave him her profile. "Man hates what is different."

He looked past her shoulder. The sun had disappeared behind the west hill, leaving the Mingo camp in shadow. But he didn't need to see them. A hundred bloodthirsty men made a lot of noise, no matter how quiet they were ordered to be.

He had to eat something because he was gut-foundered, then return to the planning. But he found himself lingering.

Pyke said, "What were you looking for? At your house?"

She smiled sadly. "It is not my house anymore."

He waited for her to answer, but instead she just walked away. He watched her until she disappeared from view behind a stretch of houses. Pyke caught a handful of boys, the ones playing ninepins earlier, watching them from behind a cart. When Pyke looked at them, they giggled hysterically and ran away, singing an old schoolboy's song about kissing he had not heard since he'd been little.

It made him feel both nostalgic and old.

Old at twenty-four.

And he might not see twenty-five. Not unless he or Wolf Tongue performed a series of miracles.

Pyke heard them arguing in the church house. It sounded like the whole town was screaming.

He pulled open the heavy door and stepped inside. Many turned at the sound of him entering, but the debate raged on.

Fletcher and Si were shouting at each other in the front of the church. Pyke scanned the crowd and found Davies. The sergeant gave him a bewildered look. Pyke nodded and excused his way through the crowd. When he reached the front, he saw Dob, Kit, and Quill as well. Another bearded man stood near them. He wore the long clerical robe of a minister and Pyke wondered where the man had been for the last day. Surely his flock needed him.

Fletcher was in the middle of saying something but stopped short when he noticed Pyke. Behind Fletcher stood his wife, Molly. Pyke smiled at her, and she smiled in return, clearly happy to see him. He understood immediately: Fletcher had been supporting Pyke's plan while Si, one of Dob's men, had been trying to undermine it. Next to Molly stood a man that resembled Fletcher. It had to be his brother, the one Fleur spoke of.

Pyke faced Si. "You wish to say something?"

Si's face was flushed. His shirt was sweated through. "We either all go, or we all stay."

Pyke wanted to jump down the man's throat. But he had to be very careful. The townsfolk would side with Dob, and challenging Si here would be tantamount to challenging Dob. He had to feign hearing the man out and then calmly refute his points. Davies would jump in and support him, he knew.

"Why do you say that?" Pyke said, as if he hadn't already anticipated this argument.

Si said, "No man will let his family flee without him. This is the frontier and savages abound. We have a duty to our families to go with them. You ask us to do the impossible."

Pyke remembered to keep his voice level. "If it comes to battle, there is a good chance we will lose. They have the numbers. If the women and children stay, they will be ..."

Pyke didn't complete the thought. There were women, and some children, in the church house listening.

"Fine," Si said. "Then under your plan some men will be charged with protecting more than one family when they flee."

"That is correct," Pyke said. "You can help each other, or die."

Si went on. "And under *your* plan, twenty to thirty men will stay to be the distraction. But in the next breath, you say that a fight is inevitable."

"That's right."

"Then men that stay will surely die."

"It is possible." Pyke nodded. "But only so that others might live."

"Why don't we ask Nyakwai to let our women and children go?" someone shouted from the back of the room.

The majority of the crowd shouted its agreement.

"The man is a savage. He will not agree." Pyke did not wait for someone else to challenge him. He had to drive home his points. "And he will not be sated until he has his daughter. The people of this town have gravely offended him. I know that some in your company are or were scalpers. You took Indian scalps for coin. How did you expect them to react?"

"No, we didn't!" Quill yelled. "Nobody ain't took any of their scalps!"

Pyke was very close to telling them he knew it for a fact, because Nederwue and other men from the town had tried to take Wolf Tongue's scalp. But in sharing that they would suspect him of Nederwue's death and he would lose them. The townfolk would likely turn him over to the Mingos as one of the five for tomorrow's deadline.

"We are past the point of lying!" Pyke yelled, even as he continued to lie by omission. "We are hours from death's door! I did not create this problem but I am trying to solve it. So we had best start working together!"

"Damned right." Davies stepped forward. "The lieutenant knows how to soldier. He's been through hell before this and if anybody can get us through, it's him. So you all better listen. Or him and me can saddle our horses and return to Jenkins Town."

It was a bluff. Pyke was duty-bound to stay and would never have left. But he said nothing to see how the townfolk reacted to Davies's challenge.

"Hold now." Dob stepped forward. "We are not soldiers. We do not take orders."

"You'd better damned well start," Davies said.

This time Pyke put his hand on the sergeant's shoulder. They shared a look and another understanding passed between them. Davies knew that Pyke was knocking him down a peg so that he looked better in the town's eyes.

"Sergeant, let's listen to what they have to say."

Dob smiled pleasantly, but there was cunning behind his eyes. "We are not *used* to taking orders. We only wished to have a discussion, Lieutenant. I'm sure you understand."

"I do. But we had better hurry it up. Night is falling and we need to prepare.

THIRTEEN – HARRIS'S FERRY

The paths where Joseph Adams led were alternately muddy and frozen. Wolf Tongue followed along behind the two brothers, who spoke little, as they picked their way among the slop of a road to the northwest. The *quhanstrono* had been cutting roads through the wilds for years, and none of them seemed remotely as useful as the paths Wolf Tongue used through the mountains.

The road they followed now was less than ten feet wide and had been cleared of most of its brush so that it made a single swath of wet mud-holes where the sun shone, and crackling ice-puddles in the shadows. The cold mud gripped at his moccasins, weighing his feet down and forcing him to pick his footing carefully to avoid the deeper ruts and puddles that would trip or bog him down.

Roads like this were meant to carry carriages, but Wolf Tongue doubted any came this way. The ground would only be passable during a few months of the year, and then if it didn't rain. With the first snow, the road would be blocked until the ground dried out enough the following summer.

Though, on a smaller path through the mountains, they would not have gone any faster. All the ground was tough now, and if this was the way the Adams brothers wanted to take him, he'd follow, at least for now. It had only been a few hours since they left Millers Town and Wolf Tongue still felt a worrying like a burr in his moccasin that Joseph Adams wouldn't lead him to where he promised.

They had left the town well before midday, and though Adams claimed it was only a half-day's walk to their destination, the forest was beginning to purple with the first setting of the sun by the time Joseph slowed and gestured ahead.

"There," he said. He spat the word over his shoulder as if begrudging Wolf Tongue the information. "Harris's Ferry. The old man Harris is dead now, but the junior runs the ferry across the water. Lots of folks come through here, some just headed somewhere else. Some to trade. French, Dutch, Prussians." He looked at Wolf Tongue with a raised eyebrow. "Even Indians."

Wolf Tongue ignored the man's tone and took in the area. From where he stood, he could just hear the rush of water. Farther down the road, he could see a sizeable log home situated beside the wide river. The ferry, a long and flat craft, dark brown against the slate gray water, lounged at the end of a dock. The water moved quickly this time of the year, even though his people called this area the "still waters." He'd been here a few times before as a young man come to trade with the whites or whoever might come—the Munsee once, though they seemed far from home.

"I know the place, Adams," he said. "Let's hope for your sake Burgess is there with the girl."

Joseph snorted again. "It ain't my sake I'm worried about." And before Wolf Tongue could reply, the man stepped off again down the hill toward the ferry.

Wolf Tongue watched the two brothers step down the hill. Joseph certainly seemed to lead the two and set their pace, and even now, they moved at a fair lope, but not with the rush that Wolf Tongue would have expected. He imagined his own village being set upon, with him as their only chance at salvation. He would have run until his lungs burst.

The Adams brothers moved at a brisk walk, but no faster. It seemed as if they didn't want or expect to find Burgess. As much as he watched, Wolf Tongue couldn't quite put together what the brothers intended to do or what they hoped to accomplish. Clearly, it seemed that their main concern was not speed to return Nyakwai's daughter as quickly as possible.

Were they devoid of hope? Resigned to failure? Irritated about being set to an errand with an Indian?

Wolf Tongue shook his head to clear it of the questions as he stepped off to follow them. He shifted his musket to the crook of his other elbow and settled his hand on the knife at his belt as he picked his way through the mud that paved the west side of the hill down to Harris's Ferry.

As they neared, Wolf Tongue saw three men milling about, chatting while they smoked pipes and carrying what seemed to be grain or other supplies from the log home to an outbuilding set farther back from the river and closer to the wide field behind them. The air smelled of mud, cold, and wood smoke.

The three followed the trail down to the cabin. A pair of dogs, shaggy and small, began to bark as they came running from behind the house. A moment later, a man came out of the door.

He was of a height with the Adams brothers, but older by nearly twenty years. He had a rounded head with hair that had just begun to gray and thin on the top of it. His soft chin strengthened with a wary smile.

He raised a hand in greeting, then walked closer to extend it. Wolf Tongue introduced himself quickly before the man turned and shook hands with Joseph and Dirch.

"Joseph Adams, it's good to see you. And Dirch, I believe? You don't come out much, eh? I haven't seen since you were here with your father. And that was when my father was alive. Must have been seven years or more!" he said.

Joseph's sharpness dulled slightly as he nodded. "Mr. Harris, it's a pleasure to see you again."

"Likewise. Dirch, you look like you father did twenty years ago, you know that?"

"I've heard so, Mr. Harris."

The older man pursed his lips. "Might I enquire to your father's health?"

Joseph shook his head. "With the Lord now, Mr. Harris. Died of the pox just before Christmas."

Harris crossed his arms and looked at the river. "I'm sorry to hear that. He was a good man and held you boys together well after your mother died. I'll remember him in my prayers. And your brother? James? Well, I hope."

At this Joseph bristled, his calm seeming to buckle. Dirch rubbed at his neck and spoke, though his voice cracked. "We … we're not sure, sir. He went out on his own and we haven't heard from him. God protect him wherever he is."

Harris' frown deepened. "I seem to remember him coming through here. I don't remember them crossing, but him and a few others. Well, I'm sorry to hear your misfortunes. But I'll pray that's the last of them."

Wolf Tongue cleared his throat. "Mr. Harris, I'm sorry to be abrupt, but we're in need of some haste."

Harris blinked and looked up at Wolf Tongue, not quite with surprise, but with a calm curiosity.

"Oh. Of course. I can ready the ferry immediately."

As Wolf Tongue took a breath to clarify, the three other men he'd seen trotted back toward them.

"Everything all right, Mr. Harris?" called the one moving the most quickly toward them. The man seemed about Wolf Tongue's own age and certainly no more than twenty-five, and moved with a heavy step and his hands tightened to fists.

"It's fine, Lazarus," said Harris with an exasperated wave of his hand.

"If you say so, Mr. Harris. But I'd watch this savage. His kind—"

"Lazarus Stewart!" Harris turned on the younger man. "My father treated all God's men with respect and helped your Presbyterians settle and make peace with the Indians here. I'll do the same. Any man, white or Indian, who makes for violence at my home will answer to me. Now, if you're finished with your trades and whatever else you may need, I suggest you retire inside to your bunk if you're still looking for lodging."

Lazarus squinted at Wolf Tongue for a long moment. It grated on him that someone else would speak up to defend him, but at the moment, he had more need of diplomacy and speed than his pride would normally allow. Wolf Tongue stared back and offered a raised eyebrow with a smile.

"Let's go, Asher," said Lazarus over his shoulder to one of the other men. "I don't think I need to stay in a building that smells of Indian."

"I understand," called Wolf Tongue to Lazarus. "Yearling bucks always run when they catch scent of a wolf." As he said it, Wolf Tongue felt a tiny pull of regret for his harsh words, given his situation. But he knew letting his words out would be better here than his tomahawk.

Lazarus glared, but then snapped his head away as he and his men stomped off on the trail Wolf Tongue had just come down. Harris spoke as Wolf Tongue watched the three men walking away.

"I do apologize about that. Let me go and get the ferry ready."

"Actually, Mr. Harris," interrupted Joseph. "We're looking for someone from Millers Town. Robert Burgess. A man about thirty, little taller than me. Might be traveling with an Indian girl."

The silence drew Wolf Tongue's eyes back to Harris. The older man frowned as he seemed to appraise the Adams brothers anew. For his part, Joseph had replaced his dour mask with one of innocence and deference to the older man.

"What are you needing with Mr. Burgess?"

Wolf Tongue sucked in his lips to watch the exchange, curious to see the change over Joseph Adams.

"Well, Mr. Harris. I'm not one to spread idle rumors or bear false witness, but I guess it's no harm in telling you why I'm here."

Wolf Tongue watched as Joseph adopted the phrases and protestations that Dob had used earlier before disassociating himself with Burgess.

"Our town's been set on by angry Indians." He raised a hand to still Harris's rebuke. "I know how much you and your father worked to build good, Christian fellowship. But the truth is we've had men killed outright, and the chief of those Indians admits he's ready to turn Millers Town into Sodom and Gomorrah. He's convinced someone in our town kidnapped his daughter."

Harris looked at Wolf Tongue, who nodded. "It's true. I came with one of the Crown's soldiers to translate and guide, to try to soothe the anger and stop the attacks. But the chief is after war, and without his daughter, he won't stop."

Joseph cleared his throat. "Some of the people think Mr. Burgess might have taken her and come through here."

Harris's shoulders slumped and he passed a hand through his hair. "He did," he said. "Yesterday."

"Did he have a girl with him?" asked Wolf Tongue.

Harris nodded. "Said it was his wife, though she didn't speak English. I thought she seemed a little young … but any woman less than thirty looks too young to me anymore." He pushed his hair back again. "Dear Lord forgive me. If he's kidnapped the poor girl …"

"Where did he go?" asked Wolf Tongue.

"Across the river. Said he was headed toward New France. Something about finding her people out there. I didn't listen much, and he didn't talk. Bought a few supplies, powder, lead, the usual." Harris seemed to come back to himself as he looked up at Joseph. "You're right, Joseph, to be wary about spreading tales that aren't substantiated. And whether he's a raper and kidnapper, I don't know. But I'll say it so that God can hear that I never rightly cared for Robert Burgess. Seemed a bit … weasely from the day I met him."

"When was he here? And do you know what direction he headed?" Wolf Tongue asked. If he had a good idea of the direction or potential destination, Wolf Tongue still might be able to track the man.

"Probably about this time yesterday. It was almost full dark by the time I got the ferry back to this side of the river. I couldn't tell you which way he was headed, but I'll tell you he wasn't moving none too fast. Had some kind of wound on his leg that seemed to bother him. He had quite a limp and the way he winced told me it hurt like the devils."

"Can you get us across tonight?"

Harris had already turned toward the river and was hurrying down to the dock.

FOURTEEN – THE ESCAPE

Forty men toiled along the wall. Last winter they had felled enough timber to ring the town, but the cold had turned the ground to stone and the many snowfalls had halted the progress. Pyke and Davies helped dig, move wood, plug holes, carry water. The men worked joylessly as night fell.

Dob arranged for campfires to be made to illuminate the work area. They were strategically placed so they drew attention to the work on the wall but did not shed light to the south, in a way that would give away their other plans.

Pyke finished digging his sixth hole and handed his shovel to Fletcher. They had agreed to rotate to keep the men fresh and able-bodied for tomorrow. Fletcher gave Pyke a look the lieutenant could not decipher, then Pyke stepped away from the wall.

Fleur walked along the line of resting men and offered them drink from a pitcher. All but two men met her eyes and actually thanked her. Pyke stood in line and patiently waited his turn. His hands felt raw from working the shovel and his back was stiff. Finally it was his turn. Fleur's pouty lips formed a playful smile as he took the pitcher from her and drank.

He'd been expecting beer and was surprised to taste water. Apparently the townfolk trusted their water. Pyke wondered if Nyakwai was evil enough to poison the supply. Too late now to worry. He'd taken a drink and it had refreshed him so he figured it was potable.

"*Merci,* Madame." Pyke handed the pitcher back to her because it was empty.

"*Je vous en prie.*" Fleur was still smiling up at him and Pyke looked into her eyes. He liked what he saw in them.

Someone cleared his throat.

Pyke looked right and saw Davies waiting for him.

It was time.

Pyke had to crouch to enter the house.

Inside, a man was hugging his wife and teenaged son. Pyke didn't even know their names. He just knew they would be the first to escape. He recognized the man from the earlier argument. He had backed Pyke and Fletcher up against those wanting to hand Fleur over to the savages.

"I'm sorry. We must go now," Pyke said.

The man let go of his family. His wife was in tears and pushed past Pyke on her way out of the hut, while the blond-haired boy stared meekly at the dirt floor.

The man said, "Tend to your mother, boy."

"Father, I want to stay with you."

The man shook his head. "You go now. You must protect her."

Pyke didn't understand. He was under the impression the man would leave with his family. "Sir, I thought—"

The man shook his head. "Can't do it. Can't run away. My boy is thirteen. He's a man now. He will tend to his mother."

Pyke looked at the boy. He might have been thirteen but looked no older than eleven. And he was skinny as a stick.

"Sir—"

"No, lieutenant. I know what you're up against and I can't leave my friends. Others will protect my family, and I'm needed here."

Pyke regarded the man. He had a family. He should have gone with them.

But he stayed.

Pyke had found another good man in this town. It raised his spirits. He stuck out his hand. "Lieutenant Hugh Pyke of Jenkins Town."

The man's hand was rough and callused, no doubt from working on the frontier or in the fields. "Bertram Miller. They named the town after me."

Pyke looked at the man.

Bertram smiled. "Joking."

Pyke laughed. "It's nice to make your acquaintance."

"Wish it were under a better situation."

They left the hut. The man's wife and son were waiting for him at the end of the road with Sergeant Davies. Two other families huddled there as well. Nobody said a word. They couldn't make any sounds. Noise carried across the fields. Pyke had ordered the men building the wall to be as loud as possible in their work, but they were a faint echo.

Three families, minus Bertram Miller. They would be the first wave. In many ways, the bravest ones.

Quietly they walked as a group to the edge of town and kneeled by the creek. The moon was a quarter full and about to slip behind some clouds. In a few minutes they would have to leave.

The river gurgled next to them. The sound would cover their footfalls. But it would also cover the footfalls of the enemy, if in fact the Mingos were out here.

Pyke looked north and south. His eyes scanned the woods for any signs of stirring. He saw nothing. He heard nothing.

He flicked a glance at Davies, who nodded. He hadn't noticed anything either. Hopefully the distraction of the fortification would prove enough and some could escape.

Pyke felt the anxiety of the group rising until clouds blotted out the moon at last.

He brought his hand to his ear and then lowered his arm in a slow chopping motion, giving the signal to leave.

The boy and his mother cleaved to Bertram one more time. Miller hugged his family and then nudged them away.

As planned, the three families stuck as close to the river line as possible and headed off. Pyke listened to them move and heard nothing. He prayed the moon would stay shrouded for as long as it took. He prayed these people would slip quietly away from the violence that tomorrow would almost certainly bring.

The nine people comprising this first party grew faint in the darkness as they moved along the riverbank. Pyke couldn't see them well but estimated they were halfway to the pass. Once through there, they would be safe. There was no reason for the Mingos to post scouts beyond the pass. If they had any sense they would keep men on this side of the river to prevent townfolk from escaping at all.

The minutes crawled by.

The moon came out again but the light was so weak Pyke couldn't discern the nine people. He prayed again to the Lord, begging for their safe passage.

Suddenly, Davies put his hand on Pyke's shoulder. Pyke was snapped out of his prayer and fully back on the moment. Davies pointed and Pyke followed his arm to the north woods. The tree line along that side of the river ran almost to the bank.

"What do you see?" Bertram said, a little too loudly.

Pyke stuck his arm out to keep Bertram in place and signaled for him to be quiet. They locked eyes for a moment until the man backed down. Finally Pyke turned back to where Davies had been pointing.

He saw nothing. Just a knot of trees and shadows melting into shadows. The three men sat in silence. Pyke closed his eyes and focused on his hearing. All he could make out was the gurgle of the river.

They waited two more minutes. Everyone in the group had been instructed to scream if they were attacked, as an alert to Pyke and Davies.

But there were no screams.

They had gotten through.

Pyke met the next group by the pile of scorched wood that had been Fleur's house.

"They're all here," Davies said.

Pyke nodded. It looked like the entire town was gathered, but Pyke knew about twenty had stayed behind to continue fortifying the wall. He took a deep breath. They had successfully spirited ten people away, but this next group dwarfed that initial party. It would be much more difficult to sneak this many out.

But they had to try.

Fleur watched him from the edge of the crowd, one hand on her hip and her head tilted to the side.

Then Dob came running up. "Your distraction has worked!"

"How do you know?" They were welcome words, but Pyke didn't want to celebrate too hastily. Saving ten people was one thing. Escaping with seventy-five more would be something else. This time, Pyke and Davies would escort the group to the pass before returning to the town.

"By the wall! The Mingos are all there, watching."

"Watching?"

Dob nodded. "And dancing, you know." He stepped closer to Pyke and lowered his voice. "They are doing their dance to intimidate the men while they work on the wall."

Pyke looked to Davies. "Sergeant, move these people into position. I will see this for myself."

Before Dob could object, Pyke marched toward the wall.

Dob was not lying.

The Mingos taunted the men building the wall. They danced and carried on no more than thirty paces from the wall. Pyke pretended to be concerned, but inside he was beaming. The savages were so busy with the men at the wall perhaps they would miss the rest of the town escaping through the east pass.

Pyke took stock of the men still working the wall. Fletcher and his brother were there. Pyke did not see any of Dob's sycophants, like Kit, Quill, or Si.

Fletcher stopped shoveling and took a rest. He looked over at Pyke. "I hope this works. I don't wanna die for nothing."

Pyke nodded. "Your wife and children will be safe. I promise you."

Fletcher nodded. "Thank you, Lieutenant. Thank you for helping us."

The Mingos continued their strange, mesmerizing dance in the firelight. Pyke watched them, until Dob said, "Come on, Lieutenant."

Pyke ignored him and spoke to Fletcher. "I will return."

Pyke had his musket out and powder and shot ready as he crept through the darkness along the riverbank. He had taken the south, Davies the north. The impossibly large group padded silently along. Some had chosen to walk through the river, even. His orders had been simple. Move slowly, move as one. Better to take an hour to reach the pass than to risk being heard. Once they reached the pass, they would be inclined to run but Pyke had urged them to stay together until they were either caught or safely within British walls elsewhere.

Fleur stayed by his side. She put on a brave, almost nonchalant face, but Pyke got the sense she was just as afraid of the townfolk as she was the Mingos possibly lurking in the shadows.

Each step was an eternity. About halfway to the pass, one of their leads called for no movement. Like a wave washing over the beach, they all sunk to the ground and went deadly still.

Pyke kept his eyes on the trees and his musket ready. He had his back to Fleur and in the sudden, gaping silence he heard her taking short, nervous breaths.

Pyke took one hand off his musket and reached behind him. He had no idea what he was doing. His hand suddenly had a mind of its own. It hung in the air till Fleur's hand met it and they interlocked fingers. He'd reached out to calm her and she'd accepted the small comfort.

Their fingers squeezed. Pyke felt each thud of his heart beat against his ribs as he watched.

They stayed like that for a long time.

Then the scout stood and the rest of the group did too, very slowly. They resumed their deliberate march through this black hell. Pyke hadn't let go of Fleur's hand yet and didn't much want to. But then her fingers slipped out of his and she stepped aside.

They drew closer to the pass. The moon had gone behind some clouds again. Pyke looked over his shoulder and saw how far they'd come. It was almost time for him to turn back.

A report shattered the silence.

And then the world was screams and war cries.

"Back to the town!" Pyke yelled.

The group had moved in careful unison up to this point. But at the sound of gunfire and the inhuman screams of the Mingos, they transformed into an unruly mob. Every man, woman, and child for themselves.

As she rushed past, Fleur gave him a panicked look. "Why do you stand there?" She did not wait for his answer.

Pyke was tempted to run like the others but that sense of duty made him stand his ground. This had been his plan and now it was backfiring. He could at least provide some cover so as many could retreat as possible.

Not that he blamed himself for the failure of this escape. They were facing impossible odds and this was the best option out of only bad ones. He'd simply had no choice and had to take this risk in the hopes of protecting the townfolk.

In the darkness, the Mingos swarmed like hornets. They descended upon the dismantled crowd quickly, and Pyke had a sudden revelation. If he lived to see tomorrow, Nyakwai would probably enjoy the opportunity to explain how Pyke had led these people right into a trap.

But Pyke would deal with that tomorrow.

In the darkness Pyke could barely see his own people, let alone the enemy. But he knew they were close. He had learned to load and fire his musket in twelve seconds, which made him quicker than most with the gun. But he did not have twelve seconds.

The Mingos were everywhere.

Not more than ten feet away, Pyke saw a family slaughtered. Two Mingo warriors hacked them down with their tomahawks.

Pyke dropped his musket and drew his saber. He was certain he was going to die. Absolutely certain. They'd been caught fleeing, a breach of the deal he'd made with Nyakwai. The chief would order his men to kill all of them.

But if Pyke was going to die, he might as well kill as many bloody savages as he could.

Pyke rushed forward, saber overhead. As he brought the blade down on the nearest warrior, he bellowed a preternatural scream. The Mingo shrieked and slumped to the ground. Pyke stepped out of the way of the second warrior, as the man swung his tomahawk wildly through the air.

Pyke ripped his saber loose of the first man's neck and slashed. The blade slowed as it sliced through the other man's flank. Warm blood sprayed Pyke's face and the man fell, clutching at his side.

More Mingos came. They were everywhere. Pyke forgot everything he'd been taught and hacked and slashed wildly, like some brute just given his first sword to play with. But his anger fueled him and more than made up for his lack of discipline in the fight.

He felled two more men and lamed a third. He was wild. Someone had opened up a gash in his leg, but Pyke barely felt it. He sliced the next warrior's hand off. The man ran away screaming bloody murder.

Before he knew it, he was out of breath and the stragglers were now running past him. Pyke feinted one way then slashed his way through a knot of three Mingos. When he was clear he sprinted for the town, the whole time expecting to feel a tomahawk in the back.

He was the last to reach the town. By then Davies—thank God Davies was alive—had set up a line. It was only eight men long, but Pyke hoped their muskets would be deterrent enough against the warriors headed their way.

Pyke took his place in the line and took out his pistol. This was it. Nyakwai would storm the town and murder everyone.

"Men, do not stand on ceremony," Pyke said. "Fire at will."

"Sir." There was a strange emotion in Davies's voice. It almost sounded like hope.

Pyke looked up from his pistol.

The Mingos warriors had not followed them into the town. He could just make them out in the blackness, slowly melting back into the shadows.

They had stopped.

They had not come.

"Why?" the man next to Pyke said, asking the question on everybody's mind.

Davies came out of his crouch, but didn't take his eyes off the stretch of land ahead of them. "They're coming back to do worse, I'll bet."

Pyke disagreed. Nyakwai didn't want his men killing everyone in the town. Not yet, anyway. If the Mingos slaughtered everyone, then the chief would never see his daughter again. Nyakwai would harass them, he would ask for five skulls tomorrow as threatened, but he would not resort to all-out battle. Not yet. Not until he was certain his daughter was gone forever.

But Pyke didn't share these sentiments with the men. He didn't want them to relax.

"Davies, set up a watch in every direction and—"

"Lieutenant!"

Dob came hurrying over. For once the man wasn't composed. His fists were clenched and his whole body looked tensed.

"You have no right to lead us!" Dob said. "How many did we lose to your damned foolish plan?"

"Too many."

"And now, what? We've just lost ten men that knew the musket. The balance tips even more in the savage's favor!"

Pyke was not going to brook these insults. He regretted seeing any townfolk killed, but the odds had always been long and everyone had understood that. Their only choice had been to make the best of a bad situation. And it hadn't worked.

"Now would be a good time to shut your bone box and magically find all that money you've got hidden away," Pyke said.

Dob hesitated, just long enough for Pyke to think he was lying. "How dare you insult me! We have offered everything we could to this man and—"

"You knew about Burgess, didn't you?"

"No. I had no idea what he was up to."

Pyke narrowed his eyes. "And the scalpers? You were ignorant?"

Dob pointed at Pyke. "I will be having words with Colonel Bennett, Pyke. You are here to help us, not accuse us. This is outrageous!"

Pyke shoved Dob out of the way. "Outrageous or not, you failed to answer my question."

Pyke stormed off, Davies in tow.

Shortly after midnight, the men ran out of wood to use for the west wall. It now stretched almost the width of the town. In some parts it was up to Pyke's shoulders, but in most stretches it met his hips. Women brought pitchers of water for the exhausted men, who slumped to the ground and looked up at Pyke pitifully. He heard one man say their time would have been better spent digging their own graves.

Pyke ordered ten rested men to take the first watch. He would come back in four hours to relieve them. Before anyone else could cast him a malevolent look, he left the wall and headed to the north field.

The digging had just started. Most of the men here had been part of the bungled escape. They worked backward, and haphazardly, hoping to leave no pattern for the Mingos to follow.

Pyke ordered them to dig ditches scattered in the field, each three feet long and a foot deep and wide. In a fight, seconds were crucial and the ditches could slow down the enemy just long enough to save lives, and possibly turn the tide of an advance. At the very least it would cause problems for the Mingos.

Pyke left Davies to supervise the digging. The sergeant hid a yawn and pretended not to be tired. Pyke slapped his shoulder and moved on.

He wended his way back to the church house. A half dozen men were carrying supplies into the building, among them Dob. Though he was in the right, Pyke didn't feel like another argument right now. He walked on.

The south field had already been taken care of. Pyke smiled at the trap they'd set for the Mingos, should they come that way. He crept back to the east, to the point where they'd tried to escape, and found that same line of men on the edge of town.

They all looked tired. Pyke smiled at Bertram Miller. The man's crooked mustache smiled back at him.

Pyke said, "Please go to the church and bring ten men and shovels here. I want them to dig an obvious ditch about twenty feet from the town's edge. Wider is more important than deep. Too wide to easily jump. We want the savages to see it tomorrow."

Bertram nodded and went off.

Pyke took his place along the line, but the men said nothing to him. When he looked over, they looked away. Obviously they were blaming him for the failed escape. That was fine. If they needed to blame someone, let it be him. He knew he wouldn't win them over unless he brought them victory. Which was a near impossibility.

Pyke stared out into the night. In the cold stillness, he could just make out what he thought was a dead body along the river bank some twenty paces ahead. An adult. Probably a woman.

He forced himself to stare at the woman till it pained him. Who was she? Did she have a husband, a child? Someone else in her life? Why had she come here, to the ends of the British Empire? Or had she been born here?

Finally Pyke's eyes drifted away. It was doing him no good to stare at a dead woman. So he did something even less productive.

He thought about Wolf Tongue.

His friend was a fighter and a good tracker, but finding Nyakwai's daughter was unlikely. As much as he hated to think it, Pyke knew he couldn't rely on his old friend returning the girl to her father.

No.

If this town was going to survive, Pyke would have to do it. With Davies. And with the few good men and women he could find.

He wanted to doze, but he stood. It was time to unveil the defensive strategy he and Davies had worked out. And he had to see if the boys in town could load muskets. And if they had enough water, food, and supplies to sustain a several-day battle.

FIFTEEN – THE BROTHERS ADAMS

Wolf Tongue pulled the blanket tighter around his shoulders. The night was warm for it not yet being spring, but it still held a biting cold if he stood unmoving too long. Or moved from the fire like he had now.

He looked over his shoulder at the Adams brothers, who sat huddled together. Joseph leaned in with his face close to his brother's while he spoke in short, curt bursts. Dirch had his blanket curled across his shoulders as he stared into the fire. Now, he turned to look at Wolf Tongue. As soon as they met eyes, the younger Adams blinked and returned his gaze to the flames.

Again, Wolf Tongue narrowed his eyes and studied them. Once they'd crossed the river, they found a few cut roads that led to the north, south, and northwest. The most recent tracks seemed to head to the northwest, which would lead them the fastest to New France. Wolf Tongue pushed the Adams brothers as much as he could, and yet, they seemed to never quite break into a run. But they had come at least four or five miles before it had gotten too dark to continue.

Joseph had complained of the constant effort, and as much as it irked Wolf Tongue to indulge him, he agreed to stop for a rest. They could have easily followed the road through the night, but he didn't want to risk stumbling upon Burgess or passing a dark camp in the night with clouds veiling the moon. And so they stopped, built a fire, and Wolf Tongue paced.

With a sigh, he returned to the circle of fire and sat down. Wolf Tongue stared at the man across the fire. Joseph's face was narrow and craggy, cast into relief by the firelight. He had his lips tightened and his eyes narrowed as he stared back. The look was intense and filled with anger before he looked away to rifle through his pouch for something.

In the firelight and darkness, the brothers reminded him of a face he'd seen before. Perhaps he'd only seen them the last time he'd come through Millers

Town. But no, it was someone else's echo he saw now only in the dark, though he couldn't quite grasp whose.

He tried to keep his voice low and calm when he spoke, though he still felt the urgency of speed only exaggerated by the brothers seeming to not feel it at all. "Where do you think Burgess is going?"

"Harris told you," said Joseph slowly. "New France."

"New France is a big place."

"Then it might take us a while to find him." Joseph stared back at him, then spat into the fire.

Wolf Tongue drew a breath and thought of his friends Pyke and Davies still at the town. If it weren't for his friendship with Pyke especially, he would have laid Joseph Adams face-first in the mud that morning before they moved a mile from Millers Town. But they had been right—Wolf Tongue needed both brothers in the case that they found Burgess in public or where they'd need to talk before Wolf Tongue could seize him and the girl.

What bothered him was that neither brother seemed to feel the press of time that threatened their town. Nyakwai would come to take his tribute the next morning, and each thereafter if they didn't return. Perhaps they had no more kin there. After all, they had said their parents and brother had died.

Now that he thought of it, he wondered why they even needed him. They could just as well find Burgess now, especially if they did in fact know where he might go to sell the girl.

Wolf Tongue decided to try the other brother.

"Dirch, what do you know about Rab?"

He looked at Joseph before answering. "Not much. He keeps to himself. Though folks don't like him much. Never took to him myself."

"Why not?"

Dirch shrugged. "He was always just off. Never seemed to laugh. Had a strange way about him that made people give him some room. And he always talked too much."

"And so do you," snapped Joseph. "Let's get some rest, Dirch. We need it."

"I'll watch," said Wolf Tongue. "We'll need to move before dawn."

Joseph grunted and spread out a blanket beneath him. "I'll watch after midnight." He laid down with his back to the fire and to Wolf Tongue while Dirch slowly did the same.

Wolf Tongue lifted his eyes from the fire to stare into the woods surrounding them. Clouds had covered them, leaving just a steel haze for light. Some of the bushes had begun to bud, but most of the forest was bones of trees and desiccated fingers in the night.

Wolf Tongue's mind flitted among the burdens he carried. He thought of Fox's Smile still at home, waiting the birth of their child. Of the empty longhouses around his village as barren as the trees around him. Of the strange behavior of his companions and his hope that they might still catch Burgess and help the girl.

Wolf Tongue wiped his hands on his face as he took a breath, then dug through his bag for his pipe. He smoked and the tobacco still tasted too bitter. As he smoked, he prayed first to the *jogah* of the woods and rivers in this place, and then to Hahgwehdiyu. Then, he stood and smoked for a while longer while he watched the forest for danger. And watched the Adams brothers.

The fire had burned low and Wolf Tongue fed another small stick into it when he reaffirmed his dedication to his mission. He decided he cared very little for the town or its people. They'd harbored the scalpers that had tried to kill him a year before and it seemed like those who remained were little better. Especially if he could judge by Joseph Adams.

But Pyke, his friend and brother in battle, felt some obligation to help them. And the more he thought about it, the more Wolf Tongue struggled with delay for the girl's sake. He didn't even know her name, but he knew whatever her life held for her now wouldn't be pleasant. If she still did indeed live, being captured and stolen as a slave by a white man was no future for any *iomwhen*, even the kin of Nyakwai.

Oddly, he felt a kinship with the girl he'd never met. Someone from Millers Town had come for him once. But he had been a grown warrior with a soldier to fight beside him.

Joseph stirred. He grunted as he sat up and glanced at Wolf Tongue. He then shuffled off a few steps to relieve himself. He shivered once, then returned to the fire.

"Sleep if you want," he said. "I can't sleep well anyway." He stared directly into the fire without looking again at Wolf Tongue.

Without answering, Wolf Tongue stepped back from the fire and sat to rest against a tree. He reclined his head against it and adjusted the blanket around him. He looked once more at Joseph sitting, frowning into the fire. Wolf Tongue loosened his tomahawk to lay it across his lap beneath the blanket.

The night passed without incident, though Wolf Tongue slept lightly and opened his eyes at every stir of his companions. Just as the sky began to bleed of its blackness in the east, Wolf Tongue rose and called to Dirch. Joseph slowly rolled from his seat and began to gather his things. Wolf Tongue smothered out the last of the fire.

"We can eat while we move," he said.

Joseph ignored him and turned to relieve himself again.

Wolf Tongue pursed his lips and stepped off to follow the road again. Dirch hustled to catch up.

"We'll follow this road to New France?" asked Wolf Tongue.

"No. We'll need to—" Dirch stopped himself with a tiny whine of an exhaled breath while he took his lip in his teeth. He looked to Joseph, then back at his feet with a resigned sag in his shoulders. Wolf Tongue suppressed a smile that so simple a ruse had taken Dirch off guard.

Joseph trotted up beside them, his frown darker than usual. He glanced between them, then settled his eyes on Dirch. "What happened?"

Dirch regained some of his height and looked at Wolf Tongue. "We think we know where Rab is headed."

"Dirch?" Joseph's voice was full of warning, but his brother continued.

"There's a lot of folks come through Harris's Ferry and Millers Town that talk about a secret trading place. A place anyone can trade whatever they want to sell, whether they're French, English, Dutch, Prussian, Spanish. They know to meet there."

Wolf Tongue's shoulders tightened as he stared at Joseph. "What do they sell there?"

Dirch answered, his voice quiet. "Anything. Muskets. Slaves. Scalps. Things stolen from churches."

Wolf Tongue's lips curled back from his teeth as he hissed, "Little girls for *quhanstrono* to fuck?"

Joseph leaned in with a terrible scowl at his brother before he turned his head to Wolf Tongue. "If you want to help save her and our town, then let's stop talking about it and get there already."

Wolf Tongue wheeled on him and grabbed his tunic in both fists. Joseph stumbled backward a few steps, off balance as Wolf Tongue lifted him. Wolf Tongue pushed his face close, baring his teeth. "You knew. You knew it was Burgess. And you knew where he was going and what he was doing."

"And you think I'd tell it all to an Indian and that dandy of a soldier?" Joseph spat back. "Whatever things Rab does never hurt Millers Town none. Not until now."

Wolf Tongue shoved him, hard. Joseph stumbled backward and fell, slapping into the mud. "Everyone in your town's about to die if you don't tell this Indian where we're going. And we need to get there fast."

Wolf Tongue raised himself up to stare down at Joseph through the bottoms of his eyes over his heaving chest. "And if you lie to me or make it so my friends die trying to help your filthy rat's hole of a town, I will take your scalp and sell it to Nyakwai."

He turned immediately to Dirch. "If you want to save your friends' lives, today we run."

Dirch hesitated for only a moment before looking at his brother. Joseph raised himself from the ground. He stared hard at Wolf Tongue, his face tight with fury, but finally he loped past and broke into a jog.

In the moment before he followed his brother, Dirch stared back at

Wolf Tongue with wide eyes and a tight mouth. It was the face of someone looking at impending death, and Wolf Tongue had seen it before.

Suddenly, his memory solidified with that horror-stricken face of Dirch. He knew now why these brothers who looked so alike seemed so familiar to him. This terrified look he saw on Dirch was the same face he'd seen on their older brother, James, when Wolf Tongue had killed him in the dark.

SIXTEEN - BLOOD-WITE

Pyke forced himself to his feet. This morning was another foggy one, the air damp and heavy.

Fleur had surprised him during the night with a blanket. It was wool and scratchy but warm. Chilled to his bones and exhausted, Pyke had accepted the gift. Only later, while wrapped in it, did Pyke realize she had probably shared it with her husband.

Now he looked down at the blanket, unsure what to do with it. Guilt filled him again. He shouldn't have accepted the gift, cold as he was. He had killed her husband. He'd been in the right, but still. And he should not have accepted a gift from a French woman. The best thing would be to return it, but he did not wish to see her this morning. He didn't trust her and her beauty was disarming.

"Your French whore left you a present?"

Pyke looked left and saw Si walking toward him, pitchfork in hand. Si grinned like the comment had been in jest, but Pyke knew better.

A few men chuckled sardonically and muttered under their breath at Si's insult. He could tell they agreed with Si's sentiment.

Pyke looked over the wall and searched the fog, thinking that would end the conversation. But Si stopped next to him.

"What's a British officer doing with a French woman? Seems kind of strange."

"She has shown me more courtesy than most people in this town, yourself included." Pyke faced the larger man. "Strange, considering I've come to help."

Si held his stare for a moment before moving on. Pyke watched him go, thinking that sooner or later they would have a serious disagreement. He folded the blanket and put it on the wall.

The air was cold and damp and through the fog Pyke could just see the edge of the Mingo camp. Already their men were stirring, engaged in their practice and banter and dancing.

Pyke turned and looked back at Millers Town. He saw a few men milling about, their faces long, their eyes downcast, their bodies shivering in the brisk March air.

They were already defeated. The real battle hadn't begun yet, and they were already dead.

Not soldiers, Pyke reminded himself.

He looked back at Si. "It's a good idea to rest whenever you can. Because you're going to need your strength today. And probably tomorrow."

"Five people." Si grimaced. "We'd better draw straws."

Pyke stared at Si till the man met his eyes. "No one is drawing bloody straws. Get that through your skull."

Pyke went to find Davis. The sergeant was sleeping in a pile of hay, snoring loudly. The man's breathing would stop for a moment after each exhale.

"Sergeant."

Davies came to suddenly, his musket in his hands. "Ah, sir. Thought you were somebody else."

Pyke smiled. "The digging is all done?"

Davies slowly climbed to his feet. "Yes, sir."

"Excellent."

"Three skips of a louse," Davies said.

Pyke shook his head. "Every little advantage helps in battle."

Davies yawned. "I'd trade my arm for some more of Molly Fletcher's cider right now. All we've got is water if you can believe it. Probably polluted."

Pyke smiled. "When this is all over, we shall have some of Molly Fletcher's cider."

"When this is all over, we'll have our pick of drinks in heaven." Davies then noticed the blanket Pyke was holding. "I didn't get one of those."

Pyke ignored the comment. "We are losing these people."

Davies nodded. "We need to give them a victory, sir."

"Agreed." Pyke looked away, toward the camp. He couldn't see it from where they were, too many houses and the fog obstructed their view. "We shall have our opportunity later today."

"Lieutenant!"

Pyke's head whipped around. The shout had come from the church house.

"Lieutenant!"

Pyke nodded at Davies, and the two men hurried toward the church. They found Bertram Miller in the crossroads, looking around frantically. When he saw them coming, his expression didn't much change.

"Bertram, what is it?" Pyke said.

"Nyakwai wants to talk."

Pyke got a chill. He'd spoken to the chief yesterday afternoon and had been given a full day. That the chief wanted to speak already was not a good sign. Pyke had feared this would happen. Presumably, Nyakwai would punish them for last night's transgression.

Pyke faced Davies. "Stay and get the town ready."

"I am coming with you this time." Dob was coming out of the church house. "To make sure this town's interests are truly being represented."

Pyke was about to protest, but then more of Dob's men came out of the church: Kit and Quill and a few others Pyke recognized as having supported the man in all public meetings so far. They watched Pyke with open hostility.

"You bloody buggerers!" Davies shouted. He stepped forward, his hand instinctively going for his belt where he kept his pistol. "The lieutenant and I have done everything possible to help you!"

Dob smirked. "Then Mr. Pyke won't mind if I accompany him. Will he?"

"*Lieutenant* Pyke to you," Davies said.

Pyke's face betrayed no emotions. "Of course not, Dob. But you'd better let me do the talking."

"We'll see about th—"

Pyke didn't let the man complete his thought. "Because Nyakwai does not respect traders. He's likely to cut your tongue out. The man only understands one thing, and that is might." Pyke nodded at Davies to stand down. The sergeant did. "So you can come along but you'd better keep quiet and let the warriors do the talking."

Pyke regretted bringing Dob with him. No doubt the man would interject at some inappropriate time, or undermine Pyke's argument by suggesting some foolish idea, or, perhaps worse, plead with Nyakwai for peace and attempt to renegotiate the terms. The chief would not take kindly to any of those suggestions.

Pyke and Dob walked in step but Dob kept a few feet between them as they tramped through the town. He was sending a clear message to his people: he was going with Pyke but he was not the man's partner. Pyke examined the faces of the townfolk in the streets watching them, hoping to find sympathetic eyes. They were few and far between. Fletcher, his wife, and his brother nodded at him, and he'd already seen Bertram at the crossroads. Just about everyone else they met ignored him and looked encouragingly at Dob.

As they neared the wall, the line of men posted there parted for them. Si and his gang waited by the makeshift gate.

"About time Dob was involved!" Si shouted.

And his men took up the cheer.

Pyke smiled ruefully. Dob had planned all this out. Not all men cheered but those that did were loud enough to quiet any potential dissent. Pyke scanned the crowd, though, and saw a few friendly faces, men that looked to him for leadership and protection.

Dob looked at Pyke and gave him an *I-told-you-so* grin. Pyke just smiled back, while his insides boiled.

Fleur appeared at the edge of the crowd. She twiddled her fingers and looked expectantly at Pyke, like she had something to tell him. Over the cheering for Dob, though, Pyke wouldn't have been able to hear it.

She mouthed some words. In school, he'd learned how to read lips well. When boredom overcame he and his classmates while the teacher droned on, they'd communicated silently.

Fleur had said, *Be careful.*

They passed over the wall and Pyke waited till they were halfway from the town limit to the Mingo camp before speaking.

"This is not child's play," Pyke said. "You've had your victory in front of your people, but when we get to Nyakwai you will defer to me."

Dob would not even look at Pyke.

They were drawing near the camp.

Pyke said, "We must project strength when we speak to him. Listen to me: he will not offer better terms. Do you understand me?"

Dob would not look at him. "We shall see. Perhaps it is time you permitted a trader to do the bargaining."

Pyke gritted his teeth. "This man is no trader. Your ways will not impress him. Quite the opposite, in fact. Now keep your jaw tight and let me do the talking."

Dob said nothing.

They had reached the Mingo camp. The warriors paced back and forth in front of them, crossing their path to Nyakwai. Dob's resolve, which had been passable a moment ago, began to melt away. He looked nervously about.

"Eyes forward, damn it!" Pyke hissed under his breath. "Remember: strength."

The dances and cries started. The noise was deafening. Pyke kept moving forward and yanked Dob's arm to keep the pace.

"Keep moving, you bloody fool."

Dob had turned ghostly pale.

The two minutes it took to reach Nyakwai were the longest in Pyke's life. They found the chief where he'd been yesterday, lazing on the felled tree. His wife sat by his side, her back stiff and her proud eyes fierce. Pyke could feel the woman's anger in her stare and in the rigid tenseness of her body. She had lost her daughter. And to the English.

Pyke wished Wolf Tongue were at his side instead of this silver-tongued devil, Dob. Walking through the camp had felt like going to the deadly nevergreen, like

Nyakwai's warriors were channeling him to the gallows.

The chief's private bodyguard danced and cursed him in their strange tongue. Pyke had picked up some Susquehannock, but neither that nor his French, nor Latin would help him here. But he did not need to know their tongue to understand the menace behind their words.

"English are dogs," Nyakwai said, once he'd settled his men. In the midst of the fray, Pyke spotted Kicks-the-Oneida. The former Susquehannock leader did not dance like the others, or call him names, or insult Dob. Instead, Kicks-the-Oneida turned a hate-filled gaze at him.

"We are dogs who killed ten of your so-called warriors last night," Pyke said.

The chief continued as if he hadn't spoken. He slapped his wife's thigh. "Last night I fucked my wife while my men split skulls."

"Your men killed women and children," Pyke said.

"They killed dogs," the chief said.

Today he wore a deerskin coat and a porcupine quill necklace. He looked like he'd slept well. The man was fresh as a daisy.

So were his warriors.

They were well-rested, well-fed, and eager for war. They served a sharp contrast to the people of Millers Town, who were beaten before the real fight had even begun.

Dob suddenly spoke. "Sir, we are wholly innocent of these crimes. We are peaceful trad—"

"HEEL, DOG!" the chief shouted.

One of his warriors broke from the group and clubbed Dob in the back of his legs. The man shrieked and fell to the ground, ending up on his knees.

Nyakwai spat at him. "Stay there until I force you to stand."

"Please, sir, we are prepared to offer you more—"

Nyakwai motioned at the warrior who'd clubbed Dob. The man raised his weapon over his head, preparing to strike and probably kill Dob.

If Pyke let them kill Dob, it would solve one of his problems. The opposing leadership in the town would be gone and Pyke could rally the people to follow his orders better. Pyke frowned at the ugly thought, though, and remembered his duty.

He stepped between the warrior and cowering Dob. "Nyakwai, this man will say no more."

The chief watched Dob with steely eyes, waiting to see if he would open his mouth again. When Dob did not, the chief motioned at his warrior and the man stepped away, the whole time keeping his eyes on Pyke.

Kicks-the-Oneida pointed at Dob. "You are a fool if you follow this man."

Pyke did not know what Kicks-the-Oneida was going to say, but it would not be good. He racked his brain to remember the last time he'd seen this man.

It had been at the Susquehannock village, when they'd celebrated the defeat of Azariah Bennett.

Wolf Tongue and Pyke had recounted their adventures for the whole tribe. Pyke had given a short accounting, but Wolf Tongue had gone into great detail beginning with their time in Millers Town.

Pyke suddenly feared he knew what Kicks-the-Oneida was going to say.

The chief sat impassively on the tree, his hand once again resting on his wife's thigh. Nyakwai was a proud man and not the sort to let others speak for him. And, Pyke guessed, Nyakwai would certainly bristle at another powerful warrior trying to establish power in this shifting collection of tribes.

Not unless there was a sinister purpose behind it.

Kicks-the-Oneida stared haughtily at Dob. "This soldier killed your people."

Pyke looked down at Dob. The man was scared out of his mind, but the warrior's words had gotten through the fear gripping his mind.

Kicks-the-Oneida continued. "You follow a man who killed your own. The men who hunted scalps. They almost had Wolf Tongue's head last year. The Dutchman and others."

"You killed—" Dob began to say.

Pyke cut him off. "You already know we did, Dob. They came for my friend's scalp. We killed them in self-defense. Now it is time you ended this pitiful charade. You are as guilty as Nederwue was."

Dob looked away.

Nyakwai spoke next. "English are dogs. They turn on each other."

Pyke said nothing.

"They break promises and steal away in darkness rather than fight, as a man should."

Pyke said nothing.

"Like dogs they lick own arsehole when they hunger."

Pyke said, "What do you want?"

Nyakwai smiled, sensing correctly that he'd gotten under Pyke's skin. "Neoke. You do not bring her."

"We have until this afternoon."

The chief's eyes turned stony. "You have until the width of one hand to bring her. Or five dogs to be killed."

"Hold on—"

"Or bring no one and we will kill all of you."

"You won't."

Nyakwai's smile turned wicked. "We enjoy killing dogs."

"You won't," Pyke said. "Because if you destroy this town and murder everyone here, you will never see your whore daughter again."

The chief's smile vanished and his eyes bulged. Pyke knew he had hit the man in his most vulnerable spot. His wife started to stand, but the chief forced her back down.

Strength, Pyke reminded himself. He'd seen Wolf Tongue interact with men of other tribes and the Susquehannock warrior always pressed on when he saw a weakness in his opponent. Pyke tried to think of what Wolf Tongue would say in this moment, no doubt it would be something vulgar and—

Then he had an idea. The girl's mother was sitting no more than ten feet away, but Pyke had to stay on the offensive. Nyakwai had to think Pyke, and by extension, the town were not afraid of him and his warriors.

Pyke said, "Neoke wasn't kidnapped from what I hear. She went with the English man willingly. He showed her his size and she said she had never seen anything that impressive amongst her own."

Nyakwai rushed him. Pyke was totally unprepared for the attack and the old man moved fast. Two of his warriors put Pyke on the ground and the chief's blade pressed into his neck. Pyke wondered if he was going to die under this man's blade. The man's wife screamed in her alien tongue from the tree, probably calling for Pyke's blood.

"Dogs do not speak of Neoke. Ever again."

Pyke stared the chief in the eye. "We need three more days, and we will bring her to you."

Nyakwai saw Pyke's defiance, and Pyke realized he'd gone too far. The man had lost a lot of face in front of his warriors and in front of his wife. So now he had to put Pyke in his place.

The chief slid the knife across Pyke's cheek. It was a short cut, but it stung and Pyke knew it would leave a permanent scar. But he pretended like it didn't hurt and just smiled.

"Three more days, then you can have your daughter back."

"Get up."

Nyakwai backed away as Pyke got to his feet.

"One hand of the sun. Bring me five."

Pyke ignored the order. "Why did you let the first group through last night?"

Nyakwai moved back to the felled tree and leaned against it. His wife was still screaming at Pyke, but the chief shot her a look and she sat obediently on the tree again.

The chief said, "So you would think it was safe."

Pyke nodded. He'd gambled last night and lost. Nyakwai hadn't been fooled by the diversions. He'd instead used them to his advantage. He could only hope the first group had truly made it past the Mingos to safety.

"One hand," Nyakwai said again. "My daughter, or five dogs."

Pyke touched his cheek where the chief had cut him. His fingers came away bloody. He wiped them on his uniform. Dob was staring at the ground, pitifully.

Pyke wanted to curse him for showing so much weakness in the face of their enemy.

"Come get your skulls, Nyakwai. It will cost you forty men to take five of ours."

The chief burst into laughter. "We will see, dog."

On their way back to the town, Dob was silent, sullen. He kept his eyes on the ground, until they drew closer to the wall.

Pyke wiped at his face. The blood was flowing freely. He needed to patch it up quickly.

He looked at Dob. "The Mingos came here because of your greed. You took their scalps and now they want blood. I can hardly blame them. If you want to survive this ordeal, you will need my help. So say nothing of what happened to Nederwue and the others that came for my friend. Do you understand?"

Dob said nothing and would not meet Pyke's eyes. They continued to walk back to the town.

Pyke said, "The Mingos *need* us to be at odds. If they can divide us they will destroy this town. So keep your bone box shut. We cannot fight amongst ourselves if we are going to defeat them."

"*Defeat* them?" Dob said. "They are more than twice our number. We asked Bennett for help and he sends three men: a savage brute, a slovenly sergeant, and an incompetent junior officer."

Pyke almost struck Dob, but they were approaching the wall and Dob's people were watching. Pyke couldn't hit the man now without further driving a wedge between himself and the townfolk.

"We will prevail," Pyke said. "You must believe that or we have no chance."

Dob looked away and shook his head.

As they drew close to the wall, Pyke heard Davies.

"Out of my bloody way. Out of my bloody way." The sergeant pushed through the crowd and his eyes bulged when he saw Pyke's face. "It's an improvement, sir."

"Thank you, Sergeant." Pyke stopped to talk to Davies, while Dob continued on. Si and his gang crowded Dob to see how it had gone. Pyke figured the man would downplay certain events and harp on Kicks-the-Oneida's revelations.

Pyke didn't want them thinking about that right now, though. He raised his voice.

"They are coming. We must get ready!"

"Now?" Davies said, under his breath.

Pyke nodded. "We can only hope Wolf Tongue is close. Perhaps he will still save us."

Si stepped forward. "We have drawn straws and we will send the French bitch first."

Si's gang, four rough-looking fellows, stepped forward and Pyke saw Fleur between them, struggling and cursing them in French.

Pyke rushed forward. "We are not handing anyone over! Let her go!"

Si put his hand on Pyke's shoulder. "Cunt for cunt. If we give him this French whore, maybe he will be appeased, at least for another day."

Pyke slapped the man's hand away. "She stays."

"Your prick clouds your judgment," Si announced, for everyone to hear. "Has her flapdragon spread to your eyes and blinded you?"

Fleur kicked and struggled between the four men and landed in the mud. Si's gang just laughed at her attempts to get away.

Pyke drew his saber. "Tell your apple polishers to let her go."

Si shook his head no. The four men started marching Fleur toward the Mingos.

"That's far enough," Davies said.

Pyke looked over his shoulder and saw the sergeant aiming his pistol at the lead man.

Davies said, "Nyakwai will gladly take her, then come for four more anyway. So we're headed for a fight, whether you like it or not, you horse's arse."

"You are no longer in charge," Si said. "Dob is."

"You are committing treason. Let her go and I will overlook the crime." Pyke tensed his hand on the handle of the saber. "Now."

Si's eyes were wide. Pyke had backed him into a corner and now the man had to make a difficult decision. If he backed down, he would look a coward.

He decided to stand his ground. "She goes to the Indians."

In the blink of an eye, Pyke slashed the saber across Si's chest. The man screamed and fell. Pyke whirled to face the four men around Fleur. With their leader writhing and screaming on the ground, they quickly lost their resolve and backed away from Davies and Fleur.

Pyke kept his eyes on the men while he helped Fleur to her feet. Fletcher stepped forward, between them and Dob's men. Pyke watched as Fletcher met the eyes of his friends, and they too came forward now, forming a wall.

Si's four men helped him to his feet. Pyke had slashed his chest. It was a long cut, but not deep. Certainly it would sting but it would not kill the man, not unless it the cut soured. Si eyed Fletcher and the men that had stood with him, then angrily turned away and left.

Pyke let him go. "The Mingos are coming! The sergeant and I have trained our whole lives to be soldiers. We have been in battle. We have stood shoulder-to-shoulder in the fray. We have seen death and we have caused it. And we are here today because we survived. Now shut up and listen, and you might yet live!"

Slowly the tension went out of the crowd.

Fletcher raised his voice. "You heard the lieutenant. Now let's get ready to give these bastards what for!"

Someone in the back of the crowd cheered. And then the others joined in.

Pyke raised his saber. "Let the savages come! Let them come!"

SEVENTEEN – RAB BURGESS

As they ran, Wolf Tongue sifted through the unanswered questions he still had about the Adams brothers and their mission. In the two hours since he'd forced them to run, he wondered about how the secretive trading occurred, and what the brothers' motives were and why they seemed so reluctant to save their town. He wondered what Joseph's plan for him might be once they found Burgess and the girl.

Mostly, Wolf Tongue wondered whether Dirch and Joseph knew that he'd killed their brother. They knew he'd gone missing a year ago, and Wolf Tongue was sure they knew he had sold scalps to the French. They even knew exactly where to go for the exchange.

Joseph, at least, was sure to know his brother had gone hunting not for game, but for victims. And the men, Nederwue and the others, had specifically followed Pyke and Wolf Tongue out of Millers Town in hopes of isolating Wolf Tongue for coin without the danger of facing a larger force.

Yes, they must have known James had gone after Wolf Tongue and Pyke and never returned. And that idea made Wolf Tongue even more wary. If the Adams brothers were selling scalps to the French and knew that Wolf Tongue had killed their brother, he had a good idea of just what Joseph had in mind for him.

He stayed behind both his companions, watching their backs as they trotted along the road. Both were breathing heavily. Mud caked on their boots for each squelching step. They didn't run quickly, but at a plodding jog that he hoped would cover more ground over time, even with the burden of running through the wet ground. The air was chill again, and Wolf Tongue felt his sweat cooling in his hair and along his neck as he ran.

Suddenly, Joseph slowed to a walk. His breath came out in gasps and he wiped at his forehead.

"We're getting close," he rasped. He waved with a hand toward a large hill ahead and to the left that rose above the trees so it was visible over their branches nearly a mile away. There seemed to be very little to separate this one hill from the others surrounding it except for a small section of sheer rock on the east side. It was as if a giant knife had shorn a projecting slice of forest and left only the blue-gray of a wall of shale. "There. Top of that ridge."

"Is there a lodge? A trading post?"

Joseph shook his head. "No. Just a clear spot. People gather, build a fire, and wait for others to see it and come."

This seemed to be the perfect place for such affairs—disputed territory getting close to the Ohio Valley and New France filled with people from every nation: French, English, Dutch, Seneca, Shawnee, Susquehannock. People could linger, come to buy what they wanted, then take it home and sell what they could. If the French were buying scalps, it would be easier, if less lucrative, to sell to an intermediary who'd then take it to contacts in New France, rather than crossing over yourself. And if you were selling slaves, you'd leave your goods here and not be tied to your merchandise or activities more than necessary.

"Burgess is a day ahead of us," said Wolf Tongue. "How long do you usually need to wait until the right buyer comes?"

Joseph looked over his shoulder at Wolf Tongue with grimace of scorn, but he answered. "Not long. People come by every few days. Especially the French. They come when they see a fire."

"So he might still be there."

"Might," replied Joseph.

"Then we run to the base of the hill."

Dirch began jogging again, but Joseph hesitated a moment to scowl at his brother before he, too, began to move faster. Wolf Tongue waited, looked once over his shoulder at the ice and mud trail behind them, and then took up his position running behind the brothers.

They ran about a half a mile before Joseph slowed and called Dirch back. They hadn't yet reached the base of the hill, but had stopped at a narrow path that broke from the main trail to lead to the west. It was barely wider than a deer trail, but the snow had been beaten to brown mush with outlines of recent boot prints.

Joseph didn't explain himself, but inclined his head toward the path for Dirch, and then stepped off the main road. Dirch followed behind, and then Wolf Tongue.

The path was worn beneath his feet, the stones exposed down to the gray and brown of the mud, and slick. But the forest seemed to try to reclaim the path as it leaned in on either side. Bare, wet branches of mountain laurel scraped at Wolf Tongue's shoulders, leaving cold streaks where they brushed or dripped on him. Chestnut trees that were as thick as Wolf Tongue's arm was long stood stoic in their crackled, gray bark while hundreds of saplings rose as if to swarm over the trail. Even the mature trees seemed to move into the way of their progress and the trail would suddenly spin to the side to circumvent a massive block that guarded the path. Here, deeper into the wood, the night's fog was still draped among the branches, leaving them blind beyond thirty strides.

As they walked, Wolf Tongue slowed his breath. Here, there was no room for them to go abreast, and the treacherous ground would have been folly to run on. They picked their way through the scratching brush, slimed stones, and low-hanging branches. The ground, the trees, and the air itself was wet and dripping, and Wolf Tongue wrapped a piece of oil cloth from his bag around his musket's breech, hoping to keep the damp from seeping into his musket.

Soon, the ground shifted, and the trail began to wind back and forth in switchbacks up the side of a steep hill. Ahead, Wolf Tongue could see the exposed slice of shale they had seen from the road, a blue smear against the hill amongst the trees and mist.

They were nearing the ridge when Wolf Tongue spotted sharp lines of white thirty strides to his right, half hidden in the leaves. There was no mistaking the pile of bones—a few long bones strewn next to a spine and human head. If the Adams brothers saw it, they made no motion or mention of it.

A few steps on, Wolf Tongue stopped abruptly as the air carried the scent of wood fire to him. Again, the Adams brothers did not slow. This time, however, Wolf Tongue grew more wary. He let the distance between him and Dirch widen a bit before he followed. He had carried his musket near the breach in one hand, but now he shifted it across his chest to hold with both.

Finally, Joseph and Dirch stopped. After a moment, a sound came again, the murmur of voices made vague by distance, mist, and the tricks of the forest. They looked at one another, then Joseph whispered, "Wait here. I'll go see," and slipped away toward the ridge.

Wolf Tongue eyed Dirch, searching for some sign of duplicity, though he saw only what he thought was simple nervousness.

They waited. The voices halted for a moment, then resumed with what Wolf Tongue thought was the lilt of Joseph's wheedling platitudes he'd offered to Harris. Then a call came. "Come on, Dirch! It's me and Burgess."

Wolf Tongue motioned for Dirch to move ahead and he followed. A moment later, the ground crested and flattened out over the ridge onto a flat expanse of rock, a half dozen saplings clinging to the cracks and standing stark in the fog. A fire crackled and smoked at its center, and around it stood five figures. On one side of the fire, Joseph stood by a broad, unshaven man with gray flecks through his red beard. Opposite them stood two other men.

Between those men stood a smaller, thin form with long, black hair.

Wolf Tongue lowered his gun, though his fingers itched to hoist it and fire.

His eyes narrowed as they approached the party and his left hand dropped to his knife hilt.

"Dirch," called the man standing by Joseph in greeting. Wolf Tongue assumed this was Burgess. He was a large man, broad in the chest and jaw, with a beard that seemed to grow up from his shoulders. When he saw Wolf Tongue, Burgess's eyes tightened and in a flick took in the Susquehannock's musket and tomahawk. One meaty paw flexed around the stock of what looked like a fowler that he held at his thigh. Wolf Tongue eyed the gun, thinking it likely loaded with shot that would scatter, rather than a single ball.

The other two men wore fur hats over long hair and sunburned faces with heavy, fur jackets. Wolf Tongue guessed them to be French fur trappers. They also tensed, one reaching for a pistol tucked into his belt while the other lifted his musket from the ground where he'd been leaning on it.

The girl had her hands bound in front of her, her one eye swollen. Her only reaction to Wolf Tongue's appearance was to stare with hatred at him, then the others. She wore a leather skirt wrapped around heavy leggings, all of which were stained with mud. She wore no jewelry or decoration and despite her filth and bruises, she stood straight with quick-darting eyes. Nyakwai was right—his daughter was beautiful.

"Who is zis? You 'ave more friends?" growled one of the two standing by the girl.

"They're friends," said Joseph. He raised his hands and stepped farther away from Burgess as if to intercept Dirch. "This is my brother. And Rab," he gestured with a placating hand, "Well … um." Joseph's smooth talk cracked for a heartbeat.

"My name is Wolf Tongue of the Wolf Clan of the Susquehannock." He looked at the girl. "*Sgëno*," he said with a nod. The girl snapped her head to look at him, her eyes blinking. Wolf Tongue was not fluent in the language of the Great Hill People, the Seneca, but their language was close enough to the others of the Six Nations and his own that he could make himself understood. He continued in her own tongue, "When the fighting starts, lay down."

"Best speak English," said Burgess in a slow voice as he lifted his fowler to hold it in both hands.

"It's a greeting," said Wolf Tongue as he angled himself to be in line with the French men's shoulders. "It means I'm here to take that poor girl back to her people."

"The hell you are," growled Burgess.

"What is zis? We bought her already! Now you cheat us?" The furtrapper drew the pistol from his belt just as Burgess lifted his fowler and aimed it at Wolf Tongue. Wolf Tongue dove headlong into a roll behind the nearest fur trapper.

As his shoulders struck the ground, he heard the snap-hiss of less than a heartbeat before the thunder of Burgess's gun. The fur trapper screamed and stumbled backward, tripping over Wolf Tongue.

Wolf Tongue went with the momentum and pulled up from a roll on the far side of the other Frenchman, who still aimed his pistol at Burgess as if waiting for the pan to fire. Wolf Tongue spun and brought the stock of his musket around, slamming it into the base of the man's skull, who toppled over the fire and into Burgess.

Burgess stumbled back and howled in pain. He staggered a step as he swung his fowler like a club down on the Frenchman once, then twice. Wolf Tongue looked to the other downed man, who now lay still except for terrible shivers of his chest. He heard two quick snaps as flint hammered down into a frizzen, but no explosions followed.

As quickly as he'd taken in the fallen fur trader, Wolf Tongue spun back to see Burgess draw a long, heavy dagger and scream as he lunged past the fire toward Wolf Tongue.

Burgess closed so quickly that Wolf Tongue barely pulled up his musket in time to jab it into Burgess's belly. The jab slowed the heavy man, but the force pushed Wolf Tongue back. He pulled the trigger. The gun fired with an explosion. Burgess twitched, then surged forward with another roar.

The dagger came slicing toward Wolf Tongue's face. He dropped his musket and spun with the direction of the dagger. It tore the leather of his sleeve as he danced away and drew his knife and tomahawk.

Burgess stumbled ahead and fell to one knee. Wolf Tongue lifted his weapons, but hesitated, thinking of their offer to bring this man to Nyakwai. Then, Burgess lumbered to his feet again. The back of his jacket was already turning black as blood poured from the gunshot through his belly. He screamed a raw, low, howl without words and limped toward Wolf Tongue. He chanced a quick glance at the Adams brothers. Both stood with their muskets half-lowered, eyes wide.

Burgess came on, his dagger flashing patterns before him. Wolf Tongue dodged and then caught it with his tomahawk. At close quarters, he managed a quick slice with his knife that scored into Burgess's belly again. Then Wolf Tongue staggered a step from the force of a meaty fist to his jaw.

"You goddamned devil-worshiper!"

That dagger came again, faster this time, as if driven by anger. Wolf Tongue countered and slashed. He scored twice more with his knife, cutting a line across Burgess's jaw, and slicing his left forearm to the bone.

Still, Burgess staggered on again, clearly favoring his right leg. Even hobbled, shot, and cut, Burgess screamed and cursed as he somehow managed to beat away each of Wolf Tongue's swings with his tomahawk.

Finally, Wolf Tongue knocked the dagger high with a swing of his tomahawk, then kicked as hard as he could into the man's wounded leg. The leg gave and Burgess toppled forward. Wolf Tongue caught him with a thrust of his knife.

He felt an instant's hesitation, then a shudder and crack as his knife broke through ribs as Burgess's weight leaned forward. Wolf Tongue stepped aside and let the big man fall forward into the mud. Burgess lay on his belly, face turned to Wolf Tongue, blinking, his teeth bared.

Still holding his tomahawk ready, he glanced around quickly. The one fur trader still shivered on the ground and his companion crashed through the brush twenty paces away, stumbling off for New France. The Adams brothers still held their weapons up as if they'd forgotten them. Both had looks of horror and fear on their faces.

And there, scrambling away from the fire was Nyakwai's daughter. She'd stolen a knife from someone, probably the shot fur trader, and now worked at her bonds.

"Goddamned devil-worshiper." Burgess's words were croaking and wet as he spat out the last of his life's blood.

He blinked for another moment, then a hollow gurgle escaped him as his lungs fell still.

Wolf Tongue turned to Joseph and Dirch. They slowly seemed to come to themselves and lowered their weapons. Dirch looked questioningly at his brother, then back at Burgess.

Wolf Tongue pointed at their muskets with his tomahawk. "The mist gets into your powder and wets your flint. You can't light water on fire."

He first went to the downed Frenchman. He still shivered, but only slightly and in short fits. His eyes were closed, his face the color of the snow. Burgess's shot had splattered across his torso and neck, puckering a dozen fatal holes through him.

Then, with one eye still watching the silent Adams brothers, Wolf Tongue approached Nyakwai's daughter.

She stared back with narrowed eyes and a scowl, clutching her stolen knife like it was the only thing that kept her soul tied to this place.

Wolf Tongue squatted on his haunches and took a breath. In his own language, he said, "Are you hurt?"

She didn't answer.

Wolf Tongue sighed. "I'm sorry this happened, and we are still in danger. Nyakwai sent me to find you. Your father wants the men who took you punished and you returned safely to him. That's why we're here. We won't harm you."

The fear and hate that showed on her face seemed to lessen at the mention of her father. She still held her knife ready to strike, but her eyes narrowed with suspicion.

"What is your name?"

"Neoke."

Wolf Tongue glanced over his shoulder at Joseph and Dirch, then back to the girl. "Neoke, if something happens to me, go with these two men. They will return you to your father."

She frowned. "What will happen to you?"

"I think they will try to kill me."

EIGHTEEN – FIVE GOOD MEN

Pyke and Davies had explained their defensive strategy in council last night. The townfolk had asked so many questions. Too many. They wanted specific direction for every possible turn of events. Finally Pyke had grown frustrated and told them, with their limited time and the town's lack of military experience, that they just had to keep in mind the main objectives of the defense and the strategy behind it. Never lose sight of the ultimate goal, he'd repeated and repeated and repeated.

To the east was a wall. It wasn't sheer like a cliff, but the slope was severe enough to be troubling. The Mingo would need to negotiate a steep descent and then cover three hundred yards of open, muddy field. They might have been fearless, but they weren't fools.

Pyke had made an approach from the north less attractive by having the men dig that long, wide ditch last night. It was difficult to jump, and failing a jump, the Mingo warriors would be slowed down by the impediment.

They were camped to the west, they had the advantage in numbers, and Nyakwai was proud. So they would come from the west or the north, despite the wall the townfolk had hastily erected. Pyke knew the chief would rely on sheer of force of numbers to win this battle. The man cared not how many warriors he lost. He just wanted this conflict brought to a close quickly.

The men on the west wall were charged with driving them to the south side of town, where they would spring their trap. Pyke told the men posted on the east end of town to do the same thing.

Pyke and Davies couldn't be everywhere at once, so they considered splitting up. Then they had thought that a bad idea, because neither knew whom here they could trust. Just as many took Dob's side as did not, but the great, unanswered question was the majority left in the middle. When the Mingo attacked and their families were in danger, would they follow Pyke? He could not sway them with rhetoric. There wasn't enough time. The only way to convince was to bring them victory. Winning changed everything.

But to claim victory, the people needed to be led. Living on the frontier had probably made them into decent marksmen, but there was much difference between shooting at small game and trying to kill a man before he hacked your neck with a tomahawk. They needed direction if their defense was going to be at all successful. So ultimately, Pyke and Davies agreed to split up.

In those mad moments before the coming hell, the Mingos sang and danced and beat their drums. The thwumping was deafening and shook the entire town. Over the drum beat, they screeched and cried.

"Who are we putting on the wall, sir?" Davies said.

"Me." Pyke looked at him. "I will drive them so they come to you."

"Good luck with that, sir." Davies looked around and lowered his voice. "You can't turn your back on any of these people."

Pyke nodded. "That's why I'm keeping Fletcher and Bertram with me."

"Thanks a lot, sir."

"You can have Fletcher's brother."

"He's not even eighteen and probably still a virgin."

"But he knows how to shoot, I'll bet."

Davies faced him again. "Now there's a wager not even I would take."

"Come now, Sergeant. Surely our luck is about to turn."

"Quite right, sir." He gave Pyke a look. "Quite right."

Pyke felt the butterflies in his stomach, but he smiled as confidently as he could. "Remember that we show these townfolk strength and they will draw theirs from our example."

"Sir."

Pyke said, "Once I have driven them, I will leave Fletcher and Bertram here and come to you."

"And remind me, sir, after you have driven them, how do you know they will loop to the south side of town?"

Pyke smirked. "Because I will encourage them."

"The timing here is everything," Davies said.

"Indeed." Pyke wished he'd had a full regiment, or even a squad to assist them. Their defense was not sophisticated, but it required some coordination. "We must show them how to soldier."

The two men shared a look. Both knew what they were up against and it was very possible they'd never see each other again, at least not in this world.

Pyke began to speak, but Davies cut him off.

"Please, sir, I cannot take any Latin right now."

Pyke laughed. "Very well, Sergeant. Then I'll just say this: through the narrows, to the glory."

"Translated from the Latin, I'll bet." Davies nodded. "Hope we run into each other soon."

"Hope springs eternal."

Davies hustled off to the south plain. Pyke watched him go for a second, until the beat coming from the Mingo drums quickened. Any minute now.

Pyke turned to the wall and was surprised to find Fleur among the men.

He ran over to her. "Madame, you cannot be here! Take shelter!"

"*Ou*?" she said. "I have no house."

"Anywhere, Fleur, dear Lord they will be here any moment and …"

"And what?"

"I will not be able to protect you," he said.

She smiled at him. "I stay. I will help. Water for the men, ammunition. I will help more than these other *women*."

He knew better than to argue. Her Gallic pride would not allow her to change her mind or admit fear. And he didn't have time to argue, anyway.

"Very well. Then stay back. When they come, they will come fast and not distinguish between man and woman."

She turned and ran to collect the pitchers. A knot of women watched her go as they rounded up ammunition. Pyke was grateful they knew how to load muskets. The women out here were a far cry from the sort he'd met in polite society: hardy and practical.

The Mingo drums beat faster. They were close and loud enough that Pyke had to shout to be heard. He motioned for Fletcher and Bertram to join him quickly. They met him behind the makeshift gate in the wall. Their muskets looked old, perhaps handed down over the generations in their families.

Pyke hoped they still fired.

He pointed to the south. "We must drive them that way. Toward Davies and the south line. Remind your men, and then remind them again. Understood?"

Both men nodded grimly.

"So we must concentrate our fire on this side. That way they will break south."

"How do we do that?" Bertram said.

"More men on one side than the other."

They both gave him a look for stating the obvious. They had apparently been hoping for him to share some well-guarded military secret.

Pyke slapped their shoulders. "They cannot get through our defense here. If they do, we are lost."

Fletcher said, "We're as ready as we are going to be."

Pyke looked around. "I want to talk to the boys first. Send them over."

Fletcher and Bertram went off in opposite directions and shouted to get their men's attention. Less than a minute later, ten boys between the ages of eleven and fourteen gathered around Pyke. Their eyes were wide and they all appeared in a daze.

Boone, the boy who'd picked up Fleur's scarf at the wall, was the smallest of the lot and stood in front of the rest, gaping up at Pyke.

"You know how to load," Pyke said. "I watched you train last night, and I can tell you I've never seen boys your age work that quickly with muskets. In His Majesty's Army, many of you would beat out some of the enlisted men."

He let that sink in before continuing.

"You have a very important job. Keep these muskets loaded and coming to the men on the wall. We have placed a big responsibility on your shoulders. Today, you are men."

The boys hadn't blinked once.

Boone said, "We won't let you down, Lieutenant Pyke!"

The other boys found their voices and repeated what he'd said, most of their words coming out as squeaks. Pyke looked into Boone's eyes and clapped the boy's shoulder.

"I need your help now, Boone. Lead the other young men."

Boone's eyes couldn't grow any wider. "I-I-I will."

"Thank you."

Boone turned to the rest. "Let's go. You heard the Lieutenant. We got a job to do."

Pyke motioned for Fletcher and Bertram to gather everybody around. He had no idea what sage advice or encouraging words he had to offer. Everything had happened so quickly, he hadn't had a chance to prepare any rousing speech. The men began hustling over and surrounded him. Their hostility and mistrust of him were gone. Now they watched him open-mouthed.

"This is your home!" Pyke shouted. "These are your families! And you are men!"

He turned and looked each in the eye. Many stood there proudly, while a few looked ready to fall over and die of fear.

"You know what it is to be a man! It is your duty to protect your family, your home, and your land. And you know what it is to be an Englishman! We have built the greatest Empire in the world together! Will we let a few backward, bloodthirsty savages take that away from us?"

"No!" Bertram said.

A few more echoed the word.

"NO!" Pyke shouted. He still didn't know where he was going with this speech, but he had to get these men excited somehow. "Today these savages come to burn your homes and rape your wives. Are you going to let them?"

"NO!" More shouting now.

"We are Englishmen!" Pyke roared. "We have sailed the world and brought our might to bear on the four corners of the globe. These brutes are nothing!"

"Nothing!" Fletcher yelled.

"Remember the ultimate plan here. We drive them to the south, and we will slaughter them!"

Now they were shouting over him and lifting their muskets into the air. His words had done the trick.

"We are going to kill all of them!" Pyke yelled.

His words were drowned out by the men, which was good because he had nothing left to say. It was time for war.

The Mingo drums suddenly stopped and everything went quiet. Pyke ordered the men to fan out along the wall and concentrate more firepower closer to the north end. When that was done, he stepped up to the gate and peered across the plain.

It was still a cold, grey day. A breeze rippled through the grass. Two hundred yards away, the Mingos stood in a long line. More warriors crowded behind that line. And more. And more.

Nyakwai stood in the middle of the line. Pyke could barely make out his crest of white hair in the distance. Many of his warriors had painted their faces white, but he had chosen red for himself. He stepped out, ahead of the line, and faced his men. Pyke watched him raise his tomahawk in the air.

His men started shouting their cries.

Pyke looked up and down his own line. The townfolk watched the spectacle nervously.

"Remember: you are Englishmen!" he roared.

Then Nyakwai faced Millers Town again and brought his tomahawk slowly down.

And the Mingos charged.

Pyke's first shot struck a warrior in the shoulder. One of the boys handed him another musket. This one was heavier than his and the weight was poorly distributed. But he put it against his shoulder, sighted, and struck the next warrior in his gut.

One-by-one, the Mingos fell as they charged the wall. But there were so many. And Pyke knew within the first minute they were advancing more quickly than the townfolk could shoot them.

They screeched their war cries and ran seemingly without fear toward the musket line. A few of them had muskets of their own and when they were inside eighty yards, these men took a knee and aimed.

"Shoot those with muskets!" Pyke ordered.

He was handed back his own musket and took aim at the nearest Mingo who was reloading. He aimed true and fired. The man jerked backward and his musket flipped through the air.

But the throng of Mingos pushed on. The ones with muskets managed to fire, but Pyke's men were protected by the wall. The bullets harmlessly struck the wood, and the Englishmen cheered.

"They can't shoot as well as you lot!" Pyke yelled. "Now keep killing them!"

The Mingos were close now. So close. There had to be nearly fifty of them still, to Pyke's twenty. They would be at the wall any moment.

"Keep firing, God damn you!" Pyke yelled, but his meaningless order was lost in the crush of sound.

Bertram's men picked up their pace, spurred on by the proximity of the enemy. They loaded and fired with reckless abandon, but their aim was true. Pyke saw another five Mingos fall and their compatriots noticed this too.

They veered south, away from Bertram's line.

It was working.

"Drive them!" Pyke shouted. "Drive the bastards!"

The men kept firing. Smoke filled the air around the wall, as thick as the fog that had swamped them yesterday morning. Pyke hadn't lost a man yet. The wall had done its job against the few muskets the Mingos had brought.

The Mingos were almost running sideways now to escape the concentrated fire coming from the north side of the line.

Pyke stepped back from the wall and waved his arms over his head to get Bertram's attention. "NOW!"

Bertram saw Pyke and shouted orders at his men. One-by-one, they began shifting the line along the wall.

The man at the far end of the line peeled away from the wall and repositioned himself about halfway down. Then the next man, then the next man, then the next man. In this way, there was no significant break in their shooting. The muskets rained hell on the approaching Mingos. Savages fell left and right.

Pyke was absolutely stunned. The townfolk were no soldiers, but they had followed the plan to the letter and hadn't broken down in the face of the enemy. And the boys continued to load with blinding speed.

The Mingos continued south, and Pyke continued to reposition his men to chase them that way. Pyke watched the Mingo camp to see what Nyakwai would do next. The chief watched the proceedings from afar and was holding many of his warriors back. So this had been only the first wave, Pyke thought grimly.

No matter. They were committed to the plan now.

The approaching Mingos continued south and Pyke was certain the plan had worked, when a dozen peeled away suddenly and changed course so they were coming straight at the wall again.

"Fletcher! With me!" Pyke ordered. "Everyone else, keep driving!"

Pyke and Fletcher edged away from the line and sighted the Mingos coming straight at them. They fired in unison and two men fell.

"Boone!" Pyke shouted at the nearest one. "Over here!"

But the boys were in the middle of reloading and had moved with the larger group, further south along the wall. Ten Mingos were almost at the wall.

"Boone!"

Finally Boone heard Pyke over the chaos and realized they needed muskets. He grabbed two that his friends had been preparing and raced them over.

"Pyke, they're almost here!" Fletcher shouted.

Boone handed Pyke the first musket. He got it around in time to blast the nearest Mingo to hell. He tossed the musket behind him and drew his pistol. Next to him, Fletcher shot another savage then tossed his musket away too. He yelled at the boy to get away.

The Mingos were five feet from the wall. At this point, it was no higher than Pyke's waist. The savages would easily get over it.

He shot the nearest Seneca in the neck. Blood sprayed as the man fell away. One of his brethren tripped over him as he writhed on the ground.

"Two men, over here!" Pyke yelled.

Seven Mingos had reached the wall. Pyke drew his saber.

Pyke and the people of Millers Town had enjoyed the advantage up until this point, armed with muskets and safely behind their wall. But now that advantage was gone.

The first man that attempted to vault the wall got a taste of Pyke's saber. He slashed wildly and cut through the man's gut, all the way up to his neck.

Six warriors left. And they were all over the wall.

Fletcher took out his butcher's knife and parried a tomahawk that would have split his skull.

"Over here!" Pyke yelled. If these men got into the town, they would get behind their defenses and all would be lost.

Pyke slashed with his blade and cut another man's arm. He howled and rolled away. Pyke stepped forward to finish the job, but another Mingo jumped forward and swung a club at him. Pyke hadn't seen the attack coming. The club smashed into his left shoulder and Pyke's arm went numb.

Pyke staggered under the blow, but with his teeth gritted painfully, he kept his feet. And brought the saber back around. The Mingo that had struck him jumped back, out of the arc of the blade. Pyke blocked an attack from another warrior and knew it would be over any moment now. He could perhaps take two of the savages in a fight by himself, but three or four was impossible. They would cut him down.

But then a musket fired, and the Mingo in front of Pyke fell. Another boom erupted, and another savage screamed and went down.

Four of them left, and one of those four injured.

Pyke looked over his shoulder. Bertram had turned from the main action to aid them. Another colonial was coming back too, musket in hand.

Pyke used the distraction to lunge at the nearest Mingo. The tip of his saber speared the man's side but instead of trying to get away, the warrior surprised Pyke by spinning and coming closer. The blade ripped through his flank but he brought his tomahawk around anyway. Pyke ducked at the last second as the weapon swung through the air right where Pyke's neck had been.

Pyke used the opportunity to spring and slashed upward. His saber cut through the man's face. The savage screamed horribly and Pyke put the man out of his misery.

More muskets roared behind him, and Pyke watched in amazement as the remaining Mingos fell. As the air cleared, Pyke found the Mingo that had only been wounded and finished the grisly job.

They had killed the men who'd gotten over the wall. And miraculously, none of the townfolk had died.

Pyke raced back to the wall and looked out. The northwest plain was littered with bodies. Most of them dead, a few of them wounded and writhing on the ground. Pyke looked past the carnage and spotted Nyakwai. The chief stood in the same spot as before, surveying the battle. He still had kept the rest of his men back.

"We drove them!" Bertram yelled. "It worked!"

Pyke looked to his left, along the wall that bent southwest. The Mingos had retreated to a relatively safe distance and were now racing west in an attempt to flank the wall.

Pyke looked back again at Nyakwai. What was the chief going to do? Would he send his remaining men to storm the wall? Pyke would have done just that. But Nyakwai stood there, doing nothing, just watching.

Pyke grabbed Fletcher. "With me!"

Fletcher nodded.

Pyke clutched Boone's shoulder. "Thank you, lad."

Boone smiled.

Pyke looked at Bertram. "Stay here and don't let those bastards anywhere near the wall! They might come back this way!"

Pyke and Fletcher raced along the wall, following its curve to the west to the end of the palisade. Sergeant Davies and his men had taken cover behind a row of huts. Their muskets were ready.

"They're coming," Pyke said.

Davies nodded and pointed his musket. "Already here."

The Mingos were running hard for them, their courage returning with each step, already forgetting the slaughter that had just occurred along the north side of the wall. Pyke marveled at their ability to recover. But only for a second.

The men grew restless beside Davies but the sergeant stood.

"Hold steady!" he shouted. "Let them get closer!"

The townfolk heeded his orders. Pyke turned back to watch as the Mingos closed now.

"Get me that torch!" Davies yelled.

A man came out of a nearby hut carrying a tarred and flaming torch. Davies had hidden him wisely out of plain view so the savages did not suspect their plan until it was too late.

Davies started to reach for the torch, but Pyke beat him to it.

"Hold here, Sergeant!"

Davies shook his head. "Fire at will!"

As one, the townfolk came out of their crouch and fired. The Indians were close now, close enough that attack was safer than retreat.

As far as they knew.

Torch in hand, Pyke sprinted to his mark some thirty yards from the town's edge. Three incoming warriors changed direction and raced toward him. Pyke waited for them to get a little closer, then lowered his torch into the tar ring they'd laid last night under cover of darkness.

The flame grew and started running in both directions.

The Mingos slowed as they saw him do this. One was shot by a musket and tumbled away. The other two stared, uncomprehending, as the fire began to run in an arc.

Pyke sprinted back to the edge of town and met Davies in front of the men.

The fire quickly zipped across the field. By the time the Mingos realized what was happening, the flames had already wrapped behind them and created a ring of fire.

They were trapped.

The Mingo war cries turned into frightened shrieks as the flames grew and the fire built in intensity. Pyke's trap had worked. As soon as he'd laid eyes on this field full of scrub, weeds, and knee-high grass, he'd known it would serve as the perfect fire trap.

Now a dozen Mingos were surrounded by a raging fire. The men defending the west field rose in unison and advanced. They took careful aim and started shooting the Mingos, who were too distracted by the fire at first.

The Indians fell. The ones that remained realized they had no choice. They ran *through* the fire, some away from the action and some toward the town. They were met with bullets and knives and Pyke's saber.

As the slaughter continued, Pyke permitted himself a moment to relax. So far, everything had gone according to plan. They had killed perhaps thirty Mingos and amazingly sustained no losses.

At the sound of more reports behind him, Pyke's head snapped around.

He couldn't believe his eyes for a moment. But Pyke forced himself out of his stupor quickly.

"Let these bastards burn!" Pyke shouted. "Everyone follow me!"

Davies looked back with a question in his eyes. Until he saw what Pyke had seen.

Somehow, Mingos had gotten into the town. Pyke lifted his saber and charged down the road. There were a dozen engaged in close-quarter fighting with townfolk, right in front of the church.

Pyke sprinted. He'd no idea where these warriors had come from and right now it didn't much matter. They had breached the town's defenses and if they weren't immediately killed or at least repelled, all would be lost.

As Pyke entered the fray, he saw houses burning on the other side of the road. Then a torch arced through the air, flipping end-over-end. It hit the front of the church house and a shower of sparks erupted.

The church was on fire. It was their stronghold, contained their supplies, and would be their last resort in the event the Mingos overran the town. If the Mingos managed to destroy it now …

Pyke cut and slashed and hacked. He let the bloodlust take him over. His mind blanked and he became an unthinking animal with only one thought: kill.

The Mingos were fierce warriors. Much fiercer than the ragtag mixed band he'd faced with the Susquehannock a year ago. These men lived and breathed war and were out to make names for themselves. They fought in the name of their chief, and they fought for glory, and they fought for the honor of killing English.

But they did not fight for their lives, as Pyke did.

He unleashed a whirl of attacks. Never once stopped moving, swinging, slashing, kicking. His saber clanged against tomahawks and he one-by-one he brought the Mingos to their knees.

But it was not enough. The front door of the church blazed. If they did not stop thc fire soon, the church would be destroyed.

He cut down another man and was free from attack long enough to take stock. All around, townfolk lay dying in the dirt road while the rest squared off against the enemy, who seemed tireless. Pyke looked around for Davies, and saw the sergeant wrestling with a savage.

Another warrior came at him, but Pyke ducked out of the way at the last minute. He swung his saber wildly and missed by a margin. The Mingo turned and brought his tomahawk down. The blade just nicked Pyke's leg. He screamed, more in frustration than in pain, and managed to bring the saber up in time to stab the warrior between the ribs.

The man backed up, surprised, and Pyke pressed forward. The blade drove home and the man's eyes rolled back in his head.

Both doors of the church were alight, and the fire licked the face of the building now.

There were just too many Mingos. The townfolk had put up a good fight but were outnumbered and outmatched.

Then Pyke heard the roar of more muskets and three Mingos fell. Dob and Si came from the east with their men. Suddenly the Mingos were outnumbered and Dob's group had loaded muskets.

The rest of the Mingos fell or fled.

The air still reeked of smoke, but the church doors were finally glossy with water over the black char marks. As Davies and some of the men had chased the final Mingos from the town, Pyke had quickly began dousing the fires with buckets with water. Now, after the strain of battle and rushing buckets of water from cisterns and the river to quell the fires, many men and women slumped to the ground or rested on buckets with their heads bowed.

As Bertram Miller stood and stretched, Pyke pulled him aside. "Where did those Mingos come from?"

Bertram's face was covered with ash and his mustache was matted with blood. "Nyakwai sent another wave. We couldn't hold them."

Pyke nodded. "How many did we lose at the wall?"

Bertram frowned. "Seven men."

Pyke cursed.

Suddenly the Mingo drums thundered again. Pyke and Bertram shared a look before hurrying back to the west wall.

When they arrived, they found three women tending to the wounded. Fleur kneeled beside a dying man and tipped the pitcher back to give him water. The man tried to sip but the water spilled down his chin. He was dead a moment later. With tears in her eyes, she looked up at Pyke. He expected a smile, but instead she made a strange, pinched face. He didn't know what the look meant.

He went to the wall and peered out.

Nyakwai stood in the middle of the field by himself.

"English!"

Pyke gripped his saber and hauled himself over the wall. He stalked across the plain and stopped five feet short of the chief.

Nyakwai smiled wickedly at him. "I took more than five."

Pyke said, "You gave up many more to get them, fool."

Nyakwai shook his head. "You should have given me my five skulls. Now your houses burn and your water is poisoned."

Pyke tried to hide his shock. Had the Mingos gotten to the cisterns? He shuddered at the thought of no more water.

Nyakwai pointed and Pyke followed his angle of his arm. In the distance, Pyke watched in horror as Nyakwai's warriors tossed two dead townfolk into the creek upstream.

The chief said, "You will die badly tomorrow if you do not have Neoke."

Pyke considered killing this man. He had his saber. Nyakwai had his tomahawk. It was a fair fight, man against man. Pyke liked his chances in a duel. He had survived others. He would take his saber over the chief's hatchet any day.

But if he killed Nyakwai, would it end the battle?

Probably not. The chief had a wife. No doubt he had sons among his warriors. They would come for Pyke. If no one else did, Kicks-the-Oneida would seek to earn a reputation after Nyakwai was gone.

Pyke eased his grip on the saber.

"I can count well," Pyke said. "And I can see with my own eyes that if you give up twenty-five to get five, you will lose this fight."

Nyakwai shrugged. "There are more. Many more. You will bring my daughter tomorrow. Or tomorrow, you will all die."

NINETEEN – NEOKE

Neoke's eyes tightened with confusion as she looked from Wolf Tongue to the brothers. "What?" she managed to say, shaking her head. "Who are you? Why are they going to kill you? What?"

Wolf Tongue didn't look directly at the brothers, who now lowered their muskets, but he kept facing them as he talked to Neoke at his side. She had cut her bonds and sat still holding the hunting knife in front of her.

"My name is Wolf Tongue," he said slowly in his own language, hoping she could understand, which she seemed to. "These men helped me find you because your father will attack their village if they don't return you to him. But I think they hate us as much as the man who captured you did. Now that they've found you and he's dead, they won't need me any more. But they won't harm you. They need to get you back to your father. So if they do attack me, just go with them and you'll be home by the end of tomorrow."

Neoke licked her lips and stared at the brothers.

"Is she coming or not?" called out Joseph. "I thought you wanted us to run today."

Wolf Tongue ignored him and spoke to Neoke. "Can you speak English?"

She shook her head in the negative. "I wouldn't taint my tongue."

Wolf Tongue smiled, then it vanished as he asked, "Are you hurt?"

She stared at the mound of Burgess's body, then back up at the Adams brothers as if they might attack her, too. "I will heal."

"Let's gather our things and go before anyone else comes."

Wolf Tongue went first to the dead trapper. He rifled through his bag and clothes, taking anything of use that wasn't too soaked with blood—lead balls, patches, a worn knife made from a file, and a purse with but three matte, silvery-copper French sols slapping loosely in the bottom.

Rab Burgess, however, carried more interesting provisions.

"That man deserves more respect," grumbled Joseph as Wolf Tongue sorted through the dead man's things, but Adams's anger was soggy with little threat behind it.

Wolf Tongue rolled Burgess over onto his back and yanked the sheath of his big knife from his belt. The knife was nearly as long as Wolf Tongue's forearm with a thick blade and no cross guard. And judging by the slice in his sleeve, sharp, too.

"He's lucky he's dead," said Wolf Tongue in English. "This is better than he'd have gotten with Nyakwai, and more than he deserves." Wolf Tongue set the dagger and its sheath aside. He bundled the rest of Burgess's worthwhile belongings, including his possibles bag, some food, a hunting knife, bag of shot, powder horn, and a purse the size of his fist filled with a mixture of sols, French card money, and silver pieces-of-eight. His hides, blankets, and anything heavy, excepting the fowler, Wolf Tongue let lie.

He again rolled Burgess onto his face.

"What are you doing?" asked Dirch, his voice pinched through a tight throat.

"What he did to the Mingos." Wolf Tongue glared at the brothers as he grasped a handful of Burgess's thick, wet hair and reached for his long dagger. He saw Joseph's jaw clench as he cut the scalp. Dirch turned away.

When he was finished, Joseph still stared back, eyes unblinking and his hands tight on his musket. Wolf Tongue tied the scalp to the bundle of Burgess's belongings and took it to Neoke.

"This is yours," he said as he held it out in front of him.

Neoke finally stood and lowered her knife. With the suspicion of a cornered animal, she said, "You killed them, not me."

"Killing is easy for me. Being bound and taken from my people would be torture. Consider it blood-wite."

Neoke kept her eyes narrowed, but nodded.

"I'll carry them for you, if you like. We'll get you back to your people, but we need to hurry."

"I'll carry the gun," she said, as she reached for the fowler. "Show me how to use it."

Wolf Tongue let her take the heavy gun, then rearranged his own gear to settle the effects of Rab Burgess on him.

"You're not giving that savage Rab's fowling piece, are you?" asked Joseph.

Wolf Tongue turned a sharp look on the brothers. "It's time we go," he said in English. "You two lead the way, since you know your way here and back so well." When the brothers looked at each other and hesitated, Wolf Tongue growled, "Now."

Joseph looked at Burgess's dead form lying sprawled on the rock for a long moment before he scowled at Wolf Tongue and turned away.

Wolf Tongue let them walk a few paces ahead before he turned to Neoke. "We'll move fast, and you'll be home by dawn tomorrow." He held out his hand to take her gun. Reluctantly, she passed it to him, though her other hand still remained on the trapper's knife.

"I'll make sure you're ready if you need it."

He stepped off and began to load the fowler. It was shorter than his musket with a wider bore, but almost as heavy. As he measured out the powder and cut a patch, he suddenly thought about Neoke and the storm that she must be enduring.

"I'm sorry," he said again, though it felt simple-minded and tentative. "I hope you really are unhurt. If you're ready, we'll take you back to your people."

Neoke stared ahead as they walked a few steps. "Their guns. Why didn't the guns go off? The French one, and those two."

"The mist is too thick," said Wolf Tongue as he rammed a wad down onto the shot. "If the powder gets wet, it won't fire."

"Yours did."

Wolf Tongue stared sidelong until she looked at him. He winked. "I'm smarter than *quhanstrono*. You can cover the breech with leather, or here." He fished out the wad of beeswax he found in Burgess's bag and smeared it over the frizzen pan. "Wax keeps the water out."

He passed the fowler back to Neoke. "Now," he said. "If you need to shoot, pull this back, hold it tight against your shoulder when you aim, and pull the trigger, here, with you finger."

Neoke took the gun and held it as if waiting for an attack.

Wolf Tongue eyed her for a moment, thinking, hoping the powder he used wasn't already too wet. Then, as the path narrowed again, he let her pass and followed behind so he could watch all three of his companions.

The brothers walked ahead of him, close enough together so that Dirch could turn over his shoulder and talk with Joseph in a whisper. As they talked, Joseph examined the breech of his musket.

Wolf Tongue reloaded his own and thought about the fight that was only moments ago. He wiggled his jaw where Burgess had hit him. The man had been a fighter, and big, too. He had wondered before why the brothers would suffer him to come along if they knew where they were going, and now, he thought he knew: if it came to trouble, they would let Wolf Tongue do the fighting.

But now that was finished. It irked Wolf Tongue that one of the trappers had escaped, but it was more important to have Neoke safe and return her to her people. Wolf Tongue had only heard rumors of Nyakwai and didn't care much for him when he finally met him. But Wolf Tongue didn't believe any gods needed

Neoke to suffer slavery or scalping or whatever path Burgess took her down.

Wolf Tongue considered returning Neoke to her father and leaving the Adams brothers to Nyakwai's vengeance. He could right the wrong that had been done, return Neoke, and leave the *quhanstrono* town to burn.

Wolf Tongue cared little for the town, and even less for the Adams brothers. But Pyke and Davies were there, and he might be able to spare them, at least. And despite his protests, Wolf Tongue knew Pyke was in the right: there were some good people in the town who didn't deserve to be slaughtered with their neighbors. Children as young as Neoke.

The Adams brothers, though. Wolf Tongue still tried to understand them. Clearly, they had no intention of fighting Burgess. Was it because they were cowards, or because they knew Burgess was formidable? Or perhaps if Wolf Tongue had fought and died, it would have simply saved them more trouble.

Or perhaps Burgess was their friend. And now Wolf Tongue had killed both a brother and a friend.

As he thought of it, he remembered they both had their guns raised as if to shoot. But Wolf Tongue wasn't sure whom they had been aiming at.

He reminded himself to make a proper offering to the *jogah* of this place to thank them for the wet weather. And for the brothers' stupidity.

The three wended through the overarching forest down the side of the hill to the main road for most of an hour. Once back on the wider road, they didn't run, but moved at a brisk walk, the Adams brothers leading while Wolf Tongue walked beside Neoke. To Wolf Tongue, it felt like an incredibly slow pace, but he could see Neoke beside him struggling with quick steps in her short stride.

Then, though, he thought again of Pyke and the town he defended. Of his friend likely striving against the stubborn Nyakwai. Of the possibility that Nyakwai had already destroyed the village and killed everyone in it.

And then he thought more of his own village, and how it, too, was under the threat of death. No violent mob waited at the palisade, though they might once the Susquehannock were weakened enough.

He clenched his teeth and turned to Neoke. "Can you run?"

"Why?" She held her gun a little tighter as she looked at him with narrowed eyes.

"We need to get back quickly, and if we run, you'll be home by dawn tomorrow."

She thought for a moment, her eyes wandering ahead to the brothers. "Why should we hurry?"

Wolf Tongue swallowed, thinking, then decided to offer the truth. "Your father has all his warriors ready to burn their town to ash. But we might save it if we hurry."

"Better if they all burned to ash."

Wolf Tongue grimaced. "Agreed," he said. "But I do have friends there. Not from the town, but soldiers duty-bound to protect their people. And they're both good men. Some of the best. And some of the people in the town are innocent. Even if they are *quhanstrono*."

Neoke grunted and shook her head. She walked on for a long time before she spoke again. "Why do you travel with them? Do you sell scalps and slaves, too?"

He took a breath to calm the urgency that burned at his chest. The brothers seemed disinclined to hurry, and now even Neoke would stymie his attempts to save Pyke. The frustration that flared and pushed the brothers earlier still smoldered in him, but he dampened it, hoping to convince Neoke of their need without threats or violence.

"I have taken scalps," he said. "But only in battle from warriors. And my people take slaves as much as yours. But I don't sell either to the French or the British." He looked again at the brothers ahead who held their muskets by their sides and traipsed sulkily through the muck.

"I travel with them because I owe a friend a debt. And I hope to save his life." He shook his head with a snort of disbelief. "My friend is a soldier, a warrior of the British chief across the water. His duty is to protect all of his people, even the ones he knows aren't worth the dirt they dig through. And so, he is bound to protect that village to his death, even though he loathes what they do. He is at the town, and, I pray, still alive."

Wolf Tongue took a long breath. "That's how I came here. But when I learned another *quhanstrono* was selling *iomwhen*, I burned with rage." He looked at her. She stared straight ahead, her chin jutting forward with a frown. "Our people have warred before. But you and I are born of the same earth. I couldn't let what happened stand. Burgess deserved to die, but I'm sad that I had to do it and couldn't leave it to you or your father."

As he spoke, Wolf Tongue realized how much he had truly felt the sting of British stealing another *iomwhen* to sell into slavery. His village hadn't seen any slavers, but he had heard stories from other nations and other villages. They'd kill the men, then steal away with boys, girls, and sometimes women if they were young enough.

Perhaps as his own village faded and died, he saw his future among the other nations. All the nations took slaves long before the *quhanstrono* arrived, and it helped keep all their blood strong. The slaves became part of their village, their family. But now, with whites coming in droves, they would make an enemy of all *iomwhen*, and make them slaves not to help at their own village and raise as family, but to sell for another white man to abuse.

"And these men?" Neoke asked, jabbing her fowler toward the brothers. "Are they the good ones, so you travel with them to save the poor, helpless girl?"

Wolf Tongue considered her. She frowned and stared with a combination of hatred and frustration.

"No," he said. "These men are not good ones. I think they would have shot me if they weren't so stupid to let their powder get wet. I don't know that they're much better than the man who kidnapped you."

She stopped walking. When Wolf Tongue also stopped and looked at her, she stared, black eyes searching, thinking for a hand of heartbeats.

"They are no better," she said. "That one, the older, was there when they took me. He shot and scalped my brother."

TWENTY – LUPUS EST HOMO HOMINI

"Thank you, Lieutenant."

"God bless you, Pyke!"

Pyke accepted the thanks from the men and women who'd found him after the battle. He was grateful for their acknowledgement, but wished more of the townfolk shared their sentiments. These few that had come to him probably equaled Dob's outspoken followers.

The fire on the west field continued to burn as night fell and showed no sign of letting up. Pyke surveyed the damage to the town with Davies. Half the homes had been destroyed. The cisterns were being looked at now, but at first blush it appeared the Mingos had left rotten vermin in most of them. The church, at least, still stood, though with smears of black soot and charred wood on the doors and one wall.

Pyke's leg throbbed from the tomahawk wound. It was a superficial cut, but it stung. Davies walked with him, back to check the west wall. It hadn't been badly damaged. Fifteen men were posted, including Bertram.

"What we really got to do is widen and deepen that ditch on the other side of town," Davies said.

"Agreed. And now that some of the houses have burned, take the wood and refortify the—"

"Is it true?"

Pyke stopped what he was saying and turned around. Fleur stood before him. She held a knife in her hand.

Pyke put his palms out. "Is what true?"

Fleur's face grew severe. Tears ran down her cheeks. "You killed him. You killed Jan."

Pyke took a deep breath.

"Fleur—"

"My name is *Madame Nederwue!*" she cried. "How dare you speak familiar to me, you murderer!"

"Madame, put the knife down so we can talk."

"English liar! Rotten two-faced English liar!"

Davies was inching forward but Pyke put a hand on the sergeant's chest.

"Madame, if we could speak in private—"

She spat in his face and stomped off.

Davies didn't say a word as thcy tromped back to the church. Pyke was grateful for the stretch of silence, for the brief moments where he wasn't being asked to make a life-or-death decision. They had lost men in the battle, but it could have been much worse. Through Pyke's plan, they had significantly weakened the enemy. He kept reminding himself of that.

The two men were almost to the church when they heard arguing in the street. They hustled to the crossroads and saw the crowd gathered in front of the church.

Si raised his arms for quiet. "The soldier's plan failed. It was Dob that saved the day when he made the decision to leave the east side unguarded and hurry back to fight here. If he hadn't, the town would be lost now."

Many in the crowd cheered. Fewer did not. Fletcher looked wearily over at Pyke and shook his head.

Pyke pushed through the crowd. "We need to refortify."

Dob cut him off. "You've had your chance, Pyke. It's my turn now. You should have turned the woman over as a sign of good faith. But you let your prick do your thinking for you and now here we are."

Pyke looked at the faces in the crowd and was surprised to find that many agreed with Dob. They blamed his decision-making for their dire straits. It was easier to count their losses and name their dead than praise God for their own lives.

Pyke turned to Dob but addressed the crowd. "You realize we won today? We cut down dozens of their men. They are badly beaten—"

"Because of our late rally, not because your damned foolish plan worked," Dob said.

"Listen to me." Pyke pushed his face to a hand's width of Dob's. "We are alive *because* of the plan. Now we must refortify. There isn't much time. I expect Nyakwai to attack at first light, after his men have rested. We don't have a minute to spare."

Dob stepped away from Pyke and turned to the crowd. "Do you trust this man?"

Pyke felt a dull ache in his chest as he realized what Dob was about to say. "Don't, Dob."

Dob ignored him. "Do you trust this man? This same man, who mur—"

"Who *defended* himself and his friend from your scalpers? Yes, that is what happened." Pyke wondered where Fleur had gone, part of him hoping she was here now to hear the full truth, not what lies Dob had fed her. "Your neighbors tried to kill Wolf Tongue so they could trade for his scalp and they were prepared to kill me for it as well."

A heavy silence fell over the crowd. Pyke surveyed the faces watching him and could not see too many supportive.

Dob was doing the same thing, and sensing blood in the water, spoke again. "This man and his heathen friend killed Nederwue to protect a savage, the very same monsters that are now here to kill us."

"The monsters are here to kill *all of us,* myself included!" Pyke said. "And the only reason they're here is because some in this town scalped their brethren for coin!"

People in the crowd began muttering. Pyke looked for friendly faces but couldn't see many. The Fletcher brothers and Molly stood almost apart from the crowd. Bertram Miller and a few other men raised shouts in Pyke's defense, but Dob's cronies drowned them out.

"Tomorrow we hand this man over to Nyakwai," Dob said.

More cheers than objections.

"He has a fondness for savages," Dob said.

Pyke knew that Dob had the crowd now. The man could make up any allegation and they would believe him. Pyke was in mortal peril.

"He fancies them," Dob said. "It was probably he who took the chief's daughter! And now we suffer the consequences."

Pyke said, "You are in this mess because Nederwue and his friends are bloody hair-dressers. Do not let this man twist the truth now! I came to help you. If I had the girl, why would I come here? It makes no sense!"

But he'd lost them. Dob's men were too many and intimidated the others. Fletcher got into a shouting match with two of them, and it was about to come to blows until Bertram Miller stepped between them and evened the odds.

The town was divided.

Dob pointed at him. "We should turn him over to Nyakwai now!"

Pyke couldn't believe what he was hearing. But that wasn't the end to his surprise.

Si, Kit, and Quill stepped forward out of the crowd and approached him.

Si said, "Come on, Pyke. No need for this to get ugly now."

Pyke drew his saber and slashed the air in front of the men. Davies rushed over, with his pistol out.

The two men walked backwards with their weapons out, until the crowd shifted and several men got between Si, Kit, and Quill. An argument ensued but Pyke and Davies didn't linger.

Pyke and Davies stood along east side of town. Ahead of them the creek gurgled and the hill sloped nearly vertically into the sky. No one else was about.

"Sir," Davies said.

"You can drop the *sir*. We're beyond that pomp and circumstance now, Davies."

"Pyke ..." Davies stepped closer to him. "It's time we left."

Pyke looked away from him, looked up at the stars in the sky. He'd thought the same thing. They had lost control of the town. Dob had twisted almost everyone's mind, blinding them to the truth. Pyke realized: when people were frightened, they would believe almost anything.

"Wolf Tongue is coming back," Pyke said.

"Not if he doesn't have the girl."

"He will find her."

"Fine. Let's say he finds her. If he brings her back to daddy, he'll be fine. He can go home. You don't need to be here for that. Do you?"

Pyke took a deep breath. The night sky was so clear. A crescent moon had risen. But all he could smell was death.

"We grab two horses and we go. Bring the Frenchie with you, I won't mind."

Pyke said nothing.

Davies sighed. "These people were ready to hand you over to that thievin' savage."

Pyke shook his head. "Not all of them."

"Enough of them."

"What about the Fletchers? And Miller? And those brave boys? Boone? The children? The wives?"

Davies said nothing.

Pyke looked at the sergeant. "I am staying."

"Why on God's earth? And don't say duty or I'll knock you over the head and throw you on a horse."

Pyke laughed. "This town is rotten, it's true, but there are good people here. So I stay. For them. I cannot abandon them. I cannot turn my back on those that stood up for us tonight."

"You are staying to die," Davies said. "Tomorrow will come and Nyakwai will send the rest of his men."

"I know."

"Don't stay for her," Davies said. "She wants to kill you."

"I don't blame her."

"You killed her man, Pyke. She won't forgive you for that."

"Maybe not." Pyke looked down. "But who will protect her? Not these people."

Davies turned to face the town. "I'm a good soldier, but I won't die for nothing. I'm no bleeding hero like you."

Pyke nodded and slapped the sergeant's shoulder. "Davies, I'm not asking you to stay."

Davies tilted his head to the side. "If you don't leave, how can I go?"

Pyke understood the sergeant's dilemma. Davies couldn't in good conscience abandon his commanding officer. If word ever got out he had, the colonel would hang him.

"Sergeant Davies, I order you to take one horse and two days of supplies and ride as hard as you can for Jenkins Town."

"Pyke—"

"There you will explain the situation to the colonel and request immediate reinforcements."

"Sir, don't—"

"And once you have those reinforcements," Pyke said. "You will ride back here, post haste so that we might crush the Mingos once and for all."

Davies was shaking his head. "I cannot obey that order, sir."

"You will obey it, and you will leave immediately."

"Pyke."

"Now, goddamnit!" Pyke yelled. He hadn't been angry with Davies, but now all the pent-up rage and frustration of the last two days had reached a boiling point inside him. "Every minute counts, Sergeant! Nyakwai returns at first light! Now bloody off with you!"

Davies walked off, without saying another word to Pyke. He watched the sergeant go and hoped the man escaped and went on to live a long, prosperous life. Or failing that, bedded a lot of women and died peacefully in his sleep.

Pyke stuck to the shadows but Millers Town was small and there weren't many places to hide. The fire in the south field was petering out, but still provided enough light that he couldn't go anywhere near it without risking detection.

Pyke had considered seeking refuge with the Fletchers, but thought better of it. They were friends to him in this otherwise hostile town, but he did not wish to jeopardize Molly and especially not their child. If it had just been Fletcher and his brother themselves, then Pyke would have asked for help.

Slowly he walked along the east edge of town. They had not posted sentries on this side, again believing the Mingos would not be foolish enough to charge a precipitous drop and slog through three hundred yards of mud before reaching the village. He trudged unmolested from one end of the small town to the other. It only took him ten minutes, and as the weather dropped after midnight he knew he could not pace back and forth all night. He would be frostbitten, exhausted, and jittery in the morning, when he most needed his wits and strength.

He cursed Rab. It was absurd that a man's disgusting sexual appetites would bring ruin to an entire town. Just like Paris had brought about Troy's downfall because he loved Helen.

A whole city lost, its people murdered.

But thinking about Rab reminded him of something. As Dob had told him, Rab had abandoned his hut here. It was the perfect place to hide.

Pyke just needed to find it.

It was slow, methodical, and careful work. Cautiously he approached each home that appeared uninhabited, listened intently, and moved on at the first sign of life inside. He realized, bitterly, he could be easily fooled in his work, as most of the townfolk were out, preparing for the battle tomorrow and possibly refortifying the town as he'd suggested.

He was about to give up altogether, when a whisper sounded behind him.

"You are looking for Rab's hut."

A cold fear gripped him. Pyke grasped his saber and spun around, but stopped short of drawing his sword.

Fleur Nederwue stood before him. She still wore the same ratty dress and had wrapped herself in a shawl. She shivered in the cold. In the scarce light, her lips appeared blue in the moonlight.

Pyke studied her. Fleur's hands were hidden inside her shawl so he couldn't tell if she was armed. There was nothing aggressive about her posture, and her face was inscrutable. She had that same pinched look about her, like she was in pain.

Pyke pushed his saber back into its scabbard and rested his hands by his sides. He spoke in a whisper too.

"They are looking for you, aren't they?"

Fleur said nothing, which told him everything. The few brave souls that had come to Pyke's defense might not be so willing to support her. She was in greater danger than him.

A cold wind blew in and Pyke felt the first drops of rain pelting his head and shoulders. Fleur wrapped herself more tightly in her shawl.

"I know where it is," she said.

"I will protect you, Fleur."

"I only help you because I need help. Otherwise I would kill you, murderer."

Pyke nodded.

Fleur continued. "Tomorrow I will leave while the battle rages. You will get me a horse."

Pyke said nothing. He didn't want to promise her something when he wasn't sure he could deliver.

She said, "Follow me."

Pyke did, keeping a good five feet between himself and her. The edge in her voice had been as sharp as a dirk. One wrong word and she would come after him with her knife. Pyke knew he could handle her if it came to a fight, but he feared if it came to that, she would be relentless and he would be forced to harm her. He didn't want to do that.

Couldn't do that.

Fleur followed a line of three houses and finally slowed when she reached a hut along the edge of the town, where the east and north sides met. Pyke didn't feel comfortable taking refuge here, but beggars couldn't also be choosers.

"In," Fleur said.

Pyke gave her a long look.

"Get in, you English bastard!"

Pyke unslung his musket and slid it through the cramped entrance to the hut. Then he removed his saber and pistol from his belt and also pushed these inside.

"Go, before they see us!"

Pyke bent at the waist and kept his head low to get into the hut. It was ten feet on each side, and the ceiling was low enough that Pyke's crown reached it. He groped in the darkness and found a chair in the corner next to a fireplace. A smoke hole had been cut in the middle of the ceiling. Pyke found two blankets and a spot on the floor, which was hard and cold, but thankfully warmer than the ground outside.

Fleur crawled into the hut. In the darkness, she was a vague shape that moved and blended with the shadows.

"Where are you?" she said.

"Here." He kept his voice low.

He heard her sit opposite him. Then, only her faint breathing. In his mind he tried to picture her. Petite, sitting cross-legged, perhaps leaning against the opposite wall.

They sat there a long time in silence. When Pyke felt himself beginning to drift, he forced his eyes wide open and would rock back and forth. The shelter was good, but he didn't want to fall asleep in here with Fleur only five feet away.

"Your conscience won't let you sleep?" she said.

It was more a declaration than a question.

Pyke's anger rose. He would not spend his final hours on this earth groveling like a dog. If he enraged her, so be it.

"Mine is clear. Your husband was a thieving murderer."

He heard the sharp intake of her breath, followed by a heavy pause. "Do not speak of my husband."

"To hell with him," Pyke said. "And to hell with you."

"Rosbif, you show your true colors."

Pyke shook his head. "Your husband tried to kill me and my friend so he could trade the man's scalp for a few French coins."

As he said *French coins,* he got a strange feeling. Like the words held some significance. But Fleur did not give him an opportunity to puzzle out the meaning.

Her voice was thick. "I loved him."

"You loved a rotten man."

She sobbed, only once. "You do not understand. You have never been in love."

Pyke laughed ruefully. "I have, and the bitch nearly killed me."

Fleur started. "*Pourquoi?*"

"What does it matter? We have both ended up here, hiding out in a pederast's abandoned home, perhaps hours from meeting our Maker."

"It matters everything," Fleur said. "The world is a cold, cruel place and the only thing that warms it occasionally is love."

"Is that what you had with Nederwue?"

"Yes." He heard her shift, perhaps sit up? "I was nothing, but he was kind."

Pyke said nothing. He didn't wish to discuss her dead husband, the man he'd helped kill. Not because he had regrets over the killing, but because he knew it pained her.

Fleur said, "My father was a lord, but my mother … she was not. So I grew up a bastard and when my mother died of the pox, I was alone. Fifteen years old and my only future was in spreading my legs for other noble men who wouldn't look twice at the children they made with a whore."

Pyke felt something inside him break. He'd suspected as much of Fleur's past, but hearing the truth laid bare devastated him.

"Nederwue saved you from that," he said.

"*Oui.*"

Pyke didn't say what he was thinking: that Nederwue had done it because he lusted for her, not because he loved her.

But Fleur anticipated his thought pattern. "He did not lay a hand on me until we were married. And then he was always tender, and never angry. I soon grew with child…"

Her sobs crushed Pyke. For as angry as he'd been minutes ago, now he wanted to reach out to her. But that would have been foolish. The last thing she wanted to feel were the hands of the man that had killed her beloved husband.

"… she died in childbirth. Our little Marie. You asked what I was looking for in my house. It was a locket Jan gave me after Marie died."

Pyke couldn't take much more of this. He wanted to comfort her but could not. And some part of him was beginning to feel sorry he'd helped kill Nederwue. The man deserved to die, but all the same, his death had led to Fleur being alone in the world again. Just like when she'd lost her mother.

It was true what his Father had once told him. Each of us was all a dozen different people. Not all good, not all bad. Before this night, Pyke had thought of Nederwue as a thief and murderer. And he *was* that.

But he wasn't *all* that.

He'd been a loving husband to this poor, wretched woman on whom the cold world had turned its back.

He said he was sorry in French. "*Je suis desolee, Madame.*"

He didn't know what else to say.

"Tell me about her." Fleur was trying to get herself under control. "The woman."

Damaris Bennett. His commanding officer's daughter. Pretty, intelligent, and older than her years. She had fiery red hair and wore the finest dresses in the Province and helped the school master. He had thought her an innocent, sweet-natured girl.

"I was wrong about her," he said. "That is all."

Fleur didn't respond. Pyke suddenly felt very tired. He laid down on his back and stared at the hole in the ceiling. The clouds had obscured the stars he'd watched earlier and rain trickled in.

"I stayed for him. Even after they turned on me, I still stayed. But now I know he is not coming back. You have freed me, in a way."

Pyke said nothing.

"The women did not like me because they thought me a whore. The men expected me to be … *loose* because I was French and grew to hate me when they realized I was not."

"*Lupus est homo homini*," he said.

"Latin? What does it mean?"

Pyke sighed. "Man is a wolf to man."

"Hugh," she said. "I do not think you are a wolf."

He didn't respond and she was silent for so long, he thought she'd fallen asleep.

But then her hand found his shoulder.

"Hugh …"

He sat up and put his arms around her. She responded by pressing her body against his and then their lips met.

Through his uniform, he felt her fingers digging into his back. When he kissed her more deeply, her lips parted and her tongue drove him wild with desire.

In the darkness, in the cold, Pyke and Fleur found warmth in one another.

TWENTY-ONE – BROTHERS

"What?" hissed Wolf Tongue. He couldn't have heard Neoke correctly. Her dialect and accent were strange to his ears.

"That man killed my brother." She stared back at Wolf Tongue with hatred and accusation in her eyes as if he'd been the one to attack her. "He and that hairy animal found me and my brother alone. They killed him. And when I started screaming, the big one attacked me. I sliced his leg before he hit me with this gun. I didn't see anything after that. But that man, the one you travel with, is a *quhanstrono* murderer. I will see him suffer."

He looked from Neoke to Joseph Adams and ran his tongue on the inside of his lip. No wonder the brothers had acted so strangely since they'd been forced to go with Wolf Tongue. They were reluctant to find and confront Burgess because they were his accomplices.

And Neoke? What would she do if she wanted her vengeance? And why hadn't she attacked them yet? In fact, why was she telling Wolf Tongue this at all? If he traveled with these men and came to help their town, it was a wonder she wasn't more suspect of him than she already was. Perhaps she had sensed the animosity among Wolf Tongue and the brothers.

Wolf Tongue rubbed at his sore jaw as he worked at the knots of everything that was happening. He turned to glare at the backs of the brothers, debating whether to simply cut them down now. Liars, slavers, murderers, the lot of them. It seemed that Wolf Tongue's father and Hugh Pyke might be the only *quhanstrono* worth the skin they occupied.

Neoke's voice brought him from his rage. "I didn't kill him yet." She lifted the gun slightly, and in her eyes Wolf Tongue saw her thanks. He thought that offering her Burgess's belongings only seemed right, and now he realized that doing so had bought a modicum of trust at least. And perhaps saved him much trouble, or even a knife in the neck when he wasn't looking.

"If we can bring him to my father, he'll get the torture he deserves."

Wolf Tongue narrowed his eyes. Many war chiefs and villages were known for horrible torture of captured warriors, particularly among the Iroquois. He wondered how many Susquehannock Nyakwai had tortured. Then again, Wolf Tongue had seen his people also capture Iroquois warriors when he was young.

He nodded and scowled as he looked at the brothers' backs. Pyke was risking his life yet a second time to protect these people, as if they were innocent rabbits set upon by wolves. They were no rabbits. They were wolves as much as the Susquehannock, the Seneca, the Shawnee, the French … but they were worse. They pretended they weren't wolves so they could kill in the dark while their victims slept. They wheedled and whined for protection, when they neither needed nor deserved it. And in the shadows, they murdered their neighbors and sold them into slavery so others of their kind could abuse them.

"He won't want to go with us, because he knows what he did. But I'll bring him to your father."

He looked back at Neoke. She stared down the road.

"If you're healthy enough to run, let's run. We'll stay behind them and push them. Tire them so when we get close to your father, they'll be too spent to fight."

Neoke immediately broke into a jog.

Neoke still cradled her fowling piece as if ready to fire at a moment's notice while they all sat on the planks of Harris's ferry. The vessel was a flat expanse of timber with huge poles that two men used to row. Another man hauled at a cable that ran through loops on one side of the ferry all the way from the western to eastern shores of the great river.

The water was matte gray and still had some few small floats of ice, though much of the winter had melted away. Wolf Tongue shivered with the west wind that blew across the water and ruffled the porcupine hair in his scalplock. It felt like rain again.

The sweat he'd worked up as they ran now cooled off him. He pulled his blanket over his shoulders as he looked at his companions. Joseph and Dirch Adams sat at the edge of the ferry, both wrapped in their own blankets with their backs decidedly to Wolf Tongue and Neoke.

Wolf Tongue had pushed the brothers hard by loping directly behind them. Neoke ran at his side, and the Adamses made no comment about the hurry this time. Instead, they quietly joined in. For a long time, the only sound was all their breathing and the slap of feet into mud. Then they came to Harris's Ferry and now enjoyed a brief rest, though the wind driving across the icy water did little to relax Wolf Tongue.

He looked to the far side where Harris's home and fields sat stark and alone against the backdrop of the forest to the east. Even without the leaves, the underside of the forest had already turned black with the coming night.

Wolf Tongue took a deep breath and closed his eyes. They would run through the night, despite the added dark with the moon shrouded by clouds. Best to rest as much as he could now.

But the rolling shake of the ferry jostled him and the wind pinched at his exposed skin. Neoke, too, did not sleep on the slow, slogging trek across the river. All the while, the Adams brothers silently watched eastward, as if Wolf Tongue and Neoke weren't there.

When they reached the eastern shore, the ferrymen hauled them against the dock. Joseph Adams passed a few coins to one of the men and stepped onto the dock with a thump of his boots. He turned as if to say something, but Wolf Tongue spoke first.

He turned to the man who'd taken the money. "Please tell Mr. Harris we're sorry we couldn't linger to talk again. Give him our news, if you like, and thank you."

With that, Wolf Tongue walked on, followed closely by Neoke. He noticed, but ignored, a scowl from Joseph as he hopped from the wooden dock onto the solid ground. Wolf Tongue took a few steps up the road before he paused and turned to look at the brothers.

Joseph glared at Wolf Tongue. Dirch watched his brother while rubbing at his shoulder. Neither said anything, but after a moment, Joseph stepped off at a brisk walk.

"Dark soon," he growled at his brother. "We'll walk all night if we have to, but we'll need to be careful. No more running today."

Wolf Tongue stared as he let Joseph and Dirch pass. He thought for a moment about forcing another run, but Joseph was right. They'd run enough. Any more and they would exhaust themselves before they reached Millers Town. And the trek through the muddy forest without so much as moonlight would be slow going.

But it still irked Wolf Tongue to let Joseph dictate their actions, even if he agreed. So he simply scowled as the brothers passed and then fell into a plodding gait alongside Neoke as they climbed the little hill that led back to Millers Town. That was, if Pyke still held Nyakwai from razing the entire place.

"What did he say?" asked Neoke as she came up beside Wolf Tongue.

"Nothing," said Wolf Tongue. "Just growling."

They walked along the road in pairs, the brothers out front, and Neoke beside Wolf Tongue behind. They walked in silence as the gray that had suffused the day bled away to leave a deepening black.

Within an hour, night had fallen and they found the forest tightened around them. The road was still wide enough for a wagon to be drawn along, and at some places two could pass. But the trees had moved to form a tight gauntlet against the edges of the carved road. They walked slowly, picking their way among the breaks in the ground, the swales, and the rocks that littered their way. Many places still had branches as thick as Wolf tongue's arm across the road from the winter storms.

Suddenly, Joseph stopped and raised a hand. Wolf Tongue brought his musket to his shoulder and tightened his eyes against the darkness. He could see ten strides ahead on the road where the moon filtered through the clouds to give an iron cast to the mud and patches of snow. But the trees around him blanketed the ground in darkness so that he could only see a few feet into the woods.

He waited, eyes searching for the slightest hint of movement. He listened, but he only heard the breath of wind through the branches and the creak of trees straining against the cold.

"I thought I saw something over that hill," hissed Joseph. "Flames coming up, or sparks."

It was unlikely that there were any other travelers out at this time of year. But the road had begun to clear, and Rab Burgess had shown that, clearly, commerce of one sort or another would not wait for summer. Wolf Tongue thought for a moment, studying Joseph, though the man had kept his back to Wolf Tongue. He didn't trust this *quhanstrono*, but he also needed to be wary of any other danger, too.

He turned to Neoke. In Susquehannock, he said, "Stay here. Keep your gun ready and don't trust the younger brother."

He narrowed his eyes on Joseph and in English added, "Let's go look. Dirch, you protect Neoke."

The two crept along the road, the darkness heavy and quiet against them. Wolf Tongue carried his musket loosely in one hand. Joseph had the butt already raised to his shoulder.

Slowly, they mounted the little rise on the road. Not a hill, really, but a hummock that obscured the path ahead. The two men separated, each to walk in the darker black of the overhanging trees on either side of the road.

With each step, Wolf Tongue took a slow breath, easing his foot down to make the least noise possible. He still strained his ears, but only heard Joseph's rustling. Ahead, he could only see the flat swath of gray mud on the road. He glanced again at Joseph through the corner of his eye. Adams faced forward, his musket readied as if to find a deer just over the hill.

Wolf Tongue paused at the crest and let his eyes slowly trace what scene he could see. Here, he could just make out the forest slightly more clearly, the top branches of a few trees like silver snakes entwined before they blended into a mass of darkness. He could see no fires or sign of life.

"*Ssssst,*" hissed Joseph. "There. To the south."

The dark shadow of his companion gestured from across the road and Wolf Tongue turned to search the forest again.

The thunder of gunfire behind him shook the air and startled Wolf Tongue. He wheeled to look back the trail from where the sound had come, but could see nothing. His eye caught movement across from him and he twisted to see Joseph aiming for him. Wolf Tongue threw himself to the ground just as Joseph fired.

A tree behind Wolf Tongue cracked. Joseph cursed and took off at a run back toward his brother and Neoke. Wolf Tongue, still lying prone, brought his musket to his shoulder, but found the trigger and breech caked with wet mud from where he landed on it.

He left his gun for later and leapt to his feet. As he closed on Joseph, he heard him yell, "Goddamn you, Dirch! I told you to get the bitch's fowling piece!"

Wolf Tongue ran, slogging through the mud. He already had his tomahawk in his hand. In a few breaths, he was nearly upon Joseph.

But Joseph stopped and spun. He brandished a pistol that he'd secreted away their whole trek.

"Die, you goddamned devil-worshiper!"

The sudden appearance of another gun took Wolf Tongue by surprise and he stumbled as he twisted away and threw his tomahawk. The road felt like liquid twisting beneath him and Wolf Tongue tumbled into it again. Joseph fired and the tomahawk hit him, but Wolf Tongue couldn't tell whether he had wounded the man or not.

Then Joseph was running again, yelling, "Dirch, you idiot!"

Wolf Tongue pushed himself from the mud and launched himself forward. In the feigned light, he could see a dark mass on the ground with Neoke standing over it, holding her gun.

As Wolf Tongue neared within steps of Joseph, the man leapt forward and tackled Neoke to the ground. He twisted and yelled, and then held still.

"Stop there, or I'll slit her throat!"

Wolf Tongue paused. He was close enough now to see them. Joseph rested on one knee with Neoke's back against his chest. The blade he held on her neck was pitted black.

Wolf Tongue forced his labored breathing to slow as he lowered the dagger he'd taken from Burgess. At his foot lay Dirch, his neck and face torn apart with lead shot.

"If you hurt her, I will kill you and your brother."

Joseph spat on Neoke and his voice trembled with tearful rage when he spoke. "She already did that for Dirch."

"Let her go. You can't win here. If you hurt her, you know your death will be terrible. And all your town, all your people will die."

"I don't care!" he screamed. "I'll cut her savage throat, then yours! And then I'll sell both your goddamned scalps, you—"

Joseph howled as Neoke slammed her hand into Joseph's groin. His grip loosened and as she tore free of his grip and stumbled forward, a wet knife glinting in her hand. Joseph's pants already bloomed with blood.

Wolf Tongue lunged with Burgess's heavy dagger drawn back. Joseph rose and brought his knife up. Wolf Tongue hacked once against Joseph's knife hand, knocking his arm wide and sending the knife flying.

Wolf Tongue's reverse swing caught Joseph across the face and he spun backward, rolling, and landed on the ground face-first. Wolf Tongue pounced onto his back and grabbed a fist full of hair. He leaned one knee onto Joseph's right arm and noticed that the swipe with the dagger had taken three fingers from his hand.

"You tried to kill me. And you killed her brother," growled Wolf Tongue through clenched teeth. "You sold his scalp and took her with Burgess."

With Joseph pinned and screaming, Wolf Tongue looked at Neoke. She stood only feet from him, and even in the shadows of night, he could see her shaking. Her shirt hung open across one shoulder where Joseph's knife had cut her by the collarbone. She held the trapper's dagger point-down in one hand, its bloody blade a shimmering black. She took in Wolf Tongue for a moment, then turned to stare at Joseph, who still struggled against Wolf Tongue's weight. Her face hardened as she straightened up and lifted her chin.

Joseph's screams echoed among the bones of the trees as Wolf Tongue tightened his grip on the man's hair, and with Rab Burgess's dagger, began to saw.

TWENTY-TWO – HONOR AMONG THIEVES

"They're in here!"

Pyke snapped awake. Fleur rolled off him and came to groggily. Pyke drew his saber and crouched in the hut. He hadn't recognized the voice, but knew that Dob and his men had found them.

"We found them!"

This time he recognized the voice. It belonged to Si.

Weak sunlight drifted in sideways through the hole in the ceiling. It was early morning and Pyke's bones were stiff from sleeping on the cold, hard ground. But at least he'd managed some sleep.

"Get your shawl," Pyke said. "And run the minute we get out of here."

Fleur nodded and wrapped the shawl around herself. He squeezed her hand and smiled. She leaned in and kissed him tenderly. Pyke felt a jolt run through his body. If last night was to be his final one on Earth, he would be at peace with that.

"Do not be afraid," Pyke said. "I will not let them harm you."

"You must be a wolf to keep that promise."

Pyke smiled. "And I will be."

Pyke stuck his saber out of the hut and swung it back and forth. The men yelled but he didn't strike anyone. Pyke hurried out of the hut and kept swinging his saber like a madman.

There were four of them: Dob, Si, Kit, and Quill. They were all armed with clubs and knives of their own, but he kept them at bay. He felt Fleur come out of the hut and cling to his back. The men tried to circle them, but Pyke flicked his saber left and right and kept them to one side.

He reached behind and squeezed Fleur's hand. "Run! I will hold them here."

Dob grinned ear-to-ear. "You think it is only us looking for you?"

Pyke smiled right back. "You are the only four I see, and I would be happy to kill all of you."

Kit looked back over his shoulder. "Over here!"

"Run, damn you!" Pyke yelled at Fleur.

"I cannot—they are this way too!"

Pyke dared to look over his shoulder for a quick second and saw another knot of men, four strong, approaching quickly.

"Then down the hill," Pyke said.

"Hugh …"

She was terrified, and had every right to be. She had no horse, no supplies, and no hope of rescue. And the Mingos lurked nearby. Nyakwai had probably posted warriors at the foot of this hill, anticipating an escape in this direction. Her eyes were frantic, but she held her pistol in both hands at arm's length as if deciding where to aim it.

"God damn you, Dob!" Pyke cursed.

Dob relaxed. "It is over, Pyke. You are done here."

A musket sounded and everybody jumped. Pyke expected to feel the sharp pain of a bullet seize him any moment, but when he felt none he realized he hadn't even been shot at. Dob and his men had all turned and were looking toward the center of town.

"Hold!"

Pyke recognized the voice and relief washed over him. The bastard had refused to follow his orders.

Davies came running from around a corner, pistol in hand and about a dozen townfolk in tow. Among them were the Fletcher brothers and Bertram Miller.

"Drop your weapons!" Davies bellowed.

When they didn't, the sergeant raised his pistol and shot Kit in the leg. The man screamed and went down. The others immediately complied with Davies's order. Dob and Si and Quill tossed their clubs and knives away. The other party that had been approaching stopped dead in their tracks and did the same.

"Put your bloody hands up!" Davies shouted. "You're all under arrest."

Dob shook his head. "No, Sergeant, you are—"

Davies smashed the butt of his pistol into Dob's jaw. The trader's knees went weak and the man fell.

"Lieutenant," Davies said with a smile. "We've been trying to find you all night."

Pyke and Davies herded the eight men back to the church. Kit hobbled on his leg but Pyke could tell by looking at it the bullet hadn't gone deep. They could dig it out easily and patch him up. He wouldn't be running any time soon, but that was fine with Pyke. The man could still shoot so Pyke could put him on the wall or elsewhere.

Pyke individually thanked all the people that had sided with Davies and helped them. He asked the Fletchers and Bertram to round everyone up and bring them to the church. Five minutes later, the entire town filed inside. Reverend Baldwin stood off to the side, his expression blank like he didn't understand what was happening. Pyke stood in the front and raised his arms for silence.

"The Mingos will come soon!" Pyke shouted. "But we will be ready for them."

The men and women of Millers Town shifted nervously.

Pyke turned to Dob and the seven men they'd arrested. "I came here to help, but these men instead wanted to offer me up to Nyakwai. I have placed them under arrest for their treason."

He allowed the townfolk to take that in.

"Make no mistake—I am in charge today. And if we are still alive tomorrow, I will be in charge tomorrow as well. And the next day. And the next day. I will not stop fighting until I am dead or we have won."

The Fletchers cheered and soon some other people joined in.

"The Mingos are fierce warriors and have the advantage of numbers." Pyke pointed at the seven men behind him. "Which means we need all the help we can get today."

He looked back at Dob.

"So here is my first—and last—offer. For everyone other than Dob, I will forget your crimes but you must take muskets and follow my lead."

His eyes tracked over each man. Dob and Si stared back at him defiantly. Kit was too busy looking at his bleeding leg. The rest of them stared at the floor.

Pyke nodded at Si. "Do you accept the terms of my offer?"

The man was a long time answering. He muttered, "Yes."

"I couldn't hear you."

"Yes," Si said louder.

Pyke walked down the line, making them all swear allegiance to him. Then he slowly walked back the other way and stopped in front of Dob.

"You, sir, are this town's leader."

Dob said nothing. He looked up at Pyke from under a furrowed brow.

Pyke said, "And a leader takes responsibility for his men's actions."

Dob clenched his jaw.

"So you are responsible for everything that has happened between us since I arrived. And, I suspect, you are responsible for the scalp-trading."

Dob couldn't hold Pyke's stare any longer. His eyes shifted and got a faraway look.

"When this is over, you will face a trial." Pyke then faced the other seven men. "There is nothing your men can do to prevent this."

Si shot him a challenging look, but the rest of the men just looked down and nodded.

Pyke turned back to Dob. "You will stay here, in this church until such time I am able to bring you to Jenkins Town. If you leave, I will kill you."

Dob didn't look up.

Then Pyke faced the crowd again. "We lost good men yesterday. But not today! Today we kill them all!"

Bertram cheered.

Pyke said, "When Nyakwai comes today, we will teach him a lesson he never forgets. No one dares challenge the British Empire!"

More cheering. And looking at the men under arrest, Pyke understood why.

Dob had ruled this town and the good men and women had lived in fear of reprisal. Now that Pyke had put Dob and his men in their place, the rest weren't as fearful to offer their support. Pyke wished he had done this earlier but there was no point looking back now.

"Now then. We must think how we can further fortify this town," Pyke said.

"Fortify?" one man called out. "We should have finished the wall!"

Fletcher spoke up. "We finished what we could and besides, we only had posts enough to stretch the wall another five paces."

That gave Pyke an idea. The wall was five feet tall ... it could work. "Where are the posts?"

Fletcher opened his mouth to speak but Davies shouted before he could.

"Sir!"

And all at once, the crowd fell silent and began parting until Pyke saw the Susquehannock warrior.

Wolf Tongue was alone. He looked tired, like he'd been up all night. His steps were as heavy as his expression. Pyke met him in the aisle.

Wolf Tongue said, "I returned the girl to her father."

The town cheered. Men and women clapped and hugged one another. With tears in her eyes, Molly Fletcher held out her hands to Wolf Tongue as if unsure whether to touch her savior or not.

Pyke could tell from the savage's eyes, though, that the news was not wholly good.

TWENTY-THREE – AN OFFER

Neoke and Wolf Tongue had said nothing as they left Joseph Adams screaming in the mud. Both paused to retrieve their weapons, left the Adams brothers as they lay, and walked on into the night.

Once they had gone far enough for the hills and forest to stifle Joseph's wordless howls, Wolf Tongue silently took Neoke's fowler and reloaded it, thinking they might still have need of a gun. His, though, would need to be cleaned before it would be any use at all.

The sound of a curling wind rasping at tree bark and the sucking of footsteps into mud became a drone in Wolf Tongue's ears as they walked on. Without the Adams brothers with them, he let his attention wander. Images of Fox's Smile glanced through his mind, followed by her weakened father. The face of Bone Snake, painted for war and sneering with a crude joke, his uncle who'd finally left their village for more prosperity.

He thought of Pyke. The soldier was the only reason he stumbled along a black road with a wounded girl. And they all were nearly killed by the people he had tried to save—the town they had come to help a year ago and found hostility and murderers. And now that town seemed even more vile. Pyke was a fool to follow his colonel this way, and so dutifully. The world had become dark in the past year, and Pyke still faced it with hope.

Or perhaps the world had always been dark. The Susquehannock conquested over the Unami and Mohicans. They fought and took slaves and scalps from the Oneida and Munsee. There had always been warriors, wars, and death. And that was good.

Now, though, Wolf Tongue thought, there were fewer warriors and more black souls. Men who sold girls for coin and murdered each other from the shadows with trickery. Even Nyakwai, whose reputation for torture and bloodlust was known even in Wolf Tongue's village, seemed more trustworthy than most. He made war on the whole village for their sins. But he screamed his hate in their faces instead of hissing death from a shadow.

And Pyke fought to protect the people Nyakwai would, perhaps justly, take his vengeance on.

No. Pyke fought for hope.

Wolf Tongue smiled. The thought was one that Fox's Smile would say to him. She would see the good deep in Pyke. Not his foolishness to be so duty-bound, but his honor to offer his life to save another's. His undying defense of the weak and his belief in good souls, despite the bloodied knife of this world slashing at him.

Fox's Smile would know that. And she would reprimand Wolf Tongue for ever calling his friend a fool.

Wolf Tongue smiled again for a breath before it drifted. Beside him, Neoke stumbled and he reached to grab her arm. She righted and continued in what had become a staggering gait.

He didn't know how long they'd been walking, or how long he'd been lost in his reverie. His stomach turned with hunger, though, and what little light there had been was now nearly gone. Though they hadn't seen it for the clouds, the moon had risen early and set. The dull iron glow off the puddles of the cleared road had darkened to a spill of shadows. They must have passed half the night.

"We need rest," said Wolf Tongue. "And food. My stomach thinks my throat's been cut."

They found a small rise on the north side of the road clear of snow where Wolf Tongue gathered some fallen leaves for a mat. They sat side by side while he portioned out what little food they carried. A chunk of hard bread, a piece of cheese taken from Burgess, and a handful of jerked venison. They ate their meal off Wolf Tongue's blanket with the quick arm movements and slow chewing of those eating only for necessity.

"Will he come?"

Wolf Tongue considered her question as he stared into the road and chewed his last bit of bread.

"Not tonight. And not for many days," he said. "Maybe never, even if he lives. But if he ever does, he will come for me."

Wolf Tongue leaned back against the tree trunk. He knew he should keep guard through the night, even to watch for wolves or cougars. But he couldn't. And the true danger had passed, at least for now.

Wolf Tongue set his tomahawk by his side, along with Joseph Adams's new rifled musket. Neoke rustled beside him and he felt her shoulder press against his arm. He covered them both with his blanket and laid his head against the tree.

When she began to cry, Wolf Tongue found her hand and wrapped it in his.

When the rain began to patter on his face, Wolf Tongue was still holding Neoke's hand. He sniffed and rubbed his face, blinking away the night, though much of it still clung to the barren trees nearby. His movements roused Neoke and she grunted and shivered.

Wolf Tongue rolled to his feet and stretched with a shudder. Dawn hadn't come yet, but the sun was nearly up so that he could again see color in the forest. The air moved with a slight breeze and with it came sporadic drips and clusters of falling mist.

Neoke stood, stretched, and then, in silent agreement, they again set off toward Millers Town.

Within less than a mile, Wolf Tongue recognized the terrain, even in the pre-dawn. The road widened and then sloped down ahead into the a valley where a wide stream would ramble lazily past the cleared fields and timber houses of Millers Town.

"We came farther last night than I thought," he said.

When Neoke didn't answer, he said. "Your father waits less than a hand's walk from here. You'll be with your family before the dawn."

"And you?" she asked. "Where will you be?"

"There, too. As long as your people don't kill me before then."

Neoke looked at him. "Why would they kill you? I thought you were sent by my father."

Wolf Tongue shrugged, shifted his musket to his left hand, and shook the tightness out of his right. "I wish I knew why so many people wanted to kill me. It seems to be a common fault."

Wolf Tongue had overestimated their walk. They heard the first shout of challenge in only about two miles. They both stopped and waited. Wolf Tongue set the butt his musket on the top of one foot in a non-threatening gesture. His fingertips brushed the haft of his tomahawk while he waited.

A moment later, two men came crashing through the wood, one carrying an old blunderbuss bigger than Neoke's fowler, the other with a ball-head war club in his hand. They stopped suddenly on sight of Neoke and she called them both by name.

The next moments came in a blur. The men did not ask Wolf Tongue to disarm, but escorted him and Neoke along a deer path another half mile where dozens of men sat bleary-eyed, or still sleeping curled beneath animal furs and rough woolen blankets. A murmur rolled through the camp as those who were awake spread the news of their arrival and woke the others.

Even in the dripping rain, the air reeked of smoke and soot, not quite wood smoke, but close. He didn't see any cooking fires around, but what he did see alarmed him. Gathered in clusters around the outskirts of the camp were rows of dead men. Wolf Tongue could see only a few bodies close enough to see the bullet wounds the width of his finger. More than a dozen bodies lay tended into death poses, cleaned and washed, but blue and stiff as they awaited someone to pray over them and offer the rites to the dead to issue their souls into their next journey.

There had been battle. Clearly, Pyke had organized his shooters and taken perhaps a fifth of Nyakwai's warriors. But how many people from the town now reposed in their god's house? And was Pyke among them?

Wolf Tongue couldn't see the town through the trees from the camp, but the reek of old smoke make a chill flash through his neck and shoulders. Could he be too late?

Then, suddenly, from the rolling mass of bodies, came Nyakwai, tall and broad. His white hair was greased high in the style of many of the Iroquois and even now, he carried his tomahawk in his hand.

At the sight of his daughter, Nyakwai dropped his weapon and leapt forward. She ran to him and jumped into a full hug where he held her off the ground.

Wolf Tongue stopped suddenly, staring at the man, a war chief known among many tribes as one of the fiercest, cruelest warriors. Then, as father and daughter put their foreheads together and began to talk in whispers, Wolf Tongue pulled his eyes from their private moment.

Around him, the men began to gather. Word had spread and now the warriors came to see for themselves. Some of the faces looked back at him with open curiosity, while others seemed already hostile with down-turned mouths and narrowed eyes.

He wondered how many of these men would resent Wolf Tongue for robbing them of the chance to earn the spoils Millers Town promised them.

Nyakwai set Neoke down and turned his eyes on Wolf Tongue.

"I would speak with my daughter alone," he said. "Take him away."

In a heartbeat, many hands grabbed hold of Wolf Tongue and dragged him backward. His hand tightened around the head of his tomahawk, ready to pull it loose, but he immediately thought better. If he fought now, he would die among so many.

Instead, he twisted, wresting his arms free from the clutching talons and throwing his arms in the air. He glared at the three men who stumbled for a moment as he broke away. "I'll go where your chief asks," he growled. "But do not haul me like a carcass or you might find yourself as one."

Two of the three young men were all arm bones and necks. They licked their lips and looked at the third, a man slightly older and thicker. Wolf Tongue grinned, knowing Nyakwai was watching their reaction.

"This way, was it?" he said as he pushed past the closest. The oldest, and likely the deadliest, turned just ahead of Wolf Tongue.

"Follow me," he said, making sure his voice was heard over the low chattering of the crowd around them.

Wolf Tongue readjusted the weight of Burgess's belongings on his shoulder before following. The man led him another hundred strides to the far side of the camp while dozens of rain-hunched shoulders turned to watch his passing.

"Wait here." The man pointed to a base of a tree well away from the rest of the huge war party. Wolf Tongue looked around, searching for a reason the man had chosen this spot. He had stepped beyond the vague outline of a camp, and had seemingly selected somewhere specific only to try to reaffirm his power.

Wolf Tongue pointed. "This spot, right here? This one by this maple?"

The man narrowed his eyes. "Just wait here."

"I'll just wait right here," said Wolf Tongue as he leaned against the tree. The man stared, but when Wolf Tongue smiled at him, he turned away and took a few steps back toward the camp, though he remained as if to be a guard. By then, the other, younger, men had taken up similar positions surrounding Wolf Tongue.

Wolf Tongue frowned at the men's backs and surveyed the camp again. The other men throughout seemed to be coming alive now, shifting in their positions, gathering in groups of three or four to lean in and talk with glances toward Wolf Tongue or toward where Nyakwai had been. Wolf Tongue saw only five women who had come with the war band from their village, though he thought it must be nearby.

He set Burgess's bundle on the ground and rolled his neck. It was stiff. His muscles ached from days of slogging through cold mud. The misty rain collected on his scalp and the patter of larger drops falling from the tree branches all seemed to push him toward sleep. But he stood and crossed his arms, fighting the urge.

Wolf Tongue swallowed. The travel back had been quick and silent, and the hustle from the road to Nyakwai's camp had seemed almost a dream in its haste and tiredness. Now, he stood, forcing himself to stay awake and vigilant, watching the camp churn through the mist.

He had been joking when he told Neoke that her people might just kill him, but all the while, he'd known Nyakwai's reputation. He might be grateful that Neoke was returned to him. Or he might take his vengeance on the traitor Susquehannock who seemed to befriend the *quhanstrono*.

Wolf Tongue didn't wait long before the slow movement of the camp quickened with a group of men bustling and making noise nearby. Though Wolf Tongue couldn't see well through the trees and other men, it seemed that Nyakwai had made a swift decision and was riling the men around him as he approached.

The drowsiness that dragged his muscles toward the ground suddenly burned away. The hill behind him rose only a few dozen strides before it peaked, and it was studded with full, thick chestnut boles. Good for cover if he could weave, but there were many men here who had muskets, too. And at least a few of them would be smarter than the Adams brothers about keeping their powder dry.

He let his blanket slough to the ground, leaned his musket against the tree, and brushed his fingers against his tomahawk. If it would be a fight, he would need to move quickly. And then run like a rabbit with its arse on fire.

Then, from the stands of trees came a figure, another man draped in a distinctive bearskin robe with the open maw hanging on his chest. Wolf Tongue's shoulders relaxed and he laughed.

His uncle Bone Snake made his way through the trees and other men and embraced Wolf Tongue.

"So," said Bone Snake as he stepped back and clapped Wolf Tongue on the shoulder. "You came to tell me your wife finally had my child?"

Wolf Tongue frowned. "You're a good warrior, Bone Snake, and you taught me a lot. But you're wrong if you think you're strong enough for what my wife put me through to get her round."

Bone Snake threw his head back with a long, rasping laugh. Wolf Tongue couldn't hold his frown and smiled. He stared at his uncle, wondering how he'd come here. Was he, too, part of Nyakwai's band now that he'd left the Susquehannock?

"Take your hand off your tomahawk and have a seat." Bone Snake adjusted his robe and sat on rock that bulged from the ground.

Wolf Tongue looked at his guards from the corner of his eye, then, with a sigh, sat.

Bone Snake picked at the stems of leaves between his feet. "I'm surprised to see you, my friend."

"As much as I'm surprised to see you with Nyakwai."

Bone Snake twisted his head to look at Wolf Tongue over his shoulder. He studied Wolf Tongue for a few heartbeats before his eyes dropped and he made a weak smile that crinkled the skin around his eyes and on his forehead. He turned back to flicking through the skeletal leaves.

"I told you I was going to the Mingos. He's not what we heard of him, to tell the truth. Every warrior wants his enemies to think he's Jahocha with a club. I think Nyakwai was just better than most at spreading his tales."

"So he's not going to kill me?"

Bone Snake hesitated. "I doubt it," he said. "You did him an incredible favor, and one I can't believe he didn't do himself." Bone Snake tossed the leaves to the ground and faced Wolf Tongue. "But I don't know. Nyakwai isn't as terrible as we heard. But, from what I've been told, he is … unpredictable."

"Sounds like I should keep my hand on my tomahawk."

"Not bad advice any time. But you won't fight alone if it comes to it. My sons are here, too."

They sat and surveyed the men around them and listened to the water dripping from barren branches onto dead leaves.

"You should join us."

Wolf Tongue's eyes flicked to Bone Snake. The older man watched him, the wrinkles of his smiles gone with a serious, plain face.

"Nyakwai and some others are the ones who started a new village a northwest of here. It's friendly enough with clear, level ground beside the Oyster River for good fishing and fresh soil. Your aunt is there with the children, but One-Who-Rides, Buckrabbit and I joined this group as soon as we arrived. Seems like Nyakwai and some others had been raiding different *quhanstrono* villages for a while. Mostly stealing supplies, tools, livestock. But then when they killed his son and took Neoke ..."

Bone Snake sighed. "Wolf Tongue, you always did everything every other man did, only better. You fought fiercer. You trained harder. You hunted longer. You learned our songs and history and dances. But you never had to."

Bone Snake pursed his lips and picked at the brown grass. "Being Susquehannock was everything to you, but you never realized that you *were* Susquehannock. No one cared that your father was English. My father loved to hunt with him. A lot of us did. The only two people who didn't see you as belonging were you and Kicks-the-Oneida. And at least one of those can eat shit."

Wolf Tongue snorted, but didn't answer.

"What I'm saying is I know how you feel. You fought when you thought you weren't one of us and now that the nation is washing away? You love our people. And I do, too. But the only way to keep us alive, to keep our history and our blood, and our songs, is to not cling so hard to them. Our village is sick. Our people are few. Soon, the *quhanstrono* will swoop in to enslave who's left like these men here are trying to do.

"I don't know if I'll stay with Nyakwai. But for now, we have a place to live where the ground is fertile and among other people. Not just ghosts. It's a chance to improve again, to give our children food and friends and strong neighbors to teach them to hunt and fight and sing and dance."

Bone Snake ducked his head to catch Wolf Tongue's eye. "New villages need good people. And dying ones can only drag you down with them. You should bring Fox's Smile and the rest of her family. Join us."

Wolf Tongue sat up and straightened his shoulders. The words unsettled him as if they'd slipped through his ribs and into his body. He tried to wrangle them together into something solid. As the thoughts of Fox's Smile and Pyke and the attacks by the people of Millers Town roiled and fought inside him, his eyes flicked through the crowded woods around him.

Suddenly, another, larger, hubbub came lurching toward him. This time, he could see at least another dozen men picking their way through the trees at a quick walk.

Wolf Tongue rose, and, settling his hand on his tomahawk again, said, "I'll think on it if Nyakwai doesn't try to kill me first."

Then, the war chief stood before him again. Neoke was at his side, as were more than a dozen warriors. His eyes glanced quickly to Bone Snake, then back to Wolf Tongue. Bone Snake rose slowly to his feet and stood beside Wolf Tongue.

Nyakwai addressed Wolf Tongue without preamble. "Your English dog promised my daughter returned two days ago."

Wolf Tongue shrugged. "I'm not bound to another man's promises. And certainly not a *quhanstrono*. But I brought your daughter back to you. And I bring more gifts."

He grabbed the remains of Rab Burgess's belongings. "Neoke, these are only a few things, but you deserve them all and more." She took the bundle, but put her hand on Wolf Tongue's arm as he reached for the dagger in his belt.

"No. This is a gift for you. You earned this much. Keep that."

Wolf Tongue hesitated, then nodded. He turned to Nyakwai. "The man who would sell girls as slaves to the French is dead. I meant to bring him to you, but he fought. His corpse sits on a pile of rock for the vultures and mice to pick at."

Nyakwai frowned and looked at Neoke with a sideways glance, then back at Wolf Tongue. "She mentioned there was more than one."

"She told me there were two that attacked her."

"You killed them both?"

"No. I killed the one who took her and tried to sell her. The other one who killed your son attacked us, along with his brother. Neoke shot the brother dead."

As he spoke, Wolf Tongue untied a thong on his belt and then tossed Joseph Adams' scalp to Nyakwai. "The one who attacked her and your son still lives. Perhaps. But he's now missing three fingers from his right hand, has a hole in his manhood, and you have his scalp."

Nyakwai examined the bloodied wad of hair and skin. His eyes lingered on it, then flicked back to Wolf Tongue. "What do you want now? You brought back my daughter and killed and maimed the men who attacked us and murdered my son. What gift do you want in return?"

Wolf Tongue drew a breath to steel himself. He knew he could ask for coin or weapons or horses. But he thought of Hugh Pyke, and his hope to save a few innocent people.

"Two things only. I have this dagger with Neoke's thanks, and both I will cherish. The other," he paused to lick his lips. "Is that now that your daughter is returned and the men punished, you leave the English village in peace."

Nyakwai bared his teeth. "These *dogs* that tried to kill you? You still plead for their lives? What has that English soldier paid you that you're so ready to come to his heel?"

Wolf Tongue fought to keep his anger in check, but it seemed that the town still stood, and that relief helped him douse the ire. "Neoke is safe and returned to you. The men who did this are punished. There needs to be no more death here. Leave them be."

"No." Nyakwai's voice was sharp, curt, but quiet. "I told your English that she was not to be harmed. But even then, if she had not so much as a scratch, it does not wash away what everyone in this town does. You say one man took her to sell as a slave? That's only one man. But there was another who attacked her and my son, the one whose scalp you bring me. And then a third attacked you?"

Nyakwai spread his arms wide. "Do you not see what these people are? While you fight one, the next prepares his blade to cut your throat from behind. The whole village is this way. We've said it for more than a year, and now we see it with our own eyes."

He gestured toward the town with one sharp finger. "Listen, Susquehannock. Those *quhanstrono* are ready to scalp one another if there would be French coin in it for them. Your friend, the soldier, was here yesterday with one of those people. I didn't kill the groveling back-biter because it seemed like the soldier might do it for me."

Wolf Tongue frowned, but tried to keep his thoughts to himself. If Pyke had been here yesterday, that meant that he was probably still alive and keeping the town the same way. In that, at least, there was some more hope.

"No," said Wolf Tongue. "Not the whole village. There are women and children like Neoke there. And good men, too."

"Bah! I don't see them. I see women who shelter their men, and men who murder and steal and lie." Nyakwai had leaned in, earnest and engaged in his talk, but suddenly he paused. Then, he drew himself up higher and stared at Wolf Tongue with narrowed eyes.

Wolf Tongue stared back in silence until the war chief spoke again.

"I don't understand you, Susquehannock. You aid the English. And then, when you are the only one who promises to save the town by finding Neoke, the people in the town attack you. And yet, you still plead for them."

Wolf Tongue couldn't hide a wry smile. "I don't care for the people of the village much. And you are right—most are rabid dogs that deserve the fate of this man." He gestured to the scalp Nyakwai still held. "But I've fought shoulder-to-shoulder with the English soldier and he is my friend. He fights to protect those innocent, those very few, who are not bloodied. They deserve their lives as much as the murderers deserve to lose theirs."

Wolf Tongue paused. He looked at Neoke, who watched him with a look that he couldn't quite understand. Was it hostility, or perhaps just intense study. "There are children like Neoke. Girls and boys not old enough to hold a hoe or knife. There are women who tend to the sick and give their food to travelers and men who take in strangers from the cold to warm by their fire.

"Nyakwai, for those people, do not attack again. Let those people be. We will deliver the scalpers and murderers to justice."

"No." His word was a single low rumble, dark and irrevocable as if it had arisen from the black parts of the earth. "These people are a blight. When you find a nest of rats in your grain stores, you don't spare the young and weak. Don't ask me again, Wolf Tongue of the Wolf Clan."

Wolf Tongue returned his baleful glare with a calm one of his own for a few breaths before Nyakwai's darkness seemed to pass. "Now," he said in a more conversational tone. "If you would fight with those who will see victory, join us. I would welcome a warrior who's already killed many of these vermin."

Wolf Tongue cocked his head and studied the old chief before letting his eyes wander to the gathered warriors around him. Many faces he didn't know stared back at him. Some wore their hair like the Mohawk or the Shawnee. Some wore distinctive jewelry that the Onondaga favored. Others, he recognized. His cousins. Kicks-the-Oneida stared back with pursed lips and narrowed eyes.

Then he looked to Bone Snake. His eyes seemed downturned somehow, his jaw jutted to one side in a look of conflicting emotions.

"I'm flattered," he said slowly.

Nyakwai smiled. "You hesitate, but you needn't. We aren't just a band of raiders. All of us have families with a village. You would be welcome with your wife."

At the mention of his wife, Wolf Tongue clenched his jaw. It should be no surprise that Nyakwai knew of Fox's Smile. There were four warriors here from Wolf Tongue's village. Or maybe Nyakwai only guessed that a grown man would have a wife. But either way, the mention reminded Wolf Tongue of the unbalanced, decaying village where she lived. Where he would return to try to raise their child.

The Susquehannock village, deserted and quiet, seemed a stark contrast to the vibrant strength of the men gathered here.

Nyakwai wanted Wolf Tongue's tomahawk and another strong warrior to strengthen his position and a new village. But what Nyakwai offered in return was a home where some of Wolf Tongue's friends already lived. He offered a larger family where there would be enough people to plant and harvest and hunt and protect one another. He offered security for Wolf Tongue's child in a growing, living village, and the chance to become one of a huge family.

As much as it burned inside Wolf Tongue to think of it, he knew he had always fought for a place among his people. He had fought to simply be Susquehannock and not a half-white Susquehannock all his life.

Now, Nyakwai offered that family, a tribe come together to make one from many. He offered something that the dying Susquehannock could never offer again.

Wolf Tongue moved his eyes from Bone Snake back to Neoke. She seemed even smaller now beside her father, though she still cradled Burgess's fowling piece in her arms. She watched him with an angle on her lips that resembled a wry smile as much as a frown.

With one more long thought, Wolf Tongue pulled his shoulders taut and turned to Nyakwai.

TWENTY-FOUR – FINAL PREPARATIONS

Pyke walked the length of the wall. It didn't take him long. Sixty paces for sixty yards. The line of men turned as he passed, their eyes either scared or wild, very few hopeful. The musket-loaders—all boys—worked feverishly to gather the town's few remaining supplies into heaps by the wall.

Boone, the boy who asked all the questions, for once was silent as Pyke stepped past. He sat somberly on the ground as the men he was helping peered over the wall. Pyke stopped and crouched.

"Boone."

"Yes, sir."

"You're a good boy. And one day you'll make a good man."

Boone gulped and didn't speak. He didn't have to. His eyes asked the question for him.

Pyke shook his head. "They do not kill children, Boone. You will be safe."

Boone looked down and played with a twig on the ground. "Begging your pardon, sir, but you're lying to me."

Pyke was about to protest but then saw little use. The boy knew better. The savages would not spare him.

"Forgive me, Boone. I made a mistake."

The boy looked up at him and squinted against the sun.

Pyke put his hand on Boone's shoulder. "Men lie to boys to protect them. We tell them falsehoods so they feel safe. But I can see it now: you are no longer a boy, Boone. Yesterday, you became a man."

Boone gulped again.

"So act like one, then." Pyke came out of his crouch and stood tall. "An Englishman stands when his enemy is near."

Boone smiled and jumped to his feet.

Pyke clamped a hand down on Boone's shoulder. "*Vale.*"
Boone frowned. "French?"
"Latin."
"I have a hard enough time learning my English letters," Boone said.
Pyke smiled. "It means *be strong.*"

Pyke continued down the line. Reverend Baldwin had come to see the men. Pyke had forgotten all about him. It was clear Dob had run this town and Baldwin was too old and feeble to do anything about it. Or he had simply looked the other way, content to have his church and live out his days in obscurity while Dob's greed endangered the entire town.

Reverend Baldwin preached and told the men they were doing God's work by killing the savages. Pyke ignored him and met Fletcher at the end of the line.

Fletcher leaned against the wall, just his head above it. He peered out to the western plain where the Mingos prepared and danced and made their strange, primitive songs.

"Lieutenant, I owe you an apology," Fletcher said.

Pyke motioned for Fletcher to come away from the wall for a moment so they could have some privacy. Fletcher handed his musket to one of the loading-boys. Under happier circumstances, it would have been a comical scene. The musket was taller than the boy and he had trouble handling it.

Fletcher followed Pyke until Pyke felt they were out of earshot.

"I'm sorry, Lieutenant."

Pyke studied the man. "Why?"

Fletcher dropped his head and looked away. "I suspected Dob or his men had caused this and yet I said nothing. I should have told you everything. It's my fault we're in this position now."

Pyke nodded. "Thank you for your apology, but it is unnecessary."

Fletcher frowned in confusion. "Lieutenant?"

"You were not privy to Dob's scalp-trading, were you?"

"No, sir. But we all suspected."

Pyke ignored the second half of the answer. "I see what happened here. It is plain as day. Dob gathered his supporters smartly to assume control of the town, until he grew so powerful no one dared challenge him. You had Molly, later you had a child, ultimately you had to protect your family."

Fletcher pursed his lips. "We could have done something. Should have, I can see now."

Pyke nodded. "Often one must learn things the hard way."

Fletcher cracked a smile. "Ain't that the truth."

"Si, Kit, and Quill would have come for you or Molly or your child. Make no mistake, they would have come." Pyke looked back at the town. He could see the church rising above the huts and small houses. It was nothing. Just a speck on a speck on a map that was constantly being redrawn. And yet it was beautiful. A man could live happily here, if it weren't for the wickedness of his neighbor. The thought made Pyke feel old.

He continued. "And you would be dead. No, Mr. Fletcher. I believe you made the choices you had to make. And when pressed, you came to my aid. I am grateful for it."

Pyke offered his hand. Fletcher pumped it.

"Thank you, Lieutenant. For everything."

"Do not speak as if these were our final words together," Pyke said. "Because we're going to kill every single bleeding savage that dares attack this town. Is that understood?"

Fletcher smiled. "Yes, sir."

"Now I need you on the wall, Fletcher. You are a natural leader. The men look up to you and will follow your example. Show them how to be brave. Do that and they will find courage they didn't know they had within themselves. Do that and we will prevail."

Fletcher pulled his shoulders back and held his head high. He was a proud Englishman and the sight of him revitalized made Pyke actually believe what he was saying. There was a chance, albeit small. Nyakwai's warriors were fierce but there was little strategy in their attack. They fought too bravely—foolishly, in other words—and without cunning. If only Pyke could get these men to follow a simple plan, perhaps they could make themselves more trouble than they were worth to Nyakwai. The chief was proud and stubborn, but even he would have to see the folly of losing dozens of men just to satisfy his pride.

Fletcher nodded and hustled back to the wall. The boy who could barely hold the musket returned it to Fletcher.

Pyke found Davies where he had expected. On the western flank. During the night they had deepened the ditch along this side of the town. Some men would be able to jump it, but most would not. And failing the jump, they would need to climb their way out of the mud-filled pit where men with muskets, standing only ten feet away, would rain death from above.

"Sir," Davies said.

"Sergeant, I came to give you your orders."

"I already have my orders, sir."

Pyke motioned for Davies to step aside. The sergeant managed to holler at one of the men on the far end of the line. The man's musket had slipped and was now in the mud.

"Next time, sir, we have to bring proper soldiers," Davies said balefully.

Pyke nodded. "Next time, indeed we will."

Davies folded his arms and looked Pyke in the eye. "We should have run when we had the chance."

Pyke measured Davies. The sergeant was being honest. But ultimately, the man hadn't run away. He'd stayed despite his inclinations. That was true courage. Doing what had to be done, when every fiber in your being told you to do the opposite.

"You are a good soldier, Davies," Pyke said.

"Lot of good that's about to do me." Davies scratched at his beard, like he always did. "Soon I'll be dead, just like this town, and history won't remember us."

Pyke smiled. "History won't remember us, that much is true. But since when did you ever give a damn about history?"

Davies managed a smile. "Sir, it has been an honor soldiering with you."

"Sergeant, the honor is all mine." Pyke shook Davies's hand. "And now for your orders."

"Sir?"

Pyke let go of Davies's hand. "Should the tide turn unfavorably, and there be nowhere left to defend, I order you to escape."

"You gave me that order last night, sir. What makes you think I'd follow it today?"

Pyke pointed toward the line of townfolk behind Davies. Women and children huddled together. "Because of them."

Davies turned. "The women and children."

Pyke nodded. "The savages will show them no mercy. Should things go … awry, take as many as you can."

Davies hesitated and Pyke knew he wanted to object. Good soldier that he was, he would have preferred to stay with Pyke until the bitter end. But realizing he would be doing a far nobler thing, he swallowed his pride and nodded.

"Never thought I'd see the day where I was the bleeding hero," Davies said.

Pyke smiled. "Let's hope we never do."

Davies laughed. "I never thought you had a sense of humor, sir."

"Gallows humor, Sergeant."

Davies flipped a casual salute—the only kind he knew how to make. "I have a feeling I'll see you at the church soon, sir."

"If it comes to that, take the children away. Don't come anywhere near that church."

Pyke stopped at the church on his way to the north field. Its exterior had blackened where the Mingos who'd breached the town's lines had set fire to it. The women and younger children were gathering outside it. Molly Fletcher was directing people inside.

"Mrs. Fletcher," Pyke said.

"Lieutenant."

He smiled at her. "I was wondering if you had any of your cider left."

She shook her head sadly. "I wish, Mr. Pyke. I could use a drink right now."

"As could we all." He nodded and let her go back to work. A few boys ran in and out of the church. They were storing some emergency muskets and provisions inside. Pyke's general orders had been basic: hold the lines till they could be held no longer, fall back, hold the savages from that point, fall back, hold them again, fall back, until finally the only place left to fall back to was the church. It was a weak, guileless plan but there was nothing else they could do now. Their only chance was in killing enough Mingos to make this petty war unprofitable for Nyakwai.

"Hugh."

He turned and found Fleur. She was wearing different clothes. A black dress and grey shawl. She had pinned her long, black hair up too so it did not wheel in the crisp March wind.

"Fleur."

He held onto her elbows, uncaring who saw them. What did it matter now if everyone in the village knew they had comforted one another on a cold, dark night, while Dob and his crew hunted them, when their lives were growing shorter by the minute?

They stood like that, not quite hugging but staring into each other's eyes. He wondered what life would be like with her, this woman of French and ignoble descent. She of the dazzling eyes and raven hair and monstrously proud personality. They had more than comforted each other last night. Perhaps they had loved each other, if only for a few hours.

"I will pray for you," she said.

"And I you, my lady."

She blushed.

"Hugh …"

He didn't know what to say and rather than blunder his way through some platitude so he slipped his arms under hers and pulled her in to kiss her. Her hands grabbed the back of his head, not letting him pull away.

He could have stayed like that forever. But war was coming. He heard it in the intensified drumming coming from the Mingos surrounding the town. Finally he pulled away, the last kiss lingering on his lips. Her taste was sweet and maddening. He rested his forehead on hers and stroked his hand once up and down her back. She smoothed her hand through his hair. And he understood, again, how men could go mad for love.

"*Merci.*" He looked into her eyes to make sure she understood.

She smiled at him, though it seemed as sad as it did sly. "*Je vous en prie.*"

Pyke let go of her and pressed on. He had to get to Wolf Tongue before the Mingos came. He stopped before he reached his turn and looked back. Fleur still stood in the middle of the dirt road, watching him. She raised her hand and held it above her head. He waved back at her.

Wolf Tongue smiled when he saw Pyke.

"I thought you had run off with the French one," Wolf Tongue said.

Pyke laughed. It felt so good to laugh, even this close to death. Perhaps because of it. He met the Susquehannock warrior on the edge of the southern plain. The brush was still scorched black from yesterday's fire and they had laid out what remaining tar they had in the town.

Pyke gazed out into the field. It was a dull grey March day. Clouds covered the sky and a chill ran through the air.

Pyke turned to his friend. "I would give you orders, but you would not follow them."

Wolf Tongue smirked. "When we first met, I told you. I don't take orders from the English."

Pyke remembered the day fondly. Though when it had happened, he'd been furious. He and Wolf Tongue had just set out to track and kill the colonel's nephew. They did not know each other at all and Pyke had discovered quickly why the man's tribe called him Wolf Tongue. He held nothing back and had a sharp, biting wit.

Wolf Tongue's face darkened. "Many from my tribe have joined Nyakwai."

"I am sorry."

"Bone Snake …" Wolf Tongue shook his head. "They asked me to join them."

Pyke nodded. "They were wise to. And you should have."

Wolf Tongue smirked. "I couldn't. Kicks-the-Oneida is with them, and I will never fight beside that traitor again."

Pyke said nothing. The force behind his friend's words had struck him.

Wolf Tongue nodded. "He's out there. We'll find each other today."

"And Bone Snake?" Pyke said.

Wolf Tongue faced him. The playfulness went out of his eyes. "I won't raise my tomahawk against him. I hope he feels the same way."

Pyke nodded. "I'm certain he does."

The two friends said nothing for awhile. The men that had volunteered to defend this side of the town were already in position. There were no musket-loaders for them, though. There were only so many boys in the town. They and some of the women who would load would be needed on the on the northern and western plains where Pyke expected the most fighting.

"And you," Wolf Tongue said. "What would you do?"

It took Pyke a moment to puzzle out what Wolf Tongue was asking. "If you and I faced each other on the field of battle?"

Wolf Tongue studied him.

Pyke laughed. "Let us hope it never comes to that."

Wolf Tongue laughed too. "An English answer, if ever there was one."

"My friend," Pyke said, "thank you again. I am in your debt."

"Remember that, *quhanstrono*," Wolf Tongue said with a twinkle in his eye. "Remember that Wolf Tongue of the Wolf Clan of the Susquehannock fought with you, because he has honor and because he is a friend to you and because he is a man among boys."

"I will remember it for as long as I live," Pyke said.

Wolf Tongue made a face. "And how long will that be?"

TWENTY-FIVE – THE STORM

Wolf Tongue lifted his chin from his chest and looked across the field to the woods. Still quiet. From where he sat, he could see across the scorched area of dirt and tawny stubble where Pyke had laid his first trap. It was more than a hundred strides to where the first trees of the forest stood—just far enough to make musket fire a gamble. A good weapon and a good man might hit a target at that distance with enough force to make it worthwhile, if Kaol favored him. But few enough of Nyakwai's warriors had muskets, and the men would need to come at least partially into the open for a sure shot, where they'd be easy prey for the Millers Town men. Untrained and as poorly armed as they were, the town still had more power in their muskets than Nyakwai.

More power, but fewer men to wield it. Pyke was right to divide the men the way he did: him with a third of the men on the north and west corner of the town facing Nyakwai's camp, Davies with a small group of muskets farther down the western wall, and Wolf Tongue here with seven men at the southwest corner. They all faced the closest approach and covered three sides of the town.

But they were too few, and Pyke's plan only left three men on the eastern side of the town. The creek lay on the east side of the town, and beyond its shores stretched three hundred strides of muck-filled fields that stopped abruptly at some scraggly trees lining a slope. The slope was no cliff, but it was steep enough that a man would need to switch back and forth, gripping trees on a descent.

Nyakwai couldn't attack in force down the slope in the east. Any men who first made it down the slope would then need to struggle through a mud pit without cover from musket fire for three hundred strides, and then cross the creek before making it into town.

Not an ideal way to plan a battle, but Pyke had done his best with what he had.

Wolf Tongue closed his eyes and let his head drop against the house behind him. No, he thought. If Nyakwai sent warriors this way, it wouldn't be a volley of lead. They would come charging from the woods to break into the town. And if that happened, the other seven men here would make enough noise to rouse Wolf Tongue. Now, there was no battle yet, and he needed as much rest as he could get.

With his eyes closed, Wolf Tongue called for sleep to come. His journey over the past two days had been rushed and exhausting, but he found himself thinking only of his brief time spent in Nyakwai's camp, of Bone Snake and Kicks-the-Oneida. Of Neoke and her dead brother.

The winds shifted and pushed Wolf Tongue's blanket off his shoulder. The cold brushed through his shirt to his skin and he resettled the blanket. Again, the wind carried the scent of ash and death, of burnt tar and earth and singed hair.

A man to his left spoke with an affected smile Wolf Tongue could hear in his voice. "They had enough of our muskets last time. Maybe they've just gone home with their precious princess." The man's voice was quiet, and Wolf Tongue could hear the struggle of hope and fear in it.

Judging by the projection of his voice, another seemed to look toward Wolf Tongue as he spoke. "Maybe. They got what they wanted." Then, the voice quieted after he cleared his throat. "Thought they'd attack at dawn to take cover in the mist and dark."

The first man seemed to take this as encouragement. "No reason to wait now. Daylight favors us."

Wolf Tongue said nothing, but recognized the nervous banter of men unaccustomed to battle. And of many who were. He was too tired to offer his own analysis and instead, recommitted himself to sleep. If Nyakwai waited a week, all the better.

Though perhaps not better for Pyke. Wolf Tongue didn't have much time to learn what had happened, but it was clear the situation for his friend had been only slightly more cordial than what Wolf Tongue had endured. Some of the men scowled and hissed curses as Pyke organized them. Others cowered sullenly as he passed.

Even in the few hours he'd been here, Wolf Tongue could clearly see a division among the people. Pyke spoke and gave orders as usual, but only a handful of the men accepted it without a grimace. Those men seemed to travel with Pyke and Davies and speak little with the others, who stood with arms crossed over their muskets and watched with hostility.

As much as Wolf Tongue would welcome a week's rest, a hot meal and some cider, leaving Pyke here without resolution would do him no good.

Wolf Tongue opened his eyes as he thought about Nyakwai's delay. The sky, a smear of gray and white, filled his vision. He had been certain Nyakwai would attack the town, and the old bear was certainly savvy enough to know to take cover of mist and darkness, especially against any kind of fortification, even as ramshackle as the town's.

Perhaps Wolf Tongue had disrupted the original strategy by appearing with Neoke so early. Though, the mist had still held for another hour, at least, after he'd left the camp. The wind, now stronger and more consistent had pushed that away, leaving only wisps of moisture clinging to the ground.

He blinked as his vision blurred suddenly.

Wolf Tongue leapt to his feet and snatched up his musket. The men around him started and, with wide eyes, turned to look across the field, searching for what he might have seen.

They watched, fingers twitching against their muskets. When no threat appeared, they slowly began to turn sideways glances back on Wolf Tongue.

But Wolf Tongue's eyes still searched. He watched the woods, then turned to search for Pyke at the other side of the town. He couldn't see anything through the hunches of houses between them, and all he could hear was the wind and the nervous shuffling of the men around him.

He held out his hand to be sure, and raindrops began to patter against his palm.

Pyke kept just his eyes above the wall as the sky grayed with clouds. He watched the Mingo camp intently. Nyakwai's warriors seemed to form an endless mass. Pyke grimly figured they outnumbered the townfolk three, possibly four, to one. He peeled his eyes away from the enemy for a moment to survey his men again. They all huddled hard against the wall now, their conversation to a minimum. His loaders sat wrapped in blankets and coats next to their piles of supplies. Their shot ran dangerously low.

Then the rain started.

And immediately Pyke grasped Nyakwai's plan.

From the look of things, the chief had not diverted too many of his warriors from the western plain. Pyke had been puzzling over this poor decision since he had finally planted himself on the wall to await the enemy's next charge. The town's best defense, such as it was, blocked their pass in this direction. Foolishly, Pyke had figured Nyakwai had stubbornly refused to employ strategy, instead relying again on sheer strength of numbers to overwhelm Millers Town in a frontal assault. In Pyke's defense, Nyakwai was the proud sort and did not think twice about sending men to their deaths.

But now Pyke realized the chief had been waiting for the rain to begin.

Operating a Brown Bess, or any gun, in the rain was a tricky business and required practice. No firearm could be made totally waterproof. In anything more than a drizzle, and in the hands of the undisciplined, the town's guns were in danger of becoming useless, taking away the only advantage Pyke and the townfolk had over the savages. Without their firearms, they would be forced to engage in hand-to-hand combat with a superior force.

Pyke grimaced as the rain started coming down. The sky was turning blacker by the minute. This was no quickly-passing storm.

"The Lord hates a coward," Pyke muttered.

"What was that?" Fletcher said.

Pyke eyed the man. Fletcher's gaze was jumping. His hands gripped and regripped his musket. His whole person seemed to fidget.

"Nyakwai waits until our muskets do not work," Pyke said.

Fletcher's mouth hung open. He said nothing.

Pyke knew then what he had to do. What they all had to do. He was proud, but not too proud to admit his plan needed to be changed.

"I need ten men," Pyke said.

Kit stepped away from the wall. "You don't expect us to go out there."

"If we leave this wall, we're dead," another man said, his voice cracking.

They were likely dead regardless, but Pyke didn't voice that defeatist thought. "We must start this battle now, while we can still use our guns."

Fletcher looked away, still coming to terms with the revised plan. The other men regarded Pyke with hostility, or like he was mad.

Pyke ignored them. "Ten men who can run quickly. Now!"

The townfolk stared in disbelief at Pyke. He feared he would not get any volunteers and failing that he would be forced to conscript, which was not ideal.

"If we wait for him to come, we are dead!" Pyke said. "We must force him to engage now."

"Our muskets are only good up to eighty paces," Kit said.

"If this rain picks up, they'll only be good at zero paces," Pyke said.

Fletcher stepped away from the wall. "The lieutenant is right. He has been right this entire time but we lived in fear of Dob and his cronies." Fletcher shot Kit a nasty look. "It's time we followed Pyke's lead."

Fletcher stood with Pyke and more men joined them. Kit went back to the wall and faced the enemy again. Soon ten men had formed around Pyke.

"Lieutenant, what is the plan?" Fletcher said.

"Seven shooters, three loaders." Pyke looked over the men. They were scared but he saw a glimmer of hope in their eyes. "When we get them to engage, we fall back to the wall."

Wolf Tongue clenched his fist and let out a frustrated breath. He looked over his shoulder, up the western palisade to where Pyke stood waiting for Nyakwai to charge the town. Except now, as the rain began to patter faster with thick, heavy drops, Nyakwai would wait. The old man knew Pyke's only hope was in his guns along that wall, and, with any luck, the pressure of battle would make his men sloppy in their loading, making the only danger at the wall the leap over it.

The rain hadn't begun in earnest, though it would come, and stay. Until then, Nyakwai would hold his men back.

Wolf Tongue looked again to the west woods. It seemed like there were no men waiting in there at all. At a hundred strides out, where the trees began, Wolf Tongue could only see darkness. The whole woodline stretched right, to the north past where Davies would be stationed halfway to the end of town, and where Pyke stood along the stronger palisade at the northwest corner. There seemed to be no movement Wolf Tongue could see. Could Nyakwai have concentrated all his men on the west for one big push against the town?

One of the townsmen watched Wolf Tongue with tightened eyebrows that seemed half question and half suspicion.

"If they come, they'll wait for rain," he said.

The man sneered and gestured to the burned fields just south of them. "We burned enough of them that they fear the fire like a dog."

"Dogs are often wiser than men." Wolf Tongue raised an eyebrow as he focused on the man's face. "How well can you reload in the rain?"

The man swallowed, looked at his companion and again out across the field.

A sudden noise caught their attention and Wolf Tongue and the men around him started and looked to the north. It wasn't battle—there were no shots fired—but murmuring and movement that hadn't been there before. Wolf Tongue spun and grasped the overhanging roof on the house behind him. With a grunt, he hauled himself up. The planks were steep and slick, and only with a squirming effort did he manage to scramble to the peak. Once he reached the top and looked down did a sudden tightening appear in his gut. His breath flew from him as his stomach clenched and he leaned down close to the peak as he straddled it.

He closed his eyes for a heartbeat, remembering the moment he and Pyke had scaled the ledges to ambush Azariah Bennett. Those cliffs were four or five times as tall as a man, but this peak was barely higher than his outstretched hand. With that thought, Wolf Tongue wrestled back control of his breath and opened his eyes.

Here, he could see over the roofs of the town and out to the wall. Pyke stood gesturing and then, with another group of about ten men, stepped over the wall and into the field.

Wolf Tongue searched the field and wood for a sign of Nyakwai, but saw none. Where was Pyke going? Could he intend to negotiate again or parley now?

Then he smiled. Pyke was not one to wait. He must have realized what the rain meant and led this group out to taunt Nyakwai into attacking. If he could draw the old man out, he could bring them within musket range before the rain ruined their powder.

Wolf Tongue's smile began to slide as he watched. If Pyke couldn't draw Nyakwai out, he'd be standing in the field with only ten men, in the open, while Nyakwai sat behind the trees and cover and shot them all down.

The thought reminded Wolf Tongue of his own position. If anyone were close enough, he'd make a pretty target here atop a house like a roosting turkey. He swiveled to his right. From here, he could see even better into the west woods. A gray squirrel skittered along the ground in short bursts. That was all that moved. And likely all that was there right now. If Nyakwai came from the west, his men were hidden farther back.

A sharp movement caught his eye and Wolf Tongue spun just in time to hear the report of Pyke's muskets firing. The soldier now stood thirty strides from the wall, exposed against the mud of the field. Two more men fired and handed their muskets back. A moment later, two more puffs of smoke followed by the blast of powder in his ears.

Wolf Tongue could just barely see into the forest where Pyke aimed. He thought he saw movement, but couldn't tell if that was a swirl of rain or his own hope.

Wolf Tongue again checked the west, but saw no movement.

Pyke and two others fired again and handed their guns back.

Wolf Tongue craned to try to see Davies farther up the wall behind another house. His weight shifted on the slippery plank and his breath seized again as he grabbed at the peak.

Then, he forgot about the height. When he twisted, he looked to see the east side of the town.

In the distance and hazy light, he could pick out perhaps three figures, no, four, picking their way down the eastern slope.

Pyke stood watch while Fletcher and the men fired and loaded. Soon the plain filled with the smoke of their muskets, but Nyakwai's warriors were loath to move from their position. They had backed out of the field and now used the trees beyond as shields.

"Closer," Pyke ordered.

"We're practically sitting down to dinner with the lot," grumbled one of the men.

Pyke seethed. "Our shot is barely making a dent in those trunks. From this distance our bullets are no more vexing than mosquito bites."

Fletcher came out of his shooter's crouch. "The lieutenant is right."

Pyke shook his head. Of course the townfolk had exaggerated the distance their guns were deadly, to remain as far from the enemy as possible. It was true what his father had always said, fear made men short-sighted. All they had done with this first series of volleys was waste precious bullets.

"Closer, God damn you!" Pyke ordered.

He had run out of wise, compelling things to say. There was no time for them anyway. The drizzle had turned into a steady, beating rain. The need to inflict as much damage as possible with their muskets in a short span was absolute.

The man that protested sluggishly fell behind but everyone else moved at an encouraging speed. After ten paces, though, the group slowed.

"Closer!" Pyke shouted as loud as he could. He wanted Nyakwai and his warriors to hear him. He wanted them to know he wasn't afraid. The warriors stuck their heads out from behind the trees and watched them. Their war chant started and the drums thundered in the distance.

Pyke ignored the sounds. He forced the men another fifteen paces, stopping only when Fletcher slowed.

"Make your shots count," Pyke said, already beginning to load his next bullet. "We can't afford to lose any more ammunition."

The men formed the standard line. The savages continued their battle cries but did not attack even though Pyke and his shooters were now fifty paces away.

"Fire at will!" Pyke yelled as he loosed his first bullet. He didn't wait to see if it struck home but instead went immediately to loading again. The rest of the men let off a volley, the dull crack of the flintlocks thundering almost in unison as the rain thickened. Pyke was careful to load.

"I got one of the bastards!" Fletcher yelled and the men let out a cheer. Pyke let himself grin. The men had gotten over their initial reluctance and fear was no longer totally controlling them. They would aim truer.

Another round and this time Pyke saw his bullet knock into a man who had dared to move from behind one tree to another. He went to load his next shot, wondering why Nyakwai did not at least send a party to contend with Pyke or fire what few muskets he had back. Nyakwai was the proud sort, unafraid to lose men indiscriminately in battle, but his failure to attack was now downright mad.

As it dawned on him what was happening, Pyke heard the crack of the first report behind him.

Wolf Tongue slid from the roof and jarred against his knees as he landed.

"You two, with me!"

He didn't wait for a response, but began to run. The ground was already wet and clinging to his moccasins as he pumped his legs through the town. He rounded a corner of a house and heard crying coming from the open doors of the church. As he passed, he heard startled wails.

By the time he arrived at the creek, his chest was heaving from the sprint. He scanned the open field for a moment. The creek, five strides wide, churned like liquid ash. Beyond it, the field was brown and barren but for scattered patches of dirty snow.

The eastern slope was a tangle of mist, scrub trees, and last year's thorns, flat like a scene painted in charcoal on an old hide. From this angle, Wolf Tongue couldn't see anything.

He looked to his left to see the three men Pyke had stationed here, all grouped together halfway to the end of town by the small bridge, not spread out like Pyke had ordered. Each cradled a musket in his arms and they stared at Wolf Tongue, confused and nervous, for a heartbeat before they also looked to the men chasing behind him.

Then one of the men shouted something and Wolf Tongue's head snapped back to look across the field.

All at once, nine Mingos broke from the trees and sprinted into the mud.

Pyke stopped firing.

"Back to the wall!" he shouted. "Now!"

His small troop, already loath to have left the safety of the palisade, needed no prodding. The loaders bolted like rabbits at the sight of a hound, and as one, the shooters came out of their crouch and broke into a run.

The war cries from the northwestern woods reached a fever pitch and all at once the Mingos burst from the forest.

At least fifty of them.

Pyke turned and ran. The field was slick with rain now as the drizzle intensified and the ground squelched with each step he took as the mud grabbed at his boots. The Mingos roared as they gave chase, their screams deafening.

He looked back over his shoulder, just in time to see the lead Mingo take a knee and bring muskets to bear.

"Don't run in a straight line!" Pyke yelled, fearing it was already too late.

The boom from the first volley was loud enough to drown out the war cries. Pyke expected to feel that hard punch of the bullet in his back. But none came. Two townfolk nearest him fell. The first was hit in the back of the head, his dark hair replaced by gore and blood. The second was shot in the leg. The man sprawled in the grass. Pyke cut over.

The bullet had torn into the man's hamstring. He screamed and clutched at his leg.

"Come on!" Pyke grabbed his arm and helped him to his feet.

Only halfway back to the wall, Pyke and this man ran a three-legged, hobbling race across the plain as the Mingos closed.

"Shoot the bastards!" Pyke shouted at his men who'd stayed behind the wall.

At once a dozen muskets moved. Pyke saw the hammer drop and waited through the agony between trigger pull and blast—a one-second eternity.

He felt the air of a few bullets as they whizzed by. He did not look back to gauge the impact of the return volley. He knew the Mingos were too many.

As one, he and the man slammed into the wall as the Mingos fired again and the townfolk loosed another volley. Fletcher helped Pyke's man over the wall, and then Pyke vaulted.

Boone grabbed Pyke's musket and handed him a loaded one. Chest heaving from the sprint, he stood back up to aim.

The Mingos were fifteen strides from the palisade, and only a few had fallen in their mad dash.

Too many to hold off.

"One more shot then fall back to the first line!" Pyke ordered.

The nine Mingos had spread out as widely as possible and charged with knees high toward the town.

Wolf Tongue fell to one knee and brought his musket to his shoulder. He tried to aim, but the men were too far. So he watched and waited as his enemy charged toward him. His breath still raged in his lungs and he closed his eyes with a breath to try to calm it.

A shot exploded beside him and Wolf Tongue looked to see one of the men he'd brought with a smoke cloud still around the end of his musket.

"Wait for a clean shot! And reload carefully!"

Wolf Tongue cursed as he brought his eyes back to the charging men. They were still more than two hundred strides away. The Mingos screamed, howled as they charged. At this distance, they looked like the *odhow* who guard the dead with white, black and red faces, teeth bared and wearing heavy furs.

When they were halfway to the creek, Wolf Tongue chose his target, a man in black fur carrying both a musket and gun-stock war club. He took another deep breath and followed the man with his barrel.

At a hundred strides, two of Millers Town men fired. Wolf Tongue did not take his eyes off his target to see whether they'd fired in vain.

Another five heartbeats. The man in black fur was ten strides closer.

Wolf Tongue let out his breath as he squeezed the trigger.

The man shuddered, then kept running. As Wolf Tongue began to reload, he saw the man stumble and fall.

Another two shots fired, their cracks sounding strangely flat against the heavy air.

Wolf Tongue jammed his ramrod down the barrel and surveyed the field for another target. Seven of nine Mingos still stood, but two of those moved more slowly now as if wounded.

As he watched, one by one, they all dropped to a knee and brought up muskets of their own.

Wolf Tongue pitched to his side, holding his musket above him when the first pops of their fire began.

Men near him began to scream.

Wolf Tongue rolled back and rose to one knee. A few of the Mingos had dropped their guns and were again charging through the mud. Three others still knelt, muzzles raised.

Wolf Tongue sighted on one of those.

A man fired beside him and Wolf Tongue's target shifted, his musket swinging wide. He heard a shout of triumph that ended abruptly as the Mingo righted himself and took aim again.

Wolf Tongue squeezed his trigger, and in the moment before his own muzzle flash, he saw his enemy's gun throw smoke and fire.

The Mingo dropped his gun and pitched forward.

Wolf Tongue made to reload, but then dropped his gun. He wouldn't have time with the Mingos within fifty strides.

He rose and drew his tomahawk and knife. Of the five Millers Town men, one lay face-down, his throat torn open. Another lay back with a bloody leg, trying to reload his musket. A third, the man beside Wolf Tongue who had wounded the Mingo in his sights, lay in the mud, twitching with a sucking wound through his sternum.

"Brace yourselves!" shouted Wolf Tongue as he eyed the oncoming Mingos. They were closer now. Close enough to see their faces scowling, teeth bared. The remaining five Mingos came screaming like the north wind, spread out wide as they had come out of the woods. For the briefest moment, Wolf Tongue wondered if any of these were men he knew.

The rain fell harder and the creek water churned and flew into the air as the Mingos kicked through it and into the town.

Pyke watched as the Mingos streamed over the wall like it was barely an impediment. They were terrifying in their fearlessness and appeared as demons with their faces painted.

The men waited for Pyke to give the order. Fletcher and Bertram shot him a pleading look to call the retreat.

But he waited. They had to time everything perfectly. Or they would all be dead in less than a minute.

"Reform at the houses!" Pyke ordered.

They hurried, stepping over the clothes they'd left on the ground between the two small houses. Hastily they reformed two lines between the chokepoint.

The Mingos, if they paused long enough to take stock, could easily flank and surround them, but Pyke figured their bloodlust would urge them forward without thought.

And he was right.

The Mingo warriors saw Pyke's line and were unafraid. The townfolk were not even a score of men, all of them wide-eyed and terrified, and the Indians gave not one thought to strategy. They saw an easy slaughter and charged bravely.

And dumbly.

"Fire!" Pyke shouted.

Not all the muskets fired. The rain had rendered many of them useless now. But some bullets found their marks. The approaching force lost men. But not enough to give them pause. They kept coming.

"Fix bayonets!" Pyke said.

But this was a ruse. The men pretended to fidget with their guns as the Mingos rushed headlong.

They were so close now. The lead men were raising their tomahawks above their heads, eager to make the first strike. Pyke could see the strains of their muscles.

"Drop your guns!" Pyke shouted, hoping the Mingos would hear him and understand, hoping the Indians would think the townfolk were surrendering.

The Mingos closed with frightening speed as half of Pyke's line dropped their muskets.

"Get ready!" Pyke said.

As one, the men who had dropped their weapons dug their fingers into the muddy street and gripped the ropes they had set up earlier.

"PULL!" Pyke shouted.

With the enemy force only five paces away, the men holding the ropes yanked. The cloths covering their trap slid away as their hastily-made spikes angled toward the oncoming Mingos. The men that had not dropped their muskets started to reload.

The spikes lifted and the Mingos were too close and moving too fast to avoid them.

The poles had been intended for the unfinished wall and they were five-feet long and lashed together. When Pyke and his men pulled, they were lifting one long stretch of deadly spikes.

Three Mingos ran right into them.

One warrior gored himself in front of Pyke, his tomahawk falling harmlessly into the mud. For a moment, time seemed to stop. Pyke took the break in action to reassess. The three Mingos that had run into the spikes were now holding up this temporary wall while the rest knotted behind their fallen brothers.

The rest of Pyke's line, the men that were now finished reloading, lifted their muskets and at close range fired into the advancing Mingos. The Indian war cries ceased as the men realized they'd been outwitted and some would die before they'd gotten a chance to even fight. Pyke saw a few more fall and the rest came to a staggering halt as they massed in front of the two homes.

Bertram Miller lifted his musket into the air. "We'll kill all of you!"

Pyke smiled as the Englishmen roared, bolstering Bertram's taunt.

A Mingo in the front line took one step forward and hurled his tomahawk. It flicked through the air and stuck Bertram between the eyes.

The man went down. For a second, the townfolk watched dumbly and the Mingos waited. One moment ago, the townfolk had been triumphant, full of belief against impossible odds. But with one throw of the tomahawk, Pyke knew the savages had just broken their spirit.

Fletcher screamed. "No!"

All hell broke loose again.

Mingos peeled away and hurried around the houses, hoping to flank and surround Pyke's men.

"Fall back!" Pyke yelled.

The men were already doing so. Pyke cast one glance back at Bertram's corpse before breaking into a run. He had no time to weep for the dead.

Wolf Tongue stood on the bank of the creek and twisted the ball of one foot deeper into the mud as the nearest Mingo came charging at him. The man had a long shirt of rabbit fur wrapped around him. His face above his nose was painted crimson and Wolf Tongue could now see the black lines of tattoos on both cheeks.

The man kicked through knee-high water before he stopped suddenly in the middle of the creek and threw his tomahawk. It hissed through the air as Wolf Tongue blinked, registering the surprise of the attack. Then he twisted his body and swung his own to knock the attack sideways.

The moment only lasted a pair of heartbeats, but when Wolf Tongue looked back, the man had changed his direction and angled toward the shore on Wolf Tongue's right.

A scream to his left drew Wolf Tongue's attention. One of the Mingos sprinted across the bridge toward one of the Millers Town men who howled in fury, teeth bared, as he fought to pull the ramrod from his musket.

Wolf Tongue made to move, but stopped. He couldn't help here. One of those two men would die before he could reach the bridge, and there were other Mingos for him to fight.

He looked again to the man in the rabbit fur. He had now cleared the creek and ran toward the center of town, another tomahawk in his hand.

Wolf Tongue pushed from the mud and tore after him.

The Mingo sprinted past the first two houses. At the third, he slowed only enough to smash his shoulder into the door. The door shattered and the man fell into the opening.

A report sounded by the creek.

Wolf Tongue reached the house a moment later and, peering in before he did, charged through the broken doorway.

The Mingo was at the far side by the fire, his back to the door. As soon as he heard Wolf Tongue enter, the man whirled. The ceiling was so low that his head nearly reached it. He held his tomahawk in one hand and burning brand in the other. He smiled as he touched the brand to the wall beside him against a smear of black above a broken jar. The oil took flame immediately.

The Mingo hurled the flaming stick at Wolf Tongue, then charged with his tomahawk swinging in quick arcs in front of him.

Wolf Tongue tried to find the balance to fight while hunched down. He was only slightly taller than the Mingo, but he couldn't stand upright in the house. He shuffled beside the wooden table and kicked the bench from beneath it. It rattled as it fell between them.

The Mingo stepped around the bench, eyes narrowed, tomahawk circling. The air was already filling with smoke.

"Why are you here, Susquehannock?"

Wolf Tongue paused, understanding why the Mingo had hesitated to attack him. He had no answer for a moment, and it surprised him. He opened his mouth to make a snide answer, but none came to him.

The Mingo shook his head. "I saw you with Neoke. You belong with us, not with these pitiful, skulking *quhanstrono*. Come, take your payment for all they've done. Join in the spoils. We will win this day."

Wolf Tongue stopped circling. "I can't let you leave."

"Then you will die."

The Mingo charged and Wolf Tongue worked his tomahawk back and forth, stopping each blow, but unable to retaliate. The smaller man moved freely while Wolf Tongue shuffled slowly, shoulders up and chin down as he ducked beneath the stripes of wood beams overhead.

He stuck his feet to the ground, unmoving as the attacks came and came again. The Mingo began to seem desperate for a score. He hammered relentlessly at Wolf Tongue.

Wolf Tongue blocked each attack and would lash out immediately, but the

Mingo would dance to the side or back out of reach before Wolf Tongue could move after him.

The flames now had crawled to the ceiling. The air was hot and so thick with smoke it was nearly unbreathable.

The attack came again, a slamming blow against Wolf Tongue's tomahawk. He let it drive him down to his knees. He saw triumph in the Mingo's eyes as he whipped his tomahawk back again for another blow.

But this time, Wolf Tongue thrust his knife out and up. The long dagger he took from Burgess sunk into the inside of the Mingo's thigh and clicked as it sliced against bone.

Wolf Tongue twisted and yanked as he threw himself backward while holding his tomahawk up high. The Mingo's tomahawk still came down and tore Wolf Tongue's from his grasp, but did no harm as Wolf Tongue fell onto his back.

The Mingo screamed in agony as he stumbled back, knocking into the table and slumping to the floor. He grabbed at his leg with both hands, murmuring something between shuddering breaths. Blood gushed in spurts onto the rabbit fur and his buckskin leggings and then out onto the dirt floor.

He would be dead in minutes.

Wolf Tongue pulled himself to his feet, snatched up his tomahawk, and ran out the door.

Outside, he again heard the spotty cracks of muskets. The howls of war from *iomwhen* and *quhanstrono*. They were all close.

The Mingo had broken into the town.

Back and back and back again. The Mingos pressed them on all sides. The town was collapsing on itself. Everywhere Pyke turned, he witnessed some new horror. At the last corner, Pyke had helplessly watched an unconscious woman being carried away by two warriors and a man being scalped while still alive. Before that, two children had …

He forced the horror from his mind.

All sense of greater purpose and higher strategy was gone, the fighting now brutal and rampant ever since the Mingos had breached the town. Pyke and Davies had met in the crush and, with Fletcher, fought their way to the church as the savages seemed to come at them from every direction.

Pyke slashed and hacked. He kept his attackers at bay with his blood-stained saber. He had lost count of the men he'd killed on this day. The dirt roads of Millers Town had turned muddy in the rain and gore-filled in the melee.

Davies batted a Mingo warrior with a war club he'd picked up somewhere along the way. "No choice now, sir!"

Davies bobbed his head backward, signaling their retreat to the church.

Pyke turned back to the knot of Mingos that had just come from around the corner. Ten warriors, all of them blood-stained and their eyes wild and savage. Pyke kept his saber pointed at them.

His heart sank. Retreat to the church was necessary but it signaled defeat. They would be safe temporarily in the church but ultimately they wouldn't be able to hold out forever. It could be over quickly, in fact, if Nyakwai set fire to the building and forced them into the street to fight.

"Sir!" Davies said. "No choice!"

Pyke knew he was right, knew his duty was to get to the church, knew he had to protect the people gathered there for as long as he could. But the foolish, pride-filled part of him preferred to stay in this street and make his last stand. He wouldn't be able to defeat all these men, but he would go out fighting. He would die on his feet, the way a soldier should. A tomahawk to the back or fleeing a smoke-filled church didn't agree with him.

Behind him a horse whinnied and Pyke hazarded a glance over his shoulder, momentarily taking his eyes off the advancing warriors. In the gloom he saw a rider urging a horse toward them. Her hair was unpinned and flew behind her as she rode hard.

Fleur briefly met his eyes as she rode past and her horse barreled through the oncoming warriors. The Mingos scrambled and jumped out of the way. Pyke saw their confusion as his opportunity.

"Now, Davies!"

The sergeant cursed as the three men advanced. Pyke slashed the first Mingo, who fumbled and howled in both fury and pain. Fletcher lost his footing during his attack and Davies averted his own attack to come to Fletcher's aid. In a matter of seconds, the eight warriors had regained their feet and now Pyke was separated from Davies and Fletcher.

He looked past the oncoming Mingos and caught one fleeting glance from Fleur. The French woman had stopped her horse and looked back at him. In the haze of rain and smoke, he could just see her eyes twinkle in the light of the fires set around the town. Her dark hair fluttered wildly.

"Go!" Pyke yelled.

Fleur flicked the reins and the horse set off. Before she disappeared up the street, Pyke was back to the fight at hand. His saber whizzed through the air. He never stopped moving. Many times a tomahawk almost split his skull, but Pyke spun and twisted and dove and rolled, fighting without conscious thought now, moving on impulse and instinct.

The Mingo warriors fell as he sliced. Pyke knew he was so close to death and any moment now his life could be ripped from him by a tomahawk, but he'd also never felt so alive at the same time. He didn't relish the violence, didn't even mildly enjoy it, but he savored his life now.

He hacked another man down and, sensing another warrior behind him, Pyke whirled. Ready to slash backhand with his saber, he turned and saw the last warrior of the party that was a danger to them. The man had raised his tomahawk over his head and Pyke saw the flash of recognition in the warrior's eyes.

Pyke stilled his arm, and Bone Snake did the same. Both men regarded each other in that way that acquaintances do. They had never had the opportunity to grow close, as Pyke had spent little time in the Susquehannock village previously. But they shared a bond deeper than friendship.

They had stood-to-shoulder in that battle against Azariah Bennett a year ago. They had fought and killed and shrugged off death. A mutual, unspoken respect passed between them and looking at the man now, Pyke couldn't imagine killing him. They had once been on the same side.

Pyke slowly lowered his blade.

"Sir!" Davies rushed forward, but Pyke pinned him back.

"Hold, Sergeant." Pyke nodded at Bone Snake. "This man is no enemy."

"Have you lost your bloody mind, sir?" Davies did not know Bone Snake and did not understand the history between them.

Pyke smiled. "Probably."

Bone Snake lowered his tomahawk and nodded at them. "Soldier Pyke of the English, I have no wish to kill you. If you see my nephew, tell him he is a great warrior and that he is missed."

Pyke nodded and turned away. "To the church now."

Davies and Fletcher preceded him as they hustled down the road. At the next intersection, townfolk and savage clashed in a wild, messy brawl. Pyke shouted his orders for the church, and the men took heed. They broke from their fighting to follow, backing away from the savages who now swelled their ranks in one huddling mass. They outnumbered the townfolk two-to-one here, and Pyke knew there were still more where they had come from.

They backed their way to the church and the townfolk filed in. Pyke and Davies hung back, waiting for the townfolk to get inside. The Mingos in front challenged them but Pyke kept them at bay.

"Get ready, Sergeant," Pyke said.

"I've been ready, Lieutenant." Davies grimaced.

Behind them there was a commotion. Pyke looked back and was confused by what he saw. Dob Sutler was fighting his way *out* of the church and clutching something. Dob was no warrior and certainly no hero, so Pyke couldn't comprehend what the man was doing. Perhaps he had figured their odds of survival as Pyke had, and Dob knew the church would ultimately be the townfolk's grave.

Anger ripped through Pyke. Dob was responsible for their current predicament. He had led his small band of traders into their unchristian business of scalping Indians, and now the man dared to escape?

Pyke pushed over to intercept Dob as the man came out of the church carrying a small chest.

"Dob!" Pyke yelled.

Dob ignored him and came to a stop in the street as he tried to find his escape route. There was nowhere to go, so Dob picked the direction with the fewest savages.

"Dob!" Pyke yelled again, but the man didn't heed him.

Dob suddenly broke into a run, hoping to surprise the oncoming warriors. Pyke knew before he did that Dob had no chance. The base side of him wanted to let Dob make his own mistake and die horribly under the tomahawk. He deserved it.

But duty reminded Pyke he was supposed to defend all the townfolk, even Dob. The man was under his arrest and therefore under his watch. As Dob raced away, two Mingos closed on him and the nearest one flicked his tomahawk. It whistled through the air and struck Dob in the leg. He screamed and went down. The strange chest he carried fell out of his hands.

Pyke hurried forward, knowing the whole way he was jeopardizing his own life to save Dob Sutler of all people. He got to the man as the Mingos did and he warded the savages off with his saber. Davies caught up with him too and the two warriors backed away cautiously. Nyakwai's men had suffered heavy losses and now that they had the townfolk cornered in the church, there was no more incentive to be so brash.

Pyke bent to assist Dob. "Stand up!"

Dob howled and clutched at the tomahawk in his thigh. Blood seeped through his fingers.

Pyke's eyes fell on the chest he'd been carrying. Its lid had come open when it crashed into the dirt road. And in the gray light, Pyke saw what was inside.

Coins.

Piles of French sols slithered over one another into the mud.

At first Pyke didn't understand why Dob Sutler, living in this tiny frontier town that did not even appear on a map, would possess these riches.

But then the horrible truth came to him. Dob and his men had been trading in Indian scalps and slaves for quite some time, exchanging them with the French and taking their money. Dob, of course, had hidden this fact from Pyke for many reasons, not the least of which because the Crown could have declared such trade treasonous and obviously inimical to its interests in the territory. They were gearing up for a war with France, and Dob had profited off the French by bringing them scalps, the scalps of the tribes friendly to the Crown.

Anger formed in his stomach and rose into his throat. Pyke roared and spun back to Dob.

"Release him, Sergeant!" Pyke shouted.

Davies saw the fire in Pyke's eyes and immediately backed away.

Dob was on his hands and knees and craned his neck to look up. Pyke's body shook with rage. He thought of all the men and women that had died. He thought of the woman those two warriors had just dragged away, the children, the man that had been scalped, Bertram Miller … Wolf Tongue, his friend, the Susquehannock who had no reason to fight except out of loyalty and friendship, probably dead. All these people had died because of Dob's greed. If they had turned these coins over to Nyakwai in the beginning, they might have been able to avoid all this bloodshed.

Pyke brought his saber up and with all the strength he could muster, hacked into Dob's neck. The man's blood fountained into the air as the life quickly drained out of him.

Davies, for once, was at a loss for words.

Pyke yanked his saber free of Dob's neck and scooped up the chest.

Men ran screaming in all directions. An occasional musket report cut through the cries of the dying and victorious. The air smelled of wet ash and cold rain that ran down Wolf Tongue's face. Despite the weather, fires had blossomed against some of the houses. Some men engaged in battle or fought in groups of two or three. Wolf Tongue ran from skirmish to skirmish, aiding Millers Town as much as he could, engaging with the Mingos who often broke away for easier prey or to loot a burning home.

Wolf Tongue now found himself on the north end of town, trying in vain to adhere to Pyke's plan to gather everyone to the church. One man ran past him. He struggled to hold on to his weapon, a new longrifle, and a bulging blanket filled with personal treasures.

Wolf Tongue chased after him a few steps. "Go to the church!"

But he stopped, knowing the man would flee and test his god's love in the wilds of the hills.

Probably more of it there than in his church today, he thought bitterly.

He caught movement and turned to his left. Ahead, he saw a couple of *quhanstrono* huddled against a house. They stood shoulder-to-shoulder with their backs against the planks, their hair coming loose in wet strands from their braids. One held a wood axe across his chest, eyes closed as his lips trembled in prayer. The other frantically slammed the ramrod down the barrel of his musket. Beyond them, a group of three Mingos who dressed as if they'd come from the Seneca came loping through the village, eyes searching.

As Wolf Tongue neared, the man with the musket whirled past the corner and brought his gun up. Wolf Tongue heard the hammer slam down, but there was no spark.

The Mingos howled and ran toward him.

The man with the axe opened his eyes and moved to run when he saw Wolf Tongue only a few strides away. He brought his axe above his head and screamed.

The swing was wild and thoughtless and Wolf Tongue slipped past it easily.

"I'm here to help you, fools!" screamed Wolf Tongue. He grabbed the axe man by the shoulder and shoved him into his companion. "Get to the church! Go!"

The man stumbled as he recovered and then stared at Wolf Tongue. Wolf Tongue slapped his face. "To the church!"

The man blinked, then, with a hurried glance at the approaching warriors who were now only forty strides away, slipped in the mud, rose, and then dashed south toward the church. The second man broke and ran to the west.

Wolf Tongue looked back at the warriors who rushed toward him now. They were only a few heartbeats from overtaking him. He glanced once more toward the church. He could see more of the townsfolk fleeing into it, but he would never reach it.

With a breath, he turned toward the attackers and twirled his tomahawk once. He slipped slightly to the side to use the house to block their progress.

"Wolf Tongue!"

He looked to his left at the sudden voice. From behind the next house over came Kicks-the-Oneida. He came at a lope, but stopped when he saw the others charging and held up one hand and yelled to them.

"No! This one is mine."

Kicks-the-Oneida glared back at Wolf Tongue with a frown, his chest heaving and speckled with blood. "You have stood in my way too long, little boy."

Wolf Tongue shrugged and before he could reply, Kicks-the-Oneida lunged. His war club sliced through the air and Wolf Tongue only managed to twist out its path by throwing his body to the side. Kicks-the-Oneida attacked again and Wolf Tongue caught the swing on the haft of his tomahawk. He pushed the attack away and danced to the side to recover his balance.

"You never were strong enough to push little boys out of your way," he said as he shifted to find a comfortable distance. "You reckon you could beat a little girl?"

Kicks-the-Oneida growled and swung. Wolf Tongue countered. The clack of wood vibrated down to his arm as he caught the swing against his tomahawk. Immediately, Kicks-the-Oneida swung again and again, his blows hammering in on Wolf Tongue. Each he caught against his own weapon, but Kicks-the-Oneida drove on so hard that it pushed Wolf Tongue back without a chance to attack.

Then, Kicks-the-Oneida's club came swinging in from the side. Wolf Tongue twisted to catch it again. Kicks-the-Oneida reversed and landed a punch to Wolf

Tongue's jaw. Wolf Tongue stumbled from the blow, trying to slip away. As he shifted, Kicks-the-Oneida swung again with his club, its ball-head glancing across Wolf Tongue's shoulder.

Wolf Tongue toppled forward and threw himself into the mud. He landed on the same, hit shoulder and fire erupted through his left arm and neck. He tried to roll forward, but the muck clung to him and he had no momentum. Instead, he rolled onto his side and found himself frozen.

Another hammer blow came down on his arm as he scrambled to get to his feet. A ragged, feral breath sliced through his teeth and he rolled the other way. He felt himself land against Kicks-the-Oneida's legs, felt them give way, slightly. He lashed out with his fists, noticing that he'd lost his tomahawk. He slammed an elbow against one knee and Kicks-the-Oneida tripped sideways with a howl.

Wolf Tongue settled his feet in the mud and launched himself. As he rose, he slammed his head up under Kicks-the-Oneida's chin. The older man staggered and caught himself while Wolf Tongue drew a knife.

The club swung in again and Wolf Tongue closed the distance, taking a lesser hit as he caught Kicks-the-Oneida's hand against his ribs. Wolf Tongue thrust with his knife and Kicks-the-Oneida swatted at the blade, catching it first against his hand. Wolf Tongue angled his next slice up at Kicks-the-Oneida's throat.

Kicks-the-Oneida raised his free arm to protect his neck. The blade caught against his shoulder and sliced the length of his upper arm. With an animal grunt, Kicks-the-Oneida brought his arm down, slammed his elbow against Wolf Tongue's nose, and then pinned Wolf Tongue's arm against his side. Wolf Tongue's eyes filled with water and fire as he fought to free his weapon.

For a moment, Wolf Tongue struggled to land a blow with his forehead while Kicks-the-Oneida did the same. The two stumbled and swayed as rain pattered against their faces. Then, Wolf Tongue slipped one leg behind the other man and threw his weight forward.

They landed in the mud on their sides, still entangled, but loosened. Wolf Tongue kicked and flailed his arms as he scrabbled backward on his back until he was free. Kicks-the-Oneida struggled to his hands and knees. His form, all blood and mud and anger, seemed to loom over Wolf Tongue like a bear.

Wolf Tongue pushed off the ground and kicked as hard as he could. His foot caught Kicks-the-Oneida against the ear and snapped his head back. Wolf Tongue rolled to the side and kicked his other foot against Kicks-the-Oneida's arm.

Kicks-the-Oneida flopped forward into the mud and in a moment Wolf Tongue was sitting on his opponent's back, holding his scalplock in one fist with his knife in the other.

"Susquehannock!"

Wolf Tongue looked up through his brows to see the three other men watching him. One of the Mingos held a musket aimed at Wolf Tongue's chest.

Pyke cradled Dob's chest of French lucre as he returned to the front of the church. The nearby Mingo taunted him but did not advance. His ignoring them served as the perfect insult—their challenges grew louder but Pyke pretended to not even hear them.

The windows of the church had been removed as he'd ordered. That way they could shoot the enemy and stave off any attack by fire. But Pyke didn't kid himself: he knew their last stand inside the church would be short.

The townfolk had crowded inside. Peering through the doors, Pyke could see they were packed in more tightly than powder and shot. Children's cries carried outside on the wind. The men watched him nervously from the windows, their muskets at the ready.

Pyke wondered how much shot they had left.

He turned back to Nyakwai's men. They flooded the street before him and wrapped around the church house. Their ranks were thick and swelled more as the stragglers fell in. The men in front began their war chant, a ceaseless dirge that Pyke knew would send the townfolk inside into a panic and render them hopeless. Balls of flame appeared as the warriors lit torches.

But they did not attack. Not yet.

Pyke knew why.

Nyakwai was coming and wished to see the end of Millers Town with his own eyes. Perhaps he would cast the first torch at the church himself.

Davies stepped beside Pyke and readied his musket. That they were both alive was a minor miracle, but it reminded Pyke they had probably used up all their luck. How much more would the Lord help him? Probably not much, now that Pyke knew Nyakwai fought with some good cause. Dob had scalped many of his people, judging by the number of coins in the chest.

"I hope that bloody savage of yours got away," Davies said. "I quite liked the brute."

Pyke kept his thoughts to himself. Wolf Tongue wasn't at the church, and it likely meant ...

Pyke looked down at Dob's chest of blood money. His anger surged again. Dob had lied to him in the hopes Pyke could resolve this conflict and Dob could secretly keep his coins. The bastard had been willing to risk the entire town so that he might preserve his minor fortune.

Money drove some men mad. These coins had presumably gotten Wolf Tongue killed.

"Blood-wite," Pyke muttered.

Davies said nothing.

The two soldiers faced Nyakwai's horde. Pyke knew he would die here, on this muddy road, in this tiny town, at the far end of the mighty British Empire. Beside Davies. But he also knew he would rather die beside no other, save Wolf Tongue.

Pyke took one step forward. "I will speak to that coward Nyakwai now!"

The Mingo song slowly died. Soon the men began to part like a curtain and the big, old, scarred warrior with the almost-white hair stood in front of his men, proud, stubborn, defiant, fearless, tomahawk in hand. He held a fist full of fresh scalps in his left and both his arms were bare and covered in gore.

"You die now." Nyakwai pointed his tomahawk at them. "I take my time."

Pyke ignored the fear knotting his stomach and stalked toward Nyakwai. The Mingo warriors cried and shouted, but the great chief lifted a palm and stilled them.

"This is your last chance, Nyakwai." Pyke stopped a few feet in front of the man. "Unless you enjoy pissing away your warriors."

The Mingos howled for Pyke's blood and again, Nyakwai commanded them to be still. A mere two strides separated them. Nyakwai sneered and let his tomahawk hang at his side, unafraid of Pyke.

Pyke suddenly dropped the chest between them. Nyakwai didn't jump. Didn't even blink. The man was utterly fearless.

Pyke said, "Take it and leave."

Nyakwai nudged the chest open with his toe and examined the contents. Then he smiled his wicked smile and looked again at Pyke.

"You English are dogs in war and whores for money."

Pyke ignored the jab. "And you throw warriors away like they were shit."

Nyakwai lost his smile. "There is no better honor than to die for Nyakwai."

"We have more than enough shot left to kill all your men ten times over." Pyke smiled. "So we'll give them all the honor they want."

Nyakwai looked back down at the coins. His expression was unreadable.

Pyke said, "Take the coins and leave. Or stay and die."

"You should have given these me on the first day. Instead your town dies."

Pyke was past caring. Now that he knew his end, he was no longer afraid. He had served honorably, the way a gentleman should. "Maybe. But we'll take your men with us."

"Or I will just take your coins and kill you anyway."

Pyke smiled. "Go ahead, you bloody savage, and watch your men fall by the dozens to satisfy your pride."

Nyakwai looked past Pyke. "Your men are women and your women are children and your children are useless."

"Then what does that make the Mingo warriors we've killed?"

The chief narrowed his eyes. "How many scalps did you take?"

Pyke had nothing else up his sleeve. He thought of the people sheltering in the church. Of the women who would be raped and probably killed. Of the children who would die, or be sold off, or even worse. Dob's petty greed had caused all this death. Pyke wished he could kill the man a hundred times. And now Wolf Tongue was probably dead. His anger nearly choked him. He let that rage carry him away when he next spoke.

"I took no scalps because I do not murder the innocent like Nyakwai, the mindless proud brute who doesn't think twice about sending his own men to die! Instead I killed the man who took the scalps. These are all his coins. If I had known about them three days ago, you would have had them. But I did not. So here we stand in this blood-soaked road now and you have your choice. Take them or don't, but know if you do not I will kill you, Nyakwai. With my musket, or with my saber, or with a tomahawk I took off your many warriors I killed. I will kill you and piss all over your dead body in front of your dried-up vicious cunt of a wife, and then perhaps I'll take your scalp. If it bloody pleases me!"

For an eternity, Nyakwai stared at him, his face expressionless.

Then the chief threw his head back and laughed.

Behind him, his warriors started their war song again. The front lines began to inch forward. Pyke looked back over his shoulder and nodded at Davies to get ready. The sergeant jutted his lower lip out and brought his musket up.

Pyke gripped his saber in its sheath. He would send Nyakwai to hell. He would slit the man's throat and send him to hell for all he had done and all his men would do. Pyke would die knowing he had bested the great man.

Nyakwai's laughter finally ceased and his warriors grew silent with anticipation. He opened his eyes and looked at Pyke.

"You amuse me, English."

Pyke loosed the saber an inch. All he had to do was take one big step forward and slash upward. He just had to be faster than Nyakwai once. Just once.

Nyakwai turned and motioned at one of his warriors to come forward. In his alien tongue, he said something incomprehensible to Pyke.

The warrior made an incredulous face and stared at Nyakwai, uncomprehending. Nyakwai barked his orders again and the man hurried forward and bent to pick up the chest as his chief walked away, pushing through his throng of warriors and barking more orders.

His men stopped their singing and fell in behind him, like a great big wave being pulled away from the shore forever.

Slowly, Wolf Tongue lowered his knife. He glanced up once more to be sure the men would allow him his trophy, then sliced the top bit of hair and hawk-feather roach from Kicks-the-Oneida's head.

With both the knife and the chunk of hair held out to his sides, Wolf Tongue rose off Kicks-the-Oneida's back, watching the three men. The youngest, a boy with long arms and prominent elbows and collar bones, looked back and forth between him and the man with the musket. He looked a year older than Wolf Tongue's nephew and held his body much the way Root Cutter would in readiness.

He brought his eyes back to the center man. "Will you shoot me?"

The man's jaw moved as he seemed to consider what to do.

Kicks-the-Oneida rose, slowly. His chest heaved with labored breath. His lips were bright with blood and it ran from his nose and dripped from the fingertips of his left hand. He spat at Wolf Tongue's feet then moved toward his war club that still lay in the mud.

"That is mine," called Wolf Tongue.

Kicks-the-Oneida glared at him, his eyes black with hatred.

"You challenged me, betrayer. You're lucky I let you have your life. But in exchange I take this," he shook the lock of hair, "and your club."

Kicks-the-Oneida sneered with red-smeared teeth. Eyes still locked on Wolf Tongue, he drew a knife from his belt. "How dare you? You're the reason your village is dying. Your *quhanstrono* father was just the first to poison it, then you bring even more to us. And then the attack by Storm-of-Villages was because you needed to show us all what a big boy you'd become. So take your trophies, but it's you who's the betrayer. You've given us all up to the *quhanstrono*."

Then, with a growl, Kicks-the-Oneida limped to the nearest house and kicked open the door. With his one arm limp at his side, he disappeared into the darkness.

Wolf Tongue looked back at the man who still held him at gunpoint. For a moment, they stared at each other, then, he lowered his musket.

"You are the one who brought Neoke to us."

Wolf Tongue nodded. In the moment of relief, he suddenly recognized his wounds and grit his teeth against the pain.

The man smiled slightly and nodded toward the house where Kicks-the-Oneida disappeared. "A friend of yours?"

Wolf Tongue smiled. "Maybe once."

The other man nodded. "He is one of us now."

The screams seemed to flourish anew behind Wolf Tongue and he glanced over his shoulder. The gunshots seemed to have stopped but for an occasional report that surged through the falling rain. But the howls of the Indians and the townsfolk alike still echoed off the clouds.

"You fight for these people?"

Wolf Tongue's smile turned to pursed lips. He looked over his shoulder. He saw only a few figures still around. A Mingo rushed from a house, a wad of dresses, shirts, and coats across his shoulder. He could still hear the fighting, though it seemed to have all relocated to the church.

"I fight for a friend. And the few good people who are here."

"Bone Snake said you might."

At the mention of his uncle, Wolf Tongue snapped his eyes back to the men. So Bone Snake had made friends with these people, too. Wolf Tongue thought about that and managed only a wry smile.

"Be careful, Susquehannock." The man nodded to his companions, and the three dispersed off into the house behind Kicks-the-Oneida.

Wolf Tongue stretched his jaw as he watched them go. Then, with a sigh, he turned to retrieve the decorated war club from the mud and his own tomahawk.

TWENTY-SIX – THROUGH THE NARROWS

The rain slowed and did little to combat the fires burning throughout Millers Town.

Pyke ordered the handful of men he trusted to stand watch on the four sides of town, in the event Nyakwai decided to renege on the deal and come back for the slaughter. His short time with the Mingo leader led him to believe this wouldn't happen, but Pyke wanted to be sure.

The muddy streets were overrun with blood. A man couldn't go far without having to step over a corpse, either white or Mingo. As they'd left, the savages had taken their spoils, gutting the unburned houses and taking what livestock the town had. Pyke passed the few houses remained as families clung to each other. A few brave souls collected water in a desperate attempt to save what homes they could. Pyke didn't have the heart to tell them it was wasted effort. One quick look told Pyke the houses would all burn to the ground and even if they didn't, no one would stay here. Too many had died, their crops had been depleted, their money was gone, and there was nothing preventing Nyakwai or some other from coming back tomorrow. They all had to leave.

Pyke walked on, passing the charred remains of Fleur's house. He wondered what had happened to her and prayed she had made it through the Mingo lines to safety. Where would she go? Back to New France, probably. The English would not accept her, not while their countries were at war.

Before he could despair over the life she would have, he reminded himself: at least she still had a life to have. Were it not for him and Davies and Wolf Tongue, Fleur would be dead now.

Or worse.

Briefly he searched the town for Dob's cronies. He found Kit dead behind the pig sty. The Mingos had opened his throat, cut out his eyes, and cut his scalp from his skull. A fitting end to the wretch as far as Pyke was concerned. He was unsurprised to find the others, including Si and Quill, had snuck away like guilty foxes from the henhouse.

Pyke let them go. He couldn't stand guard over them at all times and he would need all his strength to bring the remaining townfolk to safety in the coming days. Besides, Si and Quill's reputations would follow them anyway. Probably they would go to the French or disappear beyond the frontier. After all, they had traded scalps with the bastards. Perhaps they would be conscripted by the French army and Pyke would get his chance at revenge on the battlefield. It was a pleasing thought.

Eventually he found Davies inside the church, tending to his wounds in the candlelight. Somehow they had come out of this battle alive. Pyke still didn't know how. He had some fresh bumps, bruises, and cuts but was otherwise fine. The earlier tomahawk wound was more nuisance than anything. Nyakwai's cut to his face would leave a scar, an ever-present reminder of Millers Town.

Davies nodded as Pyke approached. "So that's that."

Pyke smiled. "That's that. We must evacuate. We can provide them with at least temporary shelter in Jenkins Town."

Davies's face twitched and he looked away.

"Come on." Pyke motioned for him to follow outside.

Reluctantly, Davies pushed away from the wall and followed.

Outside, the weather had softened to a drizzle. Men were moving supplies out of the church, while the women tended to the wounded, comforted crying children, or tried to organize what supplies that still had. Pyke caught Boone's eye and nodded at the brave lad. Boone smiled back.

The town had been headed for a disaster, but they had somehow, against all odds, avoided it.

Pyke allowed himself to smile, to take a breath, to relax even.

"Through the narrows." Pyke looked at Davies. "To the glory."

"To what glory?" Davies grumbled.

Pyke studied the man. He'd known Davies had already harbored dark thoughts, but he'd figured their victory here would have brightened the sergeant's mood. It did not appear to have done so.

"To what glory?" Davies asked, a little louder this time. "We were *lucky*, Pyke. No one will remember this town, or what happened here, or what we did. We can go back to Jenkins Town but the colonel won't thank us. He despises you and doesn't care a flea about me. We can expect nothing for this."

"Virtue is its own reward, Sergeant."

Davies made a face. "This is all we have to look forward to? Nearly getting scalped for this lot, them who deserved it in the first place?"

Pyke shook his head. "We didn't do this for Dob or his cronies, or the bastards too weak to stand up against them."

He pointed down the road at the Fletchers. Michael, his face bloody and haggard, held his infant girl in his arms while Molly wrapped a bandage around her brother-in-law's bleeding ribs.

"We did this for them. For the Fletchers. There is the glory, Sergeant, that those good people will live now. *They* will never forget us."

Davies shrugged. "I was wrong before. I know how to soldier but I ain't a good soldier. And like I said, I ain't no bloody hero like you, either."

Pyke looked away. A profound sadness welled up in him. Sergeant Davies had done the honorable thing, time and again proving his valor and worth. He was the only ally Pyke had in Jenkins Town, and truth be told, the only man who'd given him a chance when he'd arrived. The colonials didn't care for him because he was an officer and also not of the Colony, and the colonel harbored a deep-seated dislike of him. And probably always would. From a pragmatic perspective, Davies should have distanced himself from Pyke at every turn. But instead, he'd stood shoulder-to-shoulder with him every step along the way.

Pyke knew Davies had terms to his service. He could not just desert. That was a capital offense.

Pyke turned back to his friend. "I will have to inform Colonel Bennett that Sergeant Davies fought heroically at the Battle of Millers Town. He warded off ten Indians by himself at one juncture and also saved this lieutenant from certain death on multiple occasions. At the height of the battle, the sergeant broke away from the main engagement to protect a family from the hatchet. In the confusion, I was not able to find him again. His body was not recovered and he is, sadly, presumed dead. Davies died in battle, the professional soldier to the very end. He sacrificed himself to protect loyal British subjects. I will regretfully inform the colonel."

Davies's blood-spattered, grimy face didn't quite smile. "You should come with me, Pyke. We make good companions."

"Where?" Pyke said.

"Where nobody knows us. There's plenty of opportunity in this new world for a couple enterprising fellows."

There were times when Pyke secretly wished to disappear, to be out from under the colonel's malignant eye. He had served honorably but had seen no recognition. Instead the colonel lavished attention and an undeserved promotion to Captain Smith.

But deep-down Pyke knew who he was. A duty-bound soldier. And soon enough he would join the nascent war with the French, where the colonel would not be able to ignore his service any longer. He lived to serve the Crown.

"Davies, I will never forget you." Pyke extended his hand.

The sergeant nodded once. "I got two cousins up north in Boston. They're merchants and make a living. If you ever change your mind."

"I thought you dead," Pyke said.

Wolf Tongue smirked. "Not yet, Pyke. Not just yet."

They met at the unfinished palisade. It was, oddly, the only thing the Mingos hadn't tried to burn. It would remain unfinished forever now.

Pyke nodded. "I'm glad to hear it."

Wolf Tongue bore many scars of battle now, some old, but most of them new. He hadn't painted his face for this battle like the one against Storm-of-Villages, but now it was streaked with blood beneath a swollen eye. Pyke wondered grimly how many had fallen under Wolf Tongue's tomahawk on this day and what other horrors Wolf Tongue had seen and done to survive. The man carried himself heavily, with narrowed eyes and tight lips unlike when they'd first met.

Wolf Tongue said, "It will take many more than Kicks-the-Oneida and a few Mingos to kill me."

Pyke studied his friend at the mention of the other Susquehannock warrior. Wolf Tongue looked off to where Fletcher sat huddled with his family.

"Did you meet him? Kicks-the-Oneida?" Pyke asked.

Wolf Tongue nodded once, eyes still on the family crying together. He looked back and lifted a ball-head war club a few inches from his side. It was stained black by varnish or blood, Pyke did not know.

"This is his," he said. And then with his other hand, he produced from his satchel a tuft of black hair tied with a feather. "And this."

Pyke swallowed, but noticed that the hair had no skin attached to it.

He wondered at his friend, the Susquehannock, who embellished the most mundane of adventures and bragged of any feat, seemed suddenly so taciturn.

Pyke surveyed the burning houses. "This town is dead. Take what you can back to your village. You've earned it."

Wolf Tongue flashed a small smile. "I would need a horse for that, and you know I hate the beasts. Besides, you will need it for your war with the French."

"Will your people take up the tomahawk and fight with the British?"

"I don't know, Pyke." Wolf Tongue grew serious. "We have been allies in the past."

Pyke said nothing.

Wolf Tongue looked away. "For the Susquehannock to join a war, we need warriors."

Pyke looked away also and watched as the fire jumped from one house to another in the distance. By tomorrow morning, Millers Town would be no more.

Pyke felt Wolf Tongue nudge his shoulder. He turned to his friend, whose devilish smile had finally returned.

The Susquehannock held out his hand. "*Vale.*"

Pyke smiled and shook the man's hand. "Be strong."

Wolf Tongue nodded at him and then took his leave. Pyke watched him walk down the muddy road out of Millers Town. When he was twenty steps away, the Susquehannock turned to look back at Pyke.

Wolf Tongue called out. "Tell your colonel that Wolf Tongue of the Wolf Clan stood with you here! Tell him that there is no equal to a Susquehannock warrior, and of the Susquehannock warriors, there is no equal to Wolf Tongue!"

Pyke held up his hand and waved goodbye. "He already knows. I told him that a year ago."

Wolf Tongue waved back. For a moment the two warriors held each other's stare, then Wolf Tongue turned and trotted off into the darkness. He must have been exhausted from rescuing Neoke, running back to Millers Town, and fighting the Mingo all day. But he jogged like his legs were fresh and like he would never tire.

Pyke said, "I hope you and I never meet in battle, my friend."

He went back to work. He found the Fletchers and Boone and Boone's family and rounded up the remaining townfolk. They all thanked him one-by-one, even the folk that had sided with Dob earlier. They showered him with their gratitude and called him their savior, even through their tears for the dead. It took all the bitterness out of him. He made sure they had enough food to last for the march back to Jenkins Town. He prayed the few that had escaped south earlier were still alive as well.

As they set out in the darkness, Pyke took one last look at Millers Town. Davies was right: no man would remember this place or what had happened here.

But that didn't matter.

What mattered was he and Wolf Tongue and Sergeant Davies had saved these families from the tomahawk.

HISTORICAL NOTE

The names of the North American tribes are a tricky thing. Many of the indigenous peoples have come to be known by names given them by their enemies or Europeans, their exonyms, as opposed to what they call themselves, their autonyms. In fact, even when translations were attempted for nations' autonymns, most called themselves "the People."

We have attempted to apply some logic to the business of naming the tribes in our stories but ultimately had to make judgment calls. The most glaring example of this is with Wolf Tongue's own tribe. The term Susquehannock is the name given them by some tribes in the area (but of course, not all the tribes in the area!).

Also, serious students of history will be quick to point out that there was no troop of British regulars posted in Jenkins Town and Pennsylvania, under the influence of the Quakers, did not actually raise a militia until 1755, and only then after Native American raiders plundered their frontier sufficiently enough to raise citizen ire. Even then, the question became one of money as the interested parties, including Benjamin Franklin and Robert Morris, argued over who would finance the militia.

Funding the French and Indian War became problematic for the British and to recoup their massive expenses, Parliament subsequently levied more taxes on the colonies, which of course led to the War for Independence.

This is all a way of saying that Lieutenant Pyke and Colonel Bennett would not have been in Pennsylvania while the events of *Language of the Bear* and this book take place. But we thought it would be dramatically interesting to pair our young English officer, fresh from the old country, with a brash warrior of a sadly declining tribe, so we took historical liberties, again, in favor of drama.

So far, nobody has complained.

As the series continues, our characters become entwined in larger historical events of the 18th century. That is, assuming they survive …

ABOUT THE AUTHORS

Nathanael Green and Evan Ronan grew up reading thrilling adventure stories and wanted to write their own. So they did.

Nathanael Green is an author, lecturer of college students, and freelance copywriter, among other unmentionable things, living in upstate New York. He holds a master of fine arts degree in creative writing and has seen his articles, short fiction, and essays appear in national and international journals and magazines.

Despite the writer stereotype, Nate does like hearing from other readers and writers. Please feel free to contact him through his website, www.nathanaelgrcen.com, or via email at nate@nathanaelgreen.com, or subscribe to his newsletter.

Evan Ronan's stories don't always fit neatly into one genre. He reads widely and tries to write as widely. His paranormal thriller series, *The Unearthed*, features his favorite protagonist, Eddie McCloskey, a man who's constantly underestimated and always finds a way to beat long odds through hustle, brains, and hard work.

Evan also writes in the YA, sci-fi, fantasy, and mystery genres. He lives with his family in New Jersey, in the same town Eddie McCloskey grew up in.

For more information on Evan, visit his website www.ronaniswriting.blogspot.com or find him on Facebook. Join his mailing list to stay current with his new releases.

65350085R00135

Made in the USA
Middletown, DE
26 February 2018